Contents

Acknowledgements

This book is dedicated to my wonderful mother-in-law Wendy who encouraged me every step of the way. I had the privilege of her daily feedback as she read each section as it was completed. Her interest and enthusiasm spurred me on as I wrote away.

Of course my wonderful wife will always take credit for any piece of writing I complete. Her hard work, support and honest feedback throughout the completion of this book has hopefully made it the exciting read it is today.

About the book

Steve Lawson was passionate about his job as a police officer. He even chanced upon the love of his life Anna
whilst he was conducting his duties.

This story follows Steve through nearly 20 years of police work as he gets involved in a series of complex murder investigations.

When Steve chances upon the grisly murder of Landlord, Joseph Fraser he finds himself in the middle of a major investigation. Steve's career soon takes off and he sets his sights on becoming a detective.

Steve joins Westhampton CID where he has a baptism of fire into the role of family liaison officer, investigating the suspicious death of local teacher, Richard Wilson.

In search of even more challenging enquiries Steve transfers to the Metropolitan Police Murder Squad where his experiences become more and more sinister
as the facts of his latest case unfold...

Glossary

PC	Police Constable
DC	Detective Constable
DS	Detective Sergeant
DI	Detective Inspector
DCI	Detective Chief Inspector
PCSO	Police Community Support Officer
SIO	Senior Investigating Officer
FLO	Family Liaison Officer
MIR	Major Incident Room
MIT	Major *or* Murder Investigation Team
OB	Overnight (report) Book
CID	Criminal Investigation Department
CPS	Crown Prosecution Service
DNA	Deoxyribo Nucleic Acid (the genetic material of a cell)
PM	Post Mortem (autopsy)
PNC	Police National Computer
TIE	Trace Interview *and* Eliminate
OSG	Operational Support Group
ABE	Achieving Best Evidence (a video interview)
NFA	No Further Action
TOX	Toxicology (to show drugs and alcohol in the system)
HOLMES	Home Office Large & Major Enquiry System
KM	Kastle-Meyer (chemical test for blood)
FME	Forensic *or* Force Medical Examiner (doctor)

IPCC	Independent Police Complaints Commission
TFL	Transport For London
PACE	Police And Criminal Evidence *Act 1984*

Chapter 1

The Police Officer

"Beautiful!" Steve commented as he exhaled and laid back on the sun lounger.

"You deserve it darling," replied Anna.

"But do I deserve you?" Asked Steve.

"We'll have to see a little later when we get back to the cabin," Anna replied, smiling.

This was the first holiday Steve Lawson or PC948 Lawson had taken since he had joined Westhamptonshire Police two years earlier. Steve wouldn't have taken this one if it wasn't for the fact that he'd just married the love of his life, Anna who'd insisted on at least one week's honeymoon. As Steve relaxed and sipped his large frozen cocktail he was grateful that Anna had made him book the 7 night Caribbean cruise. He hadn't realised how much he needed a break until now. Of course Anna knew he was a workaholic, or 'job pissed' as his colleagues called it. Anna accepted this as part of the package when she got together with Steve. She remembered that it was because of 'the job' that they met in the first place.

"It's been a long year," Anna commented.

"I know darling but we made it didn't we?" Reassured Steve.

Steve was a professional, dedicated officer who was passionate about his job. He had not become a police officer until the age of 28 following a successful but solitary career in the army. Steve had loved that job, but this one; well the variety and opportunity overwhelmed him. Steve had vision and intended to explore his new found vocation to the full. He hadn't planned a relationship just yet and in any case spent so much time at work the chances of forging one with anyone was unlikely.

Unlikely maybe but not when a 'member of the public' falls in love with you. This all happened when Steve had the grim job of visiting Anna's flat to break the bad news of her father's suicide. Not a situation you would expect to be the foundation of a successful relationship. However Steve was a gentle man with a hidden warm heart, prepared to go that extra mile to help and support a bereaved and lonely lady. Steve still spent the following year leading up to the inquest whittling about the potential blot on his integrity that a relationship born out of a professional engagement may leave. He even secured a posting to the rural sector at the end of his probation just so he was no longer policing the main town in Westhampton where Anna lived.

Anna was five years years older than Steve. Now 35 she fell into the unconventional category of not previously married. Steve knew a few weeks before they married that Anna couldn't have children when she broke down and explained her predicament as if she was confessing to some awful crime. It broke Steve's heart to see her so upset, more upset than she'd been the night he told her that her father had died. Apparently Anna had encountered some medical complication as a teenager and following an operation she was told she was unlikely ever to be able to have children. Steve hadn't really understood or asked what the intimate medical issues were, but it didn't matter really at the time he just needed to console his devastated fiancee and convince her that it really didn't matter to him if they had a family or not. As long as they had each other he was happy. Of course Anna had thought this might be a deal breaker for the ambitious Steve who had wanted the best of everything in life, but it seemed to not be the case. Anna's love for Steve just grew stronger from there onwards and their bond was sealed for life.

Of course the wedding was a quiet affair with only Steve's parents, older brother and two work mates attending the registry office. This suited both Steve and Anna, especially as it seemed unfair that neither of Anna's parents could be there. Anna's mother was 70 when she had suffered a stroke. It occurred not long after her husband's death. Anna had no option but to put her mother in a home back in Norfolk. She had introduced Steve to her mother before the wedding and Steve was comforted by the lavish environment the home provided for his future mother in law. Both Anna's mother and father had been in their 30's before they started a family, Anna being their only child. Anna's parents were originally busy farmers, owning a large arable farm with several acres of land. Although the demise of the family business had almost certainly been a factor in her father's decision to take his own life. The land they owned had been worth a lot of money when it was eventually sold off. It therefore made sense that

Anna made sure that the money was properly invested to support the costs of her mother's care. Care that Anna could never provide alone from her small flat in Westhampton.

As Steve relaxed his thoughts drifted back to the day he'd first met Anna's mum.

'What a naturally wonderful caring woman Anna was.' Steve had thought as he smiled at his new mother-in-law and she stared back at him from the day room easy chair.

"Mary still hasn't responded that well to her speech therapy sessions," the carer commented.

She couldn't even raise her drooping face into any kind of smile, but it was still relatively early days for a victim of such a major stroke assumed Steve. Anna had told Steve her mother could speak in a very distorted manner but she was unlikely to do so whilst he was there because its so distorted and difficult to understand she gets embarrassed in front of strangers. Anna was touched by Steve's humanity as he leant over and kissed her mother on the forehead holding her more mobile hand and being reassured by the tight squeeze she had returned to his grasp.

"I'll leave you with Anna for a while, she can tell you all about the wonderful honeymoon we have planned." This had been a tactful move by Steve as he went to wander the stunning gardens. Steve knew Mary could now attempt to use some of that distorted speech in private with just her daughter there.

A familiar tone brought Steve back from his reminiscent state.

"Get your Mango Tango, medication for you vacation," the cheerful Jamaican accent sung out.

Steve returned from his daydreams to see 'the doctor' was back. Not a real doctor of course, just the nickname used by the wonderfully cheerful drinks waiter who floated around the deck serving refreshing fruity cocktails to the guests laced with dark rum. 'This was the life,' thought Steve as he reached over to hold the hand of his sun soaked new wife, she smiled contently, a week of wedded bliss followed.

Steve looked down at his simple but shiny wedding band checking it was carefully pushed into place as he closed his locker door and pulled on his leather gloves. Shutting away the small passport sized photo of his dear Anna that was carefully taped to the inside of the locker door. Steve had a knack for compartmentalising his life, it was time to focus, he was going back out on the streets and it was quick whit rather than vans full of back-up officers that would save his skin on the rural sector. Officers patrolled alone in battered old Vauxhall Astras, their boots full of traffic cones, shovels and half used first aid kits. No C/S spray, not even a personal issue stab vest. Radio signals were intermittent at best and mobile phones were for rich yuppies not police officers. Even with good comms the best Steve could expect if he got into trouble was his old mate Fred jumping in his panda at the Police House in Finborough and heading along to bail him out.

Steve was a confident chap these days, there wasn't much he hadn't seen over the last two years, including his fare share of dead bodies. Mainly suicides in locked cars full of exhaust fumes or horrible deaths from industrial accidents. Steve was fascinated by the work that the Scenes of Crime Officers did when they pitched up at these events; realising that not everything portrayed on TV and in films was as far fetched as he maybe once thought. Of course secretly Steve was also in awe of the detectives when they arrived in their sharp suits at scenes of serious crime, like celebrities attending a film premiere at Leicester Square. It was hard as a uniformed officer to secure any kind of respect from CID. The best way to get in the CID's good books was to hand them a job on a plate. Like when one of his team who had stopped and arrested a car full of post office robbers leaving the scene of the crime. They were still covered in the smashed glass from the security screen. All of this was subsequently secured by the officer in amongst their seized outer clothing and sealed in neatly labelled exhibit bags. He'd laid out all these exhibits in the CID office accompanied by every possible witness statement that he could obtain. Basically CID liked taking the glory for successful jobs and liked it even more if they didn't have to do much more than interview and charge their prisoners to achieve this. Job vacancies in the CID were often described as dead mans shoes. It was fortunate that occasionally one of the dinosaurs in their office would actually retire and provide a much sought after vacancy. Steve had his eye on one such slot and vowed to get involved in anything that looked vaguely like a job he could package up to a high standard and hand over to his detective colleagues to make his mark.

"Whisky Romeo three zero, this is Whisky Victor can you do a concern for welfare job out at Chisham."

The control room asked.

Apparently the owner of the Wheatsheaf Inn on the edge of the village hadn't opened the pub since Sunday night. It was now Tuesday morning and the driver with the weekly delivery of beer couldn't get him to answer the door.

Old man Fraser was a cantankerous old bastard at the best of times, but it didn't make any sense for him to ignore his regular delivery. His wife was away for a short period caring for her sick sister in Kent. Steve recalled Mr Fraser had been moaning about coping without her only the week before when he disturbed a lock-in at the pub. Fraser had claimed in his defence that he at least needed to keep his regulars happy whilst his pub grub business was suspended in her absence. The old man was far to tight to pay for a temporary chef whilst his wife was away.

"No problems Whiskey Victor, on my way," Steve responded.

Chapter 2

The Landlord

The tatty old coaching inn was well and truly locked, even the gates to the enclosed yard at the side were bolted secure. This was not right. 'Not another suicide, surely not,' thought Steve. Old Man Fraser was a miserable old geriatric yes, but that was when he was at his happiest. He'd been the owner of the Wheatsheaf since he inherited it from his late father. Business was okay, it must have been, as Fraser had resisted regular attempts by one of the mainstream brewery chains to buy him out. It was a popular venue with the locals even though it was right on the edge of the large village. Yes he'd had problems with a few of the travellers from a nearby permanent site but not enough to give him cause to end it all. He was an old school pub landlord, didn't even give in to the regular attempts by the local under aged hoodies to secure a drink. Most local landlords would do this just to avoid the regular nuisance of them hanging around outside instead, but not Fraser. Fraser was not easily phased.

Never the less Steve thought the worst as he gazed through the frosted glass trying to gauge what had gone wrong. He half expected to see Fraser's boots swinging at eye level within the main bar area, but he couldn't see a thing. There were absolutely no external clues as to what had happened. Continuos bursts of harsh door banging still failed to merit a response. Steve knew he had a power of entry. 'Section 17 of PACE,' he thought to himself. 'To save life and limb.' A power Steve had used many times but never successfully saved a life and he hadn't had to enter anything more than railway tunnels to save limbs before. No this was a power to break windows and kick in doors generally to find the decomposing corpse of a sadly forgotten pensioner who died quietly in their bed or even more commonly on the toilet, believe it or not.

Old Man Fraser was probably in his early 70's. Steve didn't think he was ready to pop his clogs yet. 'Oh well at least some poor bastard from Kent Police would have to do the death message,' he thought nonchalantly as he kicked hard at the double front doors. They flew open with ease. 'Maybe Fraser had shut up shop early feeling rough,' thought Steve. This might have explained why he hadn't even bolted the main doors properly from the inside when he locked up on Sunday night?

More clues confronted Steve as he entered the bar. Glasses everywhere, half a dozen of them centralised on the bar ready for washing up.

"MR FRASER, IT'S THE POLICE," shouted Steve.

Always good to shout police several times when breaking into premises on the rural sector. There were a lot of shotguns out there and many a home owner faced with an unknown visitor would shoot first and ask questions later.

"HELLO, POLICE," Steve continued. The eery silence only broken by the voice of the delivery driver squeaking out.

"Can I start bringing this lot in now?" Steve was startled looking round to see the idiot starting to push his first sack barrow full of beer crates through the broken doors.

"Fuck off out," Steve shouted having just jumped out of his skin.

Collecting himself Steve politely rephrased his instructions.

"I'm sorry Sir, no you can't come in, this is a crime scene I'm afraid."

Steve was following the golden rule of sudden deaths; regardless of the circumstances the venue is to always be treated as a crime scene until such time that the death is obviously just due to simple natural causes.

'Was this a sudden death though?' Steve thought. 'I need a dead body before I can declare that.'

'Where was Fraser?' He definitely hadn't keeled over having to clean up the bar without the assistance of his devoted and hard working spouse. Steve moved on to the obvious locations first. If Fraser had felt rough and retired early, maybe he just went straight to bed. The living accommodation was directly up the stairs behind the long open plan bar area. Steve had not been upstairs before. It was tidy and clean, a long corridor connected a lounge, small kitchen, bathroom and just two modest bedrooms. Steve began sniffing like a police dog searching for drugs, but Steve didn't expect to find drugs, no he was scanning for the distinctive smell every police officer soon learns to recognise; the smell of death. A horrible smell evident a very short time after someone passes away and more and more prominent as time goes on. 'Nothing,' thought Steve.

"Hello, Mr Fraser, it"s the police," he continued to say in a loud voice as he worked his way around the upper floor.

Alternative scenarios started to come to Steve. 'Maybe he was tied to a chair somewhere, his mouth taped shut and his safe empty?'

Bedroom 1 clear; this looked like the spare, the bed covered in boxes of miscellaneous items and a clothing rail adorned with garments even the local charity shop would struggle to sell.

The main bedroom door was shut. 'Here we go,' thought Steve as his gloved hand pushed down the handle.

"POLICE!" Steve shouted pointlessly, verbally exhaling his nervous tension.

Nothing, the room was clear, the bed was even made. 'Where the fuck is he?' Thought Steve starting to relax a little, half expecting an angry old man to suddenly return home from the cash and carry wondering what all the fuss was about. Of course he'd be insisting the police foot the bill for his broken front door.

The bathroom, lounge and kitchen were all clear with no signs of anything untoward. Just the pub kitchen and customer toilets left. The kitchen was well and truly Mrs Fraser's domain but Steve needed to check everything never the less.

'Quickly check the toilets first then do the kitchen last,' decided Steve. Wondering if the ladies would stink of stale urine as much as the gents. Steve edged through the door not surprised that they actually smelt a lot better. He was surprised however to find himself paddling across a wet floor.

"Surely it's not piss?" Questioned Steve out loud to himself as he investigated further. It wasn't of course, it was just a blocked toilet and not too bad either, just clear fresh water trickling over the rim with no obvious nasties floating on top. Steve was surprised Old Man Fraser hadn't had someone out to this, there was no way he would be able to open again until the mess was sorted out. Steve smiled thinking, 'well that's it then Fraser must have had a heart attack peeling spuds for the Wheatsheaf's world famous cottage pie,' or at least the old chalkboard claimed it's pie was world famous. If Fraser was in the kitchen, the prognosis would not be a good one, whatever it was.

Steve faced the spring loaded door that led to the large industrial style pub kitchen. He reached out to push open the door.

"Whiskey Romeo Three Zero, welfare check?" Steve jumped out of his skin for the second time in a short space of time.

'Shit,' thought Steve, 'this bloody day has more false shocks in it than a badly made horror movie.'

17

"I'm fine Whiskey Victor, still looking for signs of life," sighed the lonesome officer as he casually entered the pub kitchen.

"Oh my God," mouthed Steve staring into a blood smeared room. It looked more like an abattoir than a hygienic commercial kitchen.

'What the hell has happened in here?' Thought Steve, and 'where was Old Man Fraser?' Still nowhere to be seen. This was a major crime scene but what had happened? Scanning the room from left to right careful not to be tempted to move or touch anything Steve mentally noted several clear signs of violence. There was a large fold down griddle to the left, the kind you get your paninis toasted in at the coffee shop. It had congealed blood oozing from the closed lid and an unrecognisable mass of burnt something stuck between the plates. Across the far wall only one knife remained on the long magnetic strip that should have been full of knives attached to the wall. Hand shaped blood stains smudged the area behind it. Presumably caused by a blood soaked hand as it's owner selected the next blade. Two sets of distorted and broken cheap handcuffs hung from the pan rack that was suspended above the large stainless steel central table. Some of the knives and at least three human teeth were laid out on the table top. A tenderising hammer looking suspiciously blood stained was sat to the right hand side nearby. Someone had been tortured in this place, but why and where were they now? Using his torch for extra light Steve scanned the floor. Amongst the many pools of blood Steve could see a significant trail leading to the back door. It looked like Fraser had tried to escape into the pub garden.

The Wheatsheaf had a small pub garden with a set of swings, an old plastic Wendy house and a small slide. Somewhere for the not so conscientious parents to dump their kids whilst they got pissed in the bar and discussed the latest episode of Brookside with their friends. Steve was impressed by his clear head, given the nature of what he had just discovered. He knew with a floor like the one he was looking at and so much blood around the room that the forensic opportunities would be fantastic. Steve needed to get into that garden, but not by walking through the kitchen via the back door and risking disturbing the evidence. He needed to be methodical but quick as there was a slim chance the poor victim of this horrendous attack was still alive .

The quick thinking and adrenaline fuelled constable retraced his steps out of the building barging through the old coaching inn gates and into the yard; the wood cracking as the bolt and padlock were forced free. Steve entered the pub garden, pausing again to key his radio.

"Can I have some back-up please Whiskey Victor, a supervisor and a SOCO and you better inform CID." Reported the frantic officer with his garbled update.

"Whiskey Romeo Three Zero, what have you got?"

Steve wasn't sure, well he sort of knew, just could not believe what he'd stumbled upon thats all. Ignoring his radio Steve simply looked across at the inn's rear door. The trail of blood from what must have been serious wounds, continued soaking the paving slabs leading onto the grass and right up to the old plastic Wendy house. The little red door was shut. 'Surely no one's in there?' Thought Steve. He gingerly stepped nearer to the little brightly coloured building to get a closer look. Steve stopped, suddenly noticing a blood soaked hand sticking out of the side window, most of it's fingers missing or crushed to virtual non existence. Steve flicked out his baton, not to take this blood soaked creature on, no more to prod it at arms length staying clear of the scene but making one final check for signs of life. He wanted to confirm to himself that calling a ambulance was a pointless exercise as he prodded away. It was the hand of an old man that he gently poked, still attached to the rest of its body it seemed but totally lifeless. Steve reached forward with his baton still avoiding stepping directly where he assumed the perpetrator would have. He flicked open the door of the Wendy house to reveal the twisted remains of a man who was well and truly dead.

"Whiskey Romeo Three Zero are you receiving?" Boomed out Steve's radio.

"Yes Whisky Victor, apologies." Steve replied pausing again. "It's Old Man Fraser, I think he's been murdered." Steve reported as he stepped back. Fraser was in a battered mess and not thinking Steve was about to emerge from the pub yard, baton extended and stained with the victim's blood. Steve hurriedly took a steri-wipe from his first aid pouch cleaned and collapsed his baton before returning to the street.

"What's going on?" asked the delivery driver.

"The landlord's dead," said Steve not revealing too much.

"But what about my delivery?" Questioned the driver foolishly.

Steve's stare said it all as the delivery driver shuffled back to his truck and drove off. 'Right down to business,' thought Steve gripping himself knowing both his skipper and CID would be there in about 15 minutes.

'Scene log, inner cordon, outer cordon, request two scene tents (did the area have two?), do a sketch for the SOCO and the Detective Inspector, some notes re local knowledge and what about a brief for the family liaison officer about Fraser's wife?'

Could Steve get this all on track before the cavalry got there? He knew it would help and it wasn't just brownie points Steve was after. If his initial actions went some way to solving this old mans murder then he would be proud to have done his bit.

"Morning my darling," rung out the soft tones of Anna's voice waking Steve from a deep slumber. "What were you up to in the early hours of this morning?" She asked.

"Sorry if I woke you darling," apologised Steve. "I'd been to a bit of a messy scene and just needed to get my uniform in the machine and get scrubbed up a bit before I came to bed."

"Oh that's why there's a damp pair of boots stood on the balcony trying desperately to dry out then. Must have been a serious job you were really late?" Anna enquired.

"Yes I know I'm sorry, I really wanted to be home before you got back from your mum's, I really missed you."

Anna had been on a course in Lincolnshire for her new job the previous week and she'd stopped over for a long weekend in Norfolk to see her mother on the way back.

"I'm sure it was important Steve, was it a murder?" Asked Anna enthusiastically. Anna was almost as passionate about Steve's work as he was. So much so that her new found career was with Victim Support. She had always been very vocal about the support offenders received through probation officers, social workers and even the prison staff compared to the victims who had to rely on a registered charity and an army of well meaning volunteers for their support. Anna had trained as a mature student to qualify as a counsellor and now she had been accepted by Victim Support as an unpaid volunteer. Her week long course was the foundation of what she needed to be allowed to meet victims of various crimes and offer both practical and emotional support.

"Yes it was a murder, but I can't talk about it not even to a fully fledged Victim Support Volunteer," answered Steve smiling.

"Anyway how was your course, what were the other volunteers like?"

Anna explained how she had really enjoyed her week, very sociable and a really interesting cross section of people, a lot of whom had been victims themselves. The week had been a lot of dos and don'ts mostly involving common sense rules that Anna was surprised even needed to be included. Anna was ready and keen to get her first referral even though she knew it would be low level crime like victims of burglary or if she was lucky maybe a minor assault. Anna knew what ever it was she fully intended to make a difference.

Anna's mum was fine apparently, but Anna didn't say much more about her three nights in Norfolk. She complained as normal that her parents holiday caravan, the only residence her mother retained, was cold and stale but its occasional occupation was a worthwhile chore.

Although the family farm had been sold off it was still important that Anna's mum had the possibility of going home if she responded to the programme of rehabilitation she was undertaking following her stroke. So the least Anna could do is retain the family holiday home, a modest static caravan close to the Norfolk coast. Money was tight and it gave Anna somewhere to stay and Steve thought it was a nice rural retreat for them if they wanted a break. However, Anna had never been keen to pursue Steve's suggestion. She seemed to want to leave the sad memories of Norfolk behind her.

"I'm sorry Anna, I know I am supposed to be on my rest days and we were going to spend some time together before you start work properly next week, but they need me back in today."

"Bloody typical," responded Anna trying to sound suitably pissed off.

"I know darling but they are paying me double time and I have to report to the late turn CID Detective Sergeant for tasking to do with the murder I discovered yesterday," explained Steve trying to dull the enthusiastic tone of his voice.

"Okay," Anna said accepting the situation. "You get off back to work but on one condition; you tell me all about it tomorrow."

"Anna!" Steve complained staring back at her. Steve had been known on occasion to reveal a little too much detail of his workplace experiences, but he knew he could trust his wife's discretion not to share his revelations elsewhere. Anyway the details of Fraser's murder were going to be all over the local news by Friday evening.

"PC Lawson?"

"Yes Sarge."

"You're out with Gadget and Dave. They've got a few tasty nominals to T-I-E. So you're just there to cover their backs okay."

Steve acknowledged the instructions distantly as he pondered the term T-I-E. He knew nominals was some kind of major crime way of referring to people but even Steve's best guess was never going to work out even what the first letter T-I-E stood for. Thank God Steve knew Dave well enough to ask him before they actually got in front of any of these 'nominals.'

Dave was waiting at the back of the office for Steve to join him. Dave was a pleasant guy, always the one you homed in on if you had to go and ask CID for advice. He was not like some of the old dinosaurs in there, the kind that thought being over familiar with 'uniform' cramped their style. Dave had only been out of uniform a few years but commanded a great deal of respect from his peers as a sharp and hard working young detective.

"So you still looking to get up here one day mate?" Asked Dave.

"Yes, definitely," replied Steve enthusiastically, knowing that even being hired as CID's uniform back-up was a step in the right direction.

"Gadget's out the back having fag, you ready to go?" Asked Dave.

"Yes, just one quick question though," said Steve sheepishly as they descended the stairs towards the rear yard. "T-I-E? I think the T is trace but what's the rest of it stand for?"

"Trace, Interview and Eliminate. Apparently the E shouldn't be used these days as it suggests everyone we speak to in a major enquiry is a suspect. Subsequently we get to court, the bad guys claim we have the wrong man in the dock and the defence have a cast of hundreds of other possible suspects that were T-I-E'd to blame instead."

Steve was still a bit confused were these people suspects they were going to see, you didn't take back-up to meet your average witness? At least Steve knew what the terminology meant before he met the infamous Gadget.

Gadget was a name Steve had heard banded around before. A true detective apparently. A man in his late 40's, close to completing 30 years service, most of which had been spent in CID. Rumour had it Gadget had once earned more in a year with overtime than the Area Commander - a Superintendent cleared. 'Good Detectives don't come cheap,' was Gadget's favourite saying apparently. However, Steve knew it wasn't all about money with these guys, they cared about what they did and loved doing it too. It was often a tough job and the extra cash sometimes helped make up for the absent fathers and husbands most detectives became.

Steve jumped in the rear of the unmarked old Vauxhall Cavalier, well worn and stinking of stale cigarette smoke despite the apparent ban on smoking in all police vehicles that had recently come into force. Dave started the ropey engine sounding the horn in an effort to break Gadget away from his in depth conversation with the governor who had just gratefully scrounged one of Gadget's Benson and Hedges.

"All right, all right," groaned Gadget as his lowered himself into the passenger seat. "We're not even on overtime yet!" Gadget turned to shake hands with Steve through the gap in the front seats. "Steve Lawson yeah?"

"Yes mate," replied Steve amazed that Gadget knew his name. "I'm Gadget, or at least that's what everyone round here calls me. It's a name that has stuck with me ever since these lot found out I used to be a police cadet or a 'gadget' in my younger years. That is when police cadets were still a way into this job."

Steve was pleased to be so readily accepted by Gadget. It turned out that he had been called in from his rest day the night before to get stuck into the murder enquiry and had been impressed with Steve's actions at the scene. It was his detailed handover package that kicked off the priority actions that kept Gadget more than busy.

Steve thought back to the previous day. After he'd called in the murder he had remained at the scene as one of several officers needed to man the cordon, a mundane job, but Steve hadn't minded. From his post he'd overheard the Detective Chief Inspector or DCI getting a briefing by the crime scene manager and exhibits officer. Both had been fully clad in white paper suits.

"The victim is an older man in his 70's. The officer who found him knows him as Joseph Fraser the landlord of The Wheatsheaf Inn. I would say he's been there maybe 24 hours already, but the pathologist is coming out before we move the body. I wouldn't like to guess how he died other than from massive blood loss and multiple injuries. It appears most of the weapons used came from the pub's kitchen. There's a few footmarks in the scene but I think they are just from uniform boots tramping around before they secured the scene properly."

"So what do you know Steve?" asked Gadget pulling Steve back from his reminisce.

"It was a mess mate, I think this guy was tortured before he died."

"So does the boss," chipped in Dave as they drove out of the back yard.

"Let's see what the Pikey's think?" Said Gadget.

"The travellers?" Queried Steve using a less offensive term.

"Yeah apparently Fraser upset a whole bunch of them at the Green Spinney site last month when he refused their request to have a wedding reception at The Wheatsheaf."

Steve had been called to the back end of a few traveller weddings at clubs and pubs around the county most of the proprietors not realising what they were letting themselves in for. To say they were lively affairs was an understatement; but in an honourable way the head of the family would always deliver a sizeable wad of cash compensation the next day to make up for any problems they caused. Steve could imagine Mr Fraser taking a stance and not being foolish enough to entertain such an event. Whilst he was more than happy to have a handful of local travellers amongst his regulars, he would have drawn the line at several hundred.

"It was John Joseph junior's wedding," said Dave.

"Shit, his old man's a serious handful," responded Steve.

"Don't worry with you on board we'll have no problems," remarked Gadget. Steve had a reputation for fronting out travellers after a well talked about incident in the town centre about 18 months earlier. Naively he hadn't realised the short fat drunk he'd asked to move along late one Saturday night was a traveller, and not just any old traveller, no it was Billy Boy. One of the most notorious bare knuckle fighters the Romanies had to offer.

"That was just me as a new probationer being stupid enough to front out a gypsy full of ale mate. Thank God the control room picked up Billy Boy taking off his shirt on their CCTV monitor and sent the IRV out to back me up just in time to save my skin." Steve explained.

"It worked though mind you, standing your ground, Billy Boy wouldn't have expected that," said Gadget. "So that's what we're going to do today; stand our ground. My plan is to drive the car right into the middle of the site and front them all out."

'This was a veritable suicide mission,' thought Steve, but maybe Gadget's idea was the best approach. Most travellers admired a man with bottle and the three of them were about to pretend they had some.

"Yes officer how can we help you," rung out the Irish accent of Billy Boy, as the three of them simultaneously jumped out of the old CID car they abandoned right in the centre of the site. How unlucky could they be to have Billy Boy as the first person they met.

"Just making enquiries around the area about the murder of the landlord of the old Wheatsheaf Inn out at Chisham the other day," blurted out Dave in one long sentence addressing the ever increasing audience of mainly women and children. Travellers continued emerging from the various caravans and outhouses around the site.

"Terrible business, terrible terrible," the thick accent sung out sympathetically. "Have you caught the bastards yet?" Was the comment that followed from Billy Boy, still acting as the spokesman for the site.

'He said Bastards, not bastard,' Steve immediately thought. 'What does he know?'

Billy was as talkative as ever and went on to remark how John Joe Junior was going to have his wedding reception at the Wheatsheaf recently. He said something had gone wrong at the last minute.

An angry voice added a further response.

"Yeah the fecking old bastard said he couldn't have us all in dat place, caused my boy a shit lot of problems it did!" Boomed out the comments of a mountain of a man, John Joe senior, as he conveniently came to the the front of the group.

"Bet that was a right pain in the arse," empathised Gadget.

"Ended up at the fecking civic hall out at Ringford, fecking miles out."

'John Joe was definitely upset with our victim,' thought Steve but surely not enough to kill him and especially not to torture him. Gadget continued trying to lighten the mood.

"How did the wedding go anyway John Joe?"

"Fecking great crack me old mate, we had the boys down from Spalding and a few of the London lot up too. My boy's still out in Marbella with his missus right now living it up on the honeymoon like."

"Don't I know you from somewhere?" Billy Boy suddenly asked as he moved closer to Steve.

"Probably mate I've worked round this area for a few years now," Steve replied bracing himself for a change in atmosphere.

"You're the fucker who was ready to take me on up town that night aren't you?" Billy claimed.

"Well..." Steve begun to reply as Billy's right hand shot forward making Steve jump out of his skin.

"Put it there," Billy said laughing to himself.

Steve had fortunately resisted the temptation to draw his baton as he glanced down to see the shovel like hand of Billy Boy open and ready to receive a handshake. Steve responded relieved and momentarily honoured by the gesture, suffering only minor injuries caused by the vice like grip of Billy Boy as they shook hands.

"Listen if we can help you's out with this one we will. We'll get the boys to ask around and I'll let you know what we find out?" Billy went quiet looking at Steve inquisitively.

"Steve Lawson, PC Lawson" responded Steve guessing Billy Joe was looking for his name.

"Right Steve we'll be in touch," John Joe interjected ushering the hoard of scruffy kids away from their car implying in a polite traveller manner that it was time for them to leave. Steve looked at Gadget for the lead at that point.

"Thanks gents, that's been very useful we appreciate that, thanks for your time," he said, slightly over egging the gratitude.

Steve and the two detectives were grateful of course. They were leaving Green Spinney in one piece and had enough information to make a judgement on the traveller angle of the enquiry. By checking travel details they could probably confirm John Joe Junior was at least still out of the country and safely deposited on some cheap package deal in Spain when the murder took place. Also key was the fact that the actual wedding went well at the alternative venue so it would be less likely for Fraser to have paid such a high price for not accommodating it.

"Thanks Steve," said Dave. "I think you helped keep a lid on that." He laughed as they drove clear of the Spinney. "We'll head back to the nick and write that up. Gadget and I will pick up some new actions and you can get a change of underwear before we go out again," chuckled Dave.

The last time officers had ended up rolling around in the middle of Green Spinney site fighting travellers they'd had to call out armed response vehicles to extract them. Maybe it was a good thing that the obvious question was not uttered on that site namely, "where were you lot the night before last?" That would have been akin to lighting the blue touch paper and not walking away. Of course we did want to know where each and every one of them was, but it was pointless asking because there'd be thirty plus men, women, children and their dogs from the site who'd "swear to god" that anyone we suspected was safely tucked up in their caravans when the murder took place.

"Where to next guys?" Steve asked knowing Dave had just picked up the next T-I-E task. Steve was really getting into his new but temporary role now.

"We are off out to Mr Tucker's gaff," said Dave as they headed out to the other side of Chisham.

Mr Tucker was the Ronny Biggs of Westhants. A notorious old lag with a pair of sons who thought they were the Kray twins. Mr Tucker was even addressed as 'Mr Tucker' by most of the CID officers. They'd battled for years to try and prove he was at the head of a large drug importation business before he went legit. This was a trend for most criminals of his status, almost a retirement plan. Invest your ill gotten gains into a legitimate business and be grateful you escaped any long prison sentences whilst accumulating that wealth. In Tucker's case quite ironically, he had invested his money in the security business. Tucker ran door security for half of the county these days. It wasn't any surprise his business grew when his sales pitch included stories of pubs and clubs that he didn't do business with having such problems with undesirables that they nearly went under.

"So what has Mr Tucker got to do with Old Man Fraser?" Asked Steve.

Dave explained that he'd researched the action to T-I-E Tucker and it had originated from Old Man Fraser's handwritten account books that had been seized as exhibits.

"There's a photocopy of a page attached to the action from May / June time and it shows payments on a weekly basis to Tucker Security Services, but then they just suddenly stop," detailed Dave.

Steve recalled how there had been a period of time early in the summer when Fraser had out of the blue started to have doormen covering the main door at weekends. Steve had been making one of his occasional licensing visits when Fraser had explained he had a problem at the weekly disco and decided to take on door staff.

"So are we interested in what Mr Tucker knows about the trouble Old Man Fraser was having or simply trying to gauge whether Fraser cancelling his contract pissed him off or not?"

"Both," Gadget confirmed as they drove out to the edge of the county.

There was something rather surreal about the site of a Bentley being parked on the driveway of a council house. Well two council houses knocked into one by the council months before they were purchased for a pittance as part of a 'right to buy' scheme.'

'So this was where Mr Tucker ran his empire from,' Steve thought to himself as Gadget knocked the door, standing underneath the watchful eye of one of Tucker's many personal CCTV cameras. It seemed like overkill to have three officers make this enquiry but if Tucker and his sons were part of this gruesome crime they might stumble across something to prompt a quick decision to make an arrest. The CCTV meant the Tucker's always saw the police coming for them, they needed this early warning system in place. Had they been involved in anything they'd be out of the house like a shot and would be well and truly tucked up on the Costa del Sol before the authorities got them anywhere near a courtroom.

"You're not coming to nick me again Gadget are you?" Said the voice coming from a small intercom system next to the front door.

"No Mr Tucker course not," replied Gadget a familiar face in Tucker's previous life; so much so that Tucker used his nickname when he addressed him.

"What's with the cavalry then." Asked Tucker not convinced by Gadget's denial.

"Look John," Gadget said dropping the formalities. "We are conducting enquiries into the murder of Old Man Fraser at The Wheatsheaf. You and your lads did a bit of door work for him earlier this year so I thought if a couple of us came round we might get to speak to you and your boys as well all at the same time and not take up too much of your precious evening." Bluffed Gadget.

The door opened and there stood John Tucker, a confident looking old chap, can't have been more than six feet from the front door when he'd been talking on the intercom.

"Come on in gents I'll get Mrs T to put the kettle on. The boys have just nipped out for a quick run, I'll give em a bell and get them back." Tucker lifted his mobile phone as they entered, it was vibrating in his hand. "Yeah it's Gadget and a couple of his lot. They just want to talk to us about that bit of door work we did at Fraser's place, that's all."

Tucker had obviously received a call from one of his sons. Steve was mightily suspicious as they were led into the extended kitchen. His suspicions only made worse when within minutes two lumps of steroid induced muscle entered the house through the rear french doors.

"Here are the boys now," announced John Tucker. "I told you they wouldn't be far."

Steve knew they wouldn't either, they may have been in their sports gear and clearly not working that evening but Steve was convinced their decision to get out of the house for a run was just a contingency plan. This would have been helped of course by the delaying tactic of the intercom conversation, just in case they were coming to nick one or all of them. This was a family with a guilty conscience even if the police didn't know what crimes had been committed, the Tucker's did. That was the downside for them really, they could never tell when one such crime might come back to bite them.

"This is Robert and his younger brother Jason," introduced Mr Tucker.

Dave introduced himself with a simple, "Dave, hi," and Steve followed with "PC Lawson, Steve," a touch uncomfortable with the niceties of the situation.

"Tea, coffee?" Offered Mrs Tucker.

Steve soon realised that John Tucker was in fact a likeable rouge. Gadget was happy to let Tucker maintain control if it smoothed the team's pathway to completing their enquiries. After all it was his house and it was close to 9 pm by now.

"Gadget if you want to come with me to my study I'll dig out the invoice for the work we did at The Wheatsheaf and we'll take it from there. My boys will see what they can do for Dave and Steve in here."

Something wasn't right, the Tucker's had something to hide, but was it just their suspected protection racket or had they been the ones who'd brutally tortured that poor stubborn old man a few nights back?

"There's your drinks boys, I'm going to get back to my Cilla if that's alright with you." Announced a cheerful 'Mrs T.'

Steve was confused for a second,'who's Cilla?' He thought. Soon to realise she meant she was going back to the TV when he heard the Scouse tones of Cilla Black singing out "Surprise, Surprise," from the other room.

"Right guys what can you tell us about the work you did at the Wheatsheaf?" Asked Dave.

Robert did all the talking and seemed to be the brighter one of the pair. Jason just threw in repetitive nods and grunts of "that's right, yeah and I remember that." He might as well just said, "whatever he says," at the end of Robert's account. Robert explained that Fraser had found one of the the local hoodies dealing weed from the bar, when he'd challenged him the little shit had pulled a knife and threatened to stab Fraser if he didn't "allow it." Fraser had previously declined an offer Jason had made to provide him with security but when this happened he'd called them. Steve wasn't too happy with this account. Although Steve had decided to himself earlier that he ought to keep quiet and let either Dave or Gadget lead all the questioning, he couldn't resist chipping in when Dave paused for breath.

"So Fraser was last seen when he locked up about 11.30 pm on Sunday night. Were you two out and about then or did you see him at all on Monday?" asked Steve. He really just wanted to come out with it and get them to account for their movements right up to Tuesday just before he'd made the grisly find.

"Well err..." Robert opened paused then answered again on behalf of both of them. "Sunday night is wages night so Jay and me are out and about getting around all the staff whilst its a bit quieter. Have to say we only cover The Star in Chisham and that place closes at the same time as the Wheatsheaf so we left there by about ten maybe. Most of our places are in Wellingsby town here or out in Kithering on the top edge of the county so we have lots of ground to cover. We spent a few hours in Deevos mind, they'd had some bother with a load of boys from the Hamwell Estate over the weekend and one of our guys had been bottled, poor bastard. So we were just trying to find out a bit more about that situation really."

"And Monday?" Prompted Steve.

"Monday's or main gym day cause it's quiet and in the evening we coach the youth boxing team. It's our day off really not a lot of security work needed on a Monday." Robert said confidently.

Gadget and John Tucker emerged from the study.

"We all done here?" asked Tucker as Dave clocked the tilting of Gadget's head indicating that they might as well agree and get out of there.

"Yes thanks gents, thanks for your time," said Dave addressing the two lumps sat at the kitchen table.

"Mind those laces Jason if you are heading back out to finish your run," said Steve, who couldn't resist hinting to the confused meathead that he knew their run was a simple cover story and he'd clocked the fact that Jason hadn't even had chance to fasten his laces when they'd left the house in such a hurry.

"Thanks Mr Tucker," Gadget added as they left the house.

"Any time, don't hesitate to give me a bell if you need to come round for anything else."

Steve was slightly annoyed as they drove off. "Fucking bunch of lying bastards, I bet he'd like a call before we visit next time, give those pair of monsters the chance to splash on a bit of fake sweat to add to their charade."

"Don't worry mate John Tucker was full of the same shit." Reassured Gadget, "but we've traced and interviewed them, all we need to do now is try and eliminate them."

"Got some civvi clothes back in your locker Steve?" Asked Gadget.

"Yes mate," Steve responded.

"Right back to the nick for a quick change and then we're going out again," said Gadget as they headed back.

Real plain clothes work was an exciting prospect for Steve. He was quickly changed into his jeans, T-shirt and leather jacket heading back to the rear yard to rejoin his team.

"That was quick," remarked Dave now looking a bit more casual himself having ditched his tie and donned an old Barbour jacket.

"Where we off to then?" Steve asked excitedly.

"We're going for a beer mate," piped up Gadget.

Steve was disappointed and a little confused. He had a radio and baton shoved into the inside pocket of his jacket ready for action. He'd heard the old stories of detectives going out on the beer when they were supposed to be out doing enquiries. Steve didn't question things though, these guys hadn't let him down yet so maybe it was time to take a chance.

The Clay Pot was a real spit and sawdust place, a traditional 'boozer' that was always packed. Steve's only previous experience of this place was attending mass bar brawls there. Entering scenes that would have been better placed in an old Wild West saloon bar.

They entered the large packed bar full of old 'piss-heads' from the estates, a handful of hard drinking travellers and several other familiar local faces Steve had probably nicked before at some point.

"Shit there's a few choice characters in here," panicked Steve as they discreetly made their way to the bar.

"Don't worry," reassured Dave, "even if they know who we are they'd rather just hope we are here to enjoy a beer and keep their heads down."

Gadget lined up three pints of lager in front of them and just simply said, "watch my back," as he took his pint and walked past the other end of the bar into the empty old fashioned snug. Steve took a large glug from his glass and could just about see Gadget through the small serving area at the back of the bar. 'What was he up to? Who was the fellow in the black bomber jacket he was talking to?' Thought Steve watching carefully. This fellow was a big bloke. Steve could just about see some of his back from his obscured viewpoint. Whatever was going on it was all amicable. A few minutes later Gadget was back.

"Come on boys drink up, I've got some writing to do."

Steve and Dave gulped back their pints and the trio were soon back in the car on route back to the station.

"Nothing to do with the Tuckers," said Gadget.

"That's alright then," answered Dave.

"Probably too late to take on any more T-I-E jobs now but we'll see if there are any other actions we can get on with tonight before we knock off." Added Gadget.

Steve sat quietly in the back of the car and pieced together their last enquiry. 'That guy must have been Gadget's snout,' thought Steve. All good detectives had one or two registered informants on the books and Steve's best guess was this one was something to do with Tuckers security company given his attire. Of course Steve didn't ask, you didn't ask about another officer's source, discretion was important, you were just grateful that someone in the CID had a snout into most sections of the criminal fraternity.

"Your feet are cold," shrieked Anna as Steve slid into the warm bed next to her. "What time is it?"

"It's two thirty in the morning go back to sleep darling." Steve closed his eyes but hadn't yet switched off enough to sleep regardless of how exhausted he felt.

"Did you solve it?"

"Solve what?" replied Steve.

"The murder of course dummy," answered Anna.

"No, I'll tell you all about it in the morning go back to sleep."

"Your boss was on TV last night saying the murder could be some kind of revenge attack," stated Anna as they sat down for brunch the next morning.

"Yeah I suppose I see what he's saying, someone definitely wanted to teach Fraser a lesson, but I favour travellers or some kind of organised crime group rather than just some random individual," answered Steve basing a lot of his comment on the enquiries he still felt were incomplete from the previous day.

"So they've got a suspect then," fished Anna.

"You know I'm not allowed to tell you even if they did darling."

"So they haven't got anyone then?" said Anna.

'Shit,' Steve thought, he was such a rubbish liar when it came to Anna. "Maybe not," he admitted, "but there must be some forensic evidence that crime scene was a mess."

Steve hoped to find out a bit more about the investigation on his next shift. The exhibits officer had asked to meet him at the scene when he returned to work in two days time, so he could go over a few points with Steve about how he'd found things. He needed to know exactly what Steve did or didn't move or damage when he had first entered the scene and double check his findings with the first officer to attend.

"Anyway darling enough about my work what about your new job?" Steve asked.

"Well I start for real on Monday, I spoke to Marion on the phone yesterday and she already has two cases for me to get stuck into. One is an old lady who had her bag ripped from her shoulder in Westhampton town centre one evening and the other is a schoolgirl who saw a flasher in Beechfield Park whilst walking home from school. I'm really looking forward to it." Explained Anna.

She seemed like the obvious candidate to be a Victim Support Officer. She had not had an easy life with her father's suicide and mothers ill health, but she'd always been strong and picked herself up at each stage. Anna understood and supported the work of the police learning a lot about the real job from her long chats with Steve. Often counselling him through some mild post incident trauma. Steve was proud of what Anna was about to undertake, he was proud of his beloved wife full stop.

After two enjoyable days off with Anna, Steve was back at work dealing with more run of the mill uniform tasks like shop lifters and neighbour disputes. The murder enquiry went on and was now being run from a Major Incident Room set up at Steve's rural police station and staffed by detectives from across the county. There was no longer any need for uniform support, but at least Steve would get a chance to probe the exhibits officer for an update at 2 o'clock when he had an appointment with him back at the Wheatsheaf.

"Tim Knight, pleased to meet you Steve. Here put these on and we'll get cracking," said the very professional sounding detective as he passed Steve a fresh paper suit, face mask and over boots.

Steve donned his protective clothing feeling like a cross between a surgeon and a biochemist entering some kind of contaminated area.

"Hood up mate," instructed Tim. Steve had probably shed some hairs in the scene previously but he assumed Tim didn't want to have to seize anymore of them?

Forensic scene management was a bit like health and safety on a building site, if it was a hard hat area there were no exceptions. The suits stopped you dropping hair and fibres, whilst the masks stopped you coughing your DNA onto anything. With the special overboots preventing you putting down a new boot mark at the scene.

"So tell me about this main door Steve," Tim asked.

Steve explained how he forced it open, but whilst the latch had definitely dropped, he didn't think it had been properly secured when they were locked.

"Good that helps," Tim said. "We can't find anything to suggest the bolts were in place when the doors were locked."

"Pulled shut?" Queried Steve.

"Yes we think so." Answered Tim going on to explain that their best assessment was that the killer left via the main doors dropping the latch and pulling the doors shut as they did so. Obviously securing the doors but missing the vertical bolt at the top in their hurry.

"How did they get in then?" Asked Steve.

"They were already in when Mr Fraser locked up maybe, hidden on the premises somewhere I expect."

"But where?" Asked Steve.

"Well we are looking at the toilets for fingerprints. That may give us a steer but that isn't so easy with all the flooding."

"Yeah what was that all about?"

Tim explained how they had to get a plumber to sort it all out. One of the toilets in the ladies had been backed up by an old set of marigolds a cleaner could have dropped cleaning one of the loos and accidentally flushed them down maybe? Anyway the gents were okay and they were just starting to get some fingerprint lifts from in there.

"A load of T-I-E's then," said Steve trying to impress Tim with his little bit of knowledge about major incident work.

"Yes," Tim continued. "These empty glasses Steve, were they all just like this or did any get moved."

"No mate nothing was touched, some of them were on the bar near the glass washing sink with a fair few still at various tables, why's that important?"

"We got a fingerprint hit from a pint glass on that small corner table, it's some local scrote, deals a bit of class 'A' gear. No one's managed to trace him yet. There's also two other glasses that were on the same table. Two further sets of prints from two unknown people that could have been with him but no identification yet." Explained Tim obviously keen to pursue the possibility this dealer brought two clean skins in to do his dirty work.

"I know you went upstairs from your statement Steve and unless you're going to suggest otherwise we are not examining that at the moment as it looks untouched."

Steve agreed bracing himself as he followed Tim into the kitchen. 'It's not so bad,' thought Steve. The griddle had gone for starters. "What was that in the sandwich toaster thing?" Asked Steve.

"Fingers, all four of them from the poor bastards left hand. The pathologist confirmed from what we scraped up that this injury was definitely caused while the victim was still alive."

Tim went on to explain how he'd been given an action to confirm if Fraser was right or left handed. His right hand was still in tact and maybe there was some symbolic reason for destroying his left hand?

"Think I'll get the FLO to help me out there. Give me a body on the slab any day, but grieving relatives that's not for me, don't know how those family liaison guys do it."

Unconfirmed reports had Fraser down as left handed and the Senior Investigating Officer thought it was significant that his attacker had chosen to mutilate his lead hand, but Tim wasn't so sure.

'How well did Old Man Fraser's killer or killers know him?' Wondered Steve.

"Do you wear Magnum boots for work Steve?" Asked Tim.

"Sometimes yeah why?"

"We found one of your boot prints by the back door here, size 9 yes?"

"Yes mate I'm a 9, but it can't be one of my boot prints," answered Steve abruptly. "I made sure I stayed away from where the suspect and victim had obviously been, that's why I went to the pub garden via the side gate. Anyway I was wearing my new Danner Kinetic boots that day I'm sure. I only keep my old Magnums as spares these days."

"Alright Steve keep your hair on, must have been some idiot who came in the scene for a nose around after you." Steve was confused this was possible but unlikely he kept the scene secure and hadn't let any sightseers in whilst he was still in charge of it.

"What's all that up there?" Asked Steve pointing up towards the corner of the room.

"Well if you look at that it's a line of blood and look closely at the tails of each droplet you can see the cast off from the heavy implement that must have been used to strike Fraser. Assuming it is Fraser's blood of course, the amount of cast off shows it was a frenzied attack to start with at least and my best guess is some kind of heavy bar or club was used initially to beat him into submission. Fraser had a load of long narrow shaped areas of broken skin around his body and head with some signs of internal bleeding probably caused by numerous hard blows to the body. We're doing some forensic work to try find out if it's one of the weapons we found in here and if not, what caused that cast off."

"Sorry what actually killed Mr Fraser?" Asked Steve.

"Well basically he bled out. Apart from his fingers, torsos wounds and a load of different sized small stab wounds caused by almost every knife on that rail, two jabs that hit his femoral artery finished him off. The killers knew what they wanted to do. Fraser would have grown weaker and weaker as the blood drained from him. My guess is the last of his energy was used trying to escape to the beer garden, but why he got into that Wendy house God only knows? The SIO says this is a revenge thing, some kind of gang attack, he's adamant there would have had to be at least two or three attackers. "What do you think Tim?"

"Me I'm not so sure, this was personal, but I don't know why. I still can't eliminate the possibility this is just one person with a serious grudge, but then what do I know? You knew him didn't you Steve, have you got any thoughts?" Asked Tim.

"Fraser was a miserable old bastard I know, but likeable with it. His wife definitely loved him and has always been by his side running this place. There are a lot of arseholes in Chisham and some odd characters out in the villages round here too. So who knows but I'm with you, a single attacker with a screw loose is my best guess."

Tim was grateful for Steve's input and more than happy to share his findings. Tim had a lot to piece together and he was confident he could recreate the sequence of events accurately with the help of the forensic experts he relied upon. What was clear to Tim however was there would be no quick fix here, the killer had not left any kind of obvious biometric trace and with the absence of any eye witnesses the killer would remain at large for some time. Steve found this short insight into the world of exhibits handling and crime scene management fascinating. He had definitely added the role of exhibits officer to the bucket list of jobs he wanted to do before he retired.

"Hi Dave how you doing?" Said Steve as he joined his CID friend in the main canteen. Two months had now passed since the day Steve had discovered Joseph Fraser's body. Dave seemed genuinely pleased to see Steve who had obviously made a good impression when he had helped Dave and Gadget with their enquiries.

"I'm still seconded to the Fraser murder enquiry you know. Have been now since day one." He replied.

"So are we any closer to finding out why Old Man Fraser was so brutally murdered yet?" Asked Steve who was now a little out of touch with the investigation having returned to more mundane uniform duties.

"No not really Steve, its a real mystery this one. The governor seems to have moved away from travellers and organised crime. We had some prints for a local drug dealer and his mates in the bar but when they were eventually traced they denied any knowledge of the murder. Others in the bar saw them leave and they had weak but checkable alibis. I've spent the last month looking at a number of the local oddballs from the villages round here. Tim Knight suggested we had more than our fare share of nutters with an array of mental health problems locally during one of the SIO's office meetings," explained Dave.

Steve felt a sense of satisfaction that something he had highlighted to Tim had now become a useful line of enquiry, even if Tim probably got the credit for it.

"The trouble is Steve we've have no new forensic hits, no CCTV, no witnesses and there's not a registered informant in the county that knows anything about this case."

"So even if one of these oddballs looks promising you can't link them in with anything can you?" Stated Steve.

Dave confirmed this was correct and explained how the SIO was looking to scale this job down at the end of the month pending any new information coming to light. Steve knew it was difficult to ever stop investigating a murder totally, but realistically this was the beginning of the end. Steve still couldn't figure out who hated Fraser so much to do that to him. Someone out there knew something and maybe one day they'd come forward.

Chapter 3

The Teacher

"So I assume you'll be late home tonight darling?" Asked Anna in a jovial tone.

"I'll try not to be too late," remarked her devoted husband Steve.

"Don't worry my love you deserve a drink you're a detective now don't they all drink lots of whiskey and smoke big cigars or is that just on TV?" Joked Anna.

Steve kissed his wife goodbye and left the flat for the final day of his CID course. Steve was indeed a detective constable now and felt good dressed in his sharp suit as he got into his car to drive to the police training centre. Steve had worked really hard over the last three years to get out of uniform and into the CID office. It wasn't long after the murder at The Wheatsheaf Inn that Steve got an attachment to the area crime squad where his tenacity for pursuing criminals really shone through. His career had flourished in tandem with his wife's. She was now one of victim support's specialist children's case workers dealing specifically with child victims and their families. She had a very good relationship with the force's Child Protection Unit. Steve's credibility received an additional boost when people found out his wife was a respected member of the local Victim Support. Steve had secured a short attachment to the CID in the rural east of the county where he had previously been a uniform officer. He had enjoyed being mentored by Gadget in the months leading up to Gadget's retirement. Gadget saw Steve as the legacy he would leave behind before he moved to Spain investing his pension in a modest villa on a golf complex. That was Gadget's idea of heaven. Steve had learnt a lot in the rural sector's CID office and hadn't wanted to move outside of this comfort zone to step into a detectives shoes elsewhere. However all of the permanent vacancies for detectives were in the main town, Westhampton. So Steve moved there. They had the biggest CID office in the force and if you believed the rhetoric were the busiest detectives in the county.

"So when do you start at Westhampton?" Steve's new found colleague Julie asked.

"Straight after Christmas I think, should be the second of January, I'm just waiting for duties to confirm it."

"You'll like it in Westhampton," Julie explained. "There are five teams each with its own detective sergeant. The DCI's not bad and the DI is a great character". Julie had been on an extended attachment for over a year there now and really had her feet under the table. She was an attractive woman divorced and with a bit of a reputation. Her and Steve had really got on during the six week course both professionally and as friends. Of course Steve was the exception to the rule and intended to stay that way; he was happily married and truly in love with Anna, making no secret of it. Steve wasn't looking for any extra marital excitement, he got all the excitement he needed from the job. For Julie this was light relief if she was honest; a male colleague without a hidden agenda almost like the gay best friend analogy. Steve found it a touch worrying though when Julie once used that very term to describe their successful friendship.

It was one of those bitter cold January mornings, the kind where you could do with an ice pick to de-ice your car windscreen. Steve drove the few miles across town to his new Police Station.

"Nice and early Steve, good to see. Dump you stuff on that desk there mate and we'll nip to the canteen and grab a coffee," said the friendly voice of Ken Mayfield, Steve's new DS.

Steve had met Ken on the CID course, he'd done an input on investigating sexual offences, in particular rape. This was something Ken had a vast experience of, having been a DC then DS in the same main office for well over twenty years. Ken was expecting Steve and was ready to settle him down into his new role.

"Tea or coffee Steve?"

"I'll have a coffee thanks Ku.." Steve hesitated.

"Ken, you can call me Ken, none of that 'Sarge' shit round here, your a detective now."

Steve knew this would be the case but was momentarily stunned by Ken's vast seniority and experience thinking he maybe should call him 'sergeant' in recognition of that. There wasn't a lot Ken hadn't done in his CID centred career, he was a total guru in the world of the detectives.

"Right just to remind you of the rotation we have. One team is a duty team, one on prisoners, one enquiries, one on a late shift and the fifth on rest days. There's plenty of experience in the office and you'll always find someone who'll know the answer to your question if you get stuck on anything. Don't worry too much though because you won't be on your own much. Oh apart from when you are the nights DC, but I don't think you're rostered in for that until the end of March."

Ken went on to explain how about once every six months, when the team was on late shifts, one DC would do a night shift and be at the beck and call of the area control room to attend all reports of serious crime. Ken said not to worry because if the nights detective needed advice he would have the office mobile phone and could phone the on call Detective Inspector at home whatever the time of night was.

"But don't be the one that wakes the DI up for a crock of shit," warned Ken. "He can be a grumpy old sod in the middle of the night."

Steve settled in well, taking on a source led cocaine supply investigation and a post office robbery all in the first week. With some good colleagues around him and his allie Julie on one of the other teams Steve took most things in his stride, really enjoying his new post over the next few months.

"Are you sure you don't want me to make you a pack-up?" Anna asked.

"No darling not for tonight. I'll probably not get chance to eat it anyway, I'll just grab something at one of the 24 hour garages or maybe a kebab while I'm out."

"Don't you go eating too much junk Steve and getting indigestion, you're the sheriff of Westhampton tonight you need to be on top form," joked Anna.

"Hardly!" Exclaimed Steve, "I'm the night duty DC that's all Anna."

"You take care darling, I'll be thinking of you from my nice warm bed, with all that extra room you've left for me," laughed Anna.

Steve kissed his wife goodbye and headed out for his first ever nightshift as the 'nights DC.'

"Right Steve not a lot for you, just remember to drop that file off at the Criminal Justice Office some time during the night and if the shit really hits the fan the DI's mobile and home numbers are in the back of the O-B," instructed Ken as the rest of the shift drifted away soon after Steve entered the office.

Before he knew it Steve was alone flicking his way through the overnight book or 'O-B'; the latest acronym Steve had learnt. This made really interesting reading; in amongst the many 'quiet night - nothing to report' entries were some elaborate descriptions of serious assaults, rapes, petrol station robberies and some more diverse sudden deaths. Steve carefully assessed the standard required for writing such reports. Steve knew before the next 7 night shifts were up he'd definitely be filling in at least a few new pages of the O-B. It was essential to make sure the oncoming duty team had everything they possibly needed to start their enquiries with the next day.

Three long nights went past with Steve not writing anything meaningful in that book. It was now Sunday night and Steve knew for some reason it was always on a Sunday when things went awry. It was that false sense of security you had, having survived Friday and Saturday nights that made you think Sunday would be the quiet one, but it generally wasn't.

Steve started the shift lumbered with a load of exhibits to get booked into the store. They'd sat on the duty team's desks all day whilst they worked tirelessly on a drug rape allegation. A young female had walked into the front office of the nick at about 10 a.m. that Sunday morning, accompanied by her best friend convinced someone had had sex with her after a drink had been spiked. It had taken her over 24 hours to decide to come forward and report it. This had happened on Friday night into Saturday morning at a house party she and her friend had been invited to.

"Unfortunately it's the same old story," Ken explained. "Young girl and her mate out partying, drinking heavily, shots and all sorts of weirdly named alcopops. Then they get invited to some strangers flat for a house party and eventually both flake out. Subsequently when one of them wakes up and realises she must have had sex with the young guy next to her she cant remember a thing and therefore must have been raped. Trouble is in a lot of cases they didn't consent, they were off their heads, so they are right; they have been raped. Mind you trying to prove it is another story. Especially when nine times out of ten the toxicology shows no signs of drugs in their system, just evidence of copious amounts of alcohol having been consumed."

"So what's next then?" Asked Steve keen to educate himself on the skills needed to investigate sexual offences.

"Well the suspect has been in, claimed it was entirely consensual and they were both pretty drunk. He's been bailed for CPS advice. Turns out there was a house full of various waifs and strays most of whom we've now traced, all equally as drunk. Not one of them claiming to have seen or heard anything untoward going on in the guys bedroom."

"What about the best friend though?" Steve asked Ken.

"She's all we've got really. She sat down with her tearful friend last night not able to believe she would have had casual sex in such circumstances. It appears her friend agreed. There then follows a sustained exchange of messaging on that 'msn' thing where various other kids offer their opinion and eventually the consensus of opinion is she should report what happened as a rape."

"That sounds far from straight forward," remarked Steve, "how old are these girls then?"

"That's the icing on the cake, they're a pair of sixth formers, the victim's just turned 17 and her mate is only 16!"

"Anything I can get on with apart from getting these exhibits squared away?" Asked Steve.

Ken explained that the victims friend, 16 year old Lucy, had described a man at the party who seemed to know the suspect quite well. This man had initially tried to chat Lucy up. As far as she was concerned he seemed like a nice enough guy but she described him as ancient. When properly questioned re this description this man was in fact in his late 20's. He hadn't seemed too happy to have his advances rejected by Lucy, said he was going home just before midnight and disappeared. Ken explained that they did have a mobile phone number for this man and the first name of 'Richard'. Richard had tapped this into Lucy's phone at some point and she'd not yet deleted it. One of the team had tried ringing 'Richard' several times but it just constantly went to answer phone.

"We've asked for subscriber details," Ken explained, "but they won't come through for a few days. You're a dab hand on the Force Intelligence System Steve, see what you can do. If you can ID him from records in there, and it's not too late get round and see him. See if he can shed any light on this confusing mess." Ken grabbed his bag and begun to leave.

"Have a quiet night Steve."

'I wish he hadn't used the 'Q' word,' thought Steve. It usually had the opposite effect on events and things go crazy instead.

"Found him!" Shouted Steve aloud addressing an office full of empty desks. 'Richard Wilson, 28, victim, criminal damage to a motor vehicle,' the crime report read. Wilson had of course provided his mobile phone number to police when he was a victim of this seemingly minor crime a month earlier. The report read 'persons unknown pour unknown corrosive substance over unattended motor vehicle causing damage to paintwork for unknown reason.'

'Someone trashed his car then,' thought Steve, 'can't be a very popular guy, wonder what he does for a living.'

Richard Wilson was a supply teacher apparently and he lived in one of the new build semis just off the A485 only a few miles from the nick. That was good enough for Steve. 'Time to go and suss this guy out,' he thought. Determined to add some clarity to the scenario Ken had described and to help out the oncoming duty team in the morning Steve grabbed the car keys and headed out to where Wilson lived.

Steve pulled up outside the small unassuming semi pleased to see Mr Wilson was almost certainly still living there as he eyed the still damaged two tone Ford Fiesta on the driveway. 'The house lights are still on,' thought Steve considering whether at half past ten it was still proportionate to disturb a potential witness.

'He's a professional guy,' Steve pondered determined to assist with this line of enquiry. 'His lights are on so I'm sure he'll be happy to at least give me a quick account even though it is late?'

Steve quietly knocked on the front door of Richard Wilson's house. Nothing not even a twitching curtain. 'Theres no way someone would leave that many lights on when they go out. Maybe he's in the back watching TV?' Considered Steve. He had set a goal to trace this witness overnight and he was going to achieve it if at all possible.

Steve quietly slipped through the side gate into the rear garden hoping not to startle the poor Mr Wilson with his less than conventional approach. Yes, the rear curtains were open and Steve could see right into the lounge diner.

"Hello, Mr Wilson it's the police nothing to worry about, are you home?"

The lights were on but there was no sign of any occupants. However, the picture that faced Steve caused him immediate concern.

Steve took his radio from his pocket, "control this is November Mike three one seven have you got someone available to join me at 198 Wycombe Drive?"

"Received November Mike three one seven, what have you got Steve?" Answered the friendly voice of the controller now familiar with Steve's voice.

"I'm out tracing a possible witness for that rape that came in this morning. I'm at his house but when I couldn't get an answer I went round the back. I'm looking in the rear patio door which is slightly open, something looks to have kicked off in the lounge but there is no sign of the householder. I'm going to go in and check it out so I could just do with someone on route if that's possible, received?"

"November Mike four two, can I come in there."

"Go ahead four two."

"We're no more than three minutes away if the CID callsign wants to hang fire we'll be with him ASAP?"

It was too late Steve was already in the lounge, baton drawn and ready, concerned he may have stumbled upon an unrelated crime in progress. What could possibly go wrong when back up was so close behind. Initially Steve's approach tactic was one of stealth. Instinct told him not to call out 'police' the offender may well still be inside and Steve was going to take him on, as foolish an idea as that seemed. Steve could see the coffee table had been knocked out of place and a glass ashtray smashed with its contents spread out on the floor. Across the room Steve could see the illuminated screen of a computer sat on a small dining table. It was on and images were scrolling across the screen. Images that appeared to be pornographic pictures from a distance. The computers keyboard and mouse had been pushed out of place and the dining chair that had obviously been used to sit in front of the computer, was over on its side.

"What the fuck!" Blurted out Steve stunned as he took a closer look. The writing was literally on the wall. What Steve had initially assumed was the trendy wallpaper of a feature wall turned out to be lines of writing scrawled across the width of the main wall in the living room area.

'I'm a dirty little paedophile and I want to apologise for my sick fantasies. I have used my career as a teacher to access children and have been able to avoid detection and prosecution because the authorities are weak and can't protect children from evil monsters like me. God will be my judge.'

The message was repeated a number of times, like the lines of a naughty schoolboy in some old fashioned classroom. 'What had happened here?' Steve thought.

"RICHARD IT'S THE POLICE," He now shouted.

Steve turned, looked down and gagged uncontrollably.

"Fuck, fuck, fuck," gasped Steve as he doubled up trying desperately not to vomit all over the laminate floor. Steve had caught proper sight of the images scrolling across the computer screen. These were young girls maybe twelve, thirteen max all being horribly sexually abused in some form or another. Steve instinctively lashed out at the monitor with his baton smashing the display into submission just as two hyped up officers emerged from the rear garden.

"Where's the suspect mate, you alright?"

Asked one of them slightly confused at the sight of Steve, baton in hand, shards of shattered screen still landing around the room but no suspect anywhere to be seen.

"WILSON, WHERE THE FUCK ARE YOU, YOU SICK FUCK?" Steve shouted quite unprofessionally but justifiably so.

"Check upstairs," instructed Steve as the two uniform figures flew past him. There was a pause as the sound of the two men could be heard tramping up the stairs.

"He's in the bedroom," shouted one of the guys. Steve rushed up the stairs into the main bedroom to find the two officers stood motionless staring at the double bed.

"Looks like he's topped himself mate," said one of the officers quite casually.

Steve looked around the two men to see a very neatly laid out slightly built man, obviously dead, on a blood soaked double bed. Both wrists had been neatly sliced along the length of each artery. Almost identically sized large dried up pools of blood led down each side of the bed into congealed blobs on the carpet. In one of the blobs Steve noticed an orange craft knife lodged firmly in the centre of it. Wilson's eyes were still wide open staring up at the ceiling, maybe towards heaven wondering if his soul would ever make it there or not.

"Glove up guys and check there's no one else in this place," ordered Steve immediately taking control of the crime scene snapping out of his trance like state.

Was this a crime scene though or simply the end result of a paedophiles rage realising that his world was about to come crashing down around him. 'Surely Richard Wilson hadn't been that concerned about being a potential witness to a rape allegation that he thought the police would dig into his private life and discover his dirty secret,' thought Steve. 'Or were his advances on the victim's friend more forceful than she had actually disclosed?' Steve continued to ponder over the likely scenarios as he stood staring at the dead teacher, the two uniform officers busy cordoning off the immediate area. 'Wilson wouldn't have even known he was a witness in a rape allegation though he left the party early? Maybe someone texted him or something was sent over msn or some other web chatroom and that's how he found out?' Steve thought on.

Steve took himself back to basics. He was looking at a sudden death of a man by unnatural causes. He was in a house that Steve had found insecure. Steve's first impressions were that the lounge diner was the scene of some kind of an assault and was not the self inflicted damage of a man in anguish. The lines of confession across the walls were not the standard suicide note you'd expect to find.

Steve was pleased to see one officer stood behind tape in the alleyway at the foot of the garden as he looked out of the rear window. Steve left the house carefully via the front door, the least likely point of entry for the potential offender. The second officer had neatly boxed off the front of the house inclusive of the adjacent pathway.

"Have you called it in yet?" Steve asked.

"Just the basics mate, told them to wait for an update from you".

"Thanks," Steve responded.

"Control this in November Mike three one seven, receiving over."

"Go ahead Steve."

"Just to confirm we have one deceased male at the address, possible suspicious circumstances, if you give me a call on the CID mobile I'll let you know what I need."

"Received, standby."

That familiar Nokia ring tone soon sounded and Steve found himself speaking to the force control room inspector. A confident chap used to making his own decisions, calm in a crisis but obviously keen to get the CID management to take over responsibility for this incident as soon as he could.

"I've woken up your DI Steve, he's going to call you."

"What have you told him Sir?"

"Well just that you were at the scene of a suspicious death and you wanted him called out."

Steve cursed to himself, he hadn't asked for the DI to be called out yet and in any case Steve should be the one to call him with the full facts once he was ready to brief him properly, not some over enthusiastic uniform governor.

"Okay sir I'll speak to my DI in a minute but to update you we have an apparent suicide following a potential disturbance at the deceased house. The premises are insecure and this guy appears to be a sex offender who may have been outed recently. Both his wrists have been cut and he has been dead for several hours, maybe up to twenty four. I need a doctor out to confirm death and at present a minimum of two officers to cover the cordon for at least the next twenty four hours. I will look at additional CID resources and discuss this directly with the DI. We will also deal with identifying the next of kin." Confirmed Steve.

"I need you to draft me out a community impact assessment tonight please Steve."

"Yeah, Yes Sir," answered Steve frustrated, quickly cutting the call to take another. "Got to go sorry, I think that's the DI calling me now."

Steve was pleased to have been able to bat off the control room inspector's request for now. Why was it that senior managers and sector inspectors only ever worried about community impact and public reassurance. 'Fuck that,' thought Steve, 'what about the victim and their family. The 'community' knew extra patrols and statements saying 'this was normally a safe place to live' were just political spin and no one actually took any reassurance from it.

"Hello Boss," answered Steve accepting the call from the DI.

"How come I've got the control room inspector briefing me on a suspicious death, why didn't you call me Steve?"

"Sorry Boss but I have literally just walked out of the scene and set up the cordon, with respect though, I told the control room I would contact you myself, but that idiot took no notice and just jumped the gun before I could stop him. So you know what we've got then?" Asked Steve.

"No," laughed the DI, "that 'idiot' hadn't got a clue he said my nights DC had the full run down."

Steve explained the sequence of events and how Ken had asked him to try and locate one of the possible witnesses from the previous days rape allegation. The DI was familiar with that case and the fact that an unknown Richard was still sought. Steve explained what he'd found and what he'd now done to secure the scene.

"So what makes this suspicious Steve and not just a simple suicide uniform could deal with?"

Steve was momentarily taken aback by the DI's question, had he over egged this?

"Well one, this guy was very recently a victim of an obviously deliberate attack on his car, so he's pissed someone off. Two, inside the insecure lounge diner someone, if not the victim, has written lines and lines of confessions about being a sex offender on the wall; I believe the writer has done this under some duress. Three, he has left open what appears to be a large file of indecent images of children scrolling as a slideshow on his computer for whoever finds him which doesn't make sense. And finally his wrist cuts were almost clinical in a way; designed to cause the victim to bleed out at a rapid rate. It just doesn't make sense sir, do you think I'm wrong?"

"No Steve," chuckled the DI picking up the insecurity in Steve's final comment. "I think you're spot on. Don't let anyone go into the scene until I join you. I understand you've got a doctor on the way. Get a SOCO there; just for some scene photography and a video, then I think we'll close the scene up until daylight and leave the body in situ. It's going to be a long night Steve hope you didn't have any plans for a kip in the early hours," joked the DI. "I want you to trace the next of kin and do the death message properly before this one hits the headlines. I'll be with you in twenty minutes."

Steve was pleased with himself, all he had to do now was explain why he'd smashed a computer monitor to death with his baton and upset a scene that otherwise had been so carefully preserved.

By the time Steve had shown the DI around the scene, helped the SOCO grab some initial photography and video footage, and of course explained his act of criminal damage away, it was close to 3 a.m.

"Right Steve I really do need that next of kin tracing," remarked the boss as they stripped out of their forensic clothing outside of the scene.

"It should be doable sir, according to some cursory work I had the control room do Wilson's family may be living out in Suffolk though," commented Steve.

"Listen you can be in Suffolk in an hour at this time of night, get back to the nick, check the address yourself and get out there. Whatever you do don't get the locals to deliver the death message; this whole scenario is challenging enough and I want the information they receive to be accurate and controlled. For now just tell them his death is sudden and unexplained," instructed the DI.

'Easier said than done,' thought Steve as he headed back to the office. Steve had delivered many death messages when in uniform. He knew most grief stricken families firstly won't believe what you are telling them and secondly will want to know when, where, how and why straight away. If you don't know they rapidly drift back into denial and claim it can't be their loved one you are talking about. Steve psychologically gripped himself, reminding himself he was a detective now, the DI was busy briefing the Homicide and Major Crime Detective Chief Inspector. The DI had given Steve a task to achieve that night, unsupervised and without any need to phone him again until it was done.

Fortunately for Steve Richard Wilson had failed to inform DVLA that he didn't live with his parents any more. On the scale of Wilson's suspected criminality a bit of poetic license to maintain a cheap insurance premium was both trivial and ironically useful to the police on this occasion. Steve checked the address DVLA held and looked at the voters register to firm up his supposition that this was the family home.

'64 Newmarket Road, Long Acton - Mr Richard Wilson'

Steve checked the address for other residents listed:

'Mr James Taylor'
'Mrs Eileen Taylor'
'Ms Kathleen Taylor'

'Could they be his family with a different surname?' Steve thought. He knew from experience no family was ever straight forward. Maybe Wilson's mother was divorced and had remarried a James Taylor at some point, but who was Kathleen Taylor? Either way Wilson had previously lived at this address hidden away in the Suffolk countryside and who ever lived there now could be related to him in some way.

As Steve jumped on the brakes to avoid the flashes of yet another rural speed camera he continued to rehearse the opening lines he'd thought of out loud to himself in the car:

"Mr Taylor?"

"Is your son Richard Wilson? Do you know a Richard Wilson? A man named Richard Wilson still has a Ford Fiesta motor vehicle registered to this address can you tell me why?"

'No that's shit,' thought Steve.

"Where the fuck am I?" Complained Steve out loud as he fumbled the various sheets of route finder he'd hastily printed from a new piece of software they had in the office.

Long Acton was a quiet village about 10 miles from Newmarket. No more than maybe a hundred houses, a lot of them with names rather than numbers. Fortunately the Newmarket Road was the main 'B' road that went straight through the village. It was far to hard to see house names and numbers through the greenery adorning most of the front gardens from the car. Steve parked up by the village green hoping to find the address within the immediate area. Steve followed some numbers down the hill no more than fifty yards before he found 64. A modest stone built semi, beautifully cared for and full of character, the kind of place Steve could only dream of owning one day. It was 4:45 in the morning by now and dark as hell. The rain had stopped but the weather was very cold and unforgiving. Steve begun to shiver slightly as he stared at the dark front door, ready to lift the heavy iron door knocker, yet to decide which one of many lines he'd practised would come out of his mouth when the door was answered.

"Ruff, ruff, ruff," barked a crazed hound as Steve leapt back to see half a dogs head emerging from the cat flap in the bottom of the door. 'Never mind knocking,' Steve thought as he saw the hall light come on and could hear the angry tones of a young female telling "William" to, "get back".

"Who is it?" Asked the cautious female voice.

"It's okay, it's DC Steve Lawson from Westhamptonshire Police, sorry to wake you but I need a word," answered Steve disappointed at the latter part of his opening line.

"Hang on I need to put the dog out." She shouted.

The door opened to reveal a young woman dressed in a modest set of winter PJ's and an oversized towelling dressing gown.

"Did you say Westhamptonshire? Is it Richard?" Asked the concerned young lady.

"Can I come in please?" Asked the stoney faced Steve.

As he was shown into the cosy front room Steve asked if the young woman was alone?

"Yes mum and dad are on holiday, due back tonight, what's happened?"

"Are you Richard Wilson's sister?" Asked Steve.

"Yes, well his step-sister really. Is Richard okay?"

"I'm really sorry but the body of a young man has been found at 198 Wycombe Drive in Westhampton and we are pretty sure it is Richard."

"How do you know it's him?" Was the initial response received as the woman begun to sob.

"I'm really sorry. I'm sure it is Richard, he had his wallet on him and he is definitely the Richard Wilson shown on his driving license and school ID card," answered Steve with some certainty, having personally looked at this only a few hours earlier.

"What am I going to tell mum and dad?" Asked the woman now in full flow, crying uncontrollably as Steve watched from across the room. An unwanted voyeur in this tragic moment.

"Is there someone I can call?" Asked Steve hoping for a positive reply.

"My fiancée, I'll call him."

Before Steve had chance to offer to contact him on her behalf she had the phone in her hand and was making the desperate plea.

"Christian you need to come over her now Richard's been killed, I've got the police with me. Hurry I need you."

Concerned, Steve said, "I could have gone and picked him up for you."

"It's alright he's only in Newmarket, he'll be alright."

"When are your mum and dad due home?" Steve asked.

"They are flying home tomorrow," she answered just before she suddenly jumped up and headed out of the room.

"Oh shit William, he's still shut out in the garden, you're alright with dogs aren't you?" She asked as she passed Steve not waiting for an answer in her hurry, assuming he'd say yes.

Steve couldn't help but to fuss the slightly soggy gorgeous chocolate lab that bounded into the front room. Steve was alright with dogs of course, it came in handy in his job. Steve was just grateful his night time attire was not one of his standard formal suits that would have costed him a fortune to get cleaned after this encounter.

"He's lovely," remarked Steve wondering if this was the same monstrous beast that tried to take a chunk out of him via the cat flap.

"Where's Richard now?" asked his sister bringing Steve back from his doggy respite.

"He's going to be taken to the mortuary at Westhampton General where he'll be looked after whilst we try and find out why he died. Unfortunately I don't have a lot I can tell you at the moment other than he was found alone at home with injuries to his wrists, but we don't want to draw any conclusions until we have investigated the circumstances fully." Explained Steve wondering how that really long sentence sounded to the bereaved step sister.

"So he's killed himself then?"

"No, no I didn't say that, what I am saying is until we explore all of the possibilities we cannot rule out anything. I'm sorry it's a bit vague but I hope we will have a clearer picture later on today." Continued Steve. During pauses to allow for further tears, Steve went on to re-emphasise the fact that the death was unexplained and they would be exploring things more as time went on.

A quiet tap on the unlocked door was swiftly followed by the dashing young Christian who swept up the tear soaked sister and held her tight for a brief moment before readjusting himself to the formality of the moment.

"Christian Lomax."

"DC Steve Lawson, Westhants Police. I'm sorry to have to meet you in these circumstances." Answered Steve with a cheesy cliche he would normally try to avoid, but it did at least block the natural response of 'pleased to meet you.'

"He's cut his wrists," blurted out Wilson's sister. Again sobbing with every sentence. "How could he do this to mum and dad?"

Steve was starting to pick up some family dynamics here as he sat on the sofa warmed by the damp fur of William who'd now taken up residence next to him, presenting that confused, sad facial expression dogs are very good at.

Christian suggested he make a cup of tea and then he suggested Steve could go over everything so they could work out how they would break the news to 'mum and dad'.

"I'll make the tea," said Wilson's sister' shuffling off into the kitchen.

Steve was relieved by the presence of a slightly detached family member; clearly a long term boyfriend and now fiancée. Comfortable enough to walk straight into the family home and refer to his future in laws as 'mum and dad'. This educated professional man was going to be an asset to any family liaison officer or FLO put into this family. At this point Steve obviously didn't reveal to the sister his belief that this was the start of a murder enquiry, but he knew an FLO would be appointed in the next few hours. This role would be a challenging one. Richard Wilson's family were going to have lots of questions and the FLO would be the one who had to answer them.

Steve quickly established the slightly complicated family tree from Christian whilst his fiancée made them all tea.

Richard's mum, Eileen, had remarried a James Taylor when he was about five, hence the change of name. Richard's natural father had left his mother when he was very young hence James was virtually seen as Richard's proper father. Kathleen, the step sister, was bought up by her father and grandmother after her mother died when she was born. She was only two when her father and Richards mother married and was five years younger than Richard. He had always been like a natural brother to her even though she found out the truth about the lack of any biological link when she was in her early teens.

Both the tea making and drinking brought some calm to the room. Steve welcomed the first hot drink he'd had during that long night, but as always was now concerned that he'd have to ask to use the toilet before he left. This might seem a perfectly natural request for a visitor to make, but Steve had watched too many detective movies where one cop asks to use the bathroom and then secretly noses around the entire house only popping into the bathroom to flush the chain. Steve was paranoid that a householder would think this was what he was up to even though he did genuinely need to relieve himself.

'Find a remote hedge on the way back to Westhampton,' thought Steve as the three of them concluded there conversation having finalised the agreed plan of action.

Christian and Kathleen insisted they wanted to tell her parents the news by phone. They would be awake by now, due to travel back, but still at the hotel on the French Riviera. Steve had given the normal advice about how they wouldn't normally give people bad news over the phone, but of course it was their decision. Kathleen said they'd want to see Richard to which Steve couldn't make any promises. Steve did however promise to call at 2 p.m. and also promise that someone would come and speak to them all tomorrow afternoon sometime. Steve knew he could fulfil this commitment and he was soon to learn that a bereaved family would hang on his every word in situations like this so it was foolish to ever make promises you can't keep.

Steve drove clear of the village leaving the bereaved Kathleen in the safe hands of her fiancée and found that discreet hedgerow just before the sun came up. It was nearly six o'clock and time to update the DI.

Steve called the somewhat jaded detective inspector and gave a full brief over the phone.

"Listen mate you've done a good job. The SIO's setting up a major incident room, he thinks we could be looking at a murder here so he's putting a team together. I'm going to suggest you work with the FLO on the job if you're okay with that. Take the car home, get your head down for a few hours and be at headquarters in the briefing room for two. I'll get someone else to cover nights for the rest of the week."

Steve was excited but truly tired now, he'd get four hours kip if he was lucky. Steve could miss the early morning traffic if got a move on and be home for just after seven. He didn't even have to put in a few hours overtime writing up the O-B for this incident. The DI had already said he'd make a brief entry to log the incident and brief the teams verbally when they got in.

"Fancy a bacon sandwich darling," rung out the cheerful tones of Steve's wonderful Anna as she heard the flat door open.

"That would be lovely, thank you, after the night I've had I'm starving. Let me grab a quick shower and shove these clothes in the wash and I'll be right there." Having entered the clean confines of his own home Steve realised his chinos and shirt not only carried the lingering smell of death but also whiffed a little of wet dog. Ten minutes later Steve was sat in the kitchen diner in his fresh dressing gown admiring how good his lovely Anna looked already dressed quite formally for a day of victim support work.

"Go on then tell me all about it?" Asked Anna enthusiastically as she passed Steve his sandwich.

"Anna, you know I shouldn't," moaned Steve.

"You know it will be all over the Daily Mercury by tonight, just tell me," pleaded Anna.

Anna was right some of it would hit the local papers and anyway Steve needed a bit of counselling after the night he'd had. Anna had always been his first port of call providing a service more confidential than anyone in the force welfare department ever had.

"Well I found a horrible scene. A dead teacher with the most aggressively cut wrists I have ever seen."

"Oh Steve you shouldn't have had to find that," Anna cried out. "What were you doing being the first on the scene at something like that?"

Anna was clearly annoyed that Steve was going out to situations she thought he'd avoid more now he was no longer in uniform.

"I was hoping finding Old Man Fraser would be the last time you had to be first officer into such a bloody scene. You know how that affected you." Continued Anna.

"I'm alright darling just tired and a little sad after having to break the news to the man's step sister out in Suffolk."

"What, you've been out to Suffolk, for a suicide? Why didn't the local police tell the family?" Questioned Anna, her sharp knowledge of police procedure only enhanced by her many interactions with crime victims and the previous questions she had asked Steve as a result.

"It might not be a suicide, but I can't say too much. I'm not on nights anymore though, the DI wants to put me on the major enquiry team for this one."

"So it's a murder then?" Asked Anna.

"No, no, not necessarily but they will put a murder team on it and run the enquiry as such until the SIO deems otherwise. I need to get to bed, I've got to make a call and be in a briefing at headquarters by two. Sorry darling but I'm going to be back to long hours for a while and probably end up working the long weekend too."

"Steve you know that's okay, anyway this sounds like it will be an interesting one that you'll be able to tell me all about won't you," said Anna offering up a trade for her pleasant and flexible attitude to Steve's work routine.

Steve set his alarm for midday and slid into bed falling asleep almost instantly.

"Beep, beep, beep, beep," Steve's arm emerged from the covers hammering the tiny alarm clock into submission. 'Is that it?' Thought Steve, it seemed like he'd only been asleep five minutes. Steve gathered his thoughts and rapidly remembered the events of the previous night and the promises he'd made Kathleen and Christian. 'Shit they will have told her parents by now and they are probably returning to the family home,' thought Steve whose mind was now firmly focused on doing whatever he could to ease the pain the day would bring them.

As Steve went to the kitchen to make himself a coffee he realised he still had the CID nights mobile phone and had left it on the table. "Bollocks," moaned Steve as he saw two missed calls and the voicemail signal flashing.

"Call received on Monday at 08.23 hours - hello Steve it's Ken. I know you're probably sleeping but I just wanted to confirm you need to be at HQ for two. Keep hold of this phone you might need it if you're F-L-O ing we have a spare for the replacement nights DC. Just get that car back to the office if you're going to be on this job for more than a few days."

"Call received on Monday at 09.35 hours - Hello Steve my name's Andy Porter I'm the FLO for this job and your office has given me this number for you. Give me a bell when you get this."

"No fucking number," Steve complained quietly to himself as he scribbled the message on the back of an old Argos catalogue.

Instinctively Steve checked the missed calls on his phone. One unknown but the second showed a mobile number that he rung immediately.

"Hello Steve," answered the sharp Andy Porter who'd already stored the mobile details in his phone.

"Sorry I missed your call but I was nights last night and grabbing a few hours kip," explained Steve.

"Yeah I'm really sorry about that mate, hope I didn't wake you. They didn't tell me you'd gone home when I rang," apologised Andy.

"No, no problems I'm up and just picked up your voicemail; I'll be at force headquarters for about one if that's okay?"

Andy briefly explained that initially the SIO wanted Steve to help him out with the FLO stuff so Andy needed to pick Steve's brain before the briefing. They agreed to meet in the canteen which pleased Steve because he needed some sustenance before he embarked on another challenging shift.

As Steve entered the canteen at the grand force headquarters he was taken aback by how unusually busy it was. Suits dotted everywhere and at least a whole row of tables filled with a boisterous bunch of Operational Support Group uniformed officers. Steve did the classic police officer thing as he entered the room, not having a clue which suit contained Andy Porter, he rung him.

"Hello Andy."

"Yeah right behind you mate," was the reply.

Steve turned to see the smiling Andy Porter sat on the end of a row of tables just finishing a plate of pasta with one hand and answering his phone with the other. He put his fork down and reached across the table to shake Steve's hand.

"Starving!" Exclaimed Andy. "Been in since six and not a scrap of breakfast. You eaten Steve?"

"Not yet, I'll just grab a sandwich and let you finish that lot off. Do you want another coffee?"

"Great, yeah, no sugar, we've got plenty of time before the briefing don't rush mate," reassured Andy.

As Steve queued at the counter he reflected on his first impressions of Andy. He was a really pleasant friendly guy, very laid back but with a professional air about him. Steve was looking forward to working with him but scared to death of the family liaison role, thank God he was going to be Andy's bag man on this one.

"We've not met before have we, you're in the main office at Westhampton I understand?" Asked Andy.

"Yes, but I've only been there 3 months, before that I was in uniform out east," Steve replied honestly.

"That's where I've heard your name," Andy recalled sharply, "you were the officer who found Joseph Fraser when he was murdered."

"How did you know that?" Queried Steve wondering if this guy had properly checked Steve out before agreeing to work with him.

"That was my first FLO job, fucking hell what a job it was too. Well still is. I know that one inside out. I've read your statement many times and know the sequence of events well. I'm still in touch with Doreen periodically, Joseph's death has destroyed her, such a shame. Of course she's getting quite old now. You know the last time I visited her she said all she wanted was to know who killed her husband before she dies. How very sad. Even sadder thing is the job's been archived for over a year now, no one working on it, so unless some old villain wants a leg up and grasses up the killer out of the blue we've got no hope. Anyway this is an interesting one. I've been allowed into the scene and spoken to the high tech boys about the PC just to get my head around the victimology angle. Tell me about the family Steve."

Steve explained his findings and they laughed for some time as Steve recounted the near miss with William's head as it was thrust out of the cat flap.

"It's not funny though is it, shouldn't laugh," said Steve as he dried a laugher tear from his eye.

"No the death of Richard Wilson is not a laughing matter, but the picture I've got of you nearly getting your balls chewed off by his mum's dog is hilarious mate. Listen we are in a safe environment here, it's okay to laugh, it's okay to be happy in your work. One thing I've learnt doing family liaison is if you let yourself get too drawn into the family's grief it will destroy you and affect your ability to do a professional job for them. So in private, in the car or back in the office it's okay to unwind a little. When we are with the family, well I think you've done a good job so far and things are a lot easier when you are not on your own believe me."

"Shit the family, I promised to ring them at two, I'll have to do it before two," Steve explained.

Andy instructed Steve to call them and reassure them that we had a full briefing with the Senior Investigating Officer at two and we would head out to Long Acton straight after so should get to them before four.

Steve made the call and spoke to Mr Taylor. He was distraught but a stiff upper lip kind of gentleman. Steve made the arrangements as instructed during the brief but compassionate call.

"For those of you that don't know me I'm Detective Chief Inspector Danny Davis and for my sins I've been appointed as the senior investigating officer or SIO for this job. If you've not been on a major incident room with me before then make sure you take note from those that have. I can see a few familiar faces here, Pete Sims of course he'll be the DS acting as office manager, Harry, got your boys ready for some house to house I hope."

"Yes sir," replied the support group's uniform sergeant.

"Andy, F-L-O ing again, good to have you."

'Thank god Andy was familiar to the SIO, that would come in useful,' thought Steve.

"There's a few more faces I can see. No Gadget though?" Continued The SIO.

"He retired Sir," shouted a voice from the back.

Steve looked round to see his old friend Dave had been drafted in. He'd have to catch up with him later.

"Right down to business," the SIO announced. This is the investigation into the unexplained death of Richard Wilson, a supply teacher currently employed by the Local Education Authority at Overton Secondary School. I'm going to start by showing you an extract from the scene video to show you what young Steve Lawson, the nights DC at Westhampton found. You here Steve?"

"Yes sir," Steve shouted up feeling himself redden as almost every member of the audience turned to get a look at this unknown DC. Steve could see Dave grinning as he did so thinking to himself 'what have you stumbled upon this time Steve?'

The SIO continued "I'm going to play this first, it's obviously a bit gruesome but nothing you haven't seen before, then I'll tell you why I can't say this is a simple suicide."

The SIO didn't show the downstairs at all or show how it was found insecure with possible signs of Wilson having been put under duress and maybe attacked. Instead he simply showed a clip that went up the stairs and directly into the main bedroom. It lingered over Wilson's lifeless body and zoomed in on the congealed blood pools down the side of the bed. Steve could see clearly that it had been a craft knife used to inflict the two fatal incisions and it had apparently dropped from Wilson's right hand into the pool below it. 'What was the SIO getting at?' Thought Steve 'What had Steve missed?'

"Spotted it?" Asked the SIO faced with a room of silent individuals only broken by the odd whisper between colleagues. "Come on there's over a hundred of years of detective experience in here."

"Is it the cuts being vertical and so definite?" asked one of the officers.

"Close but not quite right. It wouldn't be the first suicide where the victim was so definite about killing themselves that they did a thorough job first time rather than make a few feeble horizontal slashes before they got it right." answered the SIO.

"What happens when you slash a couple of arteries so well?" the SIO asked.

'Fuck it,' Steve thought 'I'll answer.'

"A lot of blood Sir." called out Steve.

"You would know Steve it was still dripping from his wrists when you got there." Answered the SIO impressed with Steve's confidence. "So come on Steve tell this lot where there wasn't a lot of blood."

"Yes I missed it didn't I sir; across the bed, it doesn't make sense Wilson would have had to move at least one bleeding wrist across the bed to cut the other if he did it himself." Steve explained pleased with his eventual deduction.

"Good man and that's my problem with this job. That's before the confession stroke suicide note written across the living room wall and the possible disturbance in the same room," explained the SIO as he projected two crime scene photos onto the screen.

"Here are the priorities for the next day or so...

One - victimology. the family will be down to Andy Porter the FLO assisted by Steve Lawson who has already met some of them. There will also be some fast track actions surrounding Richard Wilson's current and previous school placements. Let's see if any of his colleagues can shed any light on what kind of man he was.

Two - the scene. That's all in hand with the scene manager and exhibits officer who have already been at it all day and have the post-mortem tonight. Andy I'm happy to get that done before the family do a formal ID. DI Stafford from Westhampton CID has offered to ID the body to the pathologists, he was the duty DI who went out to the scene with Steve Lawson last night. There are some hi-tech issues re the victims computer, or what's left of it eh Steve, and a few issues there that I'm not going to brief you on at this time.

Three - house to house and any local crime enquiries. This will be down to the OSG boys here. I'll brief Sergeant Arnold about how I want this doing, but in general I want a low key effort, mainly geared up around identifying any relevant lifestyle for the victim and any local issues that may have affected him. We know his car got damaged a while back and they'll be some actions coming out about that for some of the enquiry team to follow up on.

We don't have a huge team but I want to wrap this up as soon as we can. I'll deal with the media issues, for now the phrase we will be using to describe the death is 'unexplained'. The local news are already talking about a headline detailing the mysterious death of a local teacher. So have that in mind when you are out and about.

I'm not going to call another meeting again today, make sure you all tie in with the office manager before you finish tonight and I'll see everyone back here again at 0900 hours in the morning."

The briefing concluded and Steve and Andy were pulled to one side by Danny Davis when he finished.

"Right guys get back out to Suffolk make sure we've got mum and step dad on board and make sure there are no other close family members we've missed, especially his natural father. I don't want you to tell them anything about the possible sex offender stuff and leave the disturbance and writing on the lounge wall for now if you can. You will have to tell them his wrists were cut and that someone else could have done this. Just remember this could just be an assisted suicide or there may even be some way he'd cut them both himself and not got a load of blood across the bed. You know what, I really don't know but let's see what the background of this guy reveals. Did he have a girlfriend, ex-girlfriend, you know the sort of stuff Andy. I'll aim to meet them towards the end of the week if you can bare that in mind. Thanks guys give me a bell later when you can."

Steve was impressed with the SIO's honest and human approach. Steve had heard about Danny Davis, a respected senior career detective and now he was seconded to his team and he was also in a key role.

The next hour or so consisted on Steve driving Andy out to the family home whilst listening carefully to Andy's crash course in being an FLO. The most important thing was to keep a log and write down everything you tell the family and every question they ask and link that to when you actually answer it. It was about tea and sympathy yes, but your number one priority was to sensitively investigate the crime by using the vast and intimate knowledge the family had about the victim, adding the pieces to the jigsaw that wouldn't be found anywhere else. You were the families direct link to the SIO. It was the SIO who would decide when and how much you told the family for a number of different reasons and not you as an FLO. Andy found this aspect of the job difficult. He didn't like keeping things back from his families, even if there was a reason for it.

"Looks like Christian is still here," commented Steve noting his car on the driveway. Steve subconsciously eyed the cat flap as he knocked the front door. Steve was relieved in an odd way when the familiar face of Kathleen Taylor answered, her eyes red, exhausted with grief but surprisingly in control.

"Hello Steve thanks for coming back. It's alright William's in the back room."

"That's alright Kathleen. You didn't have to shut William out on my behalf. This is my colleague Andy. I told your father he would be coming to speak to you all," said Steve knowing Andy needed to take the lead for now.

Kathleen led the two of them into that same front room where they both introduced themselves. James Taylor was as he sounded on the phone. A refined gentlemen that Steve would later describe more colloquially as 'a posh bloke'. He remained quite formal but was clearly very protective of his grieving wife. She was distraught from the devastating news that had winded her so cruelly as she returned from a happy holiday. Eileen was a larger lady and on the surface appeared to be the kind of jolly country loving woman. Steve's own mum was very similar. She was tearful and welcomed the closeness of Kathleen by her side who she clearly had a tight bond with.

"Can you get these gentlemen a hot drink please Christian dear?" She said as she looked across at him still stood in the doorway apparently feeling a touch outside of this families grief.

"It's alright Mrs Taylor," Andy interjected, "don't go to any trouble for us.

Steve was grateful for Andy's comments. It was strange how decent people were still not prepared to ignore the social niceties of accepting visitors regardless of the situation.

"It's okay we could all do with more tea and please call me Eileen," she insisted.

"Thank you Eileen. Let me first say how sorry I am about poor Richard."

"Thank you."

"Let me tell you about the specific job Steve and I do and explain how we are going to make sure you have someone you can speak to directly throughout our investigation." Andy had now homed in on Eileen as the primary family member he would address. He had explained to Steve earlier that in nine out of ten cases it would be the wife or mother of a male victim he would address. He would subsequently identify the strengths and weaknesses of all the family members. He would use the stronger family members to help him with the more tricky aspects of his work. There was clearly a skill to this role that Steve was keen to master.

Andy continued. "Now Richard was found deceased in his house last night. I can tell you that his cause of death will be confirmed in due course but it is clear he suffered massive blood loss as both of his wrists were cut."

Although both Kathleen and Eileen knew this they burst into tears again folding into each other on the sofa. James wrapped his arm around Eileen from the other side gripping her tightly. Christian re-entered the room with a tray full of cups, saucers and a large tea pot placing it on the coffee table before joining the distraught group.

Andy went silent allowing the bereaved group a moment to re-adjust before he went on. Steve felt so sad at the sight of such distress, his own eyes filling slightly as he took in the scene.

"So was it suicide?" Asked James, breaking the silence.

"At this time Richard's death is unexplained and will be subject to a thorough investigation. There are a number of forensic tests that need to be conducted before any conclusions are drawn," explained Andy.

"But my Richard wouldn't do that to himself. He was happy at his new school, things were good why would he want to kill himself?" Sobbed Eileen.

"We don't know Eileen, I'm hoping that over the next few days we will speak more about Richard so that you can help us cover all possibilities, if that's okay?" Added Andy.

"Whatever you need, we just want some answers. What do you want us to do?" Asked James.

"Let me explain what will happen to Richard first. He has been taken to the the mortuary where we need to do a forensic post-mortem examination. That will take place this evening and I hope to have some conclusions from that tomorrow morning. The one test that takes a little longer is something called toxicology. Basically a blood test will take place to identify any prescription medications, other drugs, poisonous substances or any significant levels of alcohol that may have been in Richard's system when he died. Richard will then be taken to the main hospital mortuary where they'll look after his body for a while."

"I want to see him, can we see him, don't we need to identify him or something?" Asked Eileen.

"Yes of course you will be able to see Richard in the family viewing area at the mortuary and I do need at least one of you to formally identify him. I'm going to arrange that for tomorrow afternoon hopefully. Steve and I will either pick you up or meet you at Westhampton General Hospital, whichever you prefer. We will set aside sufficient time for you to all see Richard if that's what you decide. There's a specially laid out family waiting area there and another room where Richard will be for you to go in and spend some time with him." Andy's tone was just perfect he would have made an excellent funeral director thought Steve. Time was not an issue, even if it took until gone midnight to cover everything it wouldn't have been a problem for Andy. He paused regularly between moments of utter outpouring of grief. Andy was a very patient and caring man.

"If it's okay I'd like to find out a bit about Richard today if you feel up to talking?" Asked Andy. "Steve will just need to make some notes if that okay?" He added sensitively.

"Where do you want me to start?" Asked Eileen.

"I know it's painful but tell me a bit about your family and where Richard fits in, a bit about him and his likes dislikes, his career, his friends, things like that," summarised Andy.

"Richard has always been a clever boy, quiet but clever. His dad left us when Richard was very young and hasn't had anything to do with us ever since. Fortunately I met James and Kathleen a few years later. You'd been through a lot when I came along hadn't you dear?" Explained Eileen looking up at James.

A single tear rolled down Kathleen's cheek as Christian held her tightly.

James looked up "Kathleen's mother, my first wife died due to complications following Kathleen's birth. Until I met Eileen I was a broken man only kept going with the much appreciated help of Sarah's wonderful mother, Kathleen's grandmother."

Andy stared shocked, "I'm really sorry, what a sad story."

"It's okay" replied James, "we formed a really happy family out of all that tragedy and we're grateful for that."

"It was hard when Richard went off to university in Nottingham, but he was so dedicated to his studies and such a clever teacher we were so proud when he graduated." Eileen continued.

"How did he end up teaching in Westhampton?" Asked Steve.

"He has only been there a couple of years, his first position was actually in Nottingham. Richard had spent time on a short placement at a secondary school there whilst he was in his final year and he had impressed them so much he was offered a job there when he graduated." Recounted Eileen.

"What did he teach?" Asked Steve interjecting.

"History, English and I think some drama as well sometimes. He was very passionate about English history and literature especially," added Eileen enthusiastically already using the past tense to describe her son's attributes. Steve was not sure how to interpret this.

Andy was happy to let Steve continue to explore this angle whilst Eileen was happy to talk.

"What made him leave Nottingham and move to Westhampton then?" Was Steve's next question.

Eileen was silent momentarily. Then she answered.

"There was some issue with renewing his contract and I think Richard had had enough of Nottingham when he got offered the supply teaching job for the LEA covering the whole of Westhants. Richard said it would be more enjoyable for him as he'd get to teach in lots of different schools and it would be a new challenge for him."

"Can I just ask about Richard's natural father. I know he's not on the scene and it might not be something you like talking about, but we sometimes have an obligation to at least inform him of the death." Asked Andy conscious that the police had suffered litigation historically when they chose to ignore an estranged loved one.

"We haven't got a clue where he is," instructed James. "We even tried to find him when Richard graduated in a weak moment when we thought he should at least have the chance to see what a fine man his son had grown into, but he just ignored our letter."

"So you have an address for him?" Asked Andy.

"Probably an old one, I'm not sure its in Bury somewhere; I'll dig it out before you leave if you really must try and track him down?" Offered James.

"Yes I'm sorry we do need to at least pass on the news to him but I appreciate where he sits in all of this. I don't expect he will have any useful information for us, he just needs a visit at some stage within the next day or two that's all," detailed Andy sympathetically as Steve mentally ticked another of the key points Andy had detailed on the way up there.

"When did you both last visit Richard?" Asked Andy.

"Oh maybe a month ago, I'm not sure?" Said Eileen.

"It was the weekend of the 14th / 15th February mum," confirmed Kathleen. "Remember it was the same weekend Christian and I went away to York for Valentines."

"Yes that's right, I remember I thought we'd cheer Richard up a bit that weekend. I remember him being a bit down the weekend before when we spoke on the phone as he didn't have any plans for Valentines day and it fell on a weekend this year," explained Eileen. "James and I went across, Richard cooked us a lovely meal, but James and Richard spent most of the evening playing around with Richard's new computer."

"Its a Packard Bell, it has a built in modem and Richard has an internet account. It's really quite useful, especially for Richard's work," James added in his defence.

"When did you last speak to Richard?" Asked Andy to the group collectively.

"James and I had a telephone call with him just before we went on holiday, that was two weeks ago, but I think you spoke to him Kathleen?"

"Yes mum, Monday evening, he was fine and looking forward to payday, he'd been invited out with a group of work colleagues which would have been this last Friday night, apparently they were going to make a regular thing of it. He was really quite happy actually. I just don't understand?" She said breaking down into a gentle sob.

"That's why we are going to conduct a thorough investigation," Andy responded quite formally. Then softening his tone immediately Andy went on. "This is why it's really important you tell Steve and I everything you can remember, even if it doesn't seem important it may help in some way. Listen I'm not going to badger you anymore today, I can see its hard for you all and we'd like to give you some privacy. What I'm going to do is leave you with this notebook." Andy explained, as he took a brand new A5 pad from his case. "I'm going to put both our mobile numbers on the first page; you can ring us any time. Try me first then Steve. If you have a question please ask. If it's the middle of the night and it's driving you crazy just ring one of us don't worry, if it's such a burning issue it's just eating you up we will be happy to wake up and try and answer it. If you think it can wait or would rather discuss it face to face just use this book to make a note of all the things you think of and we will do our best to answer things when we speak. Does that make sense?" Andy scanned his audience for acknowledgement. "Use it just to make notes if you want. I will also write down the name of the Senior Investigating Officer or SIO; the boss he's a man named Danny Davis. A detective chief inspector. You will meet him soon but at present he wanted me to offer his condolences to you all and apologise for not being able to meet you straight away. He has the job of coordinating and leading all lines of enquiry so you can imagine he is very busy today. He will attend Richard's autopsy today and update me directly tomorrow morning. Anything to add Steve?"

"The media, a photo," prompted Steve bullet point style.

"Yes sorry. The local newspaper and news can sometimes be useful to us in finding witnesses and helping piece together things. At present Danny Davis has not chosen to go to the press for help. He wants to know a little bit more from our enquiries before he decides how the public could help, then he'll make a press release via our press officer. However we are conducting house to house enquiries and officers will be speaking to senior members of staff at Richard's current school. It's likely that the local paper at least will be asking us if they can release anything and they will generally want to put a photo out. We would like your input on that rather than them sourcing a photo of Richard from elsewhere. Is their a particular one you'd like to use?"

"What about that staff photo he gave us a copy of James, the one the school took of him sat at his desk for their entrance hall, where is that?" Asked Eileen.

"It's in the dresser dear I can dig it out now, come on Steve I'll get it for you it's in the dining room." Answered James beckoning Steve to follow him.

They passed through the large country kitchen to the dining room, an extension on the rear of the house. James opened a cupboard door on the dresser, pulled out a photo album and removed a loose photo from inside the front cover. He turned to Steve to hand over the photo but didn't release it until he had secured his full eye contact.

"I wanted to speak to you in private quickly Steve about something Eileen doesn't know. It would destroy her if she did. It's really difficult but you need to know."

"Go on James please, let's just sit down quickly and go through it," requested Steve as he took the photo from the concerned man knowing this might be a vital lead in the investigation. They both sat at the dining table.

"There was a bit of an indiscretion err... At Richard's school in Nottingham. He was a young guy back then; not much older than the kids he was teaching really and well, one of the girls had a silly crush, you know the sort of thing."

James paused looked down momentarily gripping the bridge of his nose between his thumb and forefinger. He looked up and continued.

"Richard was a fool; he crossed the line. Eileen knows all of this, well most of it, but it was never that clear how far over the line Richard stepped. The stupid girl thought the world of him, the police were involved but Richard was adamant he'd done nothing wrong. We obviously gave him the benefit of the doubt, but the girl's father didn't. Richard was interviewed by the police, I think, but never charged with anything. He was just a foolish and a slightly immature young man. We helped him out a lot, he obviously had to leave the job in Nottingham. Under quite a cloud unfortunately. We even paid off the negative equity he had in his flat there and helped him raise the deposit for the house in Westhampton. It just made sense, a fresh start and all that. Well I thought we were well clear of that until that email last month".

"What email?" Asked Steve quietly.

James sighed and continued.

"Richard contacted me and wanted to speak in confidence. I knew he was in trouble because it would have been a last resort for him to have to share his troubles with me and not his mum."

"So what trouble was he in?" questioned Steve.

"He received a death threat, via email from that silly girl's father I think."

"What kind of death threat? Did you get to read the email yourself?"

"Yes, Richard was scared, really scared. He kept saying how he'd let me and his mum down. He was in quite a state actually which is why I went over in the hope we could put this into some kind of rational perspective. It was the Friday before we went on holiday. Eileen doesn't know any of this please don't tell her."

"Okay, but you must tell me everything."

"The email had come from the girl's email address apparently but she was not the author. It read something like 'I'll fucking kill you if you come anywhere near my daughter again. I will find you and make your life a living hell you fucking nonse bastard.' I couldn't understand how this guy had got Richard's email address he's only been online a few months. Then he dropped the bombshell; bloody fool had tried to contact the girl on some reuniting school friends website or something like that." James explained shaking his head in disbelief.

"I could have killed him myself there and then when he admitted all that to me. Obviously her dad found out and made the threat, but I didn't think it was anything more than words on a screen. I told Richard to ignore it and we had some very strong words about his behaviour. I thought that was the end of it and hoped this final misdemeanour would be the last of Richard's childish ventures".

"James thank you. I know this is hard for you but you're right to share this with us now. You should tell Eileen about this at some point, but not now. I'll leave that up to you, when you think she's feeling up to it in the next few days maybe. We now have a line of enquiry we must follow up on and are going to have to update her about it at some point. Please ring me privately if you think of anything else or need to discuss this further. We better get back to the lounge now."

As the two men re-entered the lounge Steve felt they had been gone an uncomfortably long time. "Got it," announced Steve as he held up the photo to a trio of weak smiles; the first smiles he had seen since they arrived.

"Right Eileen so if you are okay Steve and I will get off now and I'll give you a quick call later, alright?" Andy concluded.

"Thank you Andy, Steve. You've both been very kind." Said Eileen sincerely.

"Yes thank you gentlemen, I'll show you out," added James.

As they walked out of the front door James added, "thanks Steve we'll speak again."

"Yes thanks James, I'll get our hi-tech guys to try and retrieve that email."

As they drove off Andy turned to Steve and asked, "what the fuck's that all about then?"

"Let's get out of here and find somewhere to park up we need to ring the SIO, someone threatened to kill Richard Wilson a while back, it may be the same bloke who did his car," revealed Steve who went on to recount the confidential disclosure James had made to him before they had left.

As Steve sipped the hot sweet coffee from a polystyrene cup he explained to Andy what had happened. Andy sat next to him in the passenger seat, enjoying the hot brew purchased from the lay-by's small catering van. Andy was pleased with what he was hearing from Steve. Their primary role was to investigate a murder, if that's what this was? They were already using the intimate knowledge of the victim's family to assist the enquiry which was good stuff. So many FLOs that Andy had worked with in the past had been great with the tea, sympathy and family support, but often forgot that this was a secondary thing that any good police officer could do. FLOs were recruited after they had become trained detectives for a reason.

"Thanks Andy that's good work," the SIO commented following Andy's hot briefing by phone. "I'll get some fast track research done on that and call you back in a bit."

As they drove back to Westhampton the SIO rang again.

"Right Andy it's all coming together. The intelligence research pulls up a single report that Notts Police have only fairly recently passed to us for action. A report from the girls father making an allegation that Richard Wilson had been harassing his daughter again. However that would appear to pre date the email you are on about. Obviously the father got pissed off that we didn't rush out and just nick Wilson again straight away. We've asked for a full package re what went on originally back then in Nottingham. I'm anticipating having to ask them to arrest the father later today. Get back here and get that lot written up in full. I'll speak to you again when the post-mortem has finished. I don't think this is a suicide?"

By the time Andy and Steve got back to headquarters it was early evening. They had to write up their log and collect the actions that had now been printed. These ended up in an out tray in the major incident room or M-I-R as it was referred to. Steve sifted through the actions that were all very generic; "formally ID body, obtain family background statement, produce family tree." It then dawned on Steve that there was one important gloomy task not contained in these actions. They still had to find the natural father and pass on the death message to him. Steve sifted through his notes and found the address they had been given. Jonathan Wilson, 84 Ardley Common, Bury St Edmunds. James had said he thought this was an old address, but even if it was they'd have a starter for ten by asking the current occupants where Jonathan Wilson was now. Andy went to speak with the office manager and came back to update Steve.

"Right mate the post-mortem is taking longer than expected so there's no way we'll get a face to face briefing with the boss tonight. We're still on track for the viewing in the morning so we just need to find the natural father tonight, what was his name again?"

"Jonathan Wilson... So it's back to Suffolk then? What about the geezer in Notts." Steve responded using jumbled flurry of answers and questions.

Answering the question Steve did not already know the answer to Andy confirmed a man named David Granger had been arrested by Nottinghamshire Police and a handful of the enquiry team were racing up to Notts for an overnight job to deal with him and his house.

Slightly frustrated at the administrative need to deliver a death message to an estranged father, unlikely to be able to assist the enquiry, Steve drove them both out to Bury St Edmunds.

"So Andy I bet Old Man Fraser's family were less complicated than the Taylor's and Wilson's?" Commented Steve as they negotiated the heavy traffic.

"No way. Now that is a complicated situation. Give me this family any day," exclaimed Andy.

"Why Fraser's wife always seemed so supportive of him?"

"Maybe in his latter years but only maybe after his daughter emigrated to Australia and the memories of her historic allegations faded. You see Patricia opened a whole new line of enquiry that was almost impossible to completely bottom out. Me and the SIO got a trip to Aussie land out of it, but Patricia's recall is poor and she was taking herself back up to 30 years. It emerged that Fraser had encouraged his only daughter to invite her friends around to the pub to play on a regular basis. Any excuse for a kids party and Fraser offered up the use of the pub outside of opening hours. He had a better kept garden back then with a bit more than that old Wendy house in it. Fraser would even dress up as a clown on occasions and try his hand at a bit of children's entertainment. Unfortunately according to Patricia that's not all he tried his hand at with her friends. She spent most of her childhood bribing her friends not to tell their parents about the clowns funny hands with free bags of Smiths Salt 'n' Shake and bottles of Corona. Patricia's pals came and went depriving her of any long term childhood friends. As Patricia's friends became less inclined to come round and play, Patricia herself suffered terrible abuse at her father's hands. Of course Doreen Fraser was always in denial hoping she was mistaken and her husband wasn't doing anything untoward. This was helped by the fact that Patricia kept it to herself until she was in her early 30's and was having problems in her own marriage I think. It split the small family in half and I think Doreen was glad her daughter decided to leave England and make a fresh start in Australia. Well until we dragged it all up again after the murder. All that aviation fuel and the best we could come back with was five identifiable potential victims out of a possible twenty plus first names of potential victims. Not a single one of those five really wanted to help especially when they found out Fraser had been murdered. I don't think any of them had anything to do with his murder, but I'm convinced Fraser's paedophilia is the most likely motive for his murder. There was just no sign of a recent victim or interested party that would have been motivated enough to go through with it? Of course Patricia was definitely in Australia when he was killed so it wasn't her. It's a real mystery that one Steve, maybe one day something will come up?"

Steve was intrigued by Andy's updates his mind drifting back to that torturous scene in the pub kitchen. 'Snap out of it Steve,' he thought to himself, 'back to today's job, but is this really a murder?'

Steve parked in a residents only bay, hoping Suffolk's traffic wardens didn't work late shifts. They approached the small terraced house expecting to do no more than just start a line of enquiry that might eventually lead to finding Jonathan Wilson.

"Hello sir, Steve Lawson & Andy Porter from Westhamptonshire Police I wonder if you can help me we think a Jonathan Wilson May have used to live here and we need to trace him, can you help at all?" Asked a slightly too upbeat Steve.

"I'm Jonathan Wilson, what's wrong?" The man answered as Steve stared back mute as he took in the striking resemblance to Richard Wilson he should have noticed straight away.

"Sorry, I'm sorry sir we were led to believe this would be an old address. Can we come in please?" Spluttered Steve.

Mr Wilson led them through the door that opened directly into the lounge and they were offered a seat.

"I'm really sorry but we have some very bad news. Your son Richard Wilson was found dead at his home in Westhampton yesterday evening." Explained Steve professionally.

Jonathan Wilson was clearly shocked but didn't display any overt emotion, he just quietly asked, "how did he die?"

"His wrists were cut and we believe he would have died of blood loss but a post-mortem is still being carried out," interjected Andy.

"Stupid, stupid boy," cried out Jonathan angry but clearly now showing his distress. "I suppose his mother told you where to find me?"

"Yes, it was only right you were informed as soon as we could find you sir," explained Andy.

"Were you in touch with Richard?" Asked Steve eager to establish if Jonathan Wilson could help shed some light on why Richard may kill himself or be killed.

"He used to visit me periodically when he was at University. His mother didn't know. Then when he started working and he told me what had happened in Nottingham that was it I couldn't forgive him. He sent me letters every couple of years usually inside a Christmas card. I never replied, he knew I wouldn't, not until he accepted that he had a problem and stopped pretending what he did was okay."

"How do you mean okay?" Probed Steve.

"Richard had an unhealthy interest in young pubescent schoolgirls and he knew it was wrong. It's obvious that's why he stuck with that placement in the all girls state school in Nottingham rather than trying to branch out into private education as planned. Richard needed to accept his problems and take himself out of an environment where it was going to be an issue for him. An all boys grammar school would have been the ideal place for Richard to start his career, but no it was okay and he didn't have a problem. The idiot even cited a ten year age gap in a relationship as nothing in this day and age. He insulted me further by suggesting most relationships started in the workplace and this was just his workplace; maybe so if you start shagging one of the dinner ladies but not one of your 14 year old pupils!" Explained Jonathan getting more and more upset as he detailed the cause of his estrangement with Richard.

"What made him kill himself?" He asked.

"It may not be a suicide, we can't say until we complete our enquiries and then a coroner will have the final say." Answered Steve.

"What do you mean?" He asked further.

"Well there are a few unexplained matters we need to clear up and do some enquiries on before we draw any conclusions. Such as the post-mortem. I can't tell you about all of them at this stage but I can assure you that we will keep you updated. Both Steve and I are family liaison officers and what we do is make sure Richard's family are kept up to date at all times. We may also ask you some questions about Richard so we can try and understand what kind of person he was. As you know we traced and visited Eileen first and she gave us this address but she is obviously not in touch with you. So what we will do is ring you and pass all information to you both separately if that's okay." Andy spieled off.

The rest of the meeting was quite administrative covering all the generic areas about the investigation and obtaining Jonathan's full details. Both Steve and Andy were back in the car looking for somewhere to eat before 10 p.m.

"A fucking Happy Eater!" Complained Andy as Steve pulled into the tired looking travel stop.

"It's this or that Little Chef a few miles further on mate, beggars can't be choosers anyway the chief constable is paying, fill your boots. If you're really lucky your can have one of those squirty cream banana splits for desert." Said Steve relieved at the prospect of a hot meal and a bit of light banter.

"So what's your take of Jonathan Wilson then Steve?"

"Well he hasn't been in touch with Richard for years, I'm sure that's true. He doesn't really like his son anymore, but I don't think he'd do him any harm." Concluded Steve.

"You know it never even crossed my mind he could be a suspect but I'm sure the SIO might ask us for our opinion on that at some point. All I was thinking is from an FLO point of view Jonathan Wilson is going to be easy to speak directly with and will be as happy with a quick call as he would a visit." Answered Andy.

"Yeah and he doesn't pull any punches when it comes to describing Richard Wilson's past; there's none of this 'a bit of an indiscretion' as James Taylor put it. I think we will need to spend some time getting Jonathan's take on Richard Wilson's 'indiscretion' at some point."

"Definitely," agreed Andy tucking into his mixed grill.

"Sorry I'm so late darling," whispered Steve as he slid into the bed next to Anna.

"That's alright darling I knew you'd be busy. How you feeling?"

"Tired and emotionally drained. I don't think I've ever seen so much sorrow in one day, but it's a good challenge trying to get this family liaison thing right. I suppose it's a bit like the victim support stuff you do?" Answered Steve.

"Yes and no, I don't have to work on murders or sudden deaths yet and I'm lucky I just do the tea, sympathy and practical support. I don't have to investigate the crime as well. Anyway is this a suicide? The local news report isn't saying a lot just that it's unexplained."

"You know and I shouldn't be discussing it Anna."

"Come on Steve, call it counselling you need an outlet and you know I understand the importance of confidentiality." Pleaded Anna keen to help Steve unwind and also as interested as ever in the work he does.

"Well it will be no secret he died of blood loss. Andy had a call from the SIO before we finished and the post-mortem hasn't helped that much. The pathologist has seen suicides like this before where such long precise cuts had been made but usually accompanied by signs of an alcohol or drug induced stupor giving the victim the courage to do such a thing. We won't get the toxicology result for a few days yet, but I didn't see signs of any booze at the scene." Revealed Steve.

"But he must have had a reason to commit suicide surely?" Asked Anna.

"Well yes but I really can't tell you about that at the moment. Even if I could it would take too long to explain and I'm knackered. Go to sleep we've both got to work in the morning."

Andy joined Steve for a builders breakfast at the local early morning cafe just on the edge of the industrial estate near headquarters.

"Better get a fat boy's down you Steve it's going to be a long day and we'll be at the mortuary around lunchtime," remarked Andy as upbeat and ready for the days challenges as ever.

Steve had taken families to ID their loved ones before but mainly elderly people who died suddenly and not always that prematurely. He'd never had the nightmare of showing parents their dead child before.

After breakfast and before they went to the mortuary they attended the SIO's daily briefing.

"Hello Adrian it's Danny Davis I have you on a speaker phone mate so you can update the team here re the girls father." Instructed the SIO pleased with his innovative use of technology enabling him to speak with his detached team still up in Nottingham.

"Yes sir," answered the respectful detective sergeant Adrian Thomas. "We have the family computer seized and have sent that down to you last night. Apart from that there's not a single item of blood stained clothing in the home address. We won't know about the car until they finish working on it at the forensic garage. He's been pretty cooperative throughout the whole thing I have to say and is still adamant that the only time he's been to Westhampton was for an old friend's wedding over ten years ago. On interview he admits sending the threatening email and began to quite openly state how he would have killed Richard Wilson if he hadn't have taken any notice of it. Then his solicitor stepped in and stopped him at that point. He covered his movements. He didn't do much over the weekend as the football was on Saturday afternoon so he stayed in and watched that, had a few drinks and crashed out on the sofa after tea. His wife vouches for him but then she would. We eventually managed to get her to agree to let us talk to the daughter in a video interview where she admits quite a bit of MSN chat with Richard Wilson and a full but brief sexual relationship with him when she was just fourteen. She still hasn't matured enough to realise how stupid she was and was clearly very upset at the news of his death. We opened a can of worms and we've emptied most of them out of it now."

"So let me just get this straight," interjected the SIO. "Richard Wilson is now 28. When he had the fling with this girl she was 14 (10 years his junior) and that was about 4 years ago."

"Yes boss she's just a few weeks shy of 18 now which is why I cautiously made sure we got her mums consent before speaking to her. I would call her an immature 17, not physically but certainly mentally." Adrian explained.

"Right get him bailed before the clock runs out, don't bother getting an extension of his custody time; we have what we need and I don't think he's going anywhere. Make sure you check and double check his alibi and we will see what comes out of his car and the scene. I want to know about this long lost friend as well, how close were they, is he still in Westhampton? Maybe he paid Richard Wilson a visit in the early hours of Sunday morning on behalf of the girl's father? Anyone got any questions for Adrian before I let him get on?" The boss asked.

"Yes sir," interrupted Steve. "What about the damage to Richard Wilson's car has that been put to this fellow?"

"It's alright Adrian I can answer that, Steve and Andy have been too busy with the family to have been brought up to date with the recent allegations," detailed the SIO.

"For those of you who haven't been involved in the enquiries at the victim's current school you may not know that there was a recent allegation that he was grooming a new young lady from one of the classes he taught. That was investigated by child protection down here and Wilson was interviewed under caution. The CPS advice was that there was insufficient evidence to proceed with a prosecution given the victim's previous reliability issues and her general learning difficulties. We think, but can't prove that she damaged his car in the school car park. Given all of her vulnerabilities child protection are going to deal with her as a witness at this stage but there are a few urgent actions surrounding her family and friends I want dealing with today."

Steve was intrigued but noting the concern on his colleague Andy's face soon remembered that at some point all this would have to be explained to the family. He knew like most bereaved families they would be keen to find someone to blame for their son's death.

Relieved the briefing was over Steve and Andy rushed out to Suffolk to collect the family and take them to the mortuary for an early afternoon viewing. Even though Eileen had called to say Christian wanted to come to support Kathleen so had offered to drive them all, Andy still said he'd collect Eileen and James letting Kathleen and Christian follow in their car. Andy had told Eileen this would give them chance to talk more on route. Andy knew there was a lot to discuss before the local news started putting stuff out and he picked up that Eileen felt a touch protective of her step-daughter. He really needed to get the issues surrounding the allegations against Richard out in the open at least with both Eileen and James before any of it surfaced elsewhere.

"Right, you two comfortable back there?" Steve asked as he pulled off regardless of his courteous but pointless question.

"Yes thank you Steve," responded James in his polite and well spoken tone. "I've told young Christian to get Kathleen to call me if he looses you and we will talk him in to the hospital if necessary."

"Don't worry James I'll go steady, we have plenty of time," answered Steve as he glanced back at the following car.

Andy explained again the viewing facilities and what they should expect when they saw Richard. He reassured them that the formalities of an identification were straight forward as long as one of them confirmed it was Richard they would take a statement at a later date. Andy went on to explain the post-mortem results he'd previously eluded to on the phone.

"So you understand the toxicology issues?" He asked.

Eileen responded, "yes sort of from what you told me over the phone. So you think there could be a possibility Richard was under the influence of something when he died, but that's just not like him, I don't understand. He hardly drunk a glass of wine with his dinner and he was very anti drugs always."

"I know, I know," Andy answered, "but if Richard did this to himself he definitely would have been acting out of character in a number of ways so we need to explore all of elements of this thoroughly to try and make sense of things for you."

"Yes thank you Andy I know this is going to be painful; James has told me about the threats from that silly girl's father. I just can't believe Richard could have been so foolish."

"Good I'm glad you are aware. I am sorry that we have to pry, but those are the sort of things we need to know about and James did the right thing telling us. Now you know I phoned to say a man was being questioned in Nottingham about that, I need to explain to you a little of how and why we do things. Richard has died suddenly in unexplained circumstances, therefore we have to consider all possible reasons for this from suicide right up to murder. When we question people we may arrest them if we need to use certain powers and make sure they come to the police station to answer or at least have the chance to answer our questions. We will almost always choose the most serious offence to arrest them under so all possibilities below that are covered. So just because at this early stage we arrested this man for murder, it does not mean we are sure in any way that a murder has been committed.... Sorry am I confusing you or does that make sense?" Asked Andy with his caring and professional tone.

"No I think I know what you mean," said Eileen.

"James?"

"Yes Andy I understand but who is this man, is it the girls father?"

"Yes I can confirm that now, it is not public knowledge, and what I can say at this stage is he has answered all of our questions and cooperated fully. He admits sending the email but denies even knowing where Richard lived or doing anything else. We think we will be able to verify his movements with some further enquiries and all of the forensic checks are ongoing so he has been bailed for now."

"What do you mean, have you charged him with sending the threats?" Asked James.

"No, not yet it's not that straight forward. We will fully explore his actions and make some decisions at a later stage. However at this time sending the email looks like the only thing he's done wrong. Obviously that alone would have had an impact on Richard's well being and we haven't lost sight of that." Answered Andy trying to stay on track with what the SIO's response would be to the current status of the girl's father.

"What other things are you looking at?" Asked James now taking over the conversation from Eileen and also scribbling down answers in the small notebook the family had been provided with. The notebook James had been clutching ever since they left the house like some kind of child's comfort blanket.

"Apart from the toxicology and some further forensic work at Richard's home we are doing a lot of work at Richard's current school and trying to identify any close friends or colleague that may be able to tell us more about him. We are obviously looking for any reasons anyone would have to want to hurt Richard and also anything in his life that might cause a rapid decline in his mental state. What I'm hoping to do tomorrow is arrange a time for me to bring the Senior Investigating Officer Danny Davis up to meet you. He will have all of the answers so far and you are welcome to quiz him about anything. I have a letter from him he wanted me to hand you to offer his condolences at this point as he hasn't had chance to meet you yet." Explained Andy.

"Thank you Andy," answered the ever grateful James. "Is Christian still with us?" He asked changing the subject.

"Yes he's doing well," answered Steve. "It's not a bad time of day to do this run, just let me know if you need a comfort stop anytime before we get there," added Steve setting the mode of conversation to one of lighter chit chat and small talk for the rest of the journey. He could see Andy making a few quick notes to remind himself the update he'd given Eileen and James whilst on route.

The mortuary was right in the centre of the general hospital's grounds. A miserable looking annex with lots of external pipe work and venting. Fortunately someone had remodelled the family entrance with the addition of a UPVC type porch leading into a peaceful family room not unlike what you would find in any good funeral directors. Traditional armchairs, a couple of boxes of well placed tissues and the standard vase of lilies. Steve hated it, not the room but the smell. 'Give me the smell of dead bodies any day,' he thought as they led the four worried family members into the room.

"I'll just go through and see if they are ready for us," said Steve as he carefully opened the next door knowing that in the corner of this room Richard might already be laid out. He left Andy preparing the family for the experience they were about to encounter.

Richard's body had been laid out, the top of his head neatly draped in a white band of sheeting as was his body. On top of that was a heavier embroidered blanket of traditional design, almost regal but very appropriate for a family viewing. Steve had seen how well the mortuary assistants presented bodies for viewing before and was impressed as usual. Richard Wilson looked ten times better than he had last time Steve had seen him even though he'd been dead at least three days now. 'Just those damn lilies to ruin the ambience of the viewing room,' thought Steve as he tried not to take in too much of their strong odour.

As Steve went through the next door to find the mortuary assistant he was reminded of why there were so many smelly flowers at mortuaries. The smell hit him. Just death that's all but floor to ceiling cupboards full of it. Behind each small metal door slid a body of some poor sole, waiting for a routine post-mortem or an undertaker to collect them. Two of those poor old souls lay on trolleys waiting to be examined, both no doubt very old but never the less somebody's loved one. There was little dignity after death in reality thought Steve as he edged past the dead bodies towards the office. Although not particularly religious Steve still held the belief that your soul leaves your body as you die. Leaving behind an empty shell to be disposed of in some kind of appropriate manner. This thought always helped him deal with dead bodies so suited Steve's needs.

"Hello Clive, I've got Richard Wilson's family here for a viewing," announced Steve as he entered the office and addressed its sole occupant assuming it was the same man he'd spoken to on the phone the previous day. It didn't really matter thought Steve as almost every mortuary assistant he'd met was called either Clive or Marvin it seemed. These guys were the unsung heroes of the forensic world in Steve's eyes. Never in the public domain doing the lions share of most of a post-mortem, especially the reconstruction of a body at its conclusion, but not really ever getting any recognition, let alone a decent pay scale for what they really did.

"Right mate he's all ready and you're lucky, I don't have any more viewings today so take as long as you want, just give me a shout when you're all done and I'll put him away. Will there be any more viewings of this one?" Asked Clive.

"Not sure maybe one more, I can't say yet but his natural father may want to see him," answered Steve thinking that actually it is more likely he will decline the offer but he couldn't be sure.

Steve headed back to the viewing room and just checked that Richard's hand was free in case his mother wanted to hold it at some point. It was of course freezing but now free from rigour so potentially comforting to a grieving relative. It was so much better if you could delay the viewing until after a post-mortem when the family would actually be able to touch their loved one. Steve didn't actually think viewing dead relatives was a good choice himself. He felt that every time you then tried to picture them in the future the one image that would always jump the memory queue would be that of them on the 'slab', but he'd already learnt not to influence that decision too much and let the families decide. Some bereaved families needed to see their relative properly dead to accept that this was the case and the police hadn't got the wrong person or something like that. It was the acceptance stage of bereavement that was often aided by this less than pleasant task. Of course Steve and Andy needed a formal ID of Richard Wilson so one of the family needed to see him in any case.

Andy stepped in the room having heard movement. "Everything okay Steve? So this is Richard Wilson then?"

"I fucking hope so," replied Steve in a hushed voice momentarily breaking the somber tone of the day with a brief element of private humour.

"Right mate you stay in here then you can confirm the ID as you found him at the scene. I'll stay next door and deal with the family as they come in and out. We alright for time?"

"Yes mate no other viewings today just remind me to tell Clive when we leave so he can shut up shop and put Richard away," answered Steve.

All four family members shuffled in when Andy opened the door looking like refugees in a foreign country, so far out of their comfort zone they needed physically ushering the rest of the way over to where Richard was laid out.

James looked at Steve almost for inspiration. Steve stared at him wide eyed prompting the appropriate brief response he was looking for.

"That's Richard yes," James said quietly as Eileen began to sob.

"Thank you James," replied Steve stepping back from the family group with his hands clasped in front of him in true undertaker style. Steve gave them a moment of silence as Kathleen now began to cry into the shoulder of her beloved Christian a tear now rolling down Christian's cheek. James remained as predicted, he was the stereotypical Englishman with a true stiff under lip but hurting badly inside.

"You can hold Richard's hand if you like," offered Steve as he went over to Richard to slide his right hand from under his coverings as Eileen approached. "It's okay it's very cold but it's okay. Here Eileen let me bring over a chair and you can sit with him for a while if you like?"

Eileen still sobbing welcomed Steve's instructions. The rest of the family closed in around her and Steve again took a step back. Eventually Kathleen bravely stroked Richard's forehead affectionately "goodbye my special brother" she wept and then hurried out of the room followed closely by Christian.

Eileen stood up, having contained her tears now, kissed her cold son on the cheek and calmly walked out of the room with James' arm wrapped tightly around her shoulder.

After a brief chat in the family waiting room Christian confirmed he was up to driving them all back to Suffolk. Eileen had wanted to go to Richard's house, but Andy managed to delay that based on the scene examination, ever conscious that they'd yet to discuss the writing on the walls.

The viewing may have been completed and another hurdle out of the way, but there were many challenges to come from a family liaison point of view with this enquiry. Hopefully Danny Davis' introduction to the family pencilled in for the next day would help share the burden. Andy was always relieved when the SIO was put in the hot seat for a change.

Andy and Steve were enjoying a healthy late lunch from a cardboard bucket when Andy's mobile phone rung out again for the umpteenth time that day. He struggled with his greasy fingers to accept the call as he quickly chewed down his mouthful of chicken.

"Andy it Danny Davis I need you and Steve at the video interview suite by 4 pm. I've run out of detectives and I can't use Child Protection for this bit. Most of our lot are milking a second overnight stay up in Nottingham so you are the best I have."

"Right sir no problem," answered Andy beginning to choke on a crispy piece of chicken skin and handing the phone to Steve.

"Hello sir it's Steve do you want to give me the details."

"What are you his fucking PA? Right at 4 pm young Brittany Doulton will be arriving at Child Protection Unit's video interview suite with her mum Ms Hunt. She is the 14 year old girl who made an allegation of indecent assault against Richard Wilson earlier this year. Surprise surprise she was one of his pupils. Well the CPS wouldn't run it but the advice file never mentioned Wilson's previous offending. The problem is when we gave Child Protection the task of re-visiting her she admitted pouring solvent all over his car in the school car park when she was told Wilson would be N-F-A'd. They went and fucking arrested her on the spot, a little bit over the top if you ask me. Anyway she's been de-arrested as the damage is fully admitted to and we can deal with that some other time, she's only 14 after all. Now I don't think she's capable of killing Richard Wilson she's a wee slip of a girl and not bright enough really. However her back story could be vital, maybe she has a boyfriend that has taken the law into his own hands, who knows? Get her A-B-E interviewed in as much detail as you can about everything and get back to the incident room once you're done."

"Right boss no problem," answered Steve hanging up.

"What now?" Asked Andy.

"We have to A-B-E that girl who Wilson tried it on with at his new school."

"A-B-E?" Replied Andy.

"Yeah, A-B-E, Achieving Best Evidence, you know video interviews," answered Steve.

"Oh video interview why didn't you say, are you trained then?" Replied Andy with a puzzled look on his face.

"Yes," replied Steve grateful to have been given a course at short notice when he was on his CID attachment out on the rural sector. The DC who should have done the course went sick and needed replacing. There was a knack to interviewing children and making sure you got a clear truthful picture from them on video that could be played in court to save them some of the trauma of giving evidence.

"Listen let's get to the video interview suite now, I'll show you how to do the recording bit in the monitoring room and I'm happy to crack on as soon as she arrives," reassured Steve.

Andy removed the last scrap of chicken from another drumstick and they headed off. At least they'd eaten before this next challenge.

"Hi Brittany are you comfortable in that chair," asked Steve as he opened the video interview.

"Yeah," replied the slightly rough tones of young Brittany.

"I'm a police officer, as you know, and next door in that room I showed you is another police officer Andy. Your mum is in the waiting room on the other side. Now I understand you've been interviewed like this before is that right?"

"Yeah with that Marie from the Child Protection Police innit"

Steve continued, now not so surprised why the word of this slightly wayward teenager failed to stack up against the denials of Richard Wilson. After all of the various preliminaries required at the start of an A-B-E, not least getting the child to explain their understanding of truth and lies, Brittany was asked to explain why she damaged Richard Wilson's car?

"He started touching me up in detention didn't he and the crown service don't believe me when I tried to get him done."

"Tell me about that," asked Steve.

"Well I thought Mr Wilson was okay like as a teacher, he always did the detentions, dunnow why. He was good though, used to let me do my homework in detention and he helped me when I got stuck. But the last two detentions yeah he put his hands all over me, on me shoulders and then he slip them onto me tits like. I was well embarrassed."

"Did anyone else see?"

"Nar I was the only one on detention both times. He said he liked me and I wasn't like the rest of the girls I was older and more like a young woman or summit. First time he did it I just like smiled and said okay but detention was nearly over so he let me go. Second time he was all over me straight off and the dirty fucker tried to put his hand up me skirt. Sorry, sorry for swearing like."

"That's alright Brittany I don't mind I just need you to tell me what happened in your words." Steve responded.

"Well I told him he was a dirty paedo and I was gonna get him done and run out. I thought I'd get in trouble for bunking off detention when I come in the next day but no one said nothin. I didn't report it straight away, was gonna blackmail him or summit, but I just got really vexed and told my friends when we went to the chicken shop at lunch."

"Which friends, I need to know who you told," asked Steve.

"I ain't no grass."

"No this is not about being a grass it's just important that I understand who else knew what Richard Wilson did. No one is going to get in any trouble." Steve said lying knowing full well they needed to look at further retaliation by proxy and Brittany's friends could be the source of that.

"Well I told Cheryl and Chaz like and then Chaz's boyfriend Deano was there with Animal and Menace, yeah that was it they were well vexed."

"Who are Animal and Menace?" Asked Steve immediately assuming the use of gang names was an indication of the less desirable character these individuals would be likely to hold.

"They're just boys in Deano's year not sure of their real names."

"You said they were vexed?" Steve queried.

"Yeah well mad but Cheryl told them not to do anything and told me to get the police to arrest him so he lost his job and that so I did"

"So I know all about what happened next from the reports and your first video interview. What I really wanted to know about though is what happened when the police told you he wouldn't be charged or go to court," asked Steve.

"I went mad man, it ain't fair. I just lost it when I was at school the week after and I saw him drive up and park his car like nutting had happened like. So I did that shitty little car of his. Got some stuff from the caretakers lock up and gave it a cool paint job, serves him right."

"What else did you do Brittany?" Probed Steve.

"Nutting innit. Just made sure I didn't get a detention for a while."

"Have you ever been to his house?"

"No, err course not, what would I want to go to his yard for? I ain't got nutting to do with him topping himself if that's what you are saying."

"Who says he's topped himself Brittany?"

"Everyone it's all round the school of course, can't keep nutting quiet round here. Dem teachers gossip like mad, we all know he couldn't hack it and did himself in like."

"What do you mean couldn't hack it?" queried Steve curious to explore this additional information.

"He weren't cut out for a proper school with kids from the street. His classes were a joke, you ask anyone. He was too soft man."

"Thank you Brittany, thats been very useful," concluded Steve not actually grateful for having to have had to endure the endearing nature of this wonderful example of a young person. Brittany's use of vocabulary left a lot to be desired but Steve didn't doubt her relative honesty. He tended to agree with the SIO's initial assessment, Brittany was not a murderer. Steve did however have some low level concerns about the male friends and associates she had and all that would have to be fed back in to the incident room for actions to be raised. Steve still had his family liaison head on. He was soon wondering how Andy and he would break the news of yet another revelation to Richard Wilson's family. Andy shared the same concerns when they sat down to debrief the interview and consider their next move.

Steve and Andy headed back to the Major Incident Room and sat down with the SIO to both debrief him about the lovely Brittany and highlight their concerns for the forthcoming family visit he was intending to join them on. Danny Davis accepted there were some key issues to go through and insisted that he would tell them about the latest allegation, the damage to the car and subsequent writing on the wall. Steve was quite impressed with the courage of the SIO in agreeing to cover the most sensitive points face to face with the family on the first meeting he was to have with them. Steve did have one major concern though which was the way Danny Davis kept coming back to the hypothesis that Richard Wilson may have committed suicide after all. Maybe Steve's perception was wrong, maybe this wasn't a murder after all. His head was foggy, he was worn out by the time he eventually headed home.

"Ten thirty, you feeling alright darling finishing so early," said the sarcastic Anna.

"Hello my lovely, I've missed you too," answered Steve as he leant over the sofa to kiss his darling wife.

"God you smell like an old peoples home where have you been?" Remarked Anna, "been interviewing pensioners or something?"

"It's Lilies, smelly flowers, the one's I hate."

"Lilies?"

"Yes, I've been at the mortuary for half the day in the family viewing area. Now you'll have to excuse me but I need to get out of this suit," answered Steve.

"Oh yeah sorry darling I forgot, is he still dead then?" Anna asked flippantly.

"Anna!" Retorted Steve. "The family were devastated."

"Sorry again, just trying to cheer you up darling, you must have had a horrible day?" Responded Anna sympathetically.

"Don't worry there were a few lighter moments, got to use those child video interview techniques, I learnt on that course, interviewing the charming Brittany this afternoon. Why is it when you going to meet a child named after that latest up and coming pop star you can almost predict the kind of character you will be faced with?" Chuckled Steve.

"I know," laughed Anna pleased to see her husband starting to unwind a little.

Steve changed the subject, asking Anna about her working week, ever conscious that her job in Victim Support was equally as challenging as his, but received very little interest from him sometimes. Anna never spoke of individual cases but would talk about her team and things she was learning as she went along. It was clear to Steve that Anna aspired to move onto more complex victim support cases in her role as she became more and more experienced. She was passionate about her job and keen to progress.

The next morning's briefing consisted of updates about several lines of enquiry, most of which Steve had been involved in the previous day. Towards the end of the briefing however there was one big revelation from the exhibits officer.

"Sorry boss that was the lab," explained the ever absent exhibits officer as he re-entered the room mobile phone still in hand as if he was bringing a scientist trapped in the handset back in to tell them all the news. "The tox is back, Richard Wilson had a significant amount of ketamine still in his system when he died."

"Ketamine, thats a horse tranquilliser isn't it," remarked Dave, still seconded to the enquiry and back from Nottingham where he had spent the last three days.

"It is but I thought it was a date rape drug? Go on then I can see you itching to impress us all. What is ketamine?" Responded the SIO looking back at the grinning exhibits officer.

"It's a powerful general anaesthetic which stops you feeling pain and it's used for operations on humans and animals. The effects don't last long, but until they wear off, ketamine can cause a loss of feeling in the body and paralysis of the muscles. It can also lead to you experiencing a distortion of reality."

"That would answer a lot of things," the SIO remarked. "Andy, Steve we better have a sit down after this we've got a lot of ground to cover today with the family. The briefing soon concluded and The three men sat in Danny Davis' small office.

Danny Davis let out a deep exhale as he sat behind his desk, his two family liaison officers waiting for some inspirational comment.

"I haven't got a fucking clue lads, what do you think?"

Steve was stunned, this is the SIO, he's not supposed to ask us that. "What have we got at the scene Sir?" he asked.

"Apart from what you know Steve not a lot. Richard Wilson was an unusually tidy bachelor with what looks like a pretty strict cleaning regime. Apart from the usual inordinate amount of Magnum police boot marks there's not a single footmark or fingerprint we found that doesn't belong to Wilson himself. The craft knife he used is available in most DIY stores not to mention that new

133

Hobbyworld shop that's just opened. We checked Wilson's accounts but there's not a single card transaction anywhere like that for Wilson to give us a clue where to look for CCTV. Apparently they are only about six quid for a twin pack so maybe he just used cash? The pathologist is now back tracking on his insistence that Wilson was unlikely to have been able to cut both wrists and now there's this ketamine shit, well you heard what that does; it kills pain and it can also lead to you experiencing a distortion of reality. Sounds like the ideal prerequisite for scribbling a confession on your living room wall then slicing open both your wrists," ranted the confused senior officer.

"I think we really need to tread carefully with this family boss. Tell them everything, let them ask their questions and make their suggestions and be prepared to answer anything," responded Andy keen to get on with the day's task.

"I agree, that's how we will play it. It's going to be a tough day, did you say they were expecting us at about three?" The SIO asked.

"Yes sir is that okay," answered Andy.

"Yeah I'm up for that, it'll give me time to square things away here as I'm not having a briefing tomorrow. If you want you can get us a cheap hotel in Bury then we'll have a decent meal and a beer tonight and stay over, I think we could all do with a reasonable nights kip."

"What do you want me to do about the natural father boss?" Asked Steve.

"He's quite easy going isn't he?" Checked the SIO.

"Yes sir."

"How about we take my car as well as yours and you deal with him Steve whilst me and Andy do the main family. Maybe you'll be able to bottom out all the updates with him today then just stay in touch by phone from there onwards?"

"That's fine with me sir yes," responded Steve looking over at Andy for approval.

"Yes that sounds like a plan, if me and you leave at about 1.30 that will give us loads of time boss," added Andy

Andy and Steve spent the next hour getting their paperwork in order before Steve headed off early via his flat to grab an overnight bag and leave an apologetic note in the normal place for Anna. He wanted to head up to Suffolk early hoping to get started with Jonathan Wilson as soon as he could. He stopped halfway there calling him to confirm he was on his way. It was just past midday and he knew with only one pair of hands he needed to get the lead on Andy and the SIO.

"Sorry Steve I'm stuck at work until at least 6.30, can we say 7, is that okay?" responded Jonathan.

"No problem we have a lot to get through. I'm staying local tonight so it doesn't matter how late it is when we finish."

Steve headed to Bury and easily found a suitable independent hotel, booking three rooms and texting the details to Andy and the SIO before heading out to look for some place to grab a late lunch. Steve found himself heading north and suddenly realised how close he was to Norfolk and Anna's mother's care home.

Steve had missed the last few visits Anna had paid to her mother over the previous 18 months because of work so it was only right he used a little work time to make up for that. He was no more than 10 miles from the small village south of Norwich where the care home was. Steve was sure that Anna would love to think he took time out to see her mother whilst he was in the area. By all accounts her health was improving despite being in her mid seventies now. Her mobility was still poor and she needed the constant care that the comfortable home provided. Her speech therapy had really helped according to Anna so Steve was more confident that he'd be able to hold a reasonable conversation with her now.

"How are you Edith?" Asked Steve as he came up beside the frail lady in the beautiful huge conservatory area attached to the rear of the home.

"Steven, what a wonderful surprise," Edith responded genuinely elated to see him. "Everything is okay is it, is Anna okay, where is she, why are you so smart?" Queried the now more concerned Edith.

"Yes don't worry, Anna is fine. I was in Bury St Edmunds with work. I couldn't be so close to you without dropping in for a cup of tea," answered Steve reassuringly as he leant over to kiss his mother-in-law."

"You won't get in trouble will you if you are supposed to be working?"

"No of course not, besides I haven't been able to come and visit for ages because of work. Now where's that tea trolley I'll go and get us both a nice cuppa and we can catch up."

Steve returned from the day room rattling two small cups of tea on their precarious saucers the chocolate of two digestive biscuits melting rapidly against the side of the cups.

"There you go Edith, brought you a biscuit as well."

"You eat them Steve my dinner is at five."

Steve was more than happy to oblige, tea and biscuits being his staple diet these days.

"So Steven tell me, how are you and Anna?" Edith asked quite seriously.

"We are great Edith, the picture of happiness, we just don't get to see each other much these days what with me being a detective and Anna's victim support work."

"What does Anna do with victim support?" Interrupted Edith.

"She works for them as a full time employee, she has done for a few years now," answered Steve slightly confused that this was news to Edith.

"Oh, oh yes she must have told me I'm sure. Anyway I do remember Anna telling me you had been promoted to detective now, very impressive."

"It's not really a promotion more a specialisation really but I love it."

"How do you become a detective then?" Asked Edith, genuinely interested in Steve's career.

"Well you apply, pass exams then you have to pass a course, but first you have to get recommended before any of that can happen. I'm sure the work I did in uniform on that murder in Chisham helped raise my profile."

"Oh Chisham, Anna and I used to visit her great aunt in Chisham two or three times year. Just on the edge of the village she lived. Anna loved it she'd go off and play with some of the kids around there whilst me and her great aunt caught up. I think sometimes growing up on a remote Norfolk farm was not the most social childhood for an only child," explained Edith the regret in her voice evident following her last comment.

"I didn't realise Anna had relatives in Chisham, she never mentioned it."

"Her great aunt passed away a long time ago so she probably wouldn't." Responded Edith.

"I suppose being an only child on a farm so remote was a little tough for Anna, but she turned out to be a beautiful young woman who I love dearly so it can't have been all that bad," reassured Steve.

"I'm glad, I'm really glad you are happy my dear Steven," answered Edith taking his hand in hers and looking at him, her eyes moist with emotion. "I'm so pleased you came to see me, it means so much. I know you can't get up often, that's fine but it's really good to know you are happy."

"Come on drink your tea before it gets cold." Instructed Steve breaking the intensity of Edith's sincere comments. Steve was slightly embarrassed to be in such a deep conversation with the mother-in-law he'd met only a handful of times over the last five years. Embarrassment born out of guilt if he was honest, but Anna never complained that Steve's shifts clashed with her weekends off so regularly. She used those occasions to visit her mother rather than infringe on their time together.

"Dinner in ten minutes ladies," announced a rather pleasant young care assistant.

"Oh sorry Edith I didn't time my visit that well, looks like they are going to kick me out in a minute. It's been lovely to see you looking so well though. I suppose I better get back to my work anyway." Apologised Steve.

"Thank you for visiting Steve I really appreciate it. You keep in touch now and give my love to Anna."

"I'm sorry I don't get up here more Edith, I just don't know where all the time goes."

"Don't worry my dear, I see Anna and I'm very happy here, it is my home now. I hear all about what you are up to from Anna. Just come when you get chance that's all I ask. It was lovely to see you too and I hope your job in Bury goes okay."

Steve kissed Edith affectionately on the cheek. She was a lovely old lady and Steve was so pleased to see her settled and well. As Steve walked back to his car he realised he had a voice message. He must have missed a call when he silenced his phone to visit Edith. Steve listened to the message.

"Hello DC Lawson it's Jonathan Wilson. I just wanted to let you know I'm home now. I managed to finish work early please feel free to come round a little sooner if you wish."

"Great," thought Steve he could be with Jonathan Wilson by 5.30 if he was lucky and maybe get chance to share notes with Andy and the SIO over an evening meal by 8. Steve checked his log, all that Jonathan Wilson knew was his son had died of blood loss from cut wrists and he had been found at home. He'd told us very honestly that his son had an unhealthy interest in young girls but he hadn't been told by them that one of their fathers had been arrested and questioned in Nottingham. Jonathan had sounded quite up beat in his message so hopefully he wouldn't be too emotional.

"DC Lawson thanks for coming out to see me again."

"Please call me Steve, how are you doing?" Asked Steve as he was led into the small terraced house.

"I'm okay, I really don't know how to feel. I suppose I'm still struggling to take it in," answered Jonathan. "Can I get you a drink?"

"Only if you're having one."

"Yes I've just made some fresh coffee is that okay," offered Jonathan.

"Great yes, white with one sugar please," answered Steve opening his day book to check on a few bullet points he'd made in the car before he knocked the door.

"Thank you Jonathan," Steve took the mug of coffee. "Now I wanted to start by just letting you know that Eileen has viewed Richard's body and a formal identification was made. Now his body will not be released at this stage even though the post-mortem is complete. Sadly when circumstances are unexplained there can be some delay before a funeral can take place. If you want to see Richard we can arrange it?"

"No, no.. I don't think I do. I don't need to, I don't want to see him like that if it's okay. I can remember him in better times if that makes sense."

"Yes definitely I understand, but have a think about it and let us know if you change your mind," offered Steve.

"I don't think I will. What did the post-mortem reveal?"

"As expected Richard died from blood loss. The only complication is that he had taken a drug that he wouldn't have been able to get hold of legally called ketamine."

"I've heard of that but what does this mean?" Questioned Jonathan.

"Ketamine can cause a loss of feeling in the body and paralysis of the muscles. It can also lead to you experiencing a distortion of reality." Explained Steve referring to the notes he'd made in the last briefing. "It is used in recreational drug use to get high on and equally it has appeared in date rape scenarios so it's really hard to say how Richard ended up taking it. The only thing it would explain is how he stood the obvious pain of fatal cuts to the wrists and it is highly likely that he suffered very little as he passed away."

"I don't understand. I can't understand why he wanted to kill himself. I know he'd promised to make a fresh start when he went to Westhampton. He said in one of the last letters he sent me. God I hope he didn't think that would make everything right. I didn't reply. I should have replied… maybe I should have given him a second chance. God no, but that was nearly a year ago." Reflected Jonathan momentarily putting his head in his hands and slowly pushing his hands through his hair as if to push his stress back from his forehead.

"Jonathan please don't over think your own actions. They are what they are," replied Steve meaninglessly trying to set himself up for the next revelation. "It is clear Richard was battling with the problem you told us about and it's more likely that was what was eating him up inside. You know what happened in Nottingham, well Richard had a home computer and like a lot of people these days had it connected to the internet. Stupidly it appears he made contact with the girl from his old school in Nottingham and her father found out. Richard received a threatening email from the father and we do know it caused him quite some concern. On top of that more recently it appears Richard made some

142

inappropriate advances to a young female pupil of a dubious character. He was arrested for this and denied everything so who knows. Anyway the girl would have made an unreliable witness and not a scrap of evidence existed to support her allegations so Richard wasn't charged and amazingly kept his job. Unfortunately that didn't stop her dousing his car with paint stripper or something whilst it was parked in the school car park."

"So Richard was battling his demons still right up to his death. It all makes sense now. Poor boy why didn't he just accept his lot and get some professional help, suicide was not the answer," concluded Jonathan.

"Well, we are still exploring all possibilities and there are a lot of lines of enquiry still to complete," tempered Steve. "I can tell you however that the girl in Nottingham has been spoken to, her father formally questioned and enquiries completed to establish if he had any connection with Richard's death."

"You don't think he would murder Richard though do you?" asked a confused Jonathan.

"No, but we have to eliminate all possibilities. Let me explain." Steve paused noting the despairing look on Jonathan's face. "I'm sorry this is quite distressing. Are you okay for me to go on?"

"Steve, please I just need to know everything, good or bad so I can try to make some sense of this."

"I take it you never visited Richard's house in Westhampton?" asked Steve before he explained the scene and also discreetly completed an action he had been given raised as part of the forensic strategy.

"No never, I don't actually think I've ever even been to Westhampton." Answered Jonathan confirming that any biometric evidence of his found at the scene now would put him clearly into the suspect category. Steve didn't think this was very likely.

"Richard had patio doors at the rear of his house leading into his lounge diner. Now those doors were not locked. This may not mean anything, lots of people don't lock their back doors when they are at home and who knows maybe Richard knew eventually someone would come to check on him and need a way in without breaking down the front door? Richard did not leave a suicide note. This is not unusual but what was unusual was instead Richard has hand written a brief confession on his lounge wall for everyone to see admitting to being, well a sex offender. Also his computer was left on with some indecent images of young females showing, almost to reinforce this."

"Oh God I don't believe this. This will destroy his mum, does she know?" Asked a now quite distressed Jonathan.

"Andy is visiting her today and explaining everything I am telling you." Confirmed Steve deliberately omitting the fact that the SIO had gone with Andy so as not to make Jonathan think he is being treated differently. "Are you okay Jonathan?" Checked Steve noting he had returned to his default stress position, head in hands, fingers pushed into his hair.

Jonathan looked up, "Sorry Steve please, I want to know."

"Now its hard to say but Richard may have been in a rage or an argument or even some kind of disturbance with an unknown third party as a few things are out of place downstairs. Obviously it was after this that Richard went to his bedroom and his wrists were cut. There are some inconsistencies with the blood staining in the bedroom that are still being analysed in detail to eliminate the possibility that someone helped cut Richard's wrists. Now all of these things simply mean we need to do our job and investigate thoroughly before we can conclude if this is a suicide or not."

"So who would want to kill Richard, is there something else he'd done?" Asked Jonathan.

"No, no we haven't found anything else and in answer to your other question we really don't think the father from Nottingham or the girl from Richard's school in Westhampton are capable of such a thing. Neither of them knew where he lived even. We just need to check everything and it is still only a few days since Richard died so I can't give you all the answers yet. All I can do is just explain what we have so far and why we still have more to do."

"Steve I really appreciate what you've done so far please thank your colleagues, it means a lot to me that you are checking everything. So what's next?"

"I will stay in touch by phone. As and when we complete lines of enquiry I will update you with what we found out. There will in the future be an inquest and you will be invited to attend if you wish, but the full inquest will be at least 6 months away. The coroner will simply open and adjourn it until then. I will let you know when Richard's body is released and.." Steve paused for thought, 'what should he do about letting Jonathan know the funeral arrangements Eileen will surely want to make them without his input?'

"Jonathan, are you going to make contact with Eileen before the funeral?"

"I was going to ask you about that. I can't, I don't have her number. I really don't know what to say. She's probably going to blame me. Would you... would you give her my mobile phone number and just ask her to let me know when and where the funeral is, a text will do, she doesn't even have to talk to me, but I need to go. Can you make sure she understands that, whatever she thinks. He's my son I need to pay my final respects to him."

"Of course Jonathan, that sounds like the best way forward. I understand this is difficult for you. Is there anything else you need to know?"

"No Steve, thank you, thank you very much, it can't be easy for you."

"Before I go I have a letter from Detective Chief Inspector Danny Davis who is leading the enquiry. He is on hand to answer any questions and hopefully he will meet you in due course when our enquiries have progressed," explained Steve knowing whatever his conclusion was Danny Davis would see it as his personal responsibility to deliver it face to face. "Don't forget you can call me with any questions you have as and when you think of them. I'll give you a call in a few days time anyway."

"Thanks Steve I better let you get off," said the now calm and less distressed Jonathan.

Steve knew as he stepped out of the front door that this poor man may seem okay again now but was likely to revisit the full range of emotions as the night wore on.

As Steve walked into the reception area of the hotel he spotted a couple of familiar faces perched on stools in the small bar.

"Two pints of Fosters and whatever you want Steve," the presumptuous Danny Davis requested ordering Steve's round. It was of course an unwritten rule that the SIO, who didn't qualify for overtime pay, was looked after if he ever went away with you overnight.

"Don't worry mate you're only one behind us, we only got away from the Taylor's about half an hour ago and we needed a drink after that believe me. Come on lets get a table and order some food and you can tell us how you got on," instructed Andy.

As the three detectives tucked into the array of various steaks and chips chased down by a well earned pint as they quietly discussed the family reactions to the details of the enquiry.

"The mum, what's her name, Eileen, she will never accept her son took his own life if that is the case. Just bare that in mind lads if this isn't a murder," commented the SIO.

"It might be the other way round convincing Jonathan Wilson this could be a murder. As far as he's concerned his son committed suicide and he's made his mind up on that." Responded Steve

"What's he like Steve you don't think it suits him that his son has topped himself do you," asked Danny Davis.

"No boss I can't see that nor can I see him being involved in any way. He's never even been to his son's house, he's confirmed that. Unless your going to tell me his prints are all over Wilson's house I really wouldn't say there's anything to worry about there." Answered Steve.

"Alright if that's what you think we won't worry too much about the dad. What do you think Andy?"

"I think I need another beer, I'm at a loss. We are missing something, maybe there are other girls Wilson has abused, this was almost ritualistic if it was a murder. If so I'm not sure the killer wanted it to be simply dismissed as a suicide, they were trying to make a point, 'Wilson should have killed himself but needed a helping hand?' I don't know, I've been to suicides over the years and people do the oddest things, they top themselves in a moment of madness, a moment that if they had just sat down and calmed down for half an hour they might have changed their minds forever. It's one of those jobs that we just need to dot the 'I's' and cross the 'T's' on and then have a look at everything we've got."

"And that's what we're going to do after one last round of beer and a good nights sleep. Get them in Andy," instructed the upbeat SIO as he left the table to go to the gents.

Andy headed to the bar. "I'll be with you in a minute mate just going to give the missus a quick bell then I'll join you," said Steve.

"Hi darling sorry about the note and the sudden disappearance I didn't want to ring you at work in case you were busy. You're going to have to get a mobile you know." Apologised Steve.

"Maybe you can buy me one out of your overtime you bastard." Answered a surprisingly annoyed Anna. "When I saw the envelope propped up on the breakfast bar I thought you'd left me. I'm stupid, I know but I went straight to the wardrobe to see if you'd taken your things only to see the small hold all was missing. My heart was beating so fast when I opened the note I could have killed you when I realised you were just away with work."

"I'm sorry Anna, I wanted you to see the note that's all. You know I'll never leave you, not for any reason, least of all for a night in a second rate hotel in Bury St Edmunds," laughed Steve.

"I know, I just love you so much I couldn't bare it if we were ever separated."

"Anyway I had a bit of down time when I got here so I dropped in on you mum.."

"What, why?"

"You know I haven't been able to visit for so long, I thought you'd be pleased. Her speech is doing so well now we had a nice chat," explained Steve a little bemused at not earning instant credit for his good deed.

"No Steve I am grateful really, I just worry that mum is in such a settled routine that surprises, even nice ones like you, might not be good for her, but never mind it was a really nice thing to do. What did you talk about anyway?"

"Bits and bobs just chit chat really she was in a good mood and really happy just to see me I think. Oh and you never told me you used to have a great aunt that lived in Chisham." Remembered Steve.

"Didn't I? It was a long time ago, she died years before we met and I really didn't see much of her, must have slipped my mind. What other secrets did mum reveal about me then?" Asked Anna jokingly.

"Nothing, she just kept saying she's really happy you settled down with me, so you've done the right thing obviously falling for such a wonderful fellow or at least she thinks so."

"I have Steve yes my darling of course you are well, almost perfect." Laughed Anna.

"Almost?" Replied Steve pushing his luck. "Listen Anna I'm with the boss and Andy the other FLO and believe it or not we are still discussing the case so I'm going to have to go," explained Steve exercising a little poetic license.

"Okay I suppose I'll see you tomorrow night some time?" Asked Anna. She was used to Steve never finishing anywhere near the time other normal people do.

"Well you know I don't like to promise ever finishing on time but things are slowing down a little now so I might just surprise you and get home before you go to bed."

"I'll believe it when I see it Steve. I love you darling."

"I love you too Anna, see you tomorrow."

"Bye."

"Bye, bye."

The next morning Andy and Steve enjoyed a slower start to the day than they'd had all week. Danny Davis had been glad to have his own car there as he'd had to shoot off with a slice of toast in his hand having been summoned to a gold group meeting about the job.

"What's a 'gold group meeting' anyway Andy?" Asked Steve as he tucked into his full English.

"It's basically a load of senior officers who have very little to do with the job being nosy and putting the SIO on the spot so they can pretend to make constructive suggestions about what he should do next, but only after Danny has told them what he intends to do and give them the ideas. All you need to worry about is they'll be discussing staffing levels and they are bound to be reduced even at this stage," explained Andy.

Steve looked concerned he was just starting to get a real taste for major crime enquiries.

"Don't worry mate we'll be alright, Danny will make sure of that. He likes you, says you've got real potential," revealed Andy.

"When did he say that?"

"While you were still on the phone to Your wife. Mind you he was on his fourth pint by then," laughed Andy.

The pair checked out after breakfast and headed back to the incident room. They spent most of the rest of the day writing up their logs and looking at the outstanding high priority actions. Andy was right the staffing levels had been almost halved and they were going to have to get out and do some of the other enquiries needed as well as continuing their family liaison work.

The mornings briefing was a casual affair, just in the incident room itself now there was a smaller team. All of the updates were negative at this stage. Absolutely nothing of use from the now concluded house to house, no CCTV in the local area and not even a family members fingerprint at the scene let alone a viable suspect. Andy and Steve would now be expected to complete some other enquiries individually in between their FLO work. Steve looked at his main action for the day, 'TI U/K associate of Suspect 1 who lives in Westhampton". Trace and interview of course the unknown rather than UK based friend of Suspect 1; that was the father of the girl in Nottingham. Steve remembered from his briefing notes that the father had said he'd only ever been to Westhampton before for a friend's wedding. Now all of the work surrounding his account was complete and no evidence could be found to show him coming to Westhampton at the time of the murder, it was a possibility however that he'd harmed Wilson by proxy. Steve opened up the interview transcripts now typed verbatim onto the HOLMES computer programme. Steve's mind drifted as he logged in to this amazing piece of software he'd recently received a crash course on. 'Home Office Large and Major Enquiry System' remembered Steve. A system devised after the Yorkshire Ripper enquiries. Of course like all new ideas it had its name tweaked several times probably until the title could be shortened to spell out an appropriate name. What better than one of a famous fictional detective from Baker Street. Unlike Sherlock the HOLMES system was heavily relied upon to store all material obtained during an investigation and to cross reference everything together. Actions were raised from HOLMES, sometimes pointless actions to, but it was designed to make sure investigators cover every possible angle. No stone unturned whilst still relying on good office managers and a shrewd SIO to make it work.

Steve trawled the complete range of interview transcripts realising the girl's father had not actually been named during the briefings. 'Paul Yates father of Claire Yates,' identified Steve as he opened the lengthy transcripts. Searching through the document for the word 'wedding' Steve soon identified that Paul Yates' best friend Kevin actually lived in Westhampton. When he was asked to tell the interviewing officers all about himself he explained that Kevin Houghton had actually been stationed in Westhampton when he married a local woman. He was a soldier in The Royal Pioneer Corps. Not wanting to drag his friend into things, Yates claimed to have lost contact with him in recent years and wasn't even sure if he was still in Westhampton or not. That was a enough for Steve he knew from his own army days that the military were meticulous at keeping records and with a name and a regiment he should find Kevin Houghton really easily. Steve just hoped he was still serving. Knowing what squaddies were like Steve knew if Houghton was a close friend of Paul Yates and Yates needed a visit paying to someone, most soldiers would happily step up and do that kind of favour without asking too many questions. This had suddenly become a more interesting line of enquiry in Steve's mind.

After a quick call to the Force Intelligence Bureau Steve identified the best point of liaison for the Ministry of Defence. Steve was quickly reminded that the MOD had sold the barracks in Westhampton several years early, now flattened to make way for a new housing estate. The Pioneer Corps didn't even exist anymore, they were now all part of the Royal Logistics Corps. However, Sergeant Kevin Houghton was still serving and based at some remote camp in Warwickshire no more than an hours drive away. His address was the Sergeants Mess in the camp. 'Obviously not married anymore' thought Steve. A few more phone calls and a call back from Houghton and Steve was on his way.

Steve had been deliberately vague when he spoke to him simply stating there was a serious incident in Westhampton about ten days previous and he thought Houghton might have some useful background knowledge that would help their enquiries. Houghton didn't seem to question this much, he just made a flippant comment about 'not needing his lawyer then' which Steve thought was a little odd.

"Sergeant Kevin Houghton."

"DC Steve Lawson," Steve responded as formally as he'd been greeted slightly wary of his presence in the rather grand sergeants mess. A forbidden domain for other ranks and not somewhere ex-Corporal Steve Lawson ever made it to during his army career.

"I've reserved us the ante room just off the main lounge, we shouldn't be disturbed in there," explained the smartly dressed sergeant as he ushered Steve into a small snug type room adorned with regimental oil paintings and other military memorabilia.

"You're not long back from Kosovo are you? I bet your glad to be back from that tour?" Asked Steve trying to break the formality of the situation using the small piece of information he'd managed to glean from his guardroom escort on the way to the sergeant's mess.

"Yeah it's good to be back, it was a long six months being used and abused as the Royal Engineers personal infantrymen. Ever been there yourself?" A question he knew he'd get a negative answer to and Steve detected as a status grab not unlike 'bet you've never been to a war zone, you're just a copper.'

"No mate, did twelve years in the Queens Regiment before I joined the old bill, but all they kept doing is sending us to Northern Ireland, Belfast, South Armagh, Londonderry. Got totally sick of the place." Answered Steve redressing the balance and instantly gaining the respect and interest of his interviewee.

"Right mate, how can I help you, I don't recall witnessing anything in Westhampton last time I was there."

"When was that?" asked Steve.

"Last Saturday; I get to go over at least every fortnight to see the lad like. The ex has always been good about that. What's this all about?"

"We are investigating the death of a local teacher in Westhampton that occurred about a week ago," explained Steve not wanting to totally spook this guy by pointing out the fact that it occurred on the exact day he was last in the town.

"That teacher is the same man who used to teach at the school Paul Yates' daughter went."

"Is this the same nonse bastard that fucking abused young Claire then?" Interrupted the clearly angry soldier.

"Yes it is the same teacher who had an inappropriate relationship with Claire Yates when he was based in Nottingham." Confirmed Steve using less colourful language.

"Good fucking riddance. Paul didn't have anything to do with it did he?"

"Well we have to investigate all angles and Paul Yates has helped us by answering all of our questions. I assume he hasn't told you about this?" Checked Steve.

"No, no I feel bad now because I haven't been in touch with Paul for a while. Thing is since me and the missus split two years ago we stopped going up to visit. I lost the married quarter and Paul could hardly come and stop in this place for the weekend. It was awkward you see especially as Paul's wife sort of blamed me and my stupidness for the split."

"How's that then?" Questioned Steve trying further to work this character out.

"It's my temper. Apparently I blow hot and cold too much. They thought it was a post traumatic stress thing but that's bollocks. It's just the way I am; hot headed don't really think before I do. Not the best recipe for a happy married life, but then everyone has the odd barny don't they, but that's another story."

"So I'm assuming when things happened with Claire you were still in regular contact with Paul Yates?" Checked Steve.

"Yeah, in fact he rung me the day after he found out; poor bastard was a wreck. He thought it was his fault and he should have noticed. He was worried Claire was smitten with this fucking paedo and even though he got kicked out of her school nothing else was going to be done to keep the tosser away from her. I told him what I wanted to do, but he told me the police were dealing with it so I left it. Wish I hadn't because your lot were a waste of time." Griped Kevin.

"I know what you mean, even if that's not quite the case," empathised Steve. "Did Paul ever tell you he'd found out the teacher was still working?"

"Yes, well he told me he wouldn't be struck off as a teacher. My blood boiled when he told me, poor old Paul was devastated and just hoped no one would be stupid enough to employ the nonse. Paul felt sort of responsible for the fact they had not been able to put the guy away."

"But did he tell you he'd found the teacher again and he was working in Westhampton?"

"No, no, definitely not, not back there, no. I'd have found him myself, my boy will be starting school there soon don't want no fucking sex cases teaching him."

Steve's concerns could not be quelled about this lively soldier. He had a fiery temper and a very strong contempt for the teacher that was Richard Wilson. He was in Westhampton at least the day of the death and had even admitted he wanted to take the law into his own hands. Steve needed to commit him to a couple of facts then take his conclusions away.

"When did you last speak to Paul Yates Kevin?"

"Before I went to Kosovo, a few months before. Like I said we haven't got together since my marriage went to rat shit. We promised each other we'd get together after I got back, just haven't got round to giving him a bell yet. Is it alright if I call him, he'll be in a state again now this has all been dragged up?"

"I can't stop you Kevin of course, but just bare in mind we are still eliminating him from our enquiries," answered Steve frankly.

"Eliminating him?"

"Yes it is fairly routine, we just need to cover everything when we investigate a sudden death." Explained Steve deliberately dumbing down his tone ready for one final question. "Can I just check, again just as a matter of routine, what time you left Westhampton last Saturday and where you went from there?"

"Probably about 10, 10.30 that night had a couple of beers at a little pub on the B26, only two mind I was driving. Reckon I must have been back in camp by midnight, I'm not too sure but it couldn't have been much later, last orders hadn't even been called when I left the boozer. Listen I haven't got anything to do with this mate and I don't reckon Paul has either. At least it's all over for that family now and they can try and get on with things now knowing that prick isn't going to turn up on the doorstep one day."

"Thank you Kevin I appreciate your candid answers. You understand we have to make these enquiries and it's so much easier to speak to people face to face. Listen I appreciate your time and hospitality," thanked Steve even though he'd not even been offered a cup of tea. "I'll let you get on. Thanks again."

The two men shook hands and Houghton walked Steve back to his car parked behind the guardhouse before seeing him safely out of camp.

Steve was undecided. He'd write the action up accordingly. 'Shit! The bloke didn't even ask how the teacher died,' thought Steve. That was odd, maybe he has been in touch with Paul Yates, he didn't mention reading about it in the local paper. This was unlikely anyway they'd only just printed the more detailed story indicating a possible suicide with all options being considered. Maybe his ex wife mentioned it? Frustrated Steve headed back to the incident room.

"What's going on Andy?" Steve asked his colleague when he came off the phone.

"Derek Hardwood."

"Who?"

"Derek Hardwood, one of Richard Wilson's few friends, or at least he was when they shared student digs together in Nottingham. We found Derek in Richard Wilson's email contacts. He responded to an email request to contact the incident room only yesterday and the usual suspects from our resident Nottingham team TI'd him today."

"And.." Steve asked impatiently.

"You don't want to know."

"I do."

"No honestly you don't, it's another FLO's nightmare. A clusterfuck we need to get in amongst and find out what, if any, relevance this has."

"Go on you know I like a challenge," prompted Steve.

"Not this one you won't. Anyway one drunken evening Derek, a similarly shy character, got round to discussing his short list of previous girlfriends and even shorter list of sexual conquests. Following his outpouring of not so impressive admissions he eventually forces Richard Wilson to admit that he is not the virgin his personality suggested. He admits his first love was a girl named Kathleen, but it was complicated and although they experimented sexually and eventually had full blown sex their parents didn't approve and it was a good thing he left home to go to university."

"I bet their bloody parents didn't approve, I can picture the scene when Eileen and James came home to find their individual children in some inappropriate embrace." Added Steve.

"Exactly, of course Derek didn't deduce this but I can't think of any other scenario that fits. The question is does Christian know and if so when and how did he find out?" replied Andy posing a very key question.

"Do you think Christian's in the frame then?"

"Danny Davis does, he said he wasn't sure about him after our meeting the other day. Either way there's the action, no weekend off for us. I've keyed up the family told them we need four times individual witness statements so need to speak to them each alone. Eileen and James have appointments with a funeral director and solicitor re the probate issues in the morning so have agreed to give us time with Kathleen to make a start. I've suggested to Christian that we visit him at his flat in the afternoon where we can temper our approach in line with whatever Kathleen is prepared to give up in the morning. Don't worry mate the overtime is authorised, double time of course."

"It better be, I should be rest day today remember coming off of nights, I'm going to have to work hard to make this up to Anna on Sunday. I assume we can have one day off?" asked the concerned but interested Steve.

"I think so. I know how difficult it is to keep them happy, my wife left me two years ago."

"Great!"

"Listen mate you get off now, I'll get everything together we need for the morning. Why don't I grab the car and I'll pick you up from your place say at 9 give you a bit of time with your good lady," offered Andy.

"Thanks I appreciate that mate, here let me write down my address for you," responded Andy's grateful colleague before slipping out of the incident room at an unprecedented 4 pm.

"Are you feeling alright Steve," asked Anna jokingly as the stranger walked through the flat door.

"What?"

"Well it's still daylight and you're home; I assume you've been sent home sick or maybe they've run out of money to pay you anymore overtime," laughed Anna.

"Ha, ha... Anyway don't get too excited I've got to work tomorrow and Sunday is not guaranteed either. Have you been home long?"

"No just got in."

"Right get changed we're eating out tonight, anywhere you want, it's my treat," suggested Steve.

Anna was soon heading towards the shower discarding her work clothes on the way with Steve in hot pursuit.

"That new big Italian on Bridge Street I think and you can tell me all about your week over dinner," teased Anna as she darted into the bathroom keen as ever to hear about the fascinating world of a police detective.

"That night off did you good Steve," remarked the slightly jealous Andy Porter as they drove into Suffolk. "Just remember mate 'work life balance' is not just a buzz word senior officers like to preach but not practice. Don't fucking end up like me. You can be a successful detective without a failed marriage on the bottom of your CV. It looks like you've got the right woman behind you to stand a chance of staying married. Don't you risk loosing her mate." Lectured Andy in a sincere but authoritarian manner.

Steve knew what Andy was saying it was so easy to get swept up in the pace of an interesting crime enquiry that you forgot about everything else in your life. Even more so when your role involves supporting a bereaved family.

"Today could be tough," added Andy. "If we play it right the family will understand what we are trying to achieve and it won't affect our relationship. It doesn't help that we don't have any more answers for them."

When they arrived at the house both Eileen and James were about to leave. Andy had given them a full update by phone the day before so after a few basic questions and general chat they headed out leaving the slightly nervous Kathleen behind.

Andy explained family background statements were important especially for a coroner at inquest. If Kathleen could help paint a picture of her step brother by going through her memory chronologically there might be something in his past life, no matter how insignificant she thinks it is, that helps answer a line of enquiry. Andy knew exactly what he hoped she was prepared to discuss and clear up but he needed to ease her into that chapter of her life and cognitively manage Kathleen's true recall of events.

"So tell me exactly when and how you found out Richard was not in fact your natural brother?" Asked Andy some way into the interview.

"I think I was about 13, old enough to ask all the right questions really. Richard knew long before me and had promised mum and dad he would not tell me and he'd wait until they thought I was old enough to understand. It was a confusing time, I didn't take it well. Not only did I have to suffer the grief of finding out my mum died and died because of me but also that Eileen had pretended to be my mum all those years. I can tell you adolescence and news like that didn't mix well." Explained the emotional but surprisingly controlled young woman. "At the time the only positive was it brought Richard and I closer together, too close I suppose..."

"What do you mean too close?" Mirrored Andy.

"We spent hours together talking things over and Richard really cheered me up helped me realise how mum and dad had actually done the right thing. Richard didn't have many friends and we lived out here away from school and town so we spent a lot of time together as teenagers. Oh shit this is hard I really don't know if I should be bringing all this up again?"

"Kathleen if it is about Richard I'm afraid we really need to know. We don't have to put it in this statement we can just talk in confidence if it helps," pushed Steve anticipating the forthcoming revelation.

Kathleen exhaled deeply. "We were really close, it was stupid, if only we hadn't found out we were not actually related none of this would have happened. That closeness would never have turned into what it did. When I was 14 Richard was in his last year of sixth form. I knew he didn't have a girlfriend. We used to talk about things like that. I wanted him to be happy and get on like other boys and not just academically. I would try and give him tips on how to talk to girls and what sort of things would make them laugh. He was just so nervous around girls at school and he used to worry about embarrassing himself not being able to kiss properly and things like that. That's where it all went wrong during the Easter break." Kathleen paused.

"Go on," encouraged Andy.

"We watched TV and films. Dirty Dancing and things like that and learnt how people kissed properly. Richard and I practised kissing; I was curious as well. It seemed like innocent fun at the time but like I said we got too close. It all went horribly wrong just before Richard went to university. It had gone too far by the time I was 15, I was late and Richard had insisted I get a home pregnancy test. It was negative fortunately and my period soon followed but mum found the packet in the bin and went mad. Of course she didn't suspect Richard and I had to make up some story about a boy at school that I refused to name. Richard didn't leave a happy family environment when he went off to university but it scared us so much that we vowed to stop seeing each other like we were. It would have destroyed mum and dad. You won't have to tell them will you?" Asked a worried and distressed Kathleen.

"Hopefully not no," reassured Andy, "but I do need to know if anyone else knows?"

"Only Christian but he wouldn't tell a soul".

"Why Christian?" Quizzed Steve.

"After he proposed to me I just couldn't keep things secret. It was eating me up knowing I could be deceiving him for the rest of our lives. He needed to know the truth. I thought it would freak him out but he was really good. The only problem was things between him and Richard were never the same, nothing obvious there was just an atmosphere that wasn't there before that's all."

"Thank you Kathleen we don't need to go into that detail in your background statement, but I'm glad you have told me. Is it okay if I let Christian know you've told us this in confidence just so it doesn't become a barrier when we speak to him this afternoon. I am confident we won't need to discuss it any further after that?" Asked Andy.

"Yes if you have to, I just couldn't stand the thought of mum and dad finding out especially on top of the sadness of poor Richard's death."

"I understand, don't worry I don't think we will have to ever tell them." Reassured Andy.

The interview concluded on a more positive note and a basic family statement suitable for a coroners file was completed without the revelation Kathleen had made.

As they headed to Christian's flat Steve pondered over the concept that Christian had good reason to want to bury the past, protecting his future wife from any further harm and Richard's death covered that well.

"You don't think do you Andy..."

"Nar mate can't see it, Christian hasn't got it in him to stage a murder like that, I really don't think so but let's see what he's like when we raise the subject. How did he react to the news of Richard's death?"

Steve paused, thought back then shared his thoughts with Andy. "You know I'm not sure knowing what I know now. He did all the right things and was genuinely worried about how hard the news hit Kathleen, but why do I want to say the news of the death didn't seem to surprise him. No, no I don't think he'd do that to his beloved Kathleen or her parents he thinks the world of them all. We are going to have to read him carefully."

Christian was confused. "I'm not sure why you need a background statement from me?"

"Actually I don't think we need to take a full statement at this time, we just wanted to speak to you alone and clear up a few points about Richard with you. When did you last see him?" Queried Andy.

"Christmas time I think, yes he came back for Christmas. I would have said hello on the phone when he rung home as well. Eileen had the annoying habit of putting him on speaker phone when he made his call usually on a Sunday right in the middle of lunch."

"So had you ever visited him?" Asked Andy.

"No, not at his new place no. Kath went over once with her parents but I think it was a weekend I had to work," explained Christian.

"Now I know from a confidential chat we had with Kathleen this morning that she told you about what happened between her and Richard when they were youngsters. She said it would be okay to ask you about that as long as her mum and dad didn't find out."

"Oh my god, I don't believe she told you Andy," gasped Christian.

"How did you feel when you found out Christian?"

"I was devastated and I did want to confront Richard, but Kathleen was so concerned about her parents finding out I decided not to in case Richard said something. It was so wrong Kath got into so much trouble when she was 15 and really it was all Richard's fault."

"Thank you Christian," said Andy.

"So you never did confront him then?" Interrupted Steve trying not to sound too accusatory.

"No, no I couldn't and anyway I tried to put it behind us. Couldn't change what had happened so it was best forgotten as best we could."

"Thank you we just needed to clear that up."

Andy and Steve left Christian on good terms and headed back to Westhampton.

"I don't think so Andy what do you think?" Asked Steve.

"Doesn't look like it, just another dead end, maybe this is just a suicide with complications. You couldn't blame Richard Wilson for topping himself, he had a problem and wasn't getting any help. Both his career and family life were about to implode at any point. I can see Danny Davis putting this together for the coroner to decide what actually happened, even with the blood pattern anomaly." Concluded Andy.

Steve knew this was going to make the rest of their role just as challenging. At least the SIO would rationalise his conclusions face to face with the family when the time came.

Chapter 4

The Builder

Steve sat on the Northern Line on the long trek from Bank to Colindale on route to Hendon for the last week of the much sought after advanced exhibits officer course. His mind drifted back to years of family liaison and major crime enquiries he'd since been deployed on. These stemmed right back to Richard Wilson's death seven years earlier. A lot had happened since then. Anna's career had flourished in victim support and Steve's profile was regularly raised as he worked his way through some challenging investigations and saw some very bad people put away for long periods. Steve had outgrown his small county force and like many of his colleagues in 2005 took advantage of one of the many specialist transferee posts the Metropolitan Police had to offer.

Anna had been quite excited by the prospect of moving to London. Her mother had passed away about a year before and she no longer needed to be so close to Norfolk. She sold off the old static caravan and said she didn't want to go to Norfolk ever again. As much as she enjoyed her visits to her mum, the pain of being so close to where her father died on the family farm seemed to affect her every time she went anywhere near the old run down site.

The hustle and bustle of living in E1 suited both of them and Anna soon landed a new exciting job with the NSPCC. For Steve it had been a dream come true he was on the murder squad in East London or at least one of several homicide teams that covered the one hundred plus murders London suffered on average every year. Real specialist detectives existed on these teams, all of which were totally self contained units in their own right with a host of 'Met' resources at their fingertips the constabularies could only dream of. All Steve had to do differently was get used to putting the word 'Met' in front of the name of every department and item of equipment they used, Met duties, Met HR, Met Vest. He also needed to start calling his SIO and every other inspector or above 'Governor' rather than 'Sir'. Then he could be a true Scotland Yard Detective.

Steve had passed his sergeants exams and promotion was on the near horizon, but for now Steve was about to qualify as an advanced exhibits officer responsible for working closely with crime scene managers, scene examiners and an array of forensic scientists employed at London murder scenes. He would also be a key figure at special post-mortems taking and recording exhibits and noting the findings of the various Home Office Pathologists he would meet, another fascinating area of forensic science Steve always wanted to get into. This job was worth delaying promotion for, Steve was relatively young still and at 39 had a good ten years plus to climb a few rungs on the promotion ladder before retirement loomed.

A few days later the sound of the rock band the Clash woke poor Anna, "London calling to the faraway towns, now war is declared, and battle come down," as Steve's mobile phone rung out its new ringtone slowly vibrating its way off the bedside table.

"Steve it's your phone," complained Anna

"What, what?"

"Your phone, you idiot, answer your phone," instructed Anna not really annoyed just conscious that it was now the last day of Steve's course so he'd been out for a few drinks with his classmates the night before and was somewhat worse for wear at 4.10 a.m. on that Friday morning.

"Hello, what." Answered the half asleep detective.

"You were on the fucking piss last night weren't you? Listen mate we've got a job I need you."

"Governor yeah sorry," answered Steve instantly recognising the cockney tones of his Detective Chief Inspector and new SIO Mac Spencer, referred to occasionally by his nickname 'Frank' but not often to his face. He was in fact a million miles away from the dithering comic his nickname was derived from. Mac Spencer was a sure footed man, not afraid to make a decision, a Londoner through and through, dragged up on the streets of Hackney, a borough he now regularly attended to scrape the latest knife victim up off the estate floor.

"You still living in E1 with the rest of those trendy hippies?" Asked the Mac.

"Yes gov."

"Good I'm in Tower Hamlets I need you to meet me at a scene in a couple of hours we're 'in the frame' for this one and I want you doing the exhibits. Don't worry the crime scene manager is already out here she's got everything you'll need to get started. Just come straight here." Instructed Mac.

"But gov it's the last day of my course today, I'm supposed to be back at Hendon later," explained Steve.

"Don't worry mate you can put a call in later tell them you've got some real fucking work to do at a proper murder scene. You'll know what I mean when you see it. Do you know the back of the Bathnall Estate?"

"Yes gov."

"Well just at the back of the main block of flats the railway line runs up high over the arches. There's some old lock-ups under the arches, the scene's in one of those places," detailed Mac.

"Right no problem I can be there in an hour or so," answered Steve enthusiastically.

"Don't rush mate just get there for six and I'll meet you and show you what we've got."

"No problem."

"Oh and Steve.. Don't put your best suit on geezer, this one's messy." Commented Mac hanging up.

"What's going on darling?" Asked the sleepy Anna.

"We've got a job and my teams picking it up, the SIO wants me doing the exhibits." Explained the slightly too enthusiastic Steve knowing full well that his planned weekend off was now well and truly out of the window.

"You can't you're on a bloody course for God's sake," responded an angry Anna.

"I know I'm really sorry, but it's the last day and the governor knows the course is basically over so missing that won't be a problem. I'm sorry about the weekend," apologised Steve assuming that was the main reason for Anna's outburst. "I'll make it up to you, see if you can book a couple of weeks off at the end of next month and we'll go away somewhere, a cruise maybe, sounds like I'll need a break after this next job."

"I can't believe they haven't got anyone else for this," Anna continued still quite grumpy.

"I know but you know we are short of exhibits officers, that's why I did this course," reasoned Steve.

"Okay but you take care in that scene, I love you darling."

"I love you too, now try and go back to sleep, I'll get ready in the spare room," instructed Steve slipping out of bed.

'This was going to be a proper east end murder scene,' thought Steve as he hopped off his early morning bus ride to Tower Hamlets. 'Under the arches in a real live East End lock-up like something out of the soap opera itself.' Steve still got a real buzz out of a new murder investigation, he'd seen quite a few through now to successful court cases and doing family liaison work for a few years he realised how important justice was for most families. It was a sort of closure for some, a point where they could start to rebuild their lives. Steve still felt regret that the Richard Wilson's family never made it to that point. All they had was a three day inquest and an open verdict that leant heavily on the possibility of suicide, something they could never fully accept. Steve used the regret he harboured about that case to motivate him to do better and always aim to solve deaths he investigated in whatever role he was given to perform.

Exhibits officers had a lot of say when it came to forensic strategies and DCI Mac Spencer listened to Steve, In fact he listened to the opinions of all of his trusted detectives.

As Steve approached the cordon tape he was challenged by a cold Community Support Officer or PCSO a new concept in the police service he was seeing more and more at crime scenes now. The man holding the clipboard obviously didn't know who Steve was.

"Sorry sir you can't come through this way there's been an incident"

"A murder I hope," answered Steve smiling whilst fumbling in his back pocket producing his warrant card for the somewhat confused officer. "DC Steve Lawson Homicide Command, can you log me in, I'm the exhibits officer." He said proudly.

"Hello Steve how are you," rung out the cheerful tones of Sharon Cunningham, a mature but attractive senior member of police staff employed by the Met as one of several Crime Scene Managers. Sharon was already fully clad in a white paper suit, over boots and a face mask ready to show Steve around the scene.

"Sharon, sorry I didn't recognise you with your clothes on, I mean your suit on," joked Steve as he approached the boot of her car and begun looking for a suit that might fit his slightly larger frame.

"This fucker's been tortured," heard Steve looking round to see the friendly face of Mac emerging from the railway arches behind them. "Come on Steve get your kit on and we'll take a look around. I'll tell you what we've got so far."

These arches were all over East London used for various things. Steve had been in a few in central London that were now trendy pubs, always with quite load music playing. The music was necessary to drown out the loud rumble of the trains passing overhead every ten minutes or so. This place was no different even at just past 6 a.m. in the morning the trains ran at least every 15 minutes ferrying hundreds of commuters into Fenchurch Street from out in Essex. Steve kitted up and peered into the surprisingly well lit lock up. He begun to see the beginnings of a builders workshop, ideal I suppose for this venue, no chance of the noise of a few power tools competing with the passing trains and upsetting the neighbours.

Sharon had already laid a number of large square aluminium stepping plates, essential for preserving the possibility of faint footprints on the dusty concrete floor. Steve stood on the second plate and begun to take in the ghastly scene. Mac was right this was a scene of torture, it didn't look real and was more like a scene from the recently released film 'Saw 2' thought Steve. For a moment Steve had a swift flashback to the kitchen of the Wheatsheaf. He wasn't sure why that happened, but he needed to rapidly quell any thoughts of post traumatic stress, he had a job to do.

The workshop covered the entire width of the arched cave like room, it's walls clad with boarding, but the clever brickwork of the railway arch was still exposed above them. It didn't go right under the railway and Steve assumed a similar space was accessible from the other side of the tracks divided from this one by what looked like a breeze block wall at the far end. There was a small internal room that had been created in the far right hand corner that was used as an office. Beside this was a vast array of wood and other building materials cluttering the entire back wall of the workshop. Amongst it were some larger well used pieces of equipment; a cement mixer, wacker plate and plaster soiled boxes of some heavy duty power tools. Along each side were kitchen style work tops quite neatly laid out with organised tool hanging systems above them and neat crates of various items slid underneath. Centrally there was a large island style main workbench, square with vices and a large mounted mitre saw on one corner. All of this would have been an impressively organised set up had it not been for the blood thirsty chaos that lay scattered amongst it.

"Right Sharon, from left to right talk me through what we've got here," requested Steve.

"Okay, you might have noticed I've left the double doors open inwards to protect them from the weather for now, hopefully when the borough scene examiner comes out to help us they will bring a scene tent with them so we can cover this entrance before the locals start to spectate. To me this door hasn't been forced, there are quite a few scuffs on the outside and it looks like it's been kicked a few times but that could just be a red herring and normal wear and tear for a place like this. If you look directly ahead and under the main central work bench, just below where that wood is still in the vice, you'll see two fairly evenly spaced forward projecting stains of blood and gritty bone fragments. When you see the body you'll probably agree these are likely to be from gunshot wounds to the backs of his knees. Just follow the stepping plates round to the left and you can see where a number of tools are missing from the shadow boards on the left hand wall. This guy was pretty organised because for every storage point that is vacant I think I've found a tool that fits it. There's a crowbar just to your left there under the side work top , you can see where that probably came from. Just above it on that work top are some prints in blood, possibly going to be the victims when he tried to get up and was knocked back down again. When we get some strong lighting sets in here I think we'll find some interesting blood splatter that will tell a more detailed story of what happened here. Carry on round on the plates to the far corner of the main work bench you'll notice a lot of different boot marks as you go. It's going to be a nightmare working out if any are relevant but at least our victim died with his boots on so we have a starter for ten regarding the type of sole to eliminate. We should prioritise the ones made in the victim's blood, we know they are fresh. Can you see the round disc saw thing mounted on the corner there?"

"Yes. God It's covered in claret," observed Steve using a colloquial term for the heavy blood staining.

"We'll look down around the stepping plate you're on now." Instructed Sharon.

"Fingers, one, two, three all four of them and cut at what looks like a 45 degree angle," commented Steve looking back at the mitre saw to check it was set at this common angle still.

"Yes the victim's right hand I think you'll find, even though he's been shot and battered it all seems to be about fingers and hands after that. See the nail gun on the top there?"

"Yeah."

"When we do seize it for the lab be very careful it's still live. You'll see a couple of nails have been shot halfway into the bench next to that saw there."

Steve looked at two long nails sitting about two inches high centred in a smear of dried blood. Steve continued to follow the path of stepping plates around the back of the main bench towards the far corner, where the entrance to the small office type room was. A second vice was fixed to the adjacent corner of the bench, there was some kind of flesh still squashed in its grip.

"I don't understand Sharon it looks like a couple more fingers are squashed in here but where's all the blood?"

"It's a clean up job I think."

"Why clean only one corner of the scene and leave the rest of the scene. I'm not sure that makes sense."

"Maybe they were spooked by something and had to abandon their plans and the body halfway through. They started to make a good job of sanitising that corner I know that, even the floor is scrubbed round there."

"So is the victim here or did they remove him?" Asked a slightly confused Steve.

"No he's here, poor bastard tried to grab the desk phone in the corner of his office. Just push that door there well away from the handle area and you'll see."

Steve carefully pushed the loosely swinging door and the smell really hit him. He had revealed the mutilated corpse of a man he would later find out was 53 year old Costas Salvador the self employed carpenter and builder who owned the workshop. Even though there was no blood trail leading to the office area, the floor inside was awash with dried and congealed blood. Costas was slumped on his side in a corner next to a paper filled desk. Sure enough he had no doubt tried to lift his land line phone and call for help, but as already discovered the fingers of his right hand were totally missing. His left was mutilated and no doubt some of it was still in the vice. He had massive welts of injury to the back of his head that had bled profusely. He also had a pair of half destroyed knees. If that blood loss hadn't killed him the single vertical cut to his left wrist would have rapidly finished him off. What had this poor man done to deserve this.

"Happy," asked Sharon.

"Yes," answered Steve wondering if that was an appropriate answer to the maybe inappropriate question. He knew however what Sharon meant. Yes he was happy he had a good feel for the scene now it was time for a quick hot debrief with the officers who had found Costas and to find out what Mac the SIO had in mind for this job.

The first officers on the scene had simply noticed an insecure door that had swung open in the recent high winds and thought they'd stumbled upon a burglary in progress in the early hours of that morning. Of course they'd gone right into the scene when they saw the carnage inside, they had to in case the victim was still alive. When they found him he was obviously very dead of course. For a change they'd actually withdrawn carefully and sealed the scene not letting a sole in until the homicide advisory team or HAT car arrived. These were detectives from Steve's team so they knew better than to take a peak before Sharon turned up. So things were good from a forensic point of view the uniform guys had even bagged up their own boots for Steve and were unusually happy to hand them over and be driven back to the nick in their socks. It made sense I suppose, before the stepping plates were laid anyone stepping through that scene would have virtually paddled in blood at some points. Steve thought back to a recent presentation from one of the Met's top forensic scientists.

"Luminol!" Announced Steve

"Luminol?" Questioned Sharon, knowing full well that it is a chemical that sticks to latent blood stains making them detectable under fluorescent lighting, she just couldn't work out why it was suddenly so important now.

"There's no way the people that did this left the place without blood on their feet. Luminol could tell us how many people were involved and where they went from here. For all we know they ran back into the flats over there and we could find a nice set of latent footmarks showing that?" Explained Steve.

"Or maybe they went to a vehicle?" Added Sharon.

"Maybe but where is it now?" Asked Steve.

"They probably took the fellows van," interjected Mac as he returned inside the inner cordon tape. "He was a builder, one of the locals knew him from a kitchen he fitted in her mother's house. His names Costas Salvador, Portuguese in origin she thinks. She says he has a blue transit van, she even had the reg number from a visitors parking permit she had when he did the job for her mum. She says it's not parked outside his lock-up where it normally is, hasn't been for a couple of days, just can't say what day she last saw it for definite."

"Better get this inner cordon pushed out if we are going down the Luminol route then," suggested Steve.

"Yes," agreed Sharon. "I'll give the Met Lab a call and see if Larry is on call, he's loves to play with Luminol. Have you met him Steve?"

"On the course yeah."

"When do you reckon the PM will be Sharon, tonight?" Asked Mac.

"I'm not sure, I would guess it's going to be a long one so tomorrow morning is a more likely prediction, but it will be closer to the office out at Upton Mortuary so we'll try and go for an early start if you like?"

"Good I'll leave you two to make a start, I'll get one of the skippers to circulate Costas' van on the system but I'm going ask them to put your contact details on the circulation Steve. When we find it I want a full lift done and I want it taken apart, that might be our best chance of getting these bastards. Let's just hope it's not burnt out eh." Smiled Mac as he walked off just knowing that any villain in his right mind knows fire is the best destroyer of forensic evidence.

As soon as Mac had driven off Sharon suggested a full English at a little cafe she knew round the corner. Steve's expression must had given away a hint of disapproval.

"Well I've been on all night and it'll be midday before we get the body out of there. I've already texted the scene examiner the details of the venue for a briefing. Come on dump your paper suit and dirty shit in this bag and let's go. Don't worry I'm buying."

Sharon was like a bossy older sister type so Steve gave in very easily. Anyway she knew her stuff, she'd been around a long time and examined a lot of scenes right back to when she was a young scene examiner in Islington back in the eighties. Forensic science had come a long way since then.

Steve felt energised by his fill of carbohydrates and salty bacon. He met Elizabeth at the cafe, a young well educated scene examiner and clearly mothered by Sharon in a very pleasant way. The three of them were soon back at the now extended inner cordon. A large bespoke covered working area had been constructed over the first ten feet or so of the concrete forecourt area by the Met Property on call team. The lanky figure of Larry Meakin stood next to the entrance already clad in a more heavy duty protective suit.

"Somebody call a scientist?" Asked Larry in his Northern accent.

"Hello my love, you should have said you were going to get here early for a change I'd have bought you a bacon butty back from the cafe," joked Sharon as she leant forward to hug her old familiar friend. "This is Steve he's got the exhibits on this one."

"Hi Steve, good call re the Luminol," said Larry.

Sharon had already very kindly bigged Steve up when she called Larry out.

"Here's Terry the photog," announced Sharon as another white Renault Caddy van pulled up and Steve quickly worked out the very basic colloquialism that referred to a scene photographer and video capture expert. Terry also specialised in the kind of photography Larry would require to capture the results of his Luminol tests. Terry was a cheerful chap who completed the group of paper suit cladded experts nicely.

Steve felt like he'd joined a new exclusive family, one that he was going to enjoy being part of.

Terry set about videoing every element of the scene before he set up his camera just outside the office door to record the progress as Steve and Sharon begun the task of bagging the victim's body.

Concurrent to this Larry utilised the skills of Elizabeth to begin his Luminol testing outside of the workshop.

"Will the pathologist come out to the scene?" Asked Steve as he squatted on one of the last stepping plates leaning over Costas' pale corpse.

"No, they don't very often these days, not with scene photography being so good, eh Terry?"

"The best Sharon of course," added Terry still snapping away.

"Anyway look," explained Sharon as she lifted and dropped the limp but flexible right arm of the deceased. "No rigor! This guys been dead probably more than 18 hours. He's got hypostasis in all the right places, thats blood pooling in plain English. Where the residual blood in the body comes to rest usually where it touches the floor, so this guy's not been moved since he died. Who needs a pathologist eh. Get a few close ups of that if you will Terry then we'll flip him over and start bagging him up."

Sharon knew her stuff and Steve was so fascinated by the science surrounding the scene that he was able to switch off to the horrific injuries that this man had died of; even when he had to un-stick the side of his body from the dried blood to turn him over. Steve lifted Costas' head for Sharon to slide a head bag over it. He could feel the shattered pieces of skull at the back floating around under his scalp.

"As well as the hands I think we'll improvise and slide some form of inner bag over each of those shattered knees to try and preserve and shot thats trapped in there. I'm pretty sure they are shotgun injuries rather than a normal firearm," surmised Sharon.

Steve obliged and bagged his hands and knees before they had to enlist Terry's third pair of hands to lift Costas into the body bag, making Steve wonder if that's where the phrase 'a dead weight' originated from. Body's were such heavy things and this man was large and broken in many places.

"Better change these suits," Sharon suggested.

Not only did the three of them look like Dr Death, none of them wanted to transfer the victim's blood and DNA to a part of the scene where it hadn't been deposited during his murder.

As they stood outside the workshop Sharon explained their next move.

"The body can be your first exhibit Steve, but before you zip him up you need to add as individual exhibits those four fingertips we found and undo that vice and exhibit the remains of those other fingers. Apart from blood I don't think there are any other body parts in here for the post-mortem."

"Okay, will small exhibit bags do Sharon?" Asked Steve.

"Yeah there's some small clear boxes and 'B' bags in my boot that will do the job. Once they are done we'll put them in the body bag with the main body."

Steve completed the grisly task whilst Sharon and Terry went to assist Larry. 'References SJL/1, 2, 3, 4, 5 and 6' noted Steve in his exhibits register, his initials denoting each item was his exhibit. One body, four individual fingertips from the victim's right hand and a mush of two crushed fingers from his left, squashed into one mass by the work bench's vice.

Unsure how to stop the body parts from rolling around inside the body bag with Costas, Steve neatly tucked the bags of various fingers into the pockets of the man's blue overalls. 'Must remember to point this out to the pathologist at the PM,' thought Steve as he zipped and sealed the body bag. Even Larry mucked in when the five of them got together to lift Costas' body to just inside the workshop door ready for the undertakers to collect him without them tramping all over the scene.

"Right Terry lets have a look at those UV images you took of the Luminol results," asked Larry. "I think you'll be quite surprised what they show," he continued, addressing Sharon and Steve. Terry's van was fully kitted out for the downloading and viewing of digital photography.

"There's only a single set of footprints," observed a surprised Steve.

"I think it's safe to say there's only one offender," added Sharon. "I wouldn't have guessed that, but there's no way a group could walk out of that scene with only one of them having blood on your feet."

"Over boots, removed at the exit?" Argued Steve ever the detective looking down at their feet all neatly clad in forensic over boots.

"Yeah but why make sure the group is all wearing over boots or removes their footwear when they leave and allow one idiot not to?" Questioned the more philosophical thinking scene examiner Elizabeth.

"Best we keep an open mind," concluded Larry, "but these footmarks are probably about a size 9, maybe 10 if you look at the scale and they do lead from the workshop to where I think the van was. Elizabeth is going to clarify that with the tyre print she's moulded from that dried up puddle you can see over there. We have to find that van. I think the single offender option is a safe theory at least. Enough to brief your boss up with Steve. We could just be looking for one person here as surprising as that seems. Hopefully we'll be able to identify some size 9 footmarks in the workshop to help."

"Thanks Larry, I promise I will let you loose on the workshop tomorrow, especially around the clean up area, but today's priority is to identify all possible weapons used for the pathologist and get them fast tracked to the lab for prints. Elizabeth I want you to concentrate on the entire floor area so we can get off those damn stepping plates and see if there's any confirmation of numbers of offenders for the SIO inside. Steve we'll concentrate on possible weapons, anything and everything we think the poor chap has been attacked with. Terry if you can just hang around to photograph individual marks and items as we identify them that'll be great. I'll meet you here about 9 tomorrow if that's okay Larry?" Instructed Sharon.

"I will look forward to it with pleasure," answered the charming scientist, clearly pleased with his early addition to the possible scenario.

Steve and Elizabeth walked out of the inner cordon to her van in need of a vast selection of exhibits packaging material. They were surprised to see a handful of reporters and even a TV satellite van set up on the outer cordon. Steve was grateful his hooded suit made him a fairly unrecognisable anonymous 'forensic expert' as he knew he'd be described on the midday local news.

"Hello Steve, aren't you supposed to be at Hendon still?" Sung out the familiar Welsh tones of Janet Williams as she approached. Recently promoted in house to Detective Sergeant Janet had a wealth of experience. She had over 25 years service, at least 10 of which she'd spent on the murder teams in East London. She'd looked after Steve when he first transferred to the Met dispelling any preconceived ideas he had that to fit in he'd have to learn to speak cockney.

"No Mac said he couldn't cope without me so I'm doing the last day on the job," answered Steve flippantly.

"Looks like a good one eh boyo." Commented Janet as normal playing up to everyone's love of her Welsh roots.

"So what's Mac got you doing on this one Janet?" Asked Steve knowing that a number of key roles would have been allocated by now.

Janet looked back at the two nearest five storey blocks of flat, "bloody house to house coordinator can you believe it, look at that lot. Oh and if that's not enough I'm still the Family Liaison Coordinator and there's only one FLO you see, poor Lisa so I'm going to have to help her out a bit when we find any kind of next of kin for this fellow."

"Yeah, what's the score there Janet?"

"We found his home from the reg number of the van the neighbour gave us. It's a little one bed council flat in East Ham. It's all secure, nothing suspicious and neighbours say he lived alone, we think he had a wife but we're not sure where she is now. Maybe back in Portugal, might get a trip out of this one eh."

"Don't let anyone in that flat Janet. As far as I'm concerned it will be a scene, it needs to be secured and to cover us we will need a warrant to search it for any clues as to why this man has been so brutally murdered." instructed Steve.

"Don't worry my dear, it's all in hand, Mac's happy to wait until this evening for you to have a cursory look at it, I'll get Lisa to join you if that makes sense," reassured Janet.

Steve knew being an FLO with no identified next of kin was like trying to canoe down a set of rapids without a paddle. It made perfect sense to kit up an FLO to work with the exhibits officer when it came to just searching a venue where the main aim was to seize items that helped form the victimology for a case. It would be even more important if Costas was the loner he was beginning to look like.

"Anyway Steve you take care in there, here's my new team of willing volunteers," announced Janet pointing to a Met Police minibus unloading it's cargo of bemused constables and their PCSO colleagues.

"Good luck," chuckled Steve.

Steve helped Elizabeth carry a wondrous array of cardboard boxes, plastic tubes, bags, tape and labels over the the workshop entrance. Steve also collected several large sheets of fresh brown paper that he laid out inside the covered area, away from the media's zoom lenses. He needed a sterile working area to bring his exhibits out to and carefully package them.

Terry photographed and Steve removed in close consultation with Sharon who was now working with Elizabeth on one or maybe two potentially identifiable foot marks left in blood on the workshop floor.

As Steve secured all of the confirmed weapons and a few other possible ones in boxes and bags he made detailed notes and sketches in his exhibits register:

'SJL/7 - one 90 cm blood stained crowbar with hook and chisel ends (KM positive)'

Steve had learnt about KM or 'Kastle-Meyer' testing on his course. It was a simple test to speculatively identify a stain as blood, but he felt like a real scientist when he swabbed things with his little triangle of blotting paper and carried out the chemical test as he seized items.

'SJL/8 - one large flat point screwdriver 40 cm in length (KM positive on top only)'

Steve's DIY skills came into their own when he found an obviously clean socket set to dismantle the large mitre saw that was fixed to the bench.

'SJL/9 - one apparent blood stained circular saw blade (not tested)'

Steve knew traces of blood would be present so there was no need to test this. It had obviously been used to slice off Costas' fingers.

'SJL/10 - one orange Mikita cordless nail gun (battery pack removed)'

Steve cringed at the thought of some chem-lab technician shooting themselves with the still loaded tool so made doubly sure it was safe before he packaged it.

'SJL/11 - workbench vice containing remnants of believed human tissue (not tested - handle removed see SJL/12)'

'SJL/12 - workbench handle from SJL/11'

Steve had decided that whoever trapped Costas' left
hand in this vice would have held the handle tightly. It
was statistically not unheard of for offenders to foolishly
remove gloves not thinking when they worked there way
through crime scenes. The vice was such a heavy lump
removing the handle for submission seemed the most
sensible thing to do.

'SJL/13 - one 'Stanley' type knife - blood stained (KM
positive)'

Almost certainly the tool used to make sure Costas
finished bleeding out from his left wrist.

"Think that's probably it for potential weapons what do
you think Sharon?" Asked Steve.

"I think so but we can come back and have re think after
the PM if necessary," she replied.

"Err hello, the undertakers are here," called out the
distant voice of a PCSO from just outside the tented
entrance, scared to death to enter the inner cordon any
further.

"Okay we'll be right out, thank you," shouted Steve only
just remembering the body still lay waiting for collection
all wrapped up just inside the door.

Undertakers were always cheerful characters when out
in their little black vans, well away from grieving families.
Steve noted the names of the two undertakers
confirming they knew the body was going to the old

mortuary at Upton before letting them wheel the covered corpse away to their van under the watchful eye of the media and public onlookers.

"Come and take a look at this Steve," called out Elizabeth. "That's a police boot isn't it?"

Steve had seen these kind of footmarks before. "Magnum boots I'd say, every bobbies favourite, hang on a minute I'll just confirm that."

Steve went out to his box of existing exhibits that included the boots of the two officers that had entered the scene and had been bagged up earlier. To Steve's surprise they were both Dr Martin type boots, not a Magnum boot amongst them.

"You sure only two officers went in this place before you got here Sharon?" Asked Steve.

"Definitely, your HAT car was out at Brick Lane getting their fill of salt beef bagels so they made it here before the duty officer and skipper even arrived ready to trample all over the scene like they normally do. What are you thinking Steve?"

"Surely whoever did this isn't a bloody copper!" Exclaimed a shocked Steve.

"Could be a security guard or paramedic," reasoned Sharon.

"Maybe a squaddie even," added Elizabeth

"Okay, I get your point or maybe just some tradesman who favours Magnum boots, yes I see what you mean. However all those profiles are worth bearing in mind don't you think?" Pointed out Steve adding credibility to his line of thinking.

"Yes Steve sorry, whoever it is if we get their boots it won't matter how well they've been cleaned, this footmark will be nearly as good as a fingerprint, look at the unique wear marks there. You've done an excellent job of lifting that Elizabeth, well done." Congratulated Sharon once a lowly scene examiner herself.

Elizabeth enthusiastically set about working on a second more partial footprint also pointing towards the workshop door and falling in line with where Larry had revealed the more obscure blood traced footmarks on the tarmac outside.

"Come on Steve let's take another look at this door where it looks like it was kicked open," suggested Sharon.

'Every contact leaves a trace,' thought Steve thinking back to one of the many experts who gave presentations on Steve's course.

The workshop door was an old wooden affair reinforced with metal grills on the windows and a steel frame on the interior. It consisted of two pieces with long vertical bolts top and bottom to hold one side shut. Steve noticed the bottom bolt was a poor fit into it's cracked and worn concrete recess.

"I don't think this thing would be secure if the top bolt wasn't in place. Any wimp could just kick these things open," commented Steve.

"Yeah, I don't suppose the victim would worry too much about locking it properly when he was inside. I can see black scuffs on the outside but no footmarks worth lifting… Hang on we'll have some of that." Sharon pointed out some barely visible blue cotton fibres snagged on a rough edge of the old wooden door.

Terry took some close up photography before Steve carefully plucked them free with a sterile set of tweezers securing them in a small exhibits case and bag. Steve knew some of the fibre scientists could identify a type of garment and its dye even from such a small sample. Aside from that he knew Mac would now order the seizure of every blue item of clothing a suspect had in their wardrobe for comparison. That's if they found any suspects.

"Thanks guys not a bad days work," said Sharon summarising where they were up to at that point. "We've got the murder weapons, we think we have a single offender, who is going to turn out to be a police officer eh Steve? They were probably wearing an item of blue clothing. Maybe you are right Steve, boys in blue and all that," chuckled Sharon. "We have some excellent footwear marks and luminol tests suggest they have left in the victims van. I've had confirmation Guy Hanner is doing the post mortem starting at 10 a.m. tomorrow at Upton Mortuary. Terry I've put a bid in for you to do the photography, sorry Elizabeth it's back to burglary scenes on borough I'm afraid, but I'm going to ask for you back when we start the fingerprint and blood work at the scene. Steve and I will need an extra pair of hands. I'll get Larry and his oppo started first thing with the clean up area in the scene, if you can tell Mac I won't be at his morning briefing. You can tell him what we have so far Steve."

Elizabeth kindly drove Steve and his raft of exhibits back to the murder teams headquarters and helped him unload them into their dedicated store. Steve went upstairs to the team office to find Lisa tucking into a bucket of KFC.

"Ello darling you look knackered, ere have a bit of chicken my dear." Greeted the ever friendly detective as she pushed the half full bucket across the desk. Steve was grateful to eat having lasted the day on the fry up he'd had nearly 12 hours earlier now.

"How's your day been?" Asked Steve.

"Well, one thing an FLO needs to do their job well is a sodding family and this ace detective can't fucking find one yet. Got you a very nice warrant though for the geezers pad."

"Great, let me just have a quick brew and scoff a bit more of your chicken and we'll head over there."

Steve and Lisa were soon at the 'little one bed flat' Janet had earlier described. It was a pretty sad small affair in a two story brick built block with communal doors less secure than a tent flap. Outside the flat door sat a young PC on a locally acquired polypropylene chair. The young man stood up panicked as Steve and Lisa approached.

"Relax mate DC Steve Lawson and DC Lisa Kelk from the murder team. Anyone turned up at all? Neighbours said anything?" Asked Steve

"No, no sir I think some of your team have been in and spoke to the neighbours in the block earlier." Answered the nervous PC still unsure if his laid back stance upon Steve's arrival was acceptable or not.

"Right mate do us a favour call your control room and tell them you're going to need a locksmith out to fit a new door lock to this place," instructed Steve.

"Why?" Asked the confused officer as he was ushered away from the flat door.

Steve gave the wooden door an almighty kick, smiling as it flew open with minimal damage.

"Because the bloke who lives here has had his flat keys attached to his van keys, that's been nicked and he's not in a position to tell me where he keeps his spares."

The young officer gripped his radio, "control receiving Kilo Foxtrot one nine three two..."

"Thanks mate we'll be inside if you need us," commented Steve.

"Yeah thanks love, with a bit of luck you'll be able to get off once this place is secure again." Added Lisa reassuringly as she followed Steve in.

Steve paused in the entrance hall opening his exhibits case.

"We're going to fully suit up in here if you're okay with that; don't want any hint of cross contamination so I'll let you seize any exhibits we find." It was important, no matter how minute the chance, that if Steve had picked up the minutest particle from the scene he didn't then inadvertently transfer it to another potential scene.

The flat was actually clean, tidy and in a good state of repair for local authority housing. Costas was the kind of tenant most housing officers dreamt of. Of course as a builder and a jack of all trades Costas had standards that he had clearly stamped on his own humble abode. It was as Janet had explained, a bit of a dump on the outside, but the run down block Steve and Lisa had walked through a few minutes ago was a total contrast to the cosy flat they began to inspect. It was basically four rooms off a central entrance hall. Bedroom on the left, lounge next. To the right straight ahead was the kitchen and on the immediate right the bathroom. This was not the scene of any crime. It appeared that a tidy single man might simply have left it that way before heading out for a days work. Although a touch sparse, Costas had created a comfortable home

Having made a cursory check of all rooms and established all windows were locked and secure, Lisa and Steve started their examination of the bedroom.

"Who do you think this is?" Asked Lisa picking up a framed photograph of an attractive younger woman of Mediterranean appearance.

"Maybe it's his daughter?" Surmised Steve.

"Maybe, but I'm sure the woman they found said Costas spoke about his wife to her, but there's no sign of a woman living here." Commented Lisa as she pulled open the wardrobe doors.

"Whilst your in there see if there's any blue cotton type work clothes please," asked Steve knowing that at some stage he would have to try and eliminate the fibres they found earlier.

"Where do you want me to start?" Laughed Lisa.

"Shit," Steve stared, he could see at least ten blue garments hanging in Costas' wardrobe. "Let me get some large exhibits bag from the box hang on."

Lisa helpfully set about bagging and sealing the individual items into bags whilst Steve moved on to the lounge.

"Come and have a look at this Lisa."

Steve pointed out a fairly old looking wedding photograph proudly displayed on the small wooden desk Costas had set up in the lounge.

"That's Costas Salvador on one of his better days I'm sure, albeit a lot younger and she is the same woman who smiles at him from his bedside if I'm not mistaken," concluded Steve.

"You're right you should be a detective you know," joked Lisa.

"You're going to have to be a proper family liaison officer now and find Mrs Salvador and help her come to terms with the horrific news about her husband, but where the bloody hell is she?"

"Maybe they're divorced, seems to be the norm these days?" Suggested Lisa.

"No, it doesn't make sense he still seems too smitten with her for that. Come on Costas tell me about your wife," asked Steve notionally as he opened the cabinet of the man's desk.

It was organised and neat. Not full of work related paperwork, more a filing system for Costas' private life. 'If only all places were this tidy,' thought Steve.

"How's your Portuguese Lisa I think I've found a marriage certificate but I'm confused it seems to be dated 2004 I think?"

"Don't you mean 'Pode ajudar-me, por favor?"

"Alright you flash git read that," instructed Steve.

"Not quite a marriage certificate Steve; it's a death certificate. Maria Belle Salvador, died 18th September 2004. Looks like Costas was a widower."

"That's not much help to you old girl. Here take a look at this address book it seems like a lot of it is in English with just a few Portuguese entries, maybe a sibling or even a parent is listed in there?" Pondered Steve.

The rest of the flat was very predictable, a small collection of common DVD's, the kitchen hid tins of food and frozen ready meals, comparable with the life of a lonely widower. There was also a hint of interest in the very local football team, West Ham United. Not a lot to indicate why anyone would want to brutally murder this poor man though.

Lisa decided to seize the address book and was confident it contained the next of kin she sought. "Anything else in here Steve?" She asked.

"Just one thing when was he last here do you think?"

"I'd say Tuesday night for definite, maybe went to work Wednesday morning?" Detailed Lisa.

"How the fuck do you know that?" Asked Steve wondering what he had obviously missed.

"TV book!"

"What?"

"TV book; it's neatly folded open on Tuesday's TV schedule. He's not looked at Wednesday yet so probably never made it home that night," explained a smiling Lisa.

"Very good, you should be an exhibits officer." Retorted Steve.

"No thanks doctor death, give me a grieving relative any day, you can keep your gory scenes and post-mortems thank you."

"It's not that bad and believe me murder victims are a lot easier to talk to than their relatives. I know I've done your job before." Answered Steve. "Is that locksmith here yet?"

It was another thirty minutes before the locksmith finally arrived fitting two very heavy duty locks to the premises. Steve thanked the young officer for doing the boring job of securing the scene and instructed him to tell his governor that the murder team had authorised the scene to be locked and left. Like all good exhibits officers Steve took possession of the new flat keys and temporarily added the tiny flat to his property portfolio. A railway arch workshop and an East London flat wasn't a bad start. Some exhibits officers had to retain keys for some quite swanky premises until such time they were no longer required as scenes and any ownership disputes were settled.

After another trip to the office and exhibits store Lisa dropped Steve off at Plaistow just in time for him to head home on the district line before he had to resort to a night bus.

"Steven you didn't answer my text, I've been really worried about you," declared Anna still sat up on the sofa in the half light sipping at a large glass of wine.

"Sorry darling, shit my phone's still on silent, you didn't have to wait up though, you okay," asked a concerned Steve.

"I'm just concerned, it's all over the local news. I wish you didn't have to deal with such a horrible murder."

"It's my job darling don't worry, what do you mean 'horrible murder' what did the news report say?"

"Your boss, I think it was, got interviewed on London Tonight. He called it a brutal murder and there were lots of forensic people there when the cameras zoomed in on the railway arches. Are you okay darling it must have been horrible for you?"

"I'm fine really, just want to get these clothes in the washing machine and grab a quick shower, go to bed if you want, honestly I'm okay."

Steve wondered why Anna was so concerned, maybe she thought the job of exhibits officer might be too much for him. It wasn't of course, but he had to admit to himself as he stood in the shower that the gruesome images he'd seen that day were clearly embossed in his memory. They flashed through his thoughts like an unwelcome slide show. Steve was grateful to find Anna had not turned in when he re-emerged from the bathroom and was intent of spending the next hour chatting though Steve's day over a glass of wine and a sandwich. This allowed Steve to download his thoughts and unwind before they went to bed.

The SIO sat perched on a desk surrounded by his team working his way through the first formal briefing he'd had. It was Saturday morning of course but everyone was in. He had nearly thirty detectives at his disposal. He also had a competent handful of HOLMES trained major incident room staff coupled with an intelligence analyst and researcher.

The briefing begun with the team being talked through the scene video by Mac. He then handed over the Steve to detail the work so far at the scene and what they had discovered the previous day. In particular the possibility of there being only one offender and them wearing a size 9 Magnum boot.

Lisa gave a very brief update re her current inability to trace the victims next of kin. She reassured the SIO that she intended to rectify this that day with the slightly unconventional method of trawling the seized address book.

Janet explained how the house to house had been fairly unproductive as usual. People just kept themselves to themselves these days and once they were home they shut themselves in, put the TV on and switched off to the world outside. The only positive result had been a consensus of opinion from the residents that took note of Costas' van when they parked their own cars. They were fairly confident that it hadn't been there since Wednesday night, Thursday morning. Steve concurred that the passing of rigour and congealed blood pooling supported the theory that Costas was murdered on Wednesday night.

The CCTV on the estate was poor at night, a dated system poorly managed by an underpaid caretaker.

"It's an old VHS time lapse system governor, tapes get reused so much they're half fucked when you play them back. We've confirmed how far out the system time and date is now and I've just seized every tape the old geezer has. I reckon we may be able to trace the victims van coming and going but only by shape, there's no

205

hope of getting the plates or even colour at night. As far as people go we'll do our best but all we have so far is the odd shadowy figure mooching around the estate, nothing heading towards the lock up yet and the cameras don't reach round to the arches themselves anyway."

"All good news then Bob, thanks," responded Mac looking back at the somewhat dejected officer who'd been given the thankless task of CCTV coordinator.

"Saving the best until last then give us the intel update Rob." Instructed Mac.

Rob Markham was the DS in charge of the small in-house intelligence team consisting of two desk bound detectives that were wizards with the Met's various intelligence systems that had the added luxury of two very experienced support staff providing research and analysis. They had access to all sorts of technical investigative tools and information, not least the cellphone data that they could request.

Rob referred to his notes. "Firstly Costas did have a mobile phone. We have the number from one of the customers he had that we found yesterday."

"I don't think its at the scene though, I would have found it I'm sure?" Interjected Steve.

"No Steve I don't think you've missed it. It's still raw data and for intel only but it looks like it left the scene around 20:45 hours on the Wednesday night. We've asked for more data but it was switched off or the battery died on Thursday evening out Romford Way"

"He must have left it in the van. I need that data Rob, to find out exactly where that van is. It's going to be a treasure trove of forensic evidence. When are you going to get a better location?" Asked Steve excitedly.

"Yeah don't get too excited we've been trawling the incidents for Wednesday and Thursday night in Havering and we think we have a possible. London Fire Brigade informed us they had been called to a burning van in the middle of the old derelict general hospital site up Harold Hill way on Thursday evening. Looks like they advised us not to bother attending straight away because this thing was well ablaze and there was no way anyone was getting anywhere near it to get a chassis number until it had cooled down and was safe. Trouble is Romford Town Centre kicked off big style on Thursday night and the borough are still picking up the pieces of that mayhem now. We've asked a vehicle examiner from traffic to go out and ID the van, they'll let us know if it's ours or not."

"What else have you got for us Rob?" Asked the SIO.

"Well, we've got to the bottom of that crime report I briefed you on last night gov. It's the closest thing we have to a motive so far. Four months ago Costas Salvador was completing the work on a major new kitchen stroke living area at a pricey big place in Islington. It belongs to a middle eastern family who have lived in London for over twenty years. The circumstances read that Costas was a friend or at least an associate of the owner Ahmed Akbar, a divorcee who unusually had custody of his 11 year old son Ali. Akbar is a property developer and works from home as a base.

The Child Protection guys took a referral that originated from Ali's private tutor. She had been concerned something was wrong with Ali for some time but had initially just put it down to the disruption of the building work. She eventually asked him if anyone had done anything to upset him, this was when he made the accusation. Mr Akbar went mad and confronted Costas there and then causing the tutor to call for help as it all kicked off in front of her. This really didn't help the trauma Ali was already suffering and even after completing a number of ABE interviews with the timid young boy it's still unclear how and when this abuse took place. The medical evidence however is damning, the poor boy had historic rectal damage that the FME suspects occurred over a number of incidents and he may even need some surgery to repair it. The trouble is no DNA evidence was ever found. Costas hasn't been charged yet and he's still technically on an extended bail. The last child protection case conference notes we've had faxed across basically focus on the fact that the CPS were refusing to charge Costas because they couldn't exclude the possibility of a third party being responsible. Costas had befriended the boy and he had let him watch and even sometimes help him complete his work. Costas admitted all of this on interview but he denied ever touching him inappropriately and definitely refused to accept the suggestion that he'd been the one who raped the boy."

The entire room was silent as Rob paused. A sea of detectives pondering the facts and also quite stunned by what had just been described to them.

Janet's soft Welsh voice was the first to break the momentary silence. "Suppose we're going to have to go and nick the poor father now aren't we?"

"Well volunteered DS Williams," smiled Mac. "Apart from Steve and I who have the PM to go to, everyone else hang fire, get a brew and I'll brief Janet as to how I want to play this. Whatever happens I want to keep the press well away from the back story so let's keep it tight for now."

Upton mortuary was quite an old building, built post war and filled to capacity ever since. Its interior had been patched up over the years and a modern extractor system installed. It helped a little but the entire fabric of the building was engrained with the smell of rotting corpses countered only by the faint hint of disinfectant that cut through the air. Of course Marvin the mortuary assistant was oblivious to this as he handed Steve an oversized set of Wellington boots, much better and safer than overshoes he'd had to risk at other mortuaries. After all this was going to be a wet one and Steve had a lot to do as exhibits officer on a special post-mortem.

"Am I the first here?" Asked Steve as he donned a fresh paper suit before trying his wellies for size.

"Yeah, come on I'll take you through and show you where you can set up."

Steve was led through a large spring loaded door onto the slightly greasy floor of the main mortuary. The fixed stainless steel tables or former 'slabs' were all empty except for the second one in where a full body bag bearing Steve's handwriting and some of his blood smeared finger marks had been laid out still sealed ready for the PM to begin.

"If you want to use that first slab to set up on mate that'll be okay," offered the cheerful Marvin as he exited the room to answer the slightly too domestic sound of the doorbell that was fitted to the locked mortuary entrance.

Steve laid out a fresh brown paper sheet covering the hopefully sterilised steel slab. He unpacked an array of different exhibits packaging including tubs for stomach contents, jars for liver samples and a bucket and lid that would allow him to take the brain to a neurologist for further pathological work in due course if required. Steve had observed forensic post-mortems before so any fear of the unknown didn't exist, he just had a more responsible task now and would have to be slick and prepared to keep up with the pace of Guy Hanner a notoriously thorough and progressive Home Office Pathologist.

"Hi Steve," rung out the pleasant tone of Sharon's voice. "You had some breakfast yet?"

Food was the last thing on Steve's mind as he stood in amongst the stench of death.

"Plenty of biscuits and coffee at Mac's briefing thanks," replied Steve.

"I should have thought, Larry and I just had another nice breakfast at that cafe we went to yesterday I could have bought you a bacon roll back, it would have stayed warm well wrapped."

"I'm fine Sharon honestly hopefully grab a late lunch once we're done here." Insisted Steve.

"Yeah good idea. I spoke to Mac he told me about the van being burnt out and the paedophile stuff."

"It might not be Costas' van mind," cautioned Steve.

"No sorry it is, hot off the press, he's only just spoken to me and asked what I wanted doing with it. It's seriously gutted I really don't think we'll get anything from it. You don't have to worry for now one of your team is heading out to Romford and they are going to organise a covered lift for us. They can take it to Charlton for now, it can sit there undercover until we get chance to have a proper look at it."

"That's a shame I was sort of hoping it wasn't our man's vehicle, we don't stand a chance if it's been properly burnt out."

"Some one call for a photog?" Announced Terry as his familiar face crashed through the mortuary door. Struggling away with his half extended tripod and large camera case. "Oh shit they told me it was a wedding shoot not another post-mortem," he joked.

Humour in a mortuary closed for a special PM was deemed appropriate and acceptable. It was such a grisly task that the sights, smells and sadness of sudden death laid bare would have a negative impact on all present if they walked around with long serious faces for the next 6 or 7 hours.

The appearance of Guy Hanner, kitted up and ready to go completed the ensemble with the exception of the SIO, who needed to be there to get the pathologists findings hot off the press.

"Hello Guy, how's the garden?" Asked Sharon obviously a familiar acquaintance of his.

"Good, good, just the damn peas, they just dried out and didn't do very well this year. Loads of beet root mind I'd have bought some in if I'd known you were running this one." Answered the clearly well educated but very down to earth man.

"That's alright I used some of that farmyard manure you recommended and we've had a lot of growth in our garden this time round. Right suppose we better introduce you to Costas Salvador."

"Yes a sorry tail, I've just been speaking to Mac out in the office, he'll be in in a minute, just on her phone again I think. Have you got me a set of scene photographs young Terry?"

The familiar photographer had worked with Guy Hanner many times before and knew he was old school and always insisted on a printed album of photos rather than an easier to produce CD Rom. Terry handed the album to the pathologists who begun thumbing through it.

"Steve Lawson is the exhibits officer and can ID the body to you. I don't think you've met Steve before have you?" Announced Sharon.

"No, pleased to meet you Steve, shall we say 9.35 for the ID. Then as we go through you can have all the individual clothing items as your exhibits and from there it'll be GH/1, 2 and so on okay." Instructed Guy identifying what exhibit numbers he'd allocate the various samples he'd be taking.

"Yes that's fine with me," answered Steve already making notes to keep up with events as they unfold.

"Bit of Magic FM if you will please Marvin," requested Guy never one to work in deathly silence. "Ah Mac good stuff you ready, anything to add?"

"No Guy, apologies let's crack on, just may have to take a few calls that's all. We're hoping to get someone nicked for this before the morning's out."

"Good stuff better find out what they did to this poor man then," announced Guy as he broke the seal and unzipped the body bag.

The trapped odour hit them all like a cloud of poisonous gas, each and every face looking in trying not to grimace too much.

"Bit of a pong ladies and gents sorry... Oh my gosh, this guy carries a set of spare fingers around in his pocket, what do you reckon to that eh Steve," joked Guy as he put the already bagged body parts to one side noting Steve's sensible handiwork.

Photography took place at every single stage as Sharon and Steve helped Marvin remove each item of the victim's clothing on the pathologists instructions until he was totally naked. Each item was an exhibit and most would need forensically drying before they could be re-bagged and examined further. Steve had all of this to look forward to after the post-mortem was complete. Steve had Terry specifically photograph the soles of Costas' boots confirming 100% that these were totally different steel toecap work boots definitely not Magnum branded boots.

"Right let's concentrate on the injuries we can see first?" Announced Guy working from the feet upwards, apparently one of his idiosyncrasies; most pathologists started at the head and worked down.

"Feet are all okay, those boots will have protected them. There's a couple of minor, probably historic, bruises to the right shin bone. Here Terry just put one of your sticky ruler things on here and grab a shot of each of them. Then of course we have these beauties, I would say even a very good knee surgeon would have had trouble replacing these with titanium."

Guy of course was referring to the mutilated knee joints he was now examining. Now fully exposed from the ragged overalls Steve could see the flesh and bones had virtually exploded outwards to the front of each knee.

"Shotgun, a big calibre, maybe sawn off but we will try and map the spread. Bring me one of those jars of yours Steve and I'll show you something," instructed Guy.

Steve watched as Guy slid his scalpel under the flap of flesh beside Costas right knee and scraped out a small piece of plasticky material carefully dropping it into Steve's small sterile jar.

"What's that?" Steve asked.

"GH/1," responded Guy thinking Steve needed clarification of the exhibit reference he would be using.

"That's a piece of wadding isn't it," commented the seemingly pleased Sharon.

"Shotgun wadding that's useful isn't it?" Recalled Steve not actually having seen any in a wound before but knowing he should look for it.

"Oh yes Steve," added Guy. "From that we can find out the calibre of the weapon used, the approximate range it was fired from, the make of the ammunition and sometimes if it's fired from a crudely sawn off barrel unique marks can be present on it linking it to the weapon used. Now get me another small container and we'll see if we can dig any shot from this knee".

"There you go, pretty large shot really, you wouldn't want to be the rabbit on the receiving end of a bunch of that." Guy scraped out several pieces of lead shot that he thought would be used for game shooting due to the size.

The left knee was a similar story but unfortunately only a small trace of fragmented wadding was found, not ideal for further testing but still useful for identification of the ammunition used though. The consensus of opinion was that these shots were fired into Costas' knees from a very close range.

"Pass me those scene photos Sharon please and point out to me how you think this guy was standing when he was shot from behind," requested Guy.

Sharon pointed out the front edge of the workbench adjacent to the door. The two areas of blood indicated how Costas must have been stood working near the first vice, but he would have still had his back to his attacker when they shot him.

"So he can't have heard the attacker come in then, wouldn't Costas have heard him and turned around?" Queried Guy.

"Probably not if he was using that," explained Steve pointing to the electric sander dumped down on the workbench next to the first vice still clamping a machined piece of hardwood.

"Right this is making sense, this guy would have been in trouble from the word go then, I'm surprised he managed to get to where he did. It's amazing what a bit of adrenaline can achieve, it's just short lived that's all," pondered the expert mind of this amazing pathologist.

Steve had switched off to the smell and sights surrounding him now totally fascinated by the depth of forensic pathology he was starting to witness.

By the time Guy Hanner had finished the external examination of Costas Salvador's front and back there was already evidence of a number of injuries that alone would have eventually caused death. Heavy bruising and a chipped vertebrae across his back probably from the crow bar blows. A shattered right shoulder blade so bad it would have virtually immobilised his right arm. Again inflicted from the rear and potentially from the same crow bar that had also rained blows on the rear of his head. This had two gaping flesh wounds in it with fractured and chipped pieces of skull exposed externally. Close examination of Costas' left hand revealed two small tears coming from what originally looked like neat puncture wounds behind the first and second knuckle. After close examination of the tools photographed at the scene it was agreed that the two 6 inch nails still sticking out of the workbench and fired no doubt from the nail gun once went into these holes. However Guy suspected the victim himself in a desperate panic ripped his own hand free of this restraint. Guy's conclusion was that whilst his only functioning arm was immobilised by the nails his right arm could have been lifted by a third party without Costas being able to resist and his fingers sliced off with the mitre saw. Using the last few drops of adrenaline Costas had he'd made a number of attempts to flee. However each one appeared to have been countered by a further attempt to immobilise and finish him off. The fingers of his right hand had been unpacked and laid on the adjacent slab left out for fingerprinting. Guy unpacked the squashed mess of Costas' other missing two fingers and agreed these had been crushed so hard in the vice they came from that they would have been virtually detached when Costas made his final attempt to escape into his office. Guy felt the vertical slice in Costas' left wrist was really just unnecessary as his injuries prior to that were not survivable. Guy had seen this type of cut before but only ever in very deliberate and successful suicides, never in a murder before. He was able to agree the likely use of a sharp blade not unlike a Stanley type knife, but he couldn't rule out any other similar instrument.

"So Guy what do you think?" Asked Mac interrupting proceedings momentarily.

"You want a time of death don't you, what is it with all you SIO's anyone would think you are trying to investigate a murder. When was he last seen alive?"

"About 16:00 hours on Wednesday when he left his attic conversion job in Bow to work on the stair case parts in his workshop or something." Answered Mac, filling everyone in on news they hadn't yet heard that must have been recently phoned in from one of the teams out completing actions re Costas' recent movements.

"Okay and he was found just after 3 a.m. on Friday morning is that right?" checked Guy.

"Yes."

"Well based on the lack of rigour, lividity or hypostasis you may know it as I'd say some time after 4 p.m. Wednesday and say before 6 a.m. Thursday."

"That's alight then just a 14 hour window to work with," laughed Mac.

"It's not bloody 'Silent Witness' you know Mac old boy, pass me a dissecting knife please Marvin."

Guy now set about opening up the victim's body for closer inspection assisted by Marvin. He sliced two long vertical incisions down the backs of the knees spanning the open areas of gunshot damage. He carefully peeled back large flaps of flesh and scraped clean the bone endings to show the true damage.

"Here you go Steve a few more pieces of shot there, two separate exhibits please left and right knee, quantities of lead shot from each." Instructed guy inviting Steve to help him pick out the individual pieces.

Detailed photography was taken of the excavated joints to assist should a further ballistics expert need to offer opinion.

Leaving the body face down Guy went on to cut and fold open two large flaps of skin exposing the entire back. He was then able to mark up the deep muscle bruising and internal bleeds coupled with the damaged area of vertebrae and shattered shoulder blade. Photography continued at every stage.

Steve surprised himself not being disturbed by the request for a hand as Guy, Marvin, Sharon and he helped role the partially open corpse over onto his back. There was definitely no dignity in death, but the benefits of such a detailed examination couldn't be underestimated.

Guy only opened up one hand around the knuckles of the left one where he could then use a straight metal wire to show the full penetrative path of the two nails despite the ripped flesh below each hole. This again was photographed for evidence. Guy then carefully opened the wrist up to expose the cut that had penetrated the radial artery.

When Guy opened the full torso up and began to excise each organ one by one he made two observations. Costas was a smoker but otherwise healthy and the blows from the rear had damaged his liver causing the onset of some internal bleeding. Steve then had his least favourite task to complete as he stood next to Guy, tub at the ready, as he squeezed the stinking contents of his stomach into it creating his next exhibit.

"Maybe a curry?" Sniffed Guy. "Couldn't be sure, all I can say is a Wednesday evening takeaway was probably his last meal. If you can find where he bought it you may have an advance on that 4 p.m. bracket. Better go through the bins at the scene Steve," suggested Guy.

Steve just nodded still holding his breath as he screwed on the air tight lid sealing in the last of the odorous mush.

Guy continued removing, weighing and dissecting all of Costas' remaining organs.

Steve stared at the empty shell of a corpse almost inhuman in appearance had it not been for the head still to be examined. Steve knew from experience the next stage just got worse. The way the pathologist cut and peeled back the scalp like removing a tightly fitting swimming cap was always surreal. This of course was followed by the smell and sound of Marvin removing the top of the skull with a bone saw to reveal the next fascinating organ, the brain.

Once removed and washed down it was clearly showing damage. It was not mis-shaped but bleeding was evident to the rear

"We'll have to get this to Rakesh Singh for some further work I'm afraid Steve." Requested Guy addressing Steve knowing it would be his job to take the brain over the Professor Singh's neuropathology department at his University Hospital in South London. Then about a month after depositing it he'd also have to collect it. He might also have to help the family understand why it's missing from the body and what options they had about its return before holding a funeral.

Marvin filled Steve's container with a preservative liquid and carefully placed the brain inside sealing the lid. Steve added a sticky exhibits label and it was put to one side next to a few similar looking buckets to wait for it to be ready to transport in a few days time.

As the post-mortem came to a conclusion some 6 plus hours after it had begun Guy gave the SIO a full summary of his findings. Mac had as predicted been in and out several times to take calls. Steve had been too busy to take much notice of what updates he had been getting but knew progress was obviously being made.

Steve and Sharon remained in the room as Mac, Terry and Guy shuffled out. They needed Costas' fingerprints for elimination even though a set might still be on record from his fairly recent arrest. Sharon concentrated on the remaining attached fingers, thumbs and palms whilst Steve quickly and easily took the four prints from the right hand's detached fingers. Whatever he tried though the two detached digits from the left hand were a lost cause. Sharon got two good thumbs and one and a half palms. As Steve and Sharon begin crating up the exhibits to load into Steve's van they felt some sympathy for poor Marvin as he started to load bags of organs back into the body and reconstruct it to an acceptable level for the inevitable and potentially delayed family viewing. That would be if of course Lisa could find Mr Salvador's family.

Sharon took a call as they finished loading up. "Darling Larry I forgot all about you sorry. Yes we've just finished... but we really need to get the PM stuff back to base... oh okay, it better be worth it Larry... you always say that, see you in 10 minutes or so."

"What's going on Sharon?" asked Steve.

"I don't know but Larry says its good and it takes a lot to get him excited, I should know. Come on follow me back to the scene."

Before he knew it Steve was suiting up again and heading back into the workshop behind Sharon. Larry and his team of specialists had been working all day.

"I think we've got him Sharon," announced an excited Larry.

"Go on," encouraged the curious Sharon.

"Well you know how we all said this corner had been cleaned up despite the rest of the workshop being like a horror scene."

"Yes."

"Well it got me thinking, why the clean up? Then I remembered that clean, but obviously used, Stanley knife you seized Steve. Look around." Larry paused as Sharon and Steve almost simultaneously shrugged their shoulders staring back at Larry. "No empty tool hooks for a Stanley Knife."

"And…" Prompted Steve slightly annoyed at Larry's story telling style.

"It must have come from in here," added Larry pointing down to a crowded tool box. "Now look at the Luminol results on my laptop here." Instructed Larry starting with an enhanced image of the tool box that he zoomed into showing five tiny spots that showed the presence of blood. "It looks like our suspect could have cut themselves. I've tried swabbing these spots for a meaningful trace of blood but I doubt any of them will give us a full DNA profile?"

"So how have we got him then?" asked Steve.

"Well matey I didn't stop there," said Larry scrolling through to the next Luminol pictures. "You can see this whole corner has been washed down cleaning up whats showing up there as the victims blood at a guess. It's both on the floor and this side work surface, but have a look at that." The next image showed a small circle inside a larger circle again illuminated with Luminol when something came into contact with the heavily diluted washed down side. "What do you think made those circles?"

Before either Sharon or Steve had chance to speculate Larry pointed to an orange plastic bucket, now all wrapped up carefully as one of Larry's exhibits.

"Our murderer used this to wash up the area and the Stanley knife no doubt. Now its been rinsed out so well using the outside tap. There's little point in trying to get any DNA profiles from the inside, but look at this beauty." Larry clicked and opened a further standard close up photo.

"Oh my God, Larry you're a star," congratulated Sharon.

Steve stooped in closer to the screen.

"Fucking hell! Thats a partial fingerprint and its made in blood. Are you thinking that's the offenders print and their blood?" Queried Steve.

"With some degree of confidence yes." Larry clicked through a number of identical photos but taken with various camera light filters to enhance the image. "You can see the smudged blood is actually centred on the print and not dissimilar to the blood pattern you would leave if say you nicked your finger on a blade and inadvertently blotted it on a flat surface not realising. There's too little blood for it to be the victim's fingermark I would say and if an ungloved hand of the offender became covered in the victims blood I would expect a fuller print. No my best guess is when they dipped into the tool box to grab the Stanley knife they nicked their finger and maybe snagged their glove. They didn't initially realise maybe because they were still tightening the vice on the fellows hand at the same time. They must have used the knife to inflict that final cut. Then they probably took great pleasure watching the victim use up all his reserves crawling to an office phone that the suspect knew they'd cut off. Oh did I tell you the external phone line is severed. Anyway they then realised they were bleeding, filled the bucket and frantically begun their clean up removing and maybe changing their gloves. Fortunately for us at some stage they put that bucket back under the side with an ungloved and still slightly bleeding hand. You won't get sixteen points of identification from that print, but there's more than enough blood for us to get a full DNA profile and I am feeling optimistic." Stated Larry

"Best you take your prize straight to the lab with you then Larry. Steve will get the forms faxed through with Mac's authority to fast track the DNA work. If you give me a copy of your photography I'll get it dropped off at the yard tonight so the fingerprint bureau can do the best they can with the print. Give Mac a call Steve you can tell him the good news and make sure he's going to be back in the office to sign the paperwork," directed Sharon.

"Okay but just a minute." Steve had spied a plastic bin of rubbish in the opposite corner. "The Won Key, now there can only be one curry house with a name like that in London," smiled Steve as he plucked the paper bag from the bin. Steve was mightily pleased with the results of the day making sure he reminded Mac of them all when he updated him from the cab of his van. Young Ali's father was still in custody having been arrested earlier that day. One of Mac's many calls he took during the PM. Mac intended to get an extension on his custody time limit; there was no way he was bailing him now a bloody fingerprint existed. Steve confirmed it was feasible at least that the fingerprint results would be back in time.

Steve didn't stop for the next 3 or 4 hours completing urgent lab submissions, sealing the victim's clothing in forensic drying cabinets and freezing various post mortem exhibits. It was gone 10 p.m. before he found himself in a local 24 hour Tesco's buying far too much rubbish to satisfy his now ravenous hunger, having hardly eaten since the day commenced.

Sat at his desk, grazing on his food Steve couldn't help but wonder if he'd be third time lucky. He thought back over his police career. He'd been involved in the investigation of the murders of three sex offenders now. All a mystery, some would say they all got their just deserts and the offenders deserve medals not prison sentences. All the same it was Steve's job to bring them to justice and he hoped this time he'd solve this crime.

'Shit, Anna!' Thought Steve as he grabbed his desk phone to ring home remembering he had a wife who might just be wondering if her dear husband was coming home tonight.

"Sorry darling you still up?" Apologised Steve.

"Yes, but I don't suppose you're ringing to tell me you're on your way home?" responded a rather syndical Anna.

"No you're right, it has been non stop, sorry, but we're really getting somewhere that's why I've got so much paperwork to finish here. If its alright with you I'll probably grab a couple of hours sleep in the office tonight I need to be back in at 7 and I don't expect I'll get this lot squared away until maybe 2?"

"No you stay there, I'm okay, what do you mean you're getting somewhere?"

"We've got someone in custody and we might have his blood at the scene, plus there's lot more that might help us nail him."

"What if it's not his blood?" asked Anna interested as ever in Steve's murder enquiries.

"I'm not sure, I don't think that would clear him. Depends what else we find out about him. Anyway Anna none of that has gone out to the press so keep it to yourself."

"Darling you know I do. All I care about is that you are alright having to deal with all this brutal forensic stuff on a case like this."

"I am fine honestly it's fascinating work and there are so many forensic techniques we can use to catch this man I'm really getting into this."

"Okay, just don't work too hard, you can tell me all about it if you get a day off at all in the next week. Try and book some leave soon please. I think we really do need that holiday. Now get back to work or you'll not get any sleep."

"Alright darling, I love you."

"I love you too Steve."

Steve felt warm and content momentarily. Anna had injected a sense of security and normality back into him. She was one in a million and Steve would always claim his successful career only existed because he had the backing of such a wonderful understanding wife.

"Cup of tea sleepy head?" Rung out the cheerful words of Janet. "Come on boyo Mac will be in soon look alive."

Steve dragged his crumpled body out from a nest he'd made under his desk. An old sleeping bag bunched up into a large pillow had made a quite comfortable bed for the previous 4 hours. It was just past 6:30 a.m. so Steve had time to take a quick shower in the gym changing room and chuck on a spare set of casual clothes he kept in an overnight bag under his desk.

Steve had found a cluster of exhibits sat in the transit store in the early hours. Clothes and other items seized from Ahmed Akbar when he was arrested. Steve knew all the clothing would need screening for blood and a PC, Laptop and two mobile phones would have to go to the tech lab in South London for fairly urgent examination. All these tasks usually fell to the lowly exhibits officer to arrange.

"Hello Steve, you slept?" Asked Mac from the tea making area as Steve re-entered the office.

"Morning governor, yeah I've had over four hours, not bad really this early in a new job."

"You look like shit mate. Loads to do today. Give Sharon a bell find out what's going on with the fingerprint bureau, she said she might be able to get someone to work through to get us our hit."

Steve sent Sharon a text, just in case she was actually going to take Sunday off and was at home tucked up in bed. Police staff tended to be a little more militant at times and actually protect their work life balance properly.

'call u in 5,' came back her reply.

"Hello Steve dear hope you had more sleep than I did?" said Sharon when she rung.

"Nearly 5 hours."

"Nearly 3 more than me then and not sat in an old armchair at the yard I bet. Listen I managed to get an old friend in the fingerprint bureau to work through the night with me on that partial mark. It's not the guy we have in custody, it's not Ahmed Akbar's fingerprint!"

"Shit, I suppose it would have been too good to be true. Tell me you've got a hit to one of his buddies or something like that though," pleaded the disappointed Steve Lawson.

"No, but we did manage to load it up onto the National Fingerprint ID database and guess what, it's not there either." Sharon explained.

"Shit this just gets worse Sharon tell me some good news please."

"It is sort of good news don't you see Steve. Not many people without a criminal background would get involved in such a nasty crime. Our suspect is close to Costas Salvador, a lone wolf and there was a clear motivator for their actions, we've just got to find what that is and then we will find the suspect," answered Sharon optimistically.

"Well, we know the motivator, Costas was a wrong-un, but maybe the person who sought to avenge his sick acts is the parent of a previously unknown victim and not young Ali's father. When's the DNA result due, maybe that will link into something?"

"Maybe tonight if we're lucky, Mac doesn't want to bail Ahmed Akbar until we have it. I'm back covering nights tonight still so I'm off to get my head down Steve. I've asked one of the other crime scene managers to look out for any fast track lab forms you have so you'll be able to get computers and phones in today. Oh that's what I wanted to ask you, are you sure Costas didn't have a computer of any kind?"

"No, definitely not, not even at work, he used hand written invoices on headed paper. I suppose he could have had a laptop and it's in his burnt out van, but if he did there's no modem connected either in the workplace or at home and what kind of paedophile doesn't go online for their kicks, it's 2006 for Gods sake the bloody internet is awash with that sick shit."

"Yeah, it doesn't make sense, better get Mac to raise an action re local Internet cafés and we'll drive down to Charlton early evening and get a look at that van. I'll come back in around six Steve; the old man will have to cook his own tea tonight."

"Thanks Sharon I appreciate your help on this, you know how frustrated Mac gets when he can't get someone sheeted straight away on a new job." Concluded Steve referring to having the offender identified, arrested and a charge sheet for murder read out to them within days of picking up a new job.

Mac wasn't happy that the anticipated fingerprint hit confirming Akbar was guilty didn't materialise. Not only did it not add to the circumstantial case against him, it weakened it.

"It's seriously fucking undermining that's what it is Steve, the CPS will never authorise a charge now, not even to hold the fucker. You sure it's not just the victims print or something?"

"No gov, but I suppose he could have had an accomplice who just didn't run through the blood when they left?" Surmised Steve.

"Yeah maybe and maybe they are the ones that cut themselves and left their DNA behind. We'll get that result by tonight won't we?"

"Yes gov if we're lucky they'll ring it through to Sharon before she gets in at six, well before Akbar's custody time runs out. I'm going to get his phones and computers looked at today, they will go in as an urgent submission so I may get a verbal update this afternoon. One of the parameters I've set round the computers is emails and online chatter, maybe that will identify Akbar's accomplice?"

"Right, good don't hang around for the briefing there's not a lot you don't already know. Akbar obviously went no comment on all his interviews. Child protection still haven't got young Ali settled enough to submit to a more probing ABE interview re Costas. Oh and they found the source of your stomach contents, thanks to the takeaway rubbish you found. Guy Hanner's time of death bracket has now been amended to sometime just after 1800 hours on Wednesday evening when Costas left the Won Key takeaway with his chicken curry getting back into his van that was parked outside the place. It is all shown on their CCTV. No sign of Akbar or anyone else following him though, but they wouldn't need to, they knew where he worked just had to stake that out and catch him alone one evening. Are we going to get anything from the weapons by the way?"

"Never say never, but to date all the finger marks lifted from key surfaces at the scene are gloved ones. I'll have all the weapons at the lab today for chemical testing to see if that'll bring out any prints. We will also be swabbing them for low copy DNA but any results from that will take several weeks to come back."

"Okay mate well done, let me know as soon as Sharon calls you. I assume she's gone home to her bed, I forgot she was on nights. That woman is hard as nails like a fucking Duracell bunny that never runs out of steam. Not like some of the old 'jobsworth' crime scene managers we have." Commented Mac drifting off into his own silent thoughts probably about Sharon, rabbits and batteries. Steve shuddered to think.

Steve felt like postman Pat as he drove his little white van around delivering exhibits to the various labs the Met had at its disposal, most of which were hidden deep in South London requiring regular stops to check the A to Z. Steve had only just got his head around East London since transferring to the Met. Steve's final drop off was

New Scotland Yard to deliver Costas' fingerprints to the fingerprint bureau still iconically based of the Met's headquarters. Unlike of course New Scotland Yard's finest detectives who weren't actually based there these days. There were far too many of them to house in this dated 60's tower block. Steve still felt proud to be part of the iconic brand as he passed the famous rotating sign and headed into the building.

Steve had finished at the fingerprint bureau and was sat in the fourth floor canteen enjoying a plate of spaghetti Bolognese and staring across at London Undergrounds equally as huge headquarters when his phone rung.

"DC Lawson?"

"Yes, go ahead."

"It's Jerome from the computer lab. I've got some preliminary results re GRL/5, the laptop from the Islington address. Can I just confirm, this is not the victim's laptop is it?"

"No why?" Answered a confused Steve.

"Well, I've just re read the circumstances on the lab form and it says the victim is suspected to be a child sex offender who is alleged to have raped the son of your suspect Ahmed Akbar. It just doesn't make sense."

"Go on…"

"GRL/5 was seized from Akbar's address and the operating system is registered to Akbar, the father of the abused boy. So I'm assuming it is his?"

"Yes why?"

"Well, the material found deleted on the hard drive free space and the deleted but still present internet history is well and truly that of a paedophile."

"What exactly are you saying?" Asked Steve.

"Akbar has viewed and downloaded fifty plus images of young boys, all of which would get him put away for some time and that's just a cursory check. He regularly searches the internet for such material and uses a few familiar portals embedded in seemingly legitimate sites to access it. He spends a considerable amount of his time online especially in the evenings. Unfortunately for you whilst he is banged to rights on the indecent images he was using this laptop to access the internet via his home IP address from about 1834 hours on Wednesday evening for nearly 7 hours. Not sure if that eliminates him but it puts him at home and not at the scene for a large chunk of the bracket of time detailed on the lab form."

"It just doesn't make sense Jerome." Claimed a temporarily stunned Steve.

"I know, unless two paedophiles fell out or something. Is there any news on the victims computer?" Asked the curious technician.

"No he definitely hasn't got one," answered Steve.

"No, never, this is 2006; there's not a single paedophile in London whose not exploiting every inch of the internet for their sick activities these days. Are you sure the victim was a wrong un?"

"I'm beginning to think maybe he wasn't," answered Steve in deep thought. "Thanks Jerome keep up the good work and give me a call if anything else jumps out at you like this, I appreciate it."

Steve updated Mac to a mixed response of 'fucks' and 'bollocks' as he got his head around this ever confusing scenario. "Right that's it I'm going to get Janet in front of that boy Ali, he has to be spoken to again today never mind what his bloody social workers say. I want that DNA result Steve, find me some good news please."

Having indulged in a warming bowl of spotted dick and custard Steve had regenerated his batteries ready for the next task. Steve had received a text from Marvin to confirm Costas' brain was ready for transit to the neuropathology department. Steve knew there was no rush as it would simply sit in a queue of brains once it had been booked in, but he had a few hours to spare before he was due to meet Sharon at the car pound so he made constructive use of his time.

Steve had felt quite odd walking through the outpatients department of the hospitals neurology section to get to the secure pathology lab. There were a number of patients some obviously post op whose brains were poorly but not as poorly as the one he had in the innocuous sealed bucket he was carrying.

The pleasant lady in the lab signed for the brain and Steve completed the paperwork required to ensure people's body parts don't go adrift as clearly they used to. Steve was soon juggling his A to Z again as he wormed his way through South London trying to find the vehicle pound at Charlton.

As Steve was directed into the large indoor storage facility he saw a familiar face.

"Hi Elizabeth, did Sharon drag you off of borough again?"

"Always good to get away from Tower Hamlets she replied, anyway I wanted to catch up with this job, it's really interesting. How was the post-mortem?"

"Fascinating, got some really good stuff about the gunshot wounds to the knees, probably a sawn off shotgun. The bucket print isn't on the database though, did Sharon update you?" Asked Steve.

"Yeah it's a shame, maybe the DNA will come back. I tell you this van's not going to give us much."

Steve looked across at the melted and charred cab of Costas' transit van. It was so badly burnt the front roof pillars had buckled and the top above them had warped in with the heat.

"If that's the only part of the van our suspect went into we've got no hope," suggested Elizabeth.

"Hello you pair," announced the cheerful voice of Sharon echoing in the otherwise quiet hanger.

"Hi Sharon."

"Hello Sharon, hope you got some sleep?" Asked Steve who really wanted to cut the niceties and ask, 'hope you got the DNA result?'

"Yes I did get a good few hours before Mac started calling me about 4 pm," she complained.

"I wondered why he'd left me alone all afternoon," commented Steve.

"I have updated him he's not very happy, especially as the DNA isn't our Mr Akbar." Sharon paused. "I suppose it could be Mrs Akbar if she exists, but either way its the DNA of a woman not a man. A woman whose never had her DNA taken or entered onto the database and a woman who doesn't appear to have ever left her DNA at any other crime scene before either. So we have a mystery on our hands but I would put money on it being the same woman who owns the partial fingerprint on the bucket so if we can find her I think we can convict her." Detailed Sharon optimistically.

Steve and Elizabeth stood open mouthed in silence broken only by an inspirational outburst from Elizabeth.

"A woman with very big feet as well, size 9, can't be many women capable of such a crime with such big feet!" She begun to giggle.

Sharon joined in and Steve couldn't help but laugh out load adding to the surreal chorus. The three of them were actually quite shocked by the revelation having witnessed the carnage caused by this female. The laughter was a welcome light relief before they set about the dirty task of examining the van. Steve began excavating the charred and melted cab mainly to confirm 100% that Costas hadn't left a laptop computer in there. Although there would be no chance of retrieving a readable hard drive Steve reckoned he would at least be able to find the key component parts if one did exist. Sharon and Elizabeth checked for fingerprints on any surface that had not been totally destroyed by fire or the extinguishing of it. The rear of the van was the most in tact area and they soon found the rear plate had been snapped clean off leaving the screws still in place.

"Any joy in that cab Steve?" Asked Sharon.

"No definitely no laptop in here but I have got a very melted old Nokia phone that I've managed to get the SIM card out of in tact. Don't know if we'll be able to get anything from it or not?"

"That might be useful, but I assume it will be Costas' missing phone. Have a look in that sliding side door Steve, I don't want to crack open the rear ones yet. I think whoever burnt the van ripped the plates off to make the burning vehicle hard to initially ID."

Steve slid open the side door to reveal a predictable array of tools, supplies of wood and other building materials. It was in fact a tangled mess, presumably caused by some unorthodox driving by the suspect as they fled the scene. Steve was able to locate a set of snapped front and rear plates bearing the known registration number of the van. Looking around the nearby floor area Steve also located a large flat pointed screwdriver. Steve carefully seized it securing the tool into a box before packaging up the broken registration plates.

"What to you think?" Asked Steve showing the tool to Sharon who compared it to the scratch marks at the top of where the rear plate should have been.

"That'll be it, worth a look at the lab for DNA and prints on the handle. Here have a look at this." Sharon used her torch to further enhance with light the area above the plates Elizabeth was dusting heavily with silver fingerprint powder.

"A left hand print", observed Steve revelling in the sight of yet more potentially identifiable prints.

"We can probably assume our offender is right handed", added Sharon loosely demonstrating how someone jemmying the rear plate off may steady themselves by placing their now foolishly ungloved left hand up on the back of the van to steady themselves.

It may not have been much but the profile of this offender was gradually being added to through the forensic investigation.

"Can't see any blood on this thing, but I'll book Larry and his team to give the van a more thorough going over during the week. I think we'll call it a day with what we have for now guys," confirmed Sharon.

Steve was glad to be finishing. As per normal he had a small collection of exhibits to catalogue and store back at base before he could try and get home prior to Anna turning in.

Steve returned home to find Anna had turned in early. She had been feeling a little under the weather all day and welcomed Steve's offer of a Lemsip and a hot water bottle. Anna had decided she'd probably have to call in sick this week.

"I'm sorry darling I'm never around when you need me."

"Don't be stupid, I'm a big girl, it's just a virus or something. You're better off keeping away from me for a while, you don't want my lurgy, you've got a murder to solve."

"I don't think so somehow, this isn't straight forward at all, we might never know who did this." Responded Steve not going into too much detail at this stage, even to his wife.

"Right ladies and gentleman, Monday morning and our main suspect has been bailed! To make matters worse now Sharon is telling me it was in fact a woman that did all this," announced DCI Mac Spencer rather cynically as he opened the morning briefing.

Mac summarised the enquiries conducted so far and brought the entire team up to date.

"Now here's the most significant issue. Young Master Ali Akbar is a seriously damaged child, but we are now as sure as we can ever be that Ahmed Akbar was his abuser not our victim, Janet..." Mac handed over to Janet Williams to explain.

"It's a classic mess up really, won't be the first time a child victim has been misinterpreted or the last. It's all down to the way the home tutor made assumptions and asked Ali if something was wrong with a series of leading questions. As we know she had noticed Ali was not himself and hadn't been so for quite a while. It seems it was purely coincidental that this abuse began around the time Costas begun work on the extension and new kitchen. It is also unfortunate that the young lonely boy hit it off with Costas and enjoyed spending time watching and helping him work. Classic grooming behaviour in the suspicious eyes of a child protection detective.

Unfortunately the tutor asked Ali if someone had been touching him? He said yes, confirmed it immediately and began crying. She then foolishly asked 'was it Mr Salvador?' When you tie her down to the sequence of events at this point Ali really started to bawl his eyes out as his father Ahmed came out of his home office to see who was upsetting his son. He demanded to know what was going on to which the tutor told him she thought Costas Salvador had been abusing his son. She then describes how he grabbed the petrified youngster by the shoulders looked him in the eyes and said simply 'is this right?' He nodded and it all then kicked off when Costas then walked back into the house from the back door wondering why his young friend was so upset. The police were called and the allegation was made by the adults present. Poor Costas was dragged away before he even realised what was happening. The initial ABE was a challenge especially after the intrusive medical that had to be completed on the little lamb. By the time a second ABE was attempted by child protection the boy had become almost mute. Its only over the last few days, thanks to an amazing set of temporary foster parents social services found, that he's starting to act like a normal little boy again. So we have now managed to do a further ABE interview with the mobile kit in their front room. Evidentially it's not brilliant but what we have confirmed for definite is that bastard of a father abused his boy over several weeks. When he very nearly got caught out he jumped on the opportunity to blame Costas for the situation that had been revealed by his son and it worked. It was only fortunate in a way that Ali's first two ABE's failed to meet the standard required to charge Costas."

"So with the additional charges and supporting bad character of the indecent images on Ahmed Akbar's computer the child protection guys are going out to re-arrest him now. He will not be passing go or collecting £200 this time. Ali gets to stay in the foster care where he seems happier than he's been for a long time and Costas name has been cleared. We just need to know who bloody well killed him now. Akbar didn't he was too busy pursuing his filthy perversions on the world wide web when Costas was being brutally murdered."

No matter how clear the fact that Akbar was not the murderer, Mac was still clearly annoyed to find this out and identify that this case was not so straight forward after all.

"Right so we probably have a woman, a very angry woman to identify. I want Ali's mother tracing; I know she's supposedly back in Egypt, but is she? Costas may have been a widow but what about other relationships, better go through that address book with a fine tooth comb Lisa. Did Costas have any other enemies, maybe he put a bad kitchen in and someone's missus took umbrage? Who knows? Maybe we have got some man hating psycho out there? We really need to think outside the box here. I am happy to look at anyone no matter how remote the link. We have a full DNA profile so we can eliminate people quite easily and painlessly. We won't be rushing out to arrest people, we'll make a more of a subtle approach and simply take elimination samples and wait for the positive hit before we go in heavy. Janet get hold of those crime faculty people, what are they called these days, Centrex or something? I hate to admit it but we might need a profiler on this enquiry."

Mac had his work cut out and was still reluctant to put too much out to the media at this early stage. He was still looking for a bit of luck and the right suspect to come into the frame, reliant on the ingenuity of his experienced team.

It was time for Steve to revisit the scene and walk through the offenders movements, logging every possible clue and seizing anything else that might be worthy of an examination. In any case the now tighter but permanently manned inner cordon was still in place. Steve needed secure metal shutters fitting so the workshop could be locked and sealed enabling Steve to re-open it at any time if any new information came to light.

Steve stood and stared at the closed workshop doors. The external tent had now been removed. The doors had a small mottled glass pane in the top section reinforced with mesh and large enough to see if someone was inside behind it. There was a small wooden sign to the right of the doors 'Apex Building Services.' A name no doubt Costas chose to ensure a prompt entry in the Yellow Pages, a directory still surprisingly relied upon by many when selecting trades despite the introduction of the internet. Below this at the base of the wall was the obvious location where the BT phone line entered the building. Steve took out a pair of 'tough cut' scissors from his exhibits box and snipped out the damaged section of phone line about ten inches either side of the offenders cut. He mounted it in an exhibits box ensuring he'd marked the original cut clearly. Steve knew if they could find the tool the murderer used for this precursory action, experts could match it to the characteristics of the cut.

Ensuring the top internal bolt was still in its dropped down insecure position Steve closed the doors again and stood square to the workshop entrance.

"Just ignore me, there's method in my madness." Said Steve to the interested PCSO stood at the cordon tape.

Steve kicked at the doors with a fairly gentle boot. They flung open wedging in place on the uneven concert floor. Steve was now no more than two metres from the central work top edge and exactly opposite the two exiting smears of blood that came from Costas' shattered knees.

This person had been inside the workshop before they returned to commit the murder, Steve was sure of it. There was no way you'd kick the door and go in cold if you were a lone attacker. Steve turned to the young PCSO.

"What would you do if you wanted to get a look in here but didn't want to raise the owners suspicion?" He asked.

"Sorry?"

"Let's say you wanted to see the layout of the building and maybe meet the owner before you came back and attacked him here." Rephrased Steve.

"Simple I would just come and get a quote for some kind of job. I would go in, walk around, have a look and then ask him to write me an estimate for work I don't really need doing."

"That's right thank you, excellent just what I thought," said Steve pulling on a fresh paper suit and overboots. The PCSO had done exactly what Steve wanted, given a straight forward common sense answer, not clouded by the sometimes complex and slightly warped mind of your average detective.

As Steve crouched in the blood soaked office area he began talking to himself. "Costas old boy you may have been a dinosaur but the document examiners are going to love you," said Steve as he begun sorting through the handwritten paperwork. "Got it," announced Steve to himself as he picked up an A4 pad pre printed in a generic form for customer orders, invoices and quotes. This was real old school stuff consisting of double pages carbonated so the top copy could be ripped out for the customer leaving the bottom record for Costas. Of course it relied upon the card flap that you inserted under the double page each time you wrote out a quote or invoice. This pad only went back two weeks and business was obviously slow as only four or five jobs had been written up. Steve flicked through the bottom copies. Customers names, addresses, contact details and notes re materials and labour costs; all pretty straight forward. Each and every one would need tracing. "Shit," said Steve still talking to himself and looking closely at the top inside edge of the pad just in front of the earliest completed page. Someone had ripped out the tradesman's back copy, highly irregular and obvious to Steve to have been done by the offender. Why else would anyone need to remove this. Steve held the card backing flap up to the light confirming his assumption that this would bare the indentations of the heavy writing used to ensure a carbonated copy was made. Five quotes or invoices, four of which he had copies of for elimination. Surely with some meticulous clever work the document examiners would be capable of enhancing the original invoice. Steve didn't expect for one minute the murderer would have provided true details when they visited for their reconnaissance mission but from experience Steve knew most lies were based on the truth somewhere along the lines so it could still hold vital clues. Steve carefully secured the pad and began searching for older completed pads in the desk drawer.

It was eery working quietly around the stale blood of Costas. Even more so now knowing the sad tale of false accusation that must have half destroyed him before someone else came in and finished the job off. Steve couldn't help but think this was a revenge attack for Costas' evil wrong doing, an attack that should have targeted Akbar instead.

Steve's loud ringtone made him jump.

"Hi Lisa how are you?"

"Stressed, listen I need you to work your magic Steve I need a viewing at Upton Mortuary first thing, what are the chances?"

"What's up?"

"I found Costas' sister and mother living in Portugal. After about an hour of whaling down the phone at me they just announced they will be on the next plane to Gatwick and would meet me there. Why is it when you say London, and worse still London Gatwick, people think it'll be round the corner from where your office is. Anyway I'm on the M25 now so should make it. I'm going to get them put up in a Travel Lodge out in Romford and hopefully convince them to stay away from any of the scenes. You know that geezer who works at Upton better than me can you give him a bell and text me a time if you could Steve my love?" Asked Lisa creeping to ensure Steve folded and helped her out.

"For you Lisa anything. Good luck with the family. This really will test that Portuguese of yours girl," chuckled Steve content to be dealing with scenes and exhibits instead of families.

After a quick call to Marvin and the promise of a tin of biscuits to thank him for his commitment Steve was back inside the workshop re tracing the footsteps of the murderer. In a macabre manner Steve found himself swinging an imaginary crowbar over his head in the exact location that the blood patterns marked. Before he knew it Steve was squatting behind the far left hand corner of the bench imagining being Costas now cowering on the floor. A short blood stained pencil lay innocently on the floor, clearly having fell from behind

Costas' ear as his head was pounded. Steve quickly scooped it up into an exhibits bag. Naturally Steve reached up and placed his left hand on the workbench surface to press himself to his feet only to find he'd placed it next to the two nails still stuck in the bench top. Costas must have been trying to get up when his hand got nailed to the bench. Leaving his hand in place as if it were stuck to the surface Steve was able to rein-act someone guiding his right hand through the now blade-less mitre saw. Imagining the pain he pulled his hand to his chest and found he would have instinctively pulled his other hand free to cradle his injury. This man should have been dead by now and certainly not on his feet still fighting for his life. It now made sense why the last more desperate action of the attacker was to grab that now free left hand and clamp it tightly in the vice hurriedly looking for a blade to finish him off. 'Why not the shotgun?' Thought Steve. 'Maybe they only had the two cartridges?'

There were so many things that would make sense if only they knew where they'd find an offender, maybe there was a gun toting female contract killer out there somewhere, but who else had Costas upset? Steve had to look for alternatives, if Akbar hadn't killed him or had him killed maybe there was some other event either linked to his work or home life that sparked this off. Steve made a bulk seizure of all the business paperwork he could lay his hands on, maybe Costas had ripped off one of his suppliers or one of his jobs had fallen apart at the seams. Although it didn't seem enough of a motive for murder, there were a few nasty characters in the east end of London who had a tendency to over react on occasion. Steve would make a detailed list of each and every business associate and customer so actions could be raised to eliminate them all.

Once the tradesmen had turned up and fitted a metal door to the scene Steve decided to return to the office and begin preparing the shot and wadding exhibits for submission to the firearms lab. He could get these submitted later that day and maybe finish by 9 at the latest so he could get home and check on his poorly wife.

Anna was sat up on the sofa when he got home wrapped in a fur throw comfortable and warm watching back to back recorded episodes of Eastenders on the TV.

"It's not like that out there you know," commented Steve referring to the TV. "It's far more cheerful in the real East End, even at a murder scene." Joked Steve as he plonked himself down next to his wife.

"How you feeling anyway darling?" He asked.

"Better just not 100% that's all. Work have been very good they just told me to take the rest of the week off. I think I will."

"Why not I agree. Get yourself fully fit before you go back into the murky world of abused and neglected children."

"How is your enquiry going anyway? I noticed the news has released the chaps name now."

"Anna it's really sad, really sad. I shouldn't say but this guy got accused of abusing a young boy but he didn't do it!"

"What, what do you mean he didn't do it how do you know that?" Asked Anna.

"The father did it but the boy just panicked and named the wrong man when asked. Fortunately one of our female Detective Sergeants Janet Williams is ex child protection and excellent with kids. She managed to settle him enough to get the real truth from him."

"I don't believe it, that's terrible, terrible," stated a clearly shocked Anna.

"It is yes but I'm moving away from that being the motive for the murder. There could be any number of reasons, the abuse thing just doesn't make sense any more, not now the father is out of the frame."

"Yes your boss was on the news tonight being interviewed and he said you were keeping an open mind."

"We are obviously. At the moment I think maybe it is like one of those Eastenders plots you follow, anyone could have done this and you're going to have to wait a long time before you get the answer. Unlike the TV though we might never find out in real life."

"It's like that is it?" Asked Anna.

"Yeah it is a bit, but one day they'll slip up, get arrested for something trivial and as soon as their DNA gets on that database we'll have em." Said Steve optimistically.

"You've got DNA!"

"Shh, you're not supposed to know that. Yes but there's no way of knowing who it belongs to and if they are careful we may never know, but we're not giving up yet. Anyway darling you carry on with your programme I'm just going to throw something in the microwave, I'm starving. Can I get you anything?"

"Just an orange juice when you come through please, I've eaten earlier thanks."

Three weeks had now passed since Costas Salvador was murdered and Mac had ruled out any mass DNA screening exercise across the East End. Knowing the entire job was close to review Mac set aside a full day in the base conference room to review the facts and results of various enquiries. All the team were present including Sharon to add her forensic expertise. Mac didn't invite the crime faculty profiler back having been quite unimpressed with his conclusions.

"Right I'll start with the profile for those of you that haven't been wowed by the report," opened Mac cynically. "We are apparently looking for:

A female who is relatively fit and strong aged between 18 and 40. She has no previous convictions, but may have a history of violence that has not come to the police's attention. She is likely to live in East or Central London. She may have researched forensic science.

She is able to drive. She may have killed before. She works alone. She has a reason to feel the need to take retribution against Costas Salvador.

It goes on but apart from serving to remind us what we are dealing with here, it does tend to state the bloody obvious and seriously plagiarises a number of reports we provided, not least the forensic ones. So starting with the family let us go through what 'we' know about the possible offender. Lisa?"

"Costas was until a few years ago a very devoted hard working husband. He and his wife didn't have kids, his family aren't clear why but they still remained happy regardless. Costas and his wife first settled in Madeira moving there from mainland Portugal after they married. However when development to meet the demands of tourism on the island levelled out Costas decided to scope out London for a more lucrative working environment. The couple moved to London and eventually secured the flat he still lives in. Costas ran a successful but small business and put a lot of his profits into buying and kitting out his workshop. This became his second home. It was only when his wife died suddenly in a car accident whilst she was back in Portugal visiting her parents that things went down hill for poor Costas. He withdrew from society a bit and only contacted his family occasionally after the funeral. They don't think he ever got over his wife's death. All they can say is he always seemed to be working. The only thing he seemed to have outside of his work was football. West Ham United of course who he followed on a fairly regular basis. The family cannot believe someone would want to kill him. They are now aware of the allegation obviously and are still struggling to come to terms with the possibility that this load of rubbish caused someone to want to kill him. However they have no other suggestions to make relating to a possible motive. They know about the brain and the possibility of a second post-mortem. Apart from the initial rush to fly in and insistence on an immediate viewing they've been really good. They're back in Portugal now waiting patiently for the release of the body. They intend to repatriate Costas to Portugal and they have a local solicitor dealing with probate who knows we aren't ready to release the workshop to them yet. I've asked the local authority to give us another month with the flat so the family can arrange to clear it in their own time."

"Thank you Lisa, Sharon start us off with the forensic situation please."

"We have an offender here that is forensically aware only thrown off track we think by Costas' amazing strength and survival instinct. As you know the cause of death Guy Hanner eventually concluded was multiple injuries and he explains how the injuries to the knees, head and wrist all could have proved fatal on their own. We are now confident of the sequence of events. The offender knew what she wanted to do. She would have been able to see Costas was in the workshop and had his back to the door through the window, she may have even clocked the decaying concrete bolt recess on the inside bottom of the door and knew a good kick would be enough to get her in."

"Just let everyone know why you think she knew the layout of the inside Sharon," requested the SIO.

"Steve found it and can explain, Steve."

"So it occurred to me that a single offender could have easily got it wrong if they didn't know what they were up against. Costas would hand write out quotes and estimates on a carbonated invoice pad. Most of us in here will be familiar with the type of forms, similar to some of the old police forms where we got to keep a carbonated record of what we wrote. Costas had started a new pad where one of the carbonated copies had been ripped out, we think the offender did this when they returned to kill him. Some of you will have heard of ESDA - Electrostatic Detection Apparatus. This basically reveals indentations from writing on paper or in this case the dividing card that is underneath the actual sheet being written on. After some painstaking work to eliminate all the other invoices the document examiners were able to isolate the text from the missing one. Costas quoted a 'Dorothy Butcher of 21 Turpin Road, E20' for a what appears to be a new kitchen and floor. There's a landline provided by her but it comes back to a charity shop in Bow. I know they've had the third degree off some of you lot, but our offender must have just noted it from the shop frontage at some point. We know from the workshop landline and mobile billing that Costas never actually called her back to chase this quote. Rob's team have done the name and address to death, it just doesn't exists neither does E20 of course, it's a fictitious postcode."

"So this visit was from the outset an act of deception and not a legitimate encounter. I don't believe Costas did something during that visit to make 'Dorothy' want to go back and kill him. She already had that intention before then. No, this was our killer's recognisance of the scene and victim. I'll let Sharon continue to explain the offender's plan."

"Thanks Steve. She knew she could kick the door in and providing she took Costas down quickly he would have nowhere to go but deeper into his workshop. There is only one way in and out. She also knew that the constant overhead movement of trains would easily drown out the noise of a sawn off shotgun going off and the subsequent screams from Costas. She was delivering a message to Costas whatever that was, otherwise two shots in the torso rather than the knees would have taken him out instantly at that range. No, she wanted to talk to Costas whilst he died. She must be some kind of psycho. Now the gunshot wounds clearly took him down to the left of the work bench. We assume the offender either didn't have any more cartridges or just didn't have time to reload before Costas was crawling away from her. The weapon of choice was a medium sized crowbar that had hung neatly on the wall beside where Costas had fallen. Latex glove marks and no DNA, that's all we found on that and all other weapons used. Now it's when Costas managed to get to his feet on the far side of the workbench a nail gun was used to secure his left hand to it and the fingers of his right hand were, maybe symbolically, neatly sliced clean off with a mitre saw set at a 45 degree angle. So at this point Costas would have been bleeding everywhere. He had injuries to both legs and a large combination of open head wounds to the rear of his skull. He was close to death and God only knows how he found the energy to try and escape further. It is at this point we think our offenders plan went slightly wrong; Costas should have been dead or dying by now, but when he ripped his hand free of the nails the offender grabbed it and secured it again in the nearest object, a second vice. She made sure he didn't get free again tightening the vice so hard it squashed two of his fingers into a fleshy mess. We think she was panicking at this point and just needed to kill Costas in a quick effective way. So, this is where she cocked up. Her hurried search for the Stanley knife in a nearby toolbox resulted in her getting a little cut to her finger we think, the sort of cut you don't notice until you blot blood on something. She made a neat long vertical cut in Costas exposed left wrist and would have been able to confidently leave him to bleed out. It would have been at this point she realised however that she was bleeding slightly and grabbed one of Costas' buckets filling it with water from the outside tap to wash the Stanley knife thoroughly. She also washed down the surrounding surfaces and some of the toolbox all showing up on the Luminol tests. She did however leave a minute trace to let us get a full DNA profile and a partial print in blood on the side of the bucket. We are confident then in her hurry to leave she foolishly ran through some of the victims blood diluted by her clean up activities. We do have an identifiable Magnum boot mark even though it's a rather large size 9. As you know the van was taken by her which in itself is unusual because this means she walked to the scene."

"Can we just cut in with a CCTV update at that point and then come back to you if you don't mind Sharon?"

Bob gave an update not too dissimilar to the one he gave on day one. The condition of the old CCTV tapes from the estates system was poor. However, the cameras at least covered the foot routes from the main road heading towards the arches. They also covered the road that provided the single vehicle route out. They'd done some excellent work. Bob played a compilation he had prepared on the conference rooms TV system.

"You will see if you look closely there, ignore the screen time it actually works out at real time 19:57 hours." Bob pointed out what looked like a loan figure walking between the blocks of flats in the distance. Another camera view came up, an equally as poor quality image showed what could be the same figure heading quite deliberately directly towards where the arches are.

"We've done all the buses and even the two closest tube stations but there's no way of linking the crowd of people that are out on the main road at this time and our lone figure shown on the estate CCTV. So no chance of getting a face elsewhere for this figure. However we're pretty confident this is the only figure heading towards the arches and this figure is our offender watch."

The compilation continued and switched to a view of the road through the estate. "That's real time 20:32 hours," Bob added explaining that they'd spent a considerable amount of time examining the features of Costas van and even found it heading towards the arches during daylight to help satisfy themselves that this was the offender leaving the scene.

"We have tried as you will see from the next few shots to find the van on a better colour traffic management CCTV system, but there's not a single shot where we get more than possible confirmation of a single shadowy occupant in the cab. At one point, there you see a good view of the back and you can just make out the partial plate, there. The final shots you see there is where we pick it up again in the Romford area and it finally heads towards the old derelict hospital. Even though there are a few of the external buildings still in use the site CCTV was deactivated a long time ago. Plus there are so many exits from here by foot onto a sprawling housing estate there's just no way of tracking anyone on CCTV. You are well clear before you come anywhere near the first local authority camera. If you remember the phone stuff you'll remember we think the offender went back the following evening to burn it out. Well, not a single vehicle appears to approach the main entry point to the site during a generous time slot we worked on. That is not before the fire potentially started. As for petrol stations for people buying cans of fuel well… We have now checked CCTV at a total of 17 local garages for people filling up just containers of any description, no one does, not at all."

"That's still good work Bob I know it's been pretty tedious but you've earned well out of it and we have a pretty good time for the actual murder, better than the pathologist could give and you're far cheaper than he is mate," congratulated Mac fully aware from experience that CCTV results with instant enhancements giving facial identifications of offenders were a thing you generally only found on TV dramas and they just didn't happen in real life.

"Now the firearm Sharon that's an interesting one I believe," prompted Mac.

"Right the lab have worked their magic on the shot and plastic wadding removed from Costas knees at the PM. By adding that to the pathology reports, injuries found, scene photos and measurements they conclude the following:

We are most probably looking for a crudely sawn-off shotgun that they think they would be able to match up if we ever found it.

The cartridges used are Eley Max Game but with the older plastic wadding.

Now Eley have been extremely helpful, Steve you can explain better what they said, you visited them." Sharon handed over to Steve who had completed this action raised from the firearms report.

"Max game shot is a variant favoured for duck and geese shoots mainly conducted in wetlands in the UK. For environmental reasons and new legislation Eley were one of the first manufacturers to stop using lead shot and manufacture an equally as effective steel shot. They even changed to a bio degradable wadding as opposed to the standard plastic one we have. So they haven't manufactured the type of cartridge used to shoot our victim for over seven years now. I know it seems like a lot of work for a fact that doesn't take us anywhere, but if you think about it this ammo has sat around for at least that long and probably longer. I would guess the gun was with it and both were some time back legally owned by someone who maybe lived in a rural area and went shooting in wetlands. They might have been the victim of a burglary or might even be our offender, maybe an associate of our offender. All said and done it's worthy of a national appeal bearing in mind we have a full DNA profile so we can eliminate people easily."

"I think you've just secured yourself a place on Crimewatch young Steve." Joked Mac quickly adding, "with me of course to do the speaking bit. You can

answer the phones and get to ogle Fiona Bruce from
behind mate." Mac knew that most detectives had a
Crimewatch appearance on their police career bucket
lists. "Right anything else on forensics?"

Sharon continued. "The van, totally gutted in the cab.
We did eventually identify white spirit as the likely
accelerant used. Partly through a combination of
detailed forensic science and Steve's eventual discovery
of an empty 2 litre bottle chucked in the back. Costas
had a bit of decorating gear in his van so maybe it was
already in the van. The plates were ripped off by the
offender before it was burnt out, nothing on them but we
did find an inverted hand print on the rear. It was hard to
get a full lift from the damaged paintwork but there was
enough there to confirm it matches the partial print at the
scene. So it's the same person who made this hand print
and not someone assisting the suspect. It does confirm
for sure that it was the offender who took and burnt out
the van. We also did low copy DNA testing on the
screwdriver used to jemmy the plates off but did not get
a usable profile. That's about it I think."

"Thanks Sharon great work, please pass on my thanks
to the guys at the labs. Now suspects, you better update
us about that horrible individual Ahmed Akbar Janet."

"Still in the pokey governor," sung out the charming
Janet Williams.

"Everything is going well with the prosecution against
him for what he did to that poor boy. Akbar is well and
truly eliminated for the murder though. He didn't have a
large circle of friends and associates but the ones we
have traced from his phone usage and things like that

have on the most part been alibied out of any involvement. His wife was in Egypt as were his sisters and any other female associates. They have been over to try and claim parental rights over young Ali but social services have been really good for a change and that isn't going to happen. That pissed them off a bit nearly as much as me swabbing their mouths for elimination DNA. Ali is doing well and in long term foster care now out in Essex. There's a lot of shit flying around about the initial investigation, sad really but Professional Standards and the IPCC are involved. We have provided them with a package disclosing the key facts from our side and we've had to release a more sanitised version to social services who are hauling a few of their lot over the coals. I know it's how things work buts it's so sad. There are only two guilty people here, the bitch that murdered poor Costas and that evil bastard of a father who abused that little boy and then stood by and let an innocent man take the rap for it." Explained the quite emotional detective sergeant clearly touched by the sorry set of circumstances surrounding the whole case.

After a short pause Janet pulled herself back into a more clinical frame of mind and continued. "So we've then gone to town on the profile. It turns out not only do police, security guards and soldiers like their Magnum boots, so do prison officers, ambulance crew, hospital porters, army cadets, some tradesmen, London Underground staff and even bus drivers sometimes. In fact most uniform trades and a few more. It helps that we're looking for a big footed murderess, but we've had to be a bit flexible on that and taken a handful of elimination swabs in a very low key fashion from a few less clown like females. As you know we've no hits at all there and everyone was easily eliminated. As far as other suspects go we looked closely at a number of recently arrested violent women who were not previously on the DNA database but all those were negative. Basically barring a few low priority actions we are pretty much done boss."

The SIO went through the other areas including the house to house and the actions surrounding Costas' suppliers and customers.

"So this man worked hard, kept himself to himself and didn't cross anyone to our knowledge. His suppliers were generally paid up on time and most of his customers were more than happy with the work he did. Its real a mystery this job. I think we're in good shape with what we have looked into, don't need to worry about the review team checking up on us. That's all just routine when a job like this goes on a bit. If they think we missed anything I'll be glad to hear what it is."

"Well done on all your hard work on this enquiry, it's going to be slower time now. We've got the Hackney Crew gang murder at the Old Bailey starting next week so that's going to write off half the team and we're going to have to go back in the frame for a new job by the end of next month. Rob get hold of your contact at Crimewatch and start thinking about how we're going to put that appeal together. Lisa speak to the family about that one; I'm not a fan of putting bereaved families in front of cameras so it's just more to make them aware of what will be going out. Right ladies and gents I think you're about done for today I don't want to see anyone in late today." Concluded Mac well aware that most of his team had become virtual strangers in their own homes since the job broke.

Chapter 5

The Politician

Detective Inspector Steve Lawson was back on the murder squad. It was like coming home for Steve. It had been nearly seven years since he left on promotion to Detective Sergeant going back into a mainstream CID office at Charing Cross. Steve had only just managed to fit in his promised appearance on Crimewatch before he was posted. Crimewatch hadn't produced the results Steve had secretly hoped for and he had to leave the unsolved murder of Costas Salvador behind him and focus on the challenges of running his own team of detectives. Steve had excelled in his new role and secured promotion to Detective Inspector within four years, Anna was massively proud of Steve's achievements but a little disappointed when he successfully applied for a job back on the murder teams. She said it was the hours she knew that he would be doing again; especially as Steve was posted to a team covering West and Central London based at Hendon.

Steve sat in his small side office looking out of the open door at the detectives on his team beavering away. Steve was covering for his DCI who had been off for a couple of weeks sick with a recurring back problem. One of his detectives came off the phone and called across to Steve.

"That was Shona downstairs governor, the new Detective Superintendent wants to see you."

"What new detective super?" Queried Steve.

"The one that started earlier this month while you were on one of your cruises governor, he came from an East London team, you know."

Steve didn't but just pretended he did rather than look stupid in front of his team. He headed down the stairs reminiscing about the recent cruise to the Canary Islands he and Anna had just enjoyed. They were happier than ever, but the memories of the cruise seemed like an age away. Steve had hardly been home since he'd been back; covering for his poorly DCI, long hours attending meetings, case conferences and just catching up on hundreds of emails every evening in the office. It wasn't going to get any better either, Steve was the family liaison lead for the murder command and he had to go away next Tuesday and Wednesday nights for the national conference, a great event for him, but Anna was getting a little less tolerant of his absence these days. She was over fifty now and beginning to realise that the years were flying by without them spending much time together apart from when Steve was on leave. Steve had vowed to do a couple of years on the murder teams and then find a more sedate post to see out his last years in the job. Financially they were in good shape, they had moved out of London into a swanky new build house in the commuter town of Letchworth. Anna had been promoted and moved to the head office of the NSPCC in central London where she still very much enjoyed her work from a more managerial angle. Steve could retire in less than four years time and receive a full police pension. If they played their cards right they could both retire when Steve's police career ended and use the equity they had in their current house to downsize to a tidy little mortgage free cottage in the country somewhere.

Steve knocked on the Detective Superintendent's door and was called in by a familiar sounding voice.

"Hello Steve how the devil are you? Fucking detective inspector you flash bastard. It's taken me longer just to get the next rank you've jumped three."

"Two sir, two," corrected Steve.

"Don't call me sir mate, it's Mac now unless the commander's around. Anyway it is three," answered the familiar old friend and boss of Steve's.

"I don't understand?"

"Well how about temporary Detective Chief Inspector Steve Lawson."

"Sir, I mean Mac what do you mean, why me?"

"Because you can handle it mate. I know that better than most and you've done your SIO's course haven't you so you are the ideal candidate. What you probably don't know is Derek really isn't well. He's going to be off for some time now; two of his vertebrae have crumbled and he needs a major operation and some serious recuperation before he will be fit enough to run the team again. You're alright to cover for him though, eh Steve?"

"Yeah of course it will be an interesting challenge."

"Good team 4 have just taken a job so your team's in the frame now." Smiled Mac knowing as the Detective Superintendent he didn't have to step in as the SIO much for most new murders and only really got involved in the really serious and high profile jobs. Even then most Superintendents would still let their DCI run the job and simply oversee key decisions and front up the media appeals.

Steve and Mac chatted over a coffee and shared some of the highlights of the last few years. Mac was immensely proud that since the Salvador killing all but one other job was solved and had ended in a conviction. Steve relayed some harrowing stories of serious crime investigations that he ran on his borough with a fraction of the officers deployed on most murder enquiries. Of course with Steve's tenacity and enthusiasm his teams had pulled together and still got some great results.

A few days later Steve was sat in an unconvincing presentation from the IPCC about partnership working for FLO's when his phone vibrated in his pocket on the last afternoon of the National Family Liaison Conference. It was a text message. Steve took a sly look at his phone.

"Boss can you ring me. New job in Bash."

It was from Bashir Maan one of the most experienced detective sergeants on Steve's new murder team. 'Bash' as he liked to be called was a real career detective having been a DS on the same murder team for nearly 6 years. He had been case officer for some high profile murders in Central London and was the silent hero behind a number of successful SIO's careers. If Bash needed to speak to Steve now and it couldn't wait a few hours until the conference was over then Steve needed to make the call. He shuffled his way along the line of delegates like an unwelcome cinema viewer escaping to the toilet mid film, apologising as he stumbled out of the lecture hall at the College of Policing.

"Bash, what have we got?" Asked Steve about to take on the most high profile job he'd encounter in his entire career.

"Bernard Lyle, MP - shadow Secretary of State for Education and this shit's about to hit all the news channels."

"I thought he'd resigned after all that crap in the Sunday papers. He got a 13 year old girl pregnant or something didn't he?" Asked Steve recognising the name immediately.

"No gov, didn't you see the retraction statement, the girls mother went public and admitted it had all been made up to try and get cash out of the tabloids," explained Bash.

"So what have we got Bash anyway apart from a dead MP?"

"It's complicated; Specialist Investigations got it in the early hours of this morning. Sky News had received a video confession last night from Bernard Lyle actually admitting the previous encounter and to being a paedophile, but the guy was obviously under some duress and looked quite ill. They think he had a rope round his neck. Sky obviously didn't put it out and shared it with us overnight. Specialist investigations worked with the kidnap squad and did a load of good work to ID the location. The footage had been sent to Sky via a shared wifi they located to an address in Westminster. It turned out to be a set of short term apartment rentals, almost like elaborate hotel rooms really. The bookings were checked and Lyle was found in one of the apartments there."

"Dead obviously?" Confirmed Steve.

"Yes gov, hanging but he looks a bit bashed up as well. The footage that was sent to Sky shows him in distress when he makes the confession to the camera, quite possibly doing so under duress. I'd say this is definitely a murder in some way shape or form, not a suicide."

"Right I take it Mac Spencer is aware?" Asked Steve knowing this was the kind of job that ideally a detective superintendent could provide top cover on whilst Steve actually ran the investigation.

"Yes gov, the boss told me he'd ring you in a bit but he wants you to get a look at the scene ASAP, you've got a motor up there haven't you?"

"Yes mate, where am I going?

Bashir explained the apartments were only a short walk from the Houses of Parliament just set back from the river in amongst some very expensive houses and office buildings. Steve knew about them, he'd once looked them up on the internet when he decided to stay over after a drink to celebrate his promotion but they were far too expensive. A one bed apartment would set you back around £300 a night.

"Right the scene stays exactly as it is until I get there. I assume we have one of our crime scene managers tasked and you've left an exhibits officer there?"

"Yes gov Jonno was on the homicide car," answered Bashir reassuring Steve that an exhibits officer was already on scene.

"Get Specialist Investigations out of there and keep the cordon low key just the floor that the apartment is on and the room itself please for now. I'll make some progress with the covert blues and twos on this motor and hopefully be at the scene in half an hour or so. Get the team to the yard mate. I'll be there to brief everyone at six. I'll head to the scene first then see you all at the briefing."

Steve clicked his phone into its hands free cradle as he fired up the modest but lively unmarked Mazda 3 he now had personal use of as the team's SIO on call.

"Fucking hell Steve where's the fire?" Said the voice of Mac as Steve pressed to accept his incoming call.

"Hang on boss I'll turn the toys off, I'm just on Park Lane I'll be at the scene in ten minutes." Steve deactivated the blue lights and two tone horns adopting a more sedate and safe driving stance to take Mac's call.

"Steve this is going out on the news channels tonight mate, speculation is already rife. Let me deal with the media strategy and the raft of fucking senior officers sticking their noses in just because they've got a handful of senior politicians on their shoulders. From our point of view it's just another murder and the motive is straight forward; thanks to the tabloids this guy has been labeled a paedophile and someone has decided to believe that. You just get to the scene and get started, you can brief me at the yard later. Apparently the commissioner wants to see me with our commander now; why did I take this fucking promotion?" Complained the frustrated detective superintendent who would have rather been running the murder enquiry than dealing with the bureaucracy of senior management.

Steve entered the heavily modernised complex converted from some kind of old victorian factory building. It was a mix of original features with modern touches such as individual swipe entry pads to the large apartment doors. Steve took the stairs to the first floor to be met by an officer stood guarding an internal door opening out onto a long corridor.

"DCI Steve Lawson," Steve announced producing his warrant card.

Steve walked into the corridor toward the end apartment. There he was met by the familiar face of a woman he knew. She was half clad in a white paper suit. The Met was an organisation of well over 40,000 officers and staff but it never ceased to amaze Steve what a small world the arena of serious crime investigation was, especially when it came to homicide.

"Elizabeth, what a pleasant surprise, I take it you are now a crime scene manager?" Greeted Steve.

"And you're a DCI," she smiled.

"Only temporary promotion but yes I am the SIO on this job for my sins, is my exhibits officer here somewhere?" Asked Steve.

"Yeah he's inside with the photog just doing a scene video for us. If we wait until that's done we'll get in there and have a look. There's a spare suit and all the bits in my case over there if you want to get ready?"

"Hello governor you're going to like this one," rung out the cheerful voice of Jonno as he emerged from the apartment door. Jonno was a rotund guy, an old school DC and experienced exhibits officer. Steve couldn't help but find him spookily similar and almost made from the same mould as his old CID associate Gadget.

Jonno was followed out of the scene by the photographer struggling away with a ridiculously oversized video camera probably not capable of any better footage than Steve's iPhone could capture.

"Right Jonno show us what we've got," requested Elizabeth who had yet to enter the scene.

Steve followed the pair closely behind as they entered an open plan kitchen come lounge area. Compact but tastefully decorated and seemingly undisturbed; not even a dirty cup in the sink. The room boasted a vaulted ceiling spanning the entire apartment and continuing into the single bedroom with exposed original steel roof bars. The bathroom was ensuite to the only bedroom in the apartment.

"Shit is that CS gas you can still smell?" Asked Steve.

"Yes governor I think so certainly smells familiar."
Confirmed Jonno who'd been about a bit and sprayed
his fair share of suspects with CS in his time.

Steve rubbed his slightly irritated eyes, "I think we can
open a window in here Jonno; just to vent the place a bit
or we won't last too long."

Steve looked through the bedroom door. A dressing table
stool lay on its side at the foot of the bed next which
swung the polished shoes of Bernard Lyle. He had been
strung up by the neck using a strong black nylon rope
looped over the exposed character roof strut and
stretched down to a large traditional old radiator where it
was tied off. Lyle was dishevelled but still dressed in his
business suit, his hands tightly bound behind his back
with plastic ties. His eyes bulged open and he had a
distorted look of terror on his face. This was no suicide,
neither was it made to look like one. Bernard Lyle had
been gassed and incapacitated before he was strung up
by the neck.

"What's the score on the footage that went out to the
media Jonno? You took over the scene from the team
that found him didn't you?" Asked Steve.

"I haven't seen it but they had a still image they showed
me when I got here. He was definitely stood near where
he has hung and that rope was tightly pulled around his
neck. Apparently he makes a lengthy confession in a
very distressed state, starting with confessing to being a
habitual sex offender who is guilty of grooming and
raping a 13 year old girl. He goes on to confess that she

subsequently had to abort the pregnancy he caused. He admits paying 250 K to the mother to make a retraction statement and to relocate up north. He then admits he has abused young girls for many years and only got away with it because he travelled to parts of South East Asia to satisfy his sick desires where child prostitution is rife and goes unnoticed for the right fee. Of course when your father's Lord Peter Lyle and you are as loaded as that family are, thanks to their South African mining legacy, you can have anything money can buy. Bernard Lyle bought his way out of even getting arrested for what he did, the Met didn't even get round to putting on a crime report before the mother and girl retracted everything stating it was fictitious. The Specialist Investigation guys said they had even been asked at the time to consider prosecuting the mum for attempting to pervert the course of justice but their commander saw sense and put a stop to that early doors." Detailed Jonno who was the first homicide detective to get to the scene. He explained that fortunately no one tried to cut Bernard Lyle down as it was obvious he'd been dead for hours, his body was stiff with rigour and Jonno just had an FME attend to confirm death. The rope bindings and stool were Jonno's only hope for any meaningful forensic evidence if Lyle's attacker had been careful.

"Can you see this Steve?" Asked Elizabeth using a torch to closely illuminate the underside of the rope as it sloped away from the overhead bar towards its anchor. "This wearing is significant and would not have been caused by an empty noose simply being pulled up to the required height. Our victim was hauled to his feet and I think forced to step up onto that stool or be strangled to death resisting it."

Elizabeth stooped forward her head tilted to one side as she focused on the victim's left knee. "Oh," she said carefully gripping the man's left trouser leg at the ankle between her forefinger and thumb lifting it directly outwards at an unnatural angle with very little effort. There was a faint crackle as the victims leg bent sideways. "His left knee has been smashed to bits, he would have had to balance on one leg to keep upright on that stool after sustaining an injury like that," she observed.

The two detectives watched on as Elizabeth carefully lifted the untucked shirt of Bernard Lyle, something else having caught her keen eye.

"Thats some welt," commented Jonno staring at the lateral red marking caused by a heavy swipe to the man's stomach with a narrow straight weapon.

Sympathetic to the plight of the exhibits officer and crime scene manager Steve held onto the victim assisted by Jonno whilst Elizabeth carefully cut away sections of the handled end of the rope preserving them for DNA testing. Steve and Jonno then lowered the victim's still stiffened body to the ground and laid it out on the floor.

"Right, I'm going to have to leave you with this now guys, I need to get to the yard, brief the team and tie in with Mac Spencer," apologised Steve.

"I'll brief uniform on the way out, if the media come anywhere near this place it's 'no comment' right. I'll get a house to house team to come and do the block and deal with the CCTV. If you need an extra pair of hands in here just grab one of them when they arrive Jonno."

"Thanks Governor."

"Yeah thanks Steve, I'll give you a bell later. I think we'll strip this guy before we bag him to maximise DNA and fibre opportunities and get a better look at any injuries before the PM." Added Elizabeth.

Steve abandoned his car just short of New Scotland Yard and walked into the quite grand reception, the eternal flame burning in an ornate cabinet in the middle of the main area. It made a fitting centre piece serving to remind visitors of the ultimate sacrifice many an officer had made over the years. It was of course a shame that the yard was due to be sold off to save money in the age of austerity that was now kicking in at the start of 2013. Steve headed up to the main briefing room where he hoped his team was now waiting for him.

Bash was organising MIT 12, Steve's very own murder squad. The team was carrying a few vacancies due to recent cuts, but Steve still had 18 very competent detectives and some experienced HOLMES Major Incident Room staff to back them up. Although Steve was supposed to rely on a central team for intelligence support these days he still retained the tenacious DC Graham King, a whizz with any database and excellent with open source research.

"Right Bash see if you can get this playing and I'll start with the scene." Steve handed Bashir a copy of the scene video and went on to talk through the scene.

"Now this is NOT a suicide let's be clear about that. If you hear any speculation surrounding that just be clear we are and always will be conducting a murder enquiry. Bernard Lyle was forced to hang, either by being smashed in the knee whilst he stood with a tight noose around his neck or having the stool he stood on kicked away from underneath him. The only other theory I'll accept is that he was so desperate for his ordeal to end he just decided to step off the dressing table stool and end it all. However even if that is the case this is still a murder, given the actions of the offender immediately before this."

Steve went on with his briefing around the scene and work already conducted by Specialist Investigations and the Kidnap Squad.

"Right priorities: I want a team of at least 6 doing the house to house focusing on the block itself and the CCTV. I'm expecting the footage will show our suspect arrive and leave. Once we have that I want them tracing on external cameras, all the way back to their home address if we can. Secondly forensic evidence, the crime scene manager is hopeful we will find some low copy number DNA at least where the suspect hauled on the end of the rope. I need a second exhibits officer appointing tonight and Section 8 warrants obtaining for the victim's office and home just in case we don't get family or ministerial consent. I am confident when we get his phones, computers and other media downloaded we will be able to confirm (a) the motive and (b) the contact he must of had with the suspect for them to go to that apartment. Family liaison, who do we have earmarked for this? Ah young Joseph." Remarked Steve looking back at the gently raised hand of the young officer Steve had only met recently.

Joseph or Jo was spoken of highly by Bash as an individual with excellent people skills. He was quite a camp kind of guy that you couldn't help but like. He was passionate about everything he did, never complained just got on with whatever you threw at him.

"Right Jo I need you to get in amongst the Lyle family, his wife and teenage kids. I want them on side, but I want the truth about our Bernard by the end of the week." Steve requested.

"Oh thank you sir, I love the easy jobs," joked the cheerful FLO.

"Tie in with whoever gets the warrants and see if you can't smooth the way for them. They know about the death and the detail of what's been said to them by the kidnap negotiator bloke is all in his notes, Bash has a copy for you."

"Right, Graham get online and do your thing. I want briefing tomorrow about the press attempt to out Mr Lyle and find out how far this story got. What forums did it end up being discussed on, who tweeted what and all that social media crap I don't understand."

"Finally tonight I want the mother and daughter from that earlier allegation found and under control. I want to know where they stand in this. They are 'Persons of Interest' not suspects at this time, but I want you guys in front of them first not some shit bag of a tabloid journalist waving yet more money to temp them. Detective Superintendent Spencer will deal with the media, our senior management and their MP buddies. I'm going to brief again at 09:00 hours tomorrow back here, see if you can muscle in on the room bookings please Bash. I'm sure they'll be a few noisy senior ACPO ranks want to join the audience so I'll look forward to seeing a few ties round those necks in the morning gents please." Added Steve as light hearted as he could but knowing even at times of extreme pressure the bullshit of everyday working life still continued, especially at the yard.

Steve's phone started to vibrate in his pocket. It was Mac, he'd been surprisingly patient letting Steve get on before pestering him for a face to face meeting. Steve hastily left Bashir to organise the team and set them off as he left the briefing room.

"Yes boss, I'm at the yard where do you want to meet me?"

"I'm in the commander's office Steve, on the 6th floor, you know where it is."

Steve was met by Mac, a familiar looking press officer and the commander himself. Mac did the introductions flattering Steve announcing that he was 'one of his best SIO's.' Something Mac actually said more for the commanders reassurance than to boost Steve's ego.

Steve gave an update regarding the scene and the fast track actions he'd set underway.

"Good work Steve," commented Mac. "Let me just go over the agreed holding statement we're going to put out to the press. We're going to be proactive with releasing the name, the family have ok'd this with the DI from the kidnap squad already. The press lines will read:

'The Metropolitan Police have launched a murder enquiry following the discovery of the body of Bernard Lyle MP at an apartment in the Westminster area of London. A number of lines of enquiry are already being pursued by the Homicide and Serious Crime Command. No arrests have been made at this time. Mr Lyle's family have been informed and are being supported by specially trained officers from The Met.'

Is that okay Steve?"

"Yes sir fine but when is it going out, can we delay it until say 22:00 hours give my FLO a chance to make the family aware of what we are saying exactly?" Asked Steve.

Everyone in the room agreed allowing Steve to make his excuses and get back to coordinating his team. Steve soon had Mac right on his tail though.

"Right mate when you briefing next?" Asked Mac as he followed Steve down the stairs.

"09:00 tomorrow here on the 5th floor."

"So what are our chances of detecting this one, quite good I imagine," probed Mac.

"Well DNA from the offending rope if we're lucky. Definitely some kind of CCTV trail and they'll be some technical traces on the victim's phones or computers to tell us a story." Explained Steve.

"Good so we will have someone sheeted for this within the week then?" Asked a very optimistic Mac, not a stranger to such speedy results in his day, with the exception of Costas Salvador of course.

Steve just smiled knowingly, Mac knew if the evidence was there somewhere Steve would make sure it was found. Steve and his team would have to work hard to get that speedy result though.

Steve spent most of the night making and receiving phone calls. He never did get home, exchanging only a single text message with Anna who knew how important it was for him to focus on this new job, especially now he was the SIO. Fortunately Steve had his job car nearby and even had a fresh shirt in amongst the overnight gear he'd taken to the FLO conference. Steve set about making notes of his decisions so far and preparing a professional briefing for the morning from the various updates he'd received.

After a few hours kip in one of the canteen's easy chairs Steve was up shaved and looking far fresher than he felt. Bash joined him for breakfast in the yard's canteen and Steve was ready for his formal structured briefing.

Steve looked around the stepped auditorium of the 5th Floor briefing room slightly concerned at the number of high ranking uniform officers present and quite a few unfamiliar individuals in plain clothes. As Steve settled the room down announcing he'd be starting the briefing in five minutes time he quickly formed a strategy to regain control of the situation.

"My detective sergeant will be coming round the room before we start to note the names and roles of everyone present for the minutes, I'd be grateful if you'd oblige him and confirm your need for inclusion in this sensitive briefing." Announced Steve.

At least two senior officers and three people in plain clothes quickly slipped away proving Steve's theory that whilst they were legitimate officers and staff members they had no need to hear the full briefing he was about to deliver.

As an extra precaution Steve started his briefing with a warning that no details of what was about to be disclosed could be discussed with any other officer or staff member without the authority of Detective Superintendent Mac Spencer who stood to Steve's left ready to lead the update.

Mac started the briefing introducing himself and insisting that Steve was the DCI running the day to day enquiry, Mac was just overseeing it. Mac however took the responsibility of setting the scene by playing in full the footage handed over by Sky News of Bernard Lyle making his confession.

"My name is Bernard Lyle and I am a member of parliament. I am the shadow secretary of state for education. I have betrayed you all. I am a sick child molester who has bought his way out of trouble. I have raped child prostitutes in South East Asian countries and got away with it. In November 2012 I used my position as a benefactor of my charity to groom and lure 13 year old Rosie Davis to my rented apartment under false pretences. I did dupe Rosie Davis into having sex with me on several occasions whilst she was away from home, her mother thinking she was in a safe place. She fell pregnant as a result of my abuse and told her mother who subsequently revealed the truth to the press. I paid Rosie and her mother two hundred and fifty thousand pounds to leave London and say they were making up their allegation. I am truly sorry for my sick behaviour and deserve to pay for my sins," blabbed Lyle clearly in a great deal of distress and reading from a script prepared for him it appeared. Yes the rope was tightly pulled around his neck and he was sweating profusely.

The room was silent as the footage ended and Mac said:

"Bernard Lyle died from strangulation shortly after making that film. The allegation made last November was well and truly put into the public domain even if it was retracted. I'm also sure someone close to Lyle knew of his child sex tourism. So quite simply we are looking for someone seeking to take retribution against a high profile paedophile who has been publicly exposed. Steve..." Mac handed over.

"I'm going to start with the family. For those that don't know they were initially contacted by Specialist Investigations and introduced to a kidnap negotiator before Lyle's body was later found by the police. My FLO has now been fully introduced to Mr Lyle's wife and two teenage boys at the family home in Oxfordshire. Jo where are we up to?"

"The wife is devastated but not altogether surprised by what her late husband has confessed to. She has already indicated some prior knowledge of his issues. We know from the searches we have carried out that they have separate bedrooms. His boys are very protective towards their mother and I would say a little angry at their father for doing this to her. Of course the press are camped out at the address already, but fortunately they can't get past the large electronic gates at the end of a long drive. I've set up a password for phone and door contact to safeguard them further. I'm going back up there later but I don't think they'll have a lot to add. His wife is a lovely woman she's given us free access and consent to look at anything we want even Lyle's bank accounts. They are true victims in all this I think sir." Summed up the concerned FLO.

"Thanks Jo, I'm going to be strict on this; anything whatsoever for the family then you must go through the FLO or me, no exceptions. Right where's my crime scene manager?"

"Here Steve," called out Elizabeth sat next to Jonno. "We do have a brief update."

"Good go on."

"The scene is in general very clean and sterile, it does not look like the victim had been there more than an hour or so before the attack. This ties in with the card swipe activation on the door at 7:03 p.m. About 90 minutes before the footage was uploaded to Sky News I believe. I won't steel the CCTV team's thunder re timings exactly but we appear to have an assault that lasted no more than 30 minutes. That ended with Bernard Lyle being strung up to one of the old ceiling bars so tightly anything other than an upright stance on the small dressing table stool would have strangled him to death. DC Johnson and I have studied the footage carefully comparing it to the scene and the angle and style of filming puts Lyle in that exact position when he makes his confession. We'd say filmed by someone stood a few feet in front of him with a camera or smartphone maybe. Now that rope is nylon and a very good surface for DNA. We've found a small slither of ripped latex glove on the floor by the radiator at the scene. I'm now confident that the effort needed to hoist the victim up will prove to be our offenders downfall. Especially if their gloves ripped resulting in skin to rope contact. All of this is good news because all the fibres we've found are simply black. The victim wore a black suit, the Specialist Investigations guys had dark suits on when they went in to find the victim and we now know our offender wore black so it's going to be very difficult to make use of them. We're trying hard to enhance the carpeting to see if we can get anything from footwear but I'm not holding my breath there. Subject to the swabs being tested from the victims face I can suggest CS spray was used at some point no doubt to subdue the victim in the first instance before he was beaten. The welts we've found, mostly across the centre of his body, look like they've been inflicted with a short metal bar of some sort. We've sent the photos off to the experts already to try and ID a possible weapon. The post-mortem will take place today at Kings Cross mortuary and I hope to have all the fingerprint work done at the scene by tonight."

"Thanks Elizabeth. CCTV and house to house. Bashir can you give us an overview of the findings so far please."

"Right enquires at the apartments show an online room booking was made by a Mr Bernard using a pre paid credit card a week in advance. The reception for the complex is in the main building at the front, but as you know the bulk of the apartments are in the larger building to the rear across a courtyard. The management insists that their staff keep a low profile and are very discreet as a lot of the rich and famous people use this place when they are in town. In fact after 18:00 hours only a single member of staff remains on duty and only really comes out of the office when customers arrive. There are two customer entrances, one totally insecure until 22:00 at the front and a vehicle entrance with very slow electronic gates to the side. Even whilst we were there last night people wandered in and out on foot behind the cars coming and going. Although fire exits are alarmed those alarms are silent and switch off again providing the door secures after the person uses it. Apparently resident's 'guests' are often shown out this way and staff tend to glance at the cameras when this happens but take no further action as long as the doors shut again afterwards. All entrances have overhead CCTV as does the main courtyard and stairwells. Corridors off these are not covered but never the less movement around the complex can be fairly easily tracked. As Elizabeth explained it is possible to download door card use on the main office computer system. So we have Bernard Lyle arriving with nothing more than his briefcase in hand, he's alone and seemingly relaxed, not obviously a man under duress. He very quickly books in, collects his entry card and heads across the courtyard and up the stairs towards the apartment. This happens between 18:58 and 19:03 hours. The first movement towards that apartment occurs just over an hour later at 20:08 hours. We think this is our murderer." Bash held up an A4 printed still of a figure shrouded in black. "Now that's an Abaya favoured by Arabic Muslim women complete with a Niqab which is the face veil. Let me be clear here though, we may have isolated the CCTV in this fairly quiet complex to say with some certainty that this is our killer but we CANNOT say our killer is a Muslim OR even a woman," emphasised Bash quite abruptly.

Of course Bash was right Muslim attire was available from a wide variety of sources especially in East London and even online via a vast array of merchants. It would have been easy for anyone to use this as a disguise to minimise the effects of CCTV and indeed hinder an investigation with a degree of controversy. Steve had enough controversy to deal with already and could have done without this.

Bashir continued, "so when you speak to the staff at this complex they will tell you that their high end apartments are often rented out by visiting Arabs and there wives enjoying extended visits to London. So the site of a fully covered woman is not at all unusual at this venue, it's just disgusting that such a vicious killer might choose to exploit that. Of course it's not unusual to see people from all cultures in central London either at 20:00 hours in the evening. The public areas are pretty packed with tourists and commuters well into the night. So to go back we checked all of the bookings for the complex and no Arabic customers were booked into the floor or corridor where our victim was killed. In fact on that night the place was only half booked and not one resident fitted the description of this figure. What we do know is at 20:36 hours the footage of Mr Lyle's confession was uploaded via email using the wifi provided for residents. At 20:42 hours the east fire door alarmed for a few seconds and the CCTV shows what we think is the same figure leaving the building. Now we think we've tracked them to the packed Westminster underground station and possibly onto the district line going eastbound. There is still only limited CCTV on those old district line trains so we can't locate our suspect on the actual train unfortunately. What we have been able to do is track accurately its arrival and departure times at every station all the way to Upminster. As you can imagine that's a lot of CCTV to look at and between Whitechapel and Elm Park there is a very diverse mix of population. That's a lot of potential stops where our suspect could blend in as they get off making it impossible for us to ID them."

"Thank you Bashir," said Steve. "Excellent work from those who have worked through the night to achieve all that. So let's move on to Rosie Davis. Bernard Lyle has said under duress that the initial allegation was true, but is that right? Graham you've done some cursory work on the media stuff and the background to that, what did you find out?"

"Well governor the initial newspaper story was very precise really, even named the charity that the girl used to get the fast track abortion. I've been able to look at the initial financial work that Economic Crime did on the mum for the kidnap squad yesterday. At the start of their search for Bernard Lyle, Rosie's mum was a possible suspect who they thought could have sponsored our victim's initial abduction. So, they identified the deposit of a cheque for £20,000 into her account in November last year that was almost completely withdrawn and presumably spent within about five days. Three days after that they found several accounts were opened in her name at different banks. This appears to have been done to allow a spread of deposits that stay under the financial radar. When you add the deposits up it tends to confirm that she did receive £250,000 in total from an unidentified donor. So from that angle Mr Lyle or someone else may well have paid her the hush money that he admits to under duress. I have traced the mum and she's moved from her North London address to an address in Gateshead. I think the new address is probably her mother's council house rather than some posh pad. I managed to get an early call in to a contact of mine at the local education authority there this morning and he thinks he's traced Rosie to a new school up there."

"Great thank you Graham I'll be looking to get a team on the road after this briefing if you can give DS Maan all the details please. Right where's my Search Advisor?" Asked Steve.

"Here sir," indicated the uniformed police sergeant flanked by 12 or so smart looking PC's in their blue search fatigues.

"I'm going to need a thorough search for weapons along the route identified from the CCTV up to and including Westminster Station. I don't want it to become a media circus though. In that area you guys do routine security searches all the time so there's no need for it to look any different. The parameters are simple any CS or incapacitant spray type cans and any metal bars capable of being used as weapons. It doesn't look like any clothing has been dumped so don't worry about that one." Instructed Steve.

"I'm going to get a couple of the enquiry team allocated to fast track enquiries re victimology. The FLO will deal with the family but I want everyone else that is close to our victim traced and interviewed today. I need to know if there is any other reason someone would want our victim dead and the paedophilia angle is just a good cover for them. I'll be at the post-mortem most of the day so I don't intend to brief again until tomorrow morning but I would like an update re all the areas I've covered by 20:00 hours tonight please. Any questions?"

Steve fended off a very boring question relating to community impact assessment from the Borough Commander only really asked to make himself look good in front of the Assistant Commissioner, who Steve had not managed to get to excuse himself at the start. Mac stepped in further and reassured the senior officers present that he'd be attending their Gold Group meeting later in the day and dealing personally with the Independent Advisory Group. Steve was relieved to hear that, he just wanted to get on with investigating this murder and ignore all of the politics surrounding it.

A few hours later Steve was back down to earth donning a face mask with eye shield, now required under health and safety rules, at Kings Cross mortuary.

"Steve hello, we've met before, back in the days when you were a young exhibits officer I believe?" Commented the familiar pathologists.

"Yes Guy we have several times, back when you were a young Home Office pathologist," joked Steve reassured by the presence of the very capable Guy Hanner.

"Right, down to business," announced Guy as he looked down at the now naked body of the slightly overweight Bernard Lyle MP.

"So I know he was found yesterday afternoon and Elizabeth has told me rigour was still present when he was first found. I also understand from your brief that you've got a suspect leaving the scene 8:35 ish the evening before? So I think its safe to say Mr Lyle died around that time or not to many minutes after that. It would certainly be before around 10 p.m. the night before last given the post-mortem changes I can see. Let's look at these external injuries first. We'll start from the top for a change, funny I only really do that with hangings, don't know why. Now there are some very subtle burns to the eyes and nasal openings which ties in with a good sniff of some kind of solvent based incapacitant spray. Couldn't say C/S for definite but the swabs Elizabeth already has should confirm the exact origin when tested. We'll come back to the neck when we open him up, but it's obvious to me that the rope strangled this man to death. Yes, I thought so the third and fourth ribs on his left hand side appear fractured under this red mark and that is some bruise definitely an iron bar of some kind with a rounded end. I've seen this before definitely, just can't remember where. Get the picture you have of that to the National Injuries people please; they'll help jog my memory."

"Already emailed through overnight Guy," piped up Jonno happy to be one step ahead.

"Go and give them a bell then will you DC Johnson, I know they'll want to give you a big long report and similar injury photos to back up their findings, but just see if they'll give you a verbal opinion at this point." Asked Guy before continuing as Jonno left the room.

"You see this one on the right flank is almost a back handed second blow following the left chest one. I wouldn't be surprised if we don't find a ruptured kidney when we open him up. The third welt there across the front of the stomach, very painful looks like it caught the top of the pelvis too. There's a fourth here just the tip of the weapon again on the right flank and what a clear mark, definitely some kind of finished tip to this weapon. Now we're pretty much in tact as we work down here until we get to this left knee, what a mess. Multiple blows all from the left hand side and persistently rained upon the same area until the knee was smashed and useless. No wonder our Mr Lyle came off of that stool he'd have been in agony just balancing on one leg by the time this bit of handiwork was complete."

Guy Hanner continued his examination and was soon opening up the corpse of the victim to confirm his external findings.

"It might be a bloody police baton," announced Jonno as he re-entered the mortuary clutching a number of hastily printed colour images he'd had emailed through to the mortuary assistants computer.

Guy paused and examined the pictures. "This is one of mine, yes, I remember now a young Eastern European lad with severe mental health problems took a machete to an officer nearly took his arm off. Sadly it resulted in a good few baton strikes to subdue him and a face full of C/S. It was treated as a death in custody job. He died in the ambulance on the way to hospital following arrest. A load of officers got dragged through it; but they were all cleared in the end. Yeah these photos show the injuries caused by a police baton, we know that, the officers clearly admitted that, but they are surprisingly similar to Mr Lyle's marks and bruises. Sorry Steve but these marks are from an extending baton. I know you can buy batons on the black market and probably online even; but coupled with possible C/S use it makes the use of police equipment a more likely scenario." Surmised Guy staring over his glasses at the already stressed new SIO.

Steve looked over at Elizabeth in despair his eyes searching for some positive news.

"At least there's no Magnum boot prints at the scene," she sniggered.

"That is not funny," answered the perplexed Steve Lawson.

Guy continued through the post-mortem confirming that the impact of the blows to Lyle had some deep repercussions. The top edge of his pelvic bone around the hip had fractured as had the ribs Guy had previously felt as abnormal. Lyle's right kidney had ruptured slightly and Guy confirmed may have been permanently damaged had he survived. Guy carefully dissected the area around the neck.

"There it is look," announced Guy calling his audience in closer. "The hyoid bone, snapped and bent inwards, classic sign of strangulation by hanging. There's your clear cause of death. From what I can see the ligature marks I've now examined up close fit your sequence of events well. I don't think there's any likelihood this guy was killed first then strung up. Was the killer trying to make this look like a suicide?"

"No, no they weren't, I'm sure of that." Confirmed Steve." No, they appear to have strung the victim up firstly to take control of him, beat him into helplessness then force the confession. The end result was just a convenient and quite sadistic way to get him to die when the job was done. There's no real attempt to cover up the beating they'd already given him."

When the post-mortem was complete Steve took a moment to sit down with Elizabeth and Jonno to have a quick forensic strategy meeting. The priority was clear. Get the length of rope the offender would have had to grip tightly examined along with the small piece of hopefully the offenders glove and get a DNA profile if at all possible. The scene fingerprinting was underway but so far negative. Fibre evidence was available but unlikely to help at this stage without anything to compare it to. Despite trying, any sign of footmarks were, as Elizabeth had pointed out, non existent. Mainly due to the carpeting throughout the scene. The possibility of a result from the DNA was still high but unlikely to be forthcoming for a day or two at least. Money was no object on this high profile murder so the highest level of priority was given to identifying the subject forensically.

As Steve left the mortuary on foot he took a short walk giving himself chance to collect his thoughts.

He walked through the quiet park towards the back of Kings Cross station taking in the fresh spring air.

'Must ring poor Anna.' He thought, 'haven't seen her for three days now.'

"Hi darling, I take it you are at work?"

"Yes darling, yes is everything alright Steve?" Asked the confused wife not used to getting routine calls from her missing husband during busy office hours.

"Of course it is I have every media source there is waiting to crucify me for not solving this murder by tea time, a suspect who dresses like a Muslim and a senior MP who is a predatory paedophile that bribes his way out of trouble. Oh and I forgot to mention the Met's senior management seem to think catching murderers is as easy as nicking shop lifters and think I should be stood outside the Old Bailey by now congratulating myself on a job well done." Ranted Steve cynically, knowing Anna was a safe sounding board to vent his frustrations at.

"Don't worry darling, if you can't find out who did this so what. Whoever it is has done society a favour, they deserve a medal not a prison sentence."

"You would say that doing your job, you get to see the real long term impact these bastards have on the poor kids. Sorry Anna Mac's trying to call me, should see you later tonight, love you." Anna just about got to say, "Love you to," before Steve cut the call to answer Mac.

"How's the post mortem going mate," he asked.

"All done, only one surprise," said Steve gingerly knowing neither of them wanted the complication the police baton marks added to the equation.

"Go on tell me," probed Mac.

"It looks like Bernard Lyle was beaten with a police style baton. The marks are identical to library photos of confirmed baton strikes. Normally I would just dismiss it as a baton purchased from one of these nut job martial arts weapon suppliers but the use of C/S and it was C/S, I smelt it, makes this a rather challenging problem."

"Challenging! It's totally fucked up. I've only just managed to put a lid on the media circus. Keep this one quiet for now Steve if it is one of ours I don't want them forewarned we're onto them. Listen I spoke to one of my old mates at what I still know as the National Crime Faculty, the names changed about four times now, but anyway he's done some digging on paedophile murders where confessions are believed to have been forced before death. There are a few out there; but most of them are detected and therefore not linked. All of the suspects in those cases are still well and truly behind bars. There was one however, a teacher back in your old neck of the woods I think Steve. The final report on the job tends to lean towards a probable suicide, but the way the guy wrote his confession on the lounge wall seems a bit unusual…"

"I know," interrupted Steve. "I was one of the bloody FLO's on that one, in fact I found him dead on the night it all kicked off. It's the Richard Wilson job isn't it?"

"Yeah that's the chap, what do you think?"

"I don't know, I'm not sure, but I still think it was a murder we just couldn't find a viable suspect that's all. It was a nightmare trying to get the family to accept it could have been a suicide. I'm going to jump on the tube now, I'll see you at the yard Mac and we'll have a closer look at the similarities."

Steve headed underground, almost forgetting to change tubes at Victoria as he trawled through his memories of Richard Wilson, re living the moment he entered that lounge as a newly appointed detective constable.

Steve and Mac discussed both cases over a very late lunch in the canteen. Mac couldn't help but laugh out load when Steve explained his attack on Richard Wilson's shiny new computer before he and the uniform guys found Wilson dead. Mac agreed Richard Wilson probably didn't commit suicide and could see why the coroner returned an open verdict at the inquest. Whilst there was the possibility of a link between Wilson's death and their current investigations, both men agreed to put it on the back burner for now until some tangible link came to light.

Steve continued to receive updates as the afternoon went on. He made time early evening for a face to face meeting with his FLO Joseph.

"Its even worse up there now sir, press everywhere. I've spoken with Mrs Lyle about releasing a statement to the press, maybe reading it out to them to get shut of them from her driveway. The press office have helped and it's all very bland stuff, I've made a note here for you to check." Jo showed Steve a handwritten draft of what the family would say and agreed it was bland but would help to remove the media vultures.

"I've handed Mrs Lyle the letter of condolence you signed this morning and primed her up for a visit tomorrow if that's still okay?"

"Yes should be fine, later in the afternoon, let's say aim for about 3 pm on their doorstep. Is it just the wife and sons?" Asked Steve.

"Could be his mother as well but she's very pro. I'm also anticipating Lord Lyle will show his face at some time too. I've spoken to the computer lab boys re the laptop we took from Mr Lyle. Jonno has been too busy to chase this up, what with the post mortem and searches. They tell me that the operating system has been divided into two password protected users 'work' and 'personal'. The personal section seems very interesting. This is despite Lyle's attempts to regularly clean it down. He uses a hard drive cleaning software to avoid deleted items being found and the internet history has been regularly washed down. What the idiot didn't do though is delete his cookies. This means the techcos have been able to retrieve a list of regularly visited sights he uses. Although a lot of them are innocent and predictable, they do include one site that's something like schools dating, for kids basically. It's a dating forum and chat facility that connects youngsters at various secondary schools, not the best idea in this day and age. However, using a hard drive image the tech boys have opened this site and as he had Windows set to remember passwords, the user name and password auto populated to let them log in. It appears that, 'Sugardaddy317' has been in regular contact with 'Sassygirl13'. They're still working on the results and hope to secure some cooperation from the European owners of the site to help them out. Hopefully the historic contact they have had will be fully retrievable from their server. I think Bernard Lyle groomed his attacker online. He must have thought his luck was in when 'Sassygirl13' was prepared to chat with someone calling themselves 'Sugardaddy317'. He must have been mightily disappointed when they turned out to be a cold blooded murderer instead. I hope it's okay but I've very subtly asked the two Lyle boys to verify where they were on the night of the murder and they've both given up their own laptops to be checked to assist our enquiries. I really don't think they or anyone linked to the husband had anything to do with this but I suppose you never know. They are all genuinely devastated, not just because this has confirmed their husband's and father's indiscretions, but for the loss of someone that otherwise was a good man and provided well for them." Explained Jo.

"Thank you Jo, very thorough. Did the guys doing Lyle's work colleagues speak with you at all?" Asked Steve not having had an update directly.

"Yes, all very political and pointless it seems. Lots of people happy to say he was a hard working MP and it was right for the leader of the opposition to appoint him into such a position. Not one colleague wanted to admit being a close friend of his or being involved in any way in his social activities. All very safe accounts it seems and unlikely to develop into any meaningful lines of enquiry." Relayed Jo.

"I sort of expected that, have you seen Bashir around here anywhere?"

"He's not at the yard sir, he went up to Gateshead, I assumed you told him to?" Jo said not wanting to get his immediate line manager into trouble.

"No not exactly, I think I said get a team together to go up to Gateshead."

The sniff of a trip out of London for a change had most detectives packed and on the road before you could even physically allocate them their actions. Bashir was no exception and had interpreted Steve's instructions how he wanted to hear them. Steve was in a way actually pleased Bash had made that autonomous decision as it was looking like the most important line of enquiry for now.

"Bash I'm back at the yard you around?" Asked Steve hoping to panic the cheeky detective sergeant.

"Err, no sir, I, I'm still in Gateshead, did you need me back in London?" Bumbled the slightly concerned Bashir knowing he'd been caught out.

"Gateshead who sent you there?" Asked Steve continuing to wind up the poor man.

"Err well you.. well you wanted a team up here and no one else could do it.." Bash paused hearing Steve's chuckles at the other end of the phone.

"Don't panic mate as long as you have got somewhere with young Rosie and her mum I might just authorise your hotel expenses for tonight at least."

"Yes, it's all good governor we made a load of phone calls as we headed up here managed to get the locals to visit the address and pluck Rosie out of that school Graham found. She has been in an ABE video interview all afternoon with her gran as appropriate adult. I've been giving the mum a serious talking to. Turns out Rosie was a wayward teen who ended up excluded from mainstream classes. Like all naughty kids she was rewarded for her bad behaviour with trips out organised by an outward bound charity set up by you know who. That's how she met Bernard Lyle who regularly went along on the trips to help the staff when they took the kids hill walking and camping. Rosie really got into outdoor pursuits and Lyle befriended her. He offered to take her out for days walking with him and his dog outside of these organised events. When she did it always turned out she was the only kid who'd turned up. Lyle would claim the other few kids had fallen ill or dropped out at the last minute for some other reason. Rosie really didn't mind, she had never had a father figure in her life and loved the attention Lyle gave her. Her mum thought the trips she was doing were part of the group activities. To be fair to her mum she supported these trips because Rosie's behaviour improved dramatically, she even focused better on her remedial school work. It was only when Rosie began to suffer from daily sickness and her mother took her to the GP that it all went wrong. The GP asked her about sexual activity fearing the symptoms mirrored morning sickness. He referred them to the Pregnancy Advisory Service and an abortion was the chosen option for young Rosie. You can imagine how this somewhat dysfunctional family unit dealt with the crisis, never considering making a report of the grooming and technical rape to the police. Instead Once the abortion was out of the way, she grounded her wayward daughter and sold the story to the highest bidder. She was chuffed to bits to get the 20 K for the story but even more excited about the call she took from Bernard Lyle 5 days later. The woman's a fucking mercenary boss. Rosie is a mess and back to square one. The thing is she hasn't got it in her to do the harm that was inflicted upon Lyle nor is she resourceful enough to get herself to London from up here. Her gran alibis her for what it's worth along with the mum who denies any involvement in Lyle's murder. We've got phones, an iPad, laptop and car details so we'll try and corroborate all of this, but for what it's worth she had nothing to gain outing him again in such a violent way. Clearly money talks for her."

"What about Rosie's father, I assume he's estranged?" Quizzed Steve.

"Very estranged," replied Bashir. "He died 8 years ago from a heroin overdose."

"Well enjoy the rest of your evening in Newcastle, I assume that's where you have chosen to stay. Of course I expect you all back by tomorrow afternoon, I hope to have the DNA result by then so someones door will be going in." Concluded Steve optimistically.

After updating Mac with the Gateshead results Steve decided there was little more he could do so headed home driving back to Letchworth getting there just after 9 pm.

"Hello stranger I've missed you. I don't even get to see you on TV these days, your old boss Mac Spencer is stealing the limelight. Oh and that MP's wife had some rubbish to read out." Complained Anna as Steve walked into the lounge.

"Been following my jobs on the TV again darling?" Smiled Steve.

"Well you know I like to keep tabs on you. You caught anyone yet?"

"No but I think we'll have some DNA by this time tomorrow, looks like our careful suspect shredded a little bit of their rubber gloves hanging this guy," revealed Steve not thinking.

"Shit how fucking stupid." Remarked Anna, "but what if it's not on the database you wont get anywhere with that will you?"

"Sounds to me like your siding with the fellow that did this?" Observed Steve light heartedly.

"Well no, but he did rid the world of a horrible paedophile and corrupt politician. I think his wife actually sounded quite relieved when she spoke to the press today."

"I'm not so sure Anna, anyway enough about work I fancy a glass of wine shall I open a bottle of red?"

"Yes please darling can I have my special glass please?"

Steve uncorked a bottle of Pinot Nior pouring almost half into Anna's miniature goldfish bowl of a 'special glass', taking a more modest measure himself. The two of them settled on the couch and said very little. They just enjoyed the comfort of each others embrace, reminiscing about the last time they shared a bottle of red on their last cruise prompting plans to book another one. Steve appreciated the chance to unwind and forget about his life in the murder capital of the UK for just a few hours.

The next morning Steve was pleased to see most of his team in the briefing room at the yard, with very few additions this time and certainly no unwelcome senior officers. Steve himself had received most of the significant updates from various members of his team over the previous 24 hours, but it was important they were shared with everyone else. There were some less significant lines of enquiry that Steve hadn't been briefed on, but none of them were that positive.

The search teams had worked tirelessly throughout the day and evening. They hadn't found any incapacitant spray cans of any description and the only possible weapons they found were a broken walking stick and short length of scaffold pole. Neither likely to be the weapon they were looking for.

The CCTV showing the suspect's escape route onto the district line at Westminster was now clear. Unfortunately there were so many identical passengers getting on and off at that very busy time that it was virtually impossible to work out where the suspect alighted. It was also pointed out that beyond Hornchurch station some of the carriages become virtually empty so if the suspect was still onboard they could easily have removed their disguise and walked off with it tucked away in a bag, just looking like any other commuter. It was a needle in a haystack scenario and unlikely to evidentially link anyone to the murder.

Swabs had confirmed the presence of C/S on Lyle's face and Steve felt certain the weapons used were going to turn out to be police issue.

"I want a priority action raised to identify how many losses of personal protection equipment the Met has had in recent years, especially where C/S and batons went at the same time. Better include the City Police and BTP in that as well. When he gets back from his holiday up north I want Bashir to tie in with professional standards and identify someone who he trusts to share our concerns with. Just in case they have any kind of anti corruption investigations ongoing that links in to what we have." Instructed Steve.

Steve asked the entire team to return for a briefing at 18:00 hours with a promise of the DNA results before then. Steve was hanging his hat on the chance of an early arrest based on the faith he had in Elizabeth's confident prediction of a full DNA profile from the items she and Jonno had carefully seized.

With Steve's team briefed and sent out completing their actions Steve went back to his office in Hendon and sat down with his office manager to get an overview of the actions currently raised and review the priority ones still outstanding. Steve was amazed how many actions had been completed in such a short space of time. Steve then spent some time speaking with Graham who had been trawling crime reports both for attacks on sex offenders and crimes committed in the apartments where the murder took place. Apart from a disturbance involving a high end escort and theft by one of the now ex cleaning staff the venue was clear. A number of suspected and confirmed sex offenders had been attacked over the last year but in the main they were old perverts living in local communities. They had been the subject of long term verbal abuse and vandalism due to their demeanour and general behaviour before some thug had a pop at them. Graham intended to widen his search to cover all 43 force areas in England and Wales, but this would take some time.

As Steve sat down at his desk and ripped open a pack of tuna sandwiches and a bag of ready salted crisps he was abruptly disturbed as Elizabeth marched into the room.

"I'll start with the good news," she said.

"Go on," requested Steve taking a large bite of his lunch whilst he still could.

"We have a full DNA profile from both the glove and one of the pieces of rope where the offender would have gripped it tightly."

"Good, that's good news yeah?"

"And the profile hits against the database."

"Good, and..." Said Steve getting frustrated by the drip feeding of facts taking another chunk out of his sandwich.

"The hit is against another crime scene rather than an identified suspect..." Elizabeth paused. "The crime scene for the murder of Costas Salvador!"

Steve began to choke on his lunch. "Sorry what?" He asked clearing his throat.

"The same woman who killed poor Costas has killed Bernard Lyle, I can't believe it, one more victim and we've got a serial killer Steve." Suggested Elizabeth based on a definition that describes a serial killer as a person who murders three or more people over a period of more than 30 days, with a 'cooling off' period between each murder, and whose motivation for killing is largely based on psychological gratification.

"I think we may already have one. Mac reminded me of an old unsolved case I was involved with in Westhampton. A teacher who abused young female pupils and was made to confess it all before having both his wrists sliced vertically in an identical way to how Costas was finished off."

"Shit Steve you better call Mac, we need to find this woman before she kills again."

That was Mac's thoughts exactly when he and Steve sat in his office and discussed the new investigative strategy.

"I'm bringing in our old team to make a Category 'A' murder team up," decided Mac. "I'm going to declare a confirmed link between Salvador and Lyle but also bring in the Wilson job as a possible third link. Basically you and all your key individuals are going to work closely with their opposite numbers on this one. I will be the officer in overall charge with our initial aim to confirm the link to Wilson's murder. The way I see it, the more jobs we link the better chance we have of finding this suspect. Ryan Shaw is the SIO running the old team out east now, do you know him?"

"Yes quite well he was on my SIO's course, he's a fast track guy isn't he. Young bloke but very bright made DCI in just eight years?" Recalled Steve.

"Yes that's right. I've called him he's got his team heading up here for a 7 p.m. briefing. Get your team back to Hendon as well and we'll get everyone briefed up tonight. Ryan tells me Lisa Kelk is still on the old team, a DS now so I'm going to get her coordinating family liaison for all three jobs, it's going to be vital to make sure we don't treat any family differently from any other, especially when Lyle's lot seem to have a direct line into our senior management via a few select politicians. Oh and remember Bob Fenson?"

"Yeah he was one of the DC's on the old team," Steve couldn't forget him. He was a man who probably should have retired by now but just didn't want to go.

"Bob's still there, surprisingly," confirmed Mac. "What he doesn't know about CCTV nobody does. I'm going to borrow him to work his magic and oversee all the CCTV enquiries. Elizabeth has been seconded on a permanent basis for the immediate future to link everything in; especially with the Westhamptonshire guys. She's going to review what we can do with any new techniques on the older exhibits. I think we're in a strong position and you are going to be vital for this linked enquiry, you are probably the most knowledgeable officer we could get when it comes to an intimate knowledge of all three jobs. I've got to brief the commander and he's going to speak to the Deputy Chief Constable in Westhants. Hopefully we'll have details of their appointed SIO before the briefing."

Steve set about updating Bashir so he could ring round the enquiry teams and cancel the 6 p.m. meet at the yard getting everyone back to Hendon for 7. Bashir was excited at the prospect of hunting a serial killer down. Contrary to popular fiction it was in fact very rare to have linked crimes in real life. There were plenty a murderer that SIO's would stake money on being potential serial killers, but most were caught soon after their first offence so never went on to achieve such status. It was on the bucket list of most homicide detectives to be involved in a high profile linked series of murders and of course be responsible for solving the crimes. Steve was feeling the pressure, his head was spinning as images of the three crime scenes flashed through his mind. Foolishly he questioned himself, why didn't he link Wilson and Salvador and insist Mac looked at them both together back at the time? Steve got a grip of himself 'don't be stupid' he told himself, the only distinct similarity was the precise vertical cut to the wrist, the confession is the link to Lyle not Salvador. There was no reason to link them before not without some forensic evidence to back the link up. 'Shit the Magnum boot prints around Wilson's bed, were they even lifted?' Thought Steve. So much to consider, Steve began making notes in his day book and deciding on how he'd structure the evenings briefing.

"Is that DCI Steve Lawson?" Queried the voice at the end of Steve's desk phone.

"Yes he answered".

"Do you know who this is?" Asked the voice sternly.

Steve recognised the voice but just couldn't place it and suddenly concerned it was a senior officer he replied cautiously, "No Sir?"

Laughter roared down the phone. "It's Andy Porter you twat, don't fucking sir me, I maybe a DCI as well now but it was you lot all jumping ship to the Met a few years back that gave them no choice but to promote me."

"Andy, its great to hear from you mate, don't tell me you've copped the Wilson job now?"

"Yes, I'll get to see you Met boys in action now, I'm coming down to Hendon tomorrow morning for 9, meeting you, a Ryan Shaw with your boss Mac Spencer and one of your crime scene managers."

"That's great news Andy, what a team eh," said Steve.

"Yeah, I'm happy but listen I've got just 11 months left before I retire mate and I'd like nothing more than to be visiting Eileen Taylor before that day comes and telling her we've caught her son's killer." Stated Andy.

"I will happily join you when that day comes and it will mate we're close, we're going to get this bitch. Very soon..."

Steve and Andy exchanged mobile numbers and agreed to meet for a coffee if Andy made it down to Hendon a little earlier. Steve was excited and reassured by the news that his shrewd old friend would be joining him. There would be a lot of pressure to catch this killer before they realised the police were onto them and disappeared somewhere out of reach.

"Ryan how you doing?" Greeted Steve as the familiar face walked into his office. "Coffee?"

"Please mate, black no sugar."

Steve quickly knocked up a couple of brews and returned into the office. Ryan had inherited the undetected murder of Costas Salvador only a few months ago following Mac's promotion. Steve was immensely impressed with the depth of knowledge Ryan had about the case. Ryan was a sharp intellectual man who would read documents in detail and rapidly analyse their content. He was, unlike some, very worthy of being selected for accelerated promotion and Steve was grateful for the kind of precise input Ryan was capable of giving.

Steve briefed Ryan about the current case and then went through what he knew about how the Richard Wilson job had been left.

"So how did a female suspect manage to take on Wilson and get him to write a confession before drugging him and slicing open his wrists?" Asked Ryan.

"With hindsight and given the possible link to the Salvador murder, I'd say with a persuasive sawn off shotgun in the first instance."

"Makes sense yes, so why the switch to C/S for Lyle, why not just threaten him with the shotgun?" Probed Ryan further.

"Well, we think the shotgun only had limited ammo with it, maybe it's a stolen weapon, we don't know. There's also a good chance that in the years between murders the suspect got rid of it, maybe they bottled it after we went public with the facts re the false accusation at Akbar's child abuse trial?"

"Possible yes, but why are these specific men being targeted? I know they were all alleged child abusers but its only Lyle's murder where this fact was revealed publicly before he was killed. What is the link between the killer and the victims? Apart from Lyle all the other victims were arrested as a result of the allegations weren't they?" Asked Ryan piecing together the three crimes.

"Yes, but in two different force areas," pointed out Steve.

"And our offender had access to details of these arrests either through proximity to the suspects or victims of the alleged abuse maybe. They might have been colleagues at Wilson's school, or friends of the victim but this doesn't seem to work for Costas Salvador and young Ali? This is confusing." Surmised Ryan as he tried to work through a theory.

"Unless of course our suspect is a police officer with access to the Police National Computer and trawls it like Google to trace child abusers who have got away with their crimes. Arrest records would show this nationwide?" Added Steve.

"Maybe yes but something doesn't quite add up are we missing crimes somewhere? We need to look for other links mate." Concluded Ryan.

Steve agreed and confirmed Mac was already speaking with the Serious Case Analysis guys and looking to enlist a nationally accredited profiler to assist with the overall coordination of all three murders and any more that may come to light.

The two murder teams were both shocked and excited to hear of the linked offences. Baring a few comments about Westhamptonshire detectives coming to London on their tractors, the two Met teams were enthusiastic about working with their county colleagues. The carrot cruncher jokes soon died down when Mac explained how Steve was one of the FLO's on the Wilson job and had himself been a 'carrot' before transferring to the Met.

Initially the emphasis would be to blitz the outstanding actions on the Bernard Lyle murder using both teams. Specific officers from the Lyle murder in the roles of exhibits, CCTV, FLO and intelligence would be matched to those now appointed for the Salvador Murder and if the link was confirmed with some tangible evidence, the Wilson murder too. A press strategy was to go on hold until confirmation of the triple link was made. All officers briefed were to maintain the strictest confidence, not even sharing their knowledge with other murder teams let alone any other department. Mac's theory was that once the suspect knew the police had linked the crimes they would know the end was in sight. Any evidence they still had anywhere near them would disappear as might they if they weren't brave or stupid enough to front out an arrest.

Steve went home late that night and made his excuses to Anna about being tired and not being in the mood to chat even though Anna was as keen as ever to hear how Steve's investigation was going. Steve knew how much he and Mac had emphasised to the teams not to discuss the case, so regardless of the trust Steve had in his dear wife he told her he wouldn't be able to say much about the job until they made a press release in a few days time. Anna was frustrated but understood.

"Andy you old bastard what a small fucking world this is." Greeted Steve as he shook the hand of his old colleague in the large police canteen the following morning.

"Its good to see you mate, what an interesting turn of events this is, you couldn't make it up could you."

Andy explained how Richard Wilson's death was boxed up and had been sat collecting dust in the force's archive store ever since the inquest. His family had finally accepted that no new lines of enquiry were going to come to light and they just had to get on with their lives again. Of course Andy had not contacted them about this development yet.

"There's no way I'm giving Eileen false hope until I'm 100% satisfied this is linked. You know where we got to Steve, there is still not a scrap of evidence that will ID the suspect so I really need to hear all about these new jobs and take it from there."

Steve suggested they grab a bacon sandwich and coffee and wait until they sit down with Mac, Ryan and Elizabeth before they go through it in detail. Andy explained how he'd got a new Detective Sergeant coming down for midday along with an exhibits officer and FLO so they could start to tie in with their opposite numbers on the other two jobs.

Elizabeth had prepared photo packs for both scenes and Mac had copies of the summary of evidence for each of the London murders. Andy had brought down three copies of the detailed report with graphics and photos that were prepared for the coroner in Richard Wilson's inquest. The team of experts laid everything out in the conference room and began working their way through the facts of each case.

"Footprints! Shit I forgot about the footprints we found at Richard Wilsons house," shouted Steve as he stared at the crime scene photos. "Did we ever get anywhere with them Andy I can't remember?"

"No even with the work the SOCO's did. They couldn't enhance them enough to even eliminate them against the uniform officers boots." Answered Andy.

"Yeah they're on carpet, you would really struggle even these days," added Elizabeth looking at the scene photography. "But they're definitely Magnum boots though."

The group continued their comparison and focused next on the weapons used.

"So Andy just confirm for me, apart from the long deliberate slices to Wilson's wrists did he have any other injuries?" Queried Mac.

"No apart from the heavy dose of ketamine that can't have kicked in until he'd finished scrawling his confession on the living room wall. We think he must have been threatened into submission, so the sawn off shotgun scenario fits well if these are linked. The ketamine would have had to have been timed to start taking effect in time for the suspect to order Wilson to climb the stairs to his bedroom before he collapsed on the bed in a state of semi-consciousness. It's then the suspect would have been able to kill him as he drifted into a helpless stupor. There would have been a lot of arterial bleeding and death would not have taken long. I think the suspect just watched him die and left. No doubt with some of that arterial blood on them somewhere. We just didn't find the right suspect at the time."

"Have a look at the workshop photos and the sequence of events Elizabeth has marked up. You'll see some serious injuries have been inflicted before the final long slice to the wrist was made to finish him off," pointed out Mac.

"That's pretty serious torture," Ryan noted. "I haven't ever seen such a deliberate mutilation of someone's hands before, I think this was symbolic in some way. Especially when this man had supposedly been touching children."

"Fucking hell, shit!" Swore Steve. "I've seen something like that before, so have you Andy."

"Have I? Who, where?" Andy asked looking on in anticipation.

"Old Man Fraser, the Wheatsheaf. He was a fucking nonse too, it was you who told me that Andy. Didn't you see the photos of the sandwich toaster griddle thing?"

"Yes of course, you're right," Andy answered looking shocked as he thought on.

"What, what are you saying Steve?" Quizzed Mac.

"I think we have four murders here:

1996 - Joseph Fraser - Pub Landlord, Chisham, Westhamptonshire.

1999 - Richard Wilson - Teacher, Westhampton.

2006 - Costas Salvador - Builder, Tower Hamlets, London.

2013 - Bernard Lyle - Politician, Westminster, London.

All four murders unsolved, their victims alleged or proven paedophiles, all four killed quite sadistically and a number of common features crossing two or more offences."

Andy sat nodding as Steve relayed the facts. Ryan and Elizabeth looked on in stoney silence amazed at what was being revealed, Mac being the first to break the silence.

"So who's the SIO for the Landlord murder Andy?"

"He's long gone," answered Andy, "I'm still doing the FLO work on that job, but only very remotely for a daughter in

Australia. I suppose if our boss was asked to appoint a new SIO he'd choose me, after all he's only got two DCI's to choose from in his major crime team. We're not quite the Met you know."

"Fine, how soon can you get the papers together and get an exhibits, officer and new FLO down here for the pub murder so we can hit the ground running?" Asked Mac.

"Later today if I nip out now and make a few calls. Is that okay?"

"Go for it Andy."

As Andy left the room Ryan, who'd clearly been pondering over the facts being discussed, piped up.

"So you've just linked all four just like that even though they span two parts of the UK over 70 miles apart?" Questioned the analytical young DCI.

"Yes, just two parts of the country and a full seven years between murder 2 and 3. I think its simple, the suspect must have moved down this way during that period in their life. Think about it how many people do you know who now live in London who aren't actually born and bred here. The draw of the capital brings the best and the worse of us in, eh Steve."

"Yes Mac." Interjected Steve hoping he was in 'the best' category. "I understand how sceptical you are Ryan and that's good for this enquiry. You are right to question this, but I am now convinced the four crimes are linked and you will be in time I'm sure. What I haven't said yet is I was in uniform when Fraser was murdered and was the first officer on the scene. 3 years later I was conducting some routine witness enquiries surrounding a rape when I found Wilson so I was in from day one there also. As you know I was the exhibits officer on the Salvador murder and a few days ago I walked into the scene of Lyle's murder. The scenes although very different in some ways just feel linked. The logic and method of this killer is imprinted on each crime in so many ways. It's difficult to explain but I know I'm right, we're hunting a serial killer here."

Andy re-entered the room purposefully with a slight smile on his face.

"Right I've got a new FLO and the original exhibits officer Tim Knight heading down here now. Tim went off to Special Branch to see out his last few years but their boss is happy to release him. He's got a fantastic memory of the Fraser murder, it was one of his biggest jobs. He has just reminded me they had a clear Magnum boot print at the scene. He's still adamant it must have been yours Steve. I told him he'd be able to challenge you again in person later. He soon retracted his gripe when I told him why. He remembered then you had worn some new boots when you found Fraser and they were some expensive make and not Magnums. So Elizabeth he's going to be bringing the original lifts of that footmark down with him today. How soon can you match that up to the workshop boot marks?"

"I'll get the specialist at the lab put on standby, they can usually give a provisional verbal result in a few hours. So Mac you might have your link confirmed sooner than you think."

"Great," answered Mac. "Right lets talk families and media. Steve you are due to meet Mrs Lyle and her sons I believe this afternoon at the family home. You better not cancel that, but the timing kind of forces our hand a little. I will brief the commander and the commissioner hopefully around midday. My FLO strategy is that we get out to all four families today and give them the heads up about the link, the resurrection of their investigations and the media strategy we intend to use. I am going to persuade the senior management to hold any press release for at least another 24 hours to give us some breathing space. Now I know Costas Salvador's family are as good as gold and back in Portugal in any case. The Lyle clan are happy to stay out of the media limelight given the circumstances, but what about Wilson and Fraser's family Andy?"

"Mac, believe me they are equally as sensible and will be happy to keep the news tight for a few days at least. Anyway Old Man Fraser only has his daughter still alive and she's down under so that's a telephone job, I'll make that call."

"Right what I am going to do is give the media notice of a press conference in relation to Bernard Lyle's murder and schedule it for tomorrow afternoon. I will tell them to expect a significant update but no more than that. We'll get them into the auditorium at the yard. I'll front it out and introduce you all as my Senior Investigating Officers. I will outline the key facts of all the crimes and appeal for names against the opportunity to eliminant any suspects the public suggest; you know the sort of thing. We'll get a single number set up and staff the call centre for that here at Hendon. Can you clear this with your chief constable Andy and she can talk it over with the commissioner if she needs to?" Instructed Mac.

"Sounds fine, I'm sure there won't be an issue, I'll wait until you've got the ear of the commissioner later today."

The five of them spent the next couple of hours drafting out the facts of the four cases and from their own experience a basic profile for the suspect. Before he knew it Steve found himself sat in the passenger seat of Jo's car heading out to Oxfordshire to meet some high profile family members.

"Celia it's Jo we're at your gates now." Jo had struck up a good rapport with Bernard Lyle's wife and had a paparazzi free method of driving straight through an opening set of gates rather than having to get out and press the intercom.

Steve could feel the zoom lenses of the press bearing down on him as he and Jo approached the grand front door of the Lyle residence. Of course they weren't that interested in Mrs Lyle's FLO or even Steve no they wanted to report on the opposition party leader visiting Bernard Lyle's widow and ambush him for comment as he left.

"Hello Mrs Lyle, my names Detective Chief Inspector Steven Lawson, I am one of two senior detectives leading this investigation. May I offer my sincere condolences for the loss of your husband." Announced Steve as he was greeted at the door. Wondering why he had felt the need to use his full Christian name 'Steven' just because he was meeting the upper classes.

Steve and Jo were shown into the Georgian house and taken to the front room. There Steve was introduced to Conner and Oliver Lyle, two sons who were clearly close to their mother and a rather immature 18 and 20 years of age. They remained very quiet other than to offer to prepare the tea for everyone. Steve heard a slight commotion from the front drive and stood up to look out of the veiled windows.

"That will be Bernard's mother and father. I thought I'd invite them to join us so you could meet them Mr Lawson."

"Very good idea Mrs Lyle, thank you and please call me Steve."

"As long as you stop calling me Mrs Lyle," responded the surprisingly calm woman, who was clearly still very mournful inside.

Steve stood again as Celia introduced Steve to Bernard Lyle's parents, Lord and Lady Lyle.

"Sir, madam," addressed Steve as he shook both of their hands. "I am so terribly sorry to meet you in these circumstances." Steve had never met a Lord before. I suppose this one was not unlike what he would expect. A very old looking man slightly frail but only in his early 70's Steve guessed. His wife, Lady Lyle was a dignified looking lady with the appearance of someone who enjoyed a leisurely life on a country estate somewhere close by Steve assumed.

"I'm visiting you all today for a number of reasons. Firstly to introduce myself and explain that Detective

Superintendent Mac Spencer is the second senior detective leading this investigation. You will have seen him speaking to the media during the early appeals we made. You have met Jo obviously. He gets updates directly from me and Mac so he can make sure you know everything that's going on. I will visit you periodically during the investigation and I am happy to call you if there's anything you ever want to discuss with me directly."

"What can you tell us about the possibility Bernard's murder is linked to other similar offences Detective Chief Inspector?" Interrupted Lord Lyle ambushing Steve with a hint of leaked inside information clearly caused by senior politicians badgering the Major and the Met's most senior officers for any kind of update.

"Thank you sir, yes that is one of the important matters I'm here to discuss," responded Steve calmly but cursing inside at this privileged man's ability to throw Steve off of course.

"You will know from Jo's last update that we have identified that Bernard was murdered by a female who left traces of her DNA at the scene. You will also know that this DNA is not identified to anyone on the criminal database, however a secondary search that we conduct is to compare it to any other DNA samples that are also unidentified, obtained from other crime scenes. The DNA does match 100% to a suspects blood found at a murder in 2006 in Tower Hamlets. A man named Costas Salvador had at the time been accused of abusing a child and we think murdered for this reason."

Steve deliberately didn't mention Costas' proven innocence at that point for fear of opening a whole pointless discussion about Bernard Lyle being wrongly accused. Steve knew he definitely wasn't.

"So this woman has killed twice?" Asked Celia.

"That's what we know, but we have gone further than that. Now the DNA link does not span any other offences at this time, but other slightly more circumstantial forensic evidence links Bernard's murder to two other offences in 1999 and 1996 that occurred in Westhamptonshire. These are also unsolved crimes and involve a teacher and a pub landlord. The teacher had two allegations of inappropriate conduct against female pupils made against him and some time after the pub landlord was killed historic allegations of his child abuse were discovered. Despite their history neither man was ever convicted of child sex offences."

Steve paused, the room was silent, both Conner and Oliver had tears rolling down their cheeks. The families realisation that Bernard Lyle had been just another paedophile victim of some vigilante serial killer was an immense shock to them all. Steve could only imagine the raft of thoughts that must have been going through their heads, not least the media circus that would now go on for months.

Lord Lyle broke the silence.

"So how are you going to catch this damn psychopath then Mr Lawson?"

Calmly Steve explained the investigative strategy. "Mac Spencer will hold a press conference tomorrow afternoon at New Scotland Yard. It is vital that all four families have been properly updated before this takes place. I am afraid we need the public's help to identify this suspect. We have a good spectrum of evidence and will make a speedy arrest once the person is identified. However to do that we will need to tell people what we know and make a national appeal. Someone will know this woman and when they are faced with the dates, locations and full circumstances. They will realise their friend, colleague or even family member could be the killer. When we make these kind of appeals and confirm we have DNA to eliminate anyone wrongly identified, we find people are more willing to come forward."

Steve spent some time answering further questions and reassuring the Lyle family that a very large scale enquiry was underway. Steve fully anticipated Lord Lyle would now go around him and ask the Met's most senior management for further information. However he didn't expect him to go anywhere near the press with what he had just been told so that was fine.

As Steve and Jo drove back into London his thoughts turned to the families of Costas Salvador and Richard Wilson. How would they all take the news of this unbelievable link? Steve knew that Lisa had travelled out to Portugal at short notice to speak to Costas' sister in person, his mother had sadly passed away not knowing who killed her son. Lisa would from now on coordinate family liaison for all four families making sure updates were simultaneous where possible. Steve was reassured that in his role as Westhants SIO for both murders Andy would be personally visiting his families despite new full time FLO's being put in place. Of course Fraser's wife had also passed away, but his daughter Patricia was still around in Australia. Andy would probably wait for an arrest before he flew out to speak with her face to face.

Back in his office Steve set about discussing the current new investigation with Bashir. Obtaining updates on all of the high priority actions and forensic submissions. The 'Sassygirl13' internet traffic had now been traced to a single unregistered 3G SIM operated from an IMEI that came back to a Samsung Note smartphone also unregistered. The top ups had been made by vouchers purchased in cash from a small newsagent in E1 on three separate occasions. Steve concluded that the suspect obviously knew this place was run by a man who barely spoke English. The shop was such a chaotic small business that CCTV and staff records were never on the agenda. Bashir pointed out that just because the top up vouchers were used at a specific time and date there was no way of telling when they were actually purchased. The phone itself could have been purchased anywhere, even second hand, enquiries with the manufacturer and supplier were still ongoing.

"Anything positive on that smart phone Bash or what?" Asked a frustrated Steve.

"Yes gov the cell siting... Graham has obtained the entire usage and movement of the phone. When it was switched on, which wasn't too often, it was cell sited. Generally it went from central London out east occasionally and back into central London before it was switched off. However on one occasion it was cell sited at Kings Cross at 17:34 hours a few weeks ago and the subsequent hits, before it is again switched off, show it possibly on a train towards Cambridge. There's eight possible stops between the switch off point and Cambridge. We're doing what we can with a historic CCTV trawl, but this was a main commuter train so it's packed. We also have some options re ticket purchased and season ticket card holders but that will take months to sift through."

"Hang on a minute Bash got to take this call it's Andy Porter the Westhants SIO," interrupted Steve.

"Hello mate you back out in the countryside now me duck," joked Steve using an old colloquial term familiar to Westhamptonshire.

"Yes mate the air is clear and the people actually smile occasionally up here still. Listen do you want my significant update or not you piss taking old bastard." Said Andy.

"Go on."

"Tim reminded me about the work they did on the gloves he took off the plumber who cleared the toilets at the Wheatsheaf. It was real pioneering work that our head of forensic science has spearheaded now across the UK. Basically they use a gel lifting technology to fill the retrieved gloves and can, if successful, populate the internal fingerprints left by the wearer. These gel lifts are then set and used to reproduce the wearers fingerprints. They only had partial success with the wet marigolds from the Wheatsheaf, but do have on record a set of partial prints. I never got briefed into this at the time probably because the prints didn't hit on the National database and haven't since. However when I found out today from Tim that he had these I put him in touch with Elizabeth and he emailed them down to your fingerprint bureau. Anyway one of them matches the partial print you have at the builders workshop. These crimes are definitely linked and Fraser is victim number one for sure. We just need to find out who knew all four of our victims were alleged sex offenders." Revealed Andy.

"Shit mate this is for real. I just can't get my head away from the police officer angle. Have you briefed Mac yet?"

"No not yet, you can update him if you like, that's if you are back at Hendon and near his office?"

"No problem I'm at Hendon now, I'll be here for a while yet." Confirmed Steve.

"Thanks Steve don't you go neglecting that wife of yours though, Anna wasn't it?" Recalled Andy.

"Don't you worry Andy, she'll be tucked up back home in Letchworth by now watching Eastenders in peace for a change."

"Okay mate take it easy, see you at the yard tomorrow lunchtime for a spot of the Met Police canteen's finest cuisine."

"At least we still have canteens," answered Steve having the last word remembering how Westhamptonshire Police were starting to close police canteens even as far back as when Steve transferred.

Steve went in to brief Mac to find him equally as upbeat sipping coffee with Ryan.

"Steve come in, how were the Lyle's, hard work I bet?" Mac asked.

"Not really, his wife Celia is very sensible. Lord Lyle was exactly how I imagined he would be, probably more concerned about the family name than the demise of his only son. Anyway they have the brief and I'm confident they are still on board with our media strategy."

Steve updated Mac about the fingerprint evidence confirming the link. Mac was now prepared to put his neck on the line and confirm the four murders were the work of a single female offender. Mac suggested the three SIO's and he get together about an hour before the 2 p.m. press conference. They would finalise the draft of what he was going live with at that point.

It was gone eleven by the time Steve pulled up on his driveway. The bedroom lights were still on so Anna must have waited up for him.

"You still up darling?" Observed Steve as he walked into the bedroom to find Anna vigorously tapping away on her laptop.

She looked up and closed the lid. "Yeah, just looking at some work stuff that's all."

"Everything okay?" Asked Steve detecting something might be bothering his wife.

"Yeah, yes, it's just work. We are in the middle of discussing our upgrade work for The Child-Line call centre, it just really annoys me that we rely on funding from the charity alone to do this. There just isn't enough to do the job properly, but the chances of getting any government funding are zero. They're too busy worrying about one of their own being outed as one of the bastards that makes Child-Line necessary." Ranted a somewhat annoyed Anna.

"You're working too hard darling. I know you are one of the bosses now but you can't change the world," reassured Steve as he stroked his wife's head lovingly.

"So are you, where have you been, what's going on with that MP's murder?"

"It's complicated, the last 24 hours have been a roller coaster ride. I can't say too much but it looks like this murder is linked to some others, maybe even ones back in Westhants in the 90's when we used to live there."

"What, how can you say they're linked. It doesn't make sense, you can't link them surely." Commented a confused and still slightly wound up Anna.

"All will be revealed tomorrow afternoon. Mac is going to go public on the facts at a press conference, watch it if you're interested, I'll be there, I just don't have a speaking part. It will be going out live at 2 p.m. have you got a TV in your office?"

"Yes, but I think I'll work from home tomorrow, I could do with a day away from the office to finalise this report."

"Okay darling I better get some sleep I'm going to have to leave at 6.30 if I'm driving in again."

The two of them cuddled up together in bed for what turned out to be an unsettled nights sleep. Steve wasn't sure if he was restless or Anna. In any case when he woke again to the sound of his alarm clock he concluded that they both needed a break from work and hoped the press conference would have the desired effect and result in a speedy arrest.

Steve checked in on his now much larger enquiry team first thing. He just had time to get the bullet points surrounding each line of enquiry. The most significant update came from DC Bob Fenson. He'd been drafted in to assist with the new CCTV and make comparisons to what he had discovered during the Salvador murder.

"I have completed some viewing of the TFL CCTV, but it's not compatible with this system yet so I can't play it in here. I've viewed it at the tech lab though and I can tell you it's all about height. I did a load of work on that Tower Hamlet's estate before Governor as you will remember. I have our suspect at around 5'10" tall. Now the offences are linked I have used that formula to eliminate all of the covered women leaving the District Line train at the stations where woman wearing a niqab are seen. You see without trying to sound discriminatory, most Asian woman are shorter than 5'10". So my trusted assistants have measured key points at each of the relevant station ticket barriers. I have checked the height of all of the covered individuals we previously see and I have eliminated them all. Therefore I strongly suspect our suspect must have de-robed and got off at either Elm Park, Hornchurch, Upminster Bridge or Upminster. I have a total of eleven females doing that all close to the height range of the suspect. Even better than that though it's not until Upminster that one lone blonde woman gets off an otherwise empty carriage. Its pure speculation but I think she could be our suspect."

"That's some piece of work Bob," congratulated Steve, "but as you say it is speculation at the moment albeit a very educated guess and worthy of some high priority work. Get back down the lab after the briefing and get that lot packaged up, footage, stills and a report covering the elimination process. If you can get that done in time for tomorrows briefing we will come up with a media strategy surrounding how we release that?"

"I'll try gov."

"Good, if Mac okays it we might consider asking the public to ID this blonde, but for now we'll hold it back. With a bit of luck we may get some promising calls as a result of today's press conference and be able to keep the CCTV in our back pocket. If this blonde is our killer it will be great to be able to drop the stills in front of her once she's arrested on interview."

Steve continued briefing his team about how he wanted the team to be in a position to respond to the anticipated calls following the press appeal.

Steve was shattered and still running on adrenaline as he ploughed through the central London traffic on his way to New Scotland Yard. As expected several news crews were set up opposite that famous revolving sign. Speculation about what they expected to hear was rife. The suggestions being broadcast in the preamble to the live news conference were frustratingly accurate. 'Someone had leaked something already,' thought Steve as he carefully passed the reporters from behind the cameras.

"You look about as tired as I feel Andy," remarked Steve as he sat down to eat with his old friend.

"You're lucky I'm here at all. If it wasn't for the old lady who woke me up on the train at Euston I'd be halfway back to Birmingham by now." He laughed.

Andy still had concerns about the linking of Richard Wilson's murder being purely circumstantial.

"Evidence of similar fact." Asserted Steve. "When we get this killer on the sheet with the evidence we have they'll have to plead guilty to murder, surely."

"Manslaughter Steve, manslaughter. This one's got a screw loose you wait and see." Andy responded.

"Fucking pessimist," cursed Steve.

"Realist," corrected Andy.

"What you two arguing about?" Asked Mac as he and Ryan joined the table.

"Diminished responsibilities," answered Andy.

"Okay I'll accept your plea Andy, what you done now?" Joked Mac.

"Caused the Chief Constable of Westhamptonshire Police a world of stress." Replied Andy smiling to himself.

Andy went on to explain how he'd spent over two hours in the Chief Constable's office that morning trying to justify his intention to strip the force of its handful of experienced detectives, spend a fortune in expenses housing them in London and go public with the failings of his small county force who needed the Met to detect their historic unsolved murders.

"Oh and did I mention one of those murders we wrote off as a suicide!" He concluded.

"So you had a good morning then Andy," Ryan added.

The four men continued the light hearted banter as they ate their lunch. Then they reconvened in one of the side conference rooms for their final scrum down before the press conference.

Steve had never seen the auditorium so packed with people and camera gear. The small stage area was set with the usual corporate Metropolitan Police frontage clad on one long table adorned with bottles of mineral water, desk mounted microphones and five chairs laid out behind it. One central for Mac the main speaker flanked to his right by the commander and Ryan and tactfully to his immediate left by Andy with Steve relieved to find himself on the outside left and presumably on the edge of any camera view.

2 o'clock came and they went live. The commander spoke first announcing he had a significant development to reveal in relation to the investigation of Bernard Lyle's murder and revealed that it had been linked to three previous homicides. The commander introduced Mac as

his Senior Investigating Officer in overall command and handed over the floor to him.

"My name is Detective Superintendent Mac Spencer. I want to speak to you today about four separate murder enquiries that we suspect a single female offender is responsible for."

There were a few gasps from within the room and the sound of keyboards tapping rapidly updating editors by email or posting live Twitter feeds. Mac paused, momentarily waiting for the room to settle before continuing.

"Today I am asking for the public's help to identify the woman responsible for these attacks. I am going to spend some time providing details of these four murders and the evidence we have obtained. Hopefully someone out there will know this woman and have the courage to contact us in confidence with a name. I am told that you will be able to see the dedicated phone number on your screens. My detectives will be staffing this number twenty four hours a day to take your calls.

We are investigating the murder of Bernard Lyle MP. This occurred only a few days ago.

We have linked that murder to the murder of self-employed builder Costas Salvador that occurred in 2006 in Tower Hamlets, London.

Prior to that we believe the same woman murdered school teacher Richard Wilson in Westhampton. That murder took place back in 1999.

The earliest linked murder we have now identified is that of Joseph Fraser, an elderly man who was a pub landlord in a village called Chisham that is in Westhamptonshire. That murder took place in 1996.

Each man had at some stage been accused of sex offences against children. I have to emphasis that not one of them had been prosecuted for any offence and it is proven without doubt that Costas Salvador was wrongly accused in lieu of the real offender who is currently serving a lengthy prison sentence."

Mac had felt strongly about adding that comment to the script he had prepared, not just for the memory of poor Costas but also to knock down the vigilante supporters he knew at that point would be dismissing any idea of helping to stop this killer. Mac continued.

"There are similarities and provable areas of forensic evidence that span the four crimes. I can confirm I have a full DNA profile of the suspect and therefore can discreetly eliminate anyone who is wrongly identified. I have worked with national police advisors to fully profile this killer and can today reveal the following characteristics we strongly believe she has.

This woman is most likely white and aged over 35 now. She is between 5 foot 6 and 6 foot in height.

She may have had access to a shotgun previously, possibly even legally through a family member maybe.

She will have lived in Westhamptonshire at some time in her life and potentially between 1996 and 1999.

We think she moved to London between 1999 and 2006. She has knowledge of East London and may have some link to the E1 area of the city.

This woman is likely to be someone who over the years has taken a keen interest in forensic science and police investigations.

She has no previous convictions and may well not have ever had contact with the police as a suspect before. She may however have had historic contact with the police as a victim in some way.

She is a physically fit woman, able to drive and capable of taking on these four men.

Her motive is one of revenge. The common theme of this is knowledge of four totally unrelated alleged sex offenders. This woman had access to the details of each and every allegation. She may have worked in jobs that gave her that insight?"

Steve's stomach churned, he rushed out of the auditorium and vomited violently into a nearby waste paper bin.

"Governor, you alright?" Asked a concerned Bashir who had slipped out of the side of the auditorium to check on his poorly boss.

Steve wiped his mouth and spluttered "I need to get out of here Bash, I just need to go." That was all he said as he dashed toward the doors and headed down the stairwell.

Bash slipped into Steve's seat next to Andy and whispered, "he's got some serious food poisoning or something, it's bad you're going to have to write him off for at least 24 hours sir." Andy slipped a note in front of a Mac who annoyed just carried on hoping the exit of Steve from the side of the camera angle would not distract from the impact of his appeal.

The unmarked police car sped through North London, blue lights and two tones blaring away from its interior. Steve gripped the steering wheel, tears flooding down his face as he rushed back to Letchworth Garden City in a virtual trance. Steve didn't want to believe it, surely Anna couldn't have committed these horrendous crimes!

Chapter 6

The Suspect

"Anna where the fuck are you?" Shouted Steve as he entered the house realising Anna's car was absent from the driveway.

"Anna, please Anna where are you?" Screamed Steve as he searched the ground floor praying she would be home working away on her laptop and wondering what all the fuss was. Instead all he was met with was the TV still blurting out updates on Mac's press release tuned into the Sky News channel.

"Oh Anna please, God no," wailed Steve as he continued his search, distraught and physically pained by the grim realisation that his wife was a serial killer. Steve buckled over the kitchen sink vomiting again struggling to breath. Looking up he saw a scribbled note laid out on the kitchen side weighted down under Anna's mobile phone in the exact location he and Anna had often left messages for each other in the past.

'Steven darling please don't hate me, goodbye my love, Anna x'

"Anna!" Roared the stricken man as he rushed up the stairs dreading what he might find. The bathroom and spare bedroom were clear, Steve kicked open the master bedroom door. Nothing, the fitted wardrobe doors were all open and the holdalls and cases stored under the bed were disturbed and half out. Steve spotted the corner of his police holdall in the back of the end wardrobe.

"Oh no, no please Anna what have you fucking done to me?" He groaned. It was only the sight of this bag that reminded Steve of how he'd brought his officer safety kit and various other seldom used items home when he'd moved offices. Steve hurriedly pulled the bag from the wardrobe ripping open the zip and tipping out the contents on the bed. Grabbing the loose can of C/S spray he shook.

"Fucking empty," he complained as he stared at the half closed baton that lay amongst the contents of his bag knowing for sure he was now looking at a murder weapon.

The realisation was dawning on the panicked detective as he dropped the offending canister and headed for the garden shed.

Throwing items of gardening equipment out, as he burrowed into the chaos like a mole blindly digging away, Steve found what he feared he would. His old Magnum work boots Anna had told him she'd relegated them for gardening duty only. For a split second Steve could not help but reflect on the ingenuity of wearing oversized police boots at a murder scene to cover your tracks.

Steve still feared the worse, to him the words "goodbye my love" meant only one thing; Anna had gone off to end her life somewhere.

Steve staggered back into the lounge slumping down on the sofa in despair. He placed his head into his hands and sobbed like baby, distraught and lost. What should he do? His wife was the very woman only a few hours ago he'd been excited about the prospect of hunting down. Steve's love for Anna was so strong as hard as he tried he just could not bring himself to hate her. He needed to find her, he just wanted to know why?

Steve fumbled for his mobile phone and sent a text message to Andy Porter:

'I HAVE ID OF THE SUSPECT SHE LIVES AT 22 EVERGREEN DV, LETCHWORTH, SG29 8PQ GET A TEAM HERE I AM GOING AFTER HER SHE IS ON THE RUN'

Steve switched his phone off stripping out the battery and SIM and dropping it back in his pocket. He ran out of the house leaving the back door wide open, jumping in his car and driving off at speed.

Steve just drove north for a while. Although Andy didn't know the address Steve had texted him, Steve knew he would soon find out it was his home. Steve wanted to do the right thing and the evidence he'd uncovered was in tact and awaiting their collection, but Steve wasn't giving Anna up, not yet anyway, not before he found her. Steve knew he'd be tracked by the murder teams and probably even arrested, he didn't care he just needed to find Anna alive and well. Steve pulled into a service station and headed straight for the cash machine so he could end his reliance on traceable card transactions from there onwards.

'Shit she's cleared the current account,' thought Steve surprisingly relieved by his discovery. This meant Anna was more likely to be on the run than intending suicide, at least for the immediate future anyway. Steve had to find her. Steve took a large chunk of money out on his credit card and moved on immediately.

'Norfolk, that's it Norfolk,' he thought. Steve knew Anna had talked about her happier days roaming her fathers land with its many barns and small derelict outhouses where she simply got lost in herself and played all alone. Of course the land had been sold on a long time ago but its many acres were criss-crossed with footpaths and bridleways, still very accessible. For now anyway it was the only place Steve could think of to start looking for his deranged wife.

Steve had driven past the farmland once owned by Anna's father when he and Anna had visited her mother. Steve had a knack of remembering areas he had previously visited so knew where he was heading. Within an hour or so he found himself parking his car in a remote gateway. There was a public footpath he knew cut straight through the middle of the farmland he wanted to search. Steve's sharp suit had long since lost it glamour, his tie had been ditched and his shiny shoes were about to face the dirt tracks of rural Norfolk. Steve rummaged around in the boot of his unmarked police car, now no longer lawfully in his possession. He grabbed a large torch from the spattering of equipment he carried conscious that darkness would soon be upon him.

The peace and quiet was therapeutic and calming from the outside, but the fire inside of Steve's head was still burning strong. He just walked and walked. Steve headed towards a familiar looking open sided hay barn he spotted in the distance. He ploughed straight through the crops at a fast pace in the dusky evening light. Steve scrambled to the top of a high stack of bales at one end of the barn sure he'd fine a bolt hole hiding Anna up high on the plateau of bails.

Nothing, Steve flopped onto his back with exhaustion looking up at the high beams that crossed the roof space above him. A short length of scrappy rope tightly knotted around the beam above him fluttered in the wind. Steve took a sharp intake of breath.

"Oh my fucking God," Steve said out loud. It had just dawned on him why the barn had seemed familiar. This was the barn that Anna's father had hung himself in back in 1995. Steve had been shown scene photos of the barn by the Norfolk case officer when they came down to Westhampton to visit Anna before her father's inquest. He recognised the interior of the barn, this was the last place Anna would want to hide out, Steve had to move on.

Now totally reliant on his torch to find his way Steve was not going to stop until he physically dropped. A copse in the distance was a good bet. Steve soon found himself on what appeared to be the straight cut of an old disused railway line that would take him right past it. The partial moonlight cut through the evening mist to illuminate the partially in tact slate roof of a building at the edge of the copse. It was a small brick and flint built railway hut with a little chimney at one end. The crumbling roof had the fairly recent addition of a green tarpaulin strung over a damaged section. The smell of woodsmoke was still evident in the air.

Suddenly Steve became drenched in fear, the cold damp night chilling him to the bone. Would Anna turn on him? Images of the violent murders flashed through Steve's mind as he rummaged around amongst the edge of the trees looking for a weapon. He selected a thick heavy branch gripping it like a club as he approached the derelict hut. A glimmer of candlelight flickered around the sides of the ill fitting door. Clicking off his torch and shoving it in his pocket Steve took hold of the outward opening door raising his ragged piece of timber ready to defend himself as he ripped open the door.

The broken man just stood and stared exhausted in his grief. He just wanted to find Anna, he wanted to ask her why she committed those gruesome murders, but she was not inside, she had already fled. Steve was so close, this was definitely her hastily occupied bolt hole. Steve instantly recognised the camping gear they had once purchased but never got round to using. A single sleeping bag and roll mat had been laid out. A small fire had been set in the old fireplace and a steel pan sat propped up on it. A couple of Co-op carrier bags lay dumped in one corner containing freshly purchased groceries. Steve's large North Face holdall lay partially open full of Anna's most practical clothes. Two pieces of old pipe were propped up next to the fireplace. 'Maybe Anna was ready to fight,' thought Steve cautiously, full of fear. He dropped his wooden club and grabbed the double metal pole turning to face the doorway.

"Anna where the fuck are you?" He shouted ready to confront the wife he was still trying hard to detest.

Hopelessly wishing that he was wrong about her being the killer.

"Come on show yourself you fucking evil bitch, I need to know why you've done this to me." He screamed out in desperation. "This ends now!"

Nothing, not a sound. Steve's legs buckled, he was exhausted and distraught, he dropped to his knees. He just stared ahead at the doorway waiting clutching the pole still in fear of being Anna's final victim. Steve looked down at the weapon he was still holding realising this was no ordinary old pole. Like a hot poker he suddenly threw the item to the side in realisation. Steve had been holding the double barrels sawn from a shotgun.

"Oh God please help me," cried Steve having just discarded final confirmation of his wife's guilt.

Instinctively Steve fumbled in his suit pocket retrieving his mobile phone and hurriedly refitting the SIM and battery, powering it up again.

"Come on, come on for fucks sake," complained Steve as he watched it searching for a network.

"Shit, Shit, Shit…" Enraged he launched the useless item out of the open door and into the darkness collapsing onto the sleeping bag his heart breaking.

The morning chorus of wild birds began to rouse Steve. He sucked in the sweet smelling country air comfortable in the arms of his darling Anna.

"Darling you came to me," she said gently.

"Shit," Steve leapt up and backed into the corner pushing himself against the cold stone wall. Anna had waited until he'd simply crashed out before re-entering the small derelict building. She had calmly cradled him as he slept enjoying the privilege of being close to him once again, something she never thought would happen after he'd found out what she'd done.

"Anna, what the fuck, don't come near me, I'm fucking warning you. Oh God Anna why?" asked Steve his heart racing.

"Steven darling I would never hurt you, please don't worry, I'm so so sorry. It's just those evil perverts they were just like my father, you have to understand."

"I don't Anna, I never will."

"Please Steve don't, please understand. I thought after I killed that sick bastard father of mine I would be able to put it all behind me, especially when I met my knight in shining armour."

"Are you saying you fucking killed your dad, Anna no, no. You're fucking sick you need help," responded Steve angrily.

"Don't you fucking judge me," came the heated response. "That bastard abused me for years, got me pregnant, nearly killed me the evil bastard. Listen to me, I nearly died, don't you understand, why do you think I can't have kids, why?"

"I don't know Anna you would never talk about it!"

"I had a ruptured ectopic pregnancy with serious internal bleeding. It was only when they rushed me to hospital with a suspected ruptured appendix that they found out I was pregnant. The damage was so severe I had a full hysterectomy at the age of just 14, 14 Steve. Thats why I had to kill him, don't you judge me."

"ARMED POLICE COME OUT WITH YOUR HANDS ON YOUR HEAD." Boomed the voice coming from outside of the hut.

"Steve hold me," begged Anna like a frightened child. "Just hold me please."

Steve wrapped his arms around his wife. They stood tightly embraced in the centre of the room weeping into each others shoulders.

"It's going to be okay Anna, you need help. You are going to be arrested now it's out of my hands, they must have traced my phone, I'm so sorry but we need to walk out of here now together."

Anna just looked into Steve's eyes and nodded, tears still rolling down her face.

"DCI STEVE LAWSON," shouted Steve. "Lower your weapons, she's unarmed I'm bringing her out."

Steve slowly walked out holding Anna closely behind him making it impossible for even the most over zealous firearms officer to take a shot. Steve looked through the ring of armed police locking his eyes on the serious face of Andy Porter. The eye contact reassured Andy who walked forward and was handed a set of handcuffs as he broke through the armed line up.

Anna held out her hands submissively as Andy gently fitted the handcuffs.

"Anna Lawson, my name is DCI Andy Porter. I'm arresting you for the murders of Joseph Fraser, Richard Wilson, Costas Salvador and Bernard Lyle. You do not have to say anything but it may harm your defence if you do not mention when questioned something you later rely on in court. Anything you do say can be used in evidence."

"I'm sorry, so sorry," replied Anna as she was led away by two uniformed officers looking back at Steve, who was blocked from following by Andy.

Steve knew this might be the last time he would ever see Anna, her sad face peering out of the rear window of a police Landrover as she was driven away down the grassy track.

Steve was in deep shock, shivering and staring into nowhere.

"She killed her dad Andy," he croaked his throat as dry as sand.

"What was that Steve?"

"She killed her fucking dad, he was the first, she killed five men. I just don't believe it, what am I going to do Andy?" Steve was lost with the demeanour of a scared child.

"Come on mate I have to take you back to London. Bashir is with me he's going to look after you."

Bash draped a large warm overcoat around Steve's shoulders. With a friendly arm placed around him he guided him in the opposite direction some distance down the disused railway line. Steve was quiet and withdrawn. Bash had a car waiting with the reassuringly familiar Graham sat in the driver's seat.

Steve was driven at speed back into London. He sat in the rear of the car silent, lost in his many thoughts.

"We're just passing Marble Arch Sir," said Bash to someone at the end of his phone. "Mac is at the yard governor, he needs to speak to you, then we'll get you cleaned up."

"The yard! You're taking me to the yard?" Asked Steve knowing full well it would be under siege by every single media organisation there was.

"It's okay gov we're driving straight into the underground car park and this things got blacked out windows, no one will take any notice." Reassured Bashir. "They'll be round the front not by where we go in."

As they entered the gloomy tight basement Steve could see the solitary figure of Mac stood amongst the Range Rovers and high powered cars of the various specialist units. Graham and Bashir stayed in the car, Mac approached and opened the rear door.

"Come on Steve we need to talk," instructed Mac. The two men walked clear of the car stopped and faced each other.

"I need your warrant card and car keys Steve please."

Steve handed them over without hesitation. Of course he would be suspended, that just had to happen.

"The DPS are all over this, they wanted you locked up mate. Listen the commander has stepped in and we've agreed Bashir will look after you until tomorrow. Then the professional standards guys will debrief you as a potential witness but under caution I'm afraid. The federation have sorted you out some legal advice and Bash has got you one of the duty officer's bunks at the section house so you can freshen up and get your head down."

"She needs help Mac, she killed five men, oh God what have I done I should have just told you after the press conference, Mac I'm sorry." Apologised Steve pouring out his heart to the trusted friend.

"Steve listen to me this is important. You were emotional and not thinking straight, instinctively you went after the suspect, that's all. You identified the scene and exhibits for us at your home and when you found Anna and ended up in close company with her you made sure your phone was on so we could geo-locate you. That's all Steve." Scripted Mac.

"But.."

"Steve listen to me listen, Anna needs you. She never intended to take you down with her. You can't even be compelled to give evidence against her, she's your wife for God's sake. Just stay strong for me mate, this is fucked up enough. I don't want to see a good man go away for assisting an offender when you did nothing of the sort. I understand Steve just stick to the facts don't let those fuckers play on your distress and convince you otherwise." Asserted Mac.

"Don't crucify her Mac, her head is not right." Pleaded Steve.

"You just look after yourself mate, she's got a good brief. Listen I won't be seeing you for a while now mate. Remember what I have said."

Mac held out his hand and shook Steve's hand gripping his upper arm with the other hand with reassuring sincerity.

The next few days were a blur. Steve ended up withdrawing into the comforting arms of his elderly distraught parents. Like a child in a man's body. The media eventually found him some weeks later forcing him into seclusion at the family's North Devon holiday cottage. Steve was a shell of a man. Living a broken empty existence, cut off from his police colleagues, still suspended pending the outcome of the case against Anna. He didn't dare watch the TV even, it wasn't just the news, Anna's story would crop up on daytime TV and even Panorama did a piece on vigilante attacks against sex offenders linking in to her case. Steve just walked, long walks in all weathers hoping one day the sea air would finally clear the dirty fog of what had happened from his mind.

Steve woke from his late afternoon nap to the sound of a vehicle pulling up on the gravel driveway. 'Shit the press' thought Steve knowing that Anna's trial was listed to start any day now.

"BANG, BANG," sounded the old iron door knocker. Steve looked out of the window but could only make out the side of two men dressed in suits, from the angle he was looking. Steve rushed to the front door and opened it not really knowing what to expect.

"Andy, Mac what are you doing here?"

"Sorry mate we got a number from your parents but just couldn't get hold of you to let you know we were on our way." Apologised Andy.

"That's alright the signal's shit out here, I have to go up on the cliffs to make a call, but that's how I like it these days. It's great to see you both come in come in, I'll put the kettle on you've come a long way."

The two men looked surprisingly glum considering Steve's warm welcome. They followed Steve into the cosy lounge and were offered a seat.

"I'll just stick the kettle on the Aga it takes a few minutes to boil I'll be right back."

Steve was back within a minute and as he walked into the room the gloomy faces of his two friends suddenly registered with him.

"What is it, is it Anna, is she okay, please tell me she's okay," pleaded a desperate Steve thinking the worse and still deeply concerned for his wife's welfare despite what she had done to him.

"Relax Steve Anna is fine, she's okay, nothing happened to her, we were at The Old Bailey with her this morning for the start of her trial. That's what we've come to speak to you about," explained Mac.

"What, what… What's happened?"

"Anna has pleaded guilty to five counts of Manslaughter and the associated firearms offences on the grounds of diminished responsibility. Based on the initial phycologist's report the judge has sentenced her today. All the reports he needed had already been prepared for the trial. Anna's defence team welcomed this and obviously had prior knowledge of the judges intentions. Anna is to be detained indefinitely by way of a hospital order with restrictions under section 37."

The kettle whistled loudly, Andy leapt up and headed for the kitchen leaving the room. Steve remained rooted to the armchair, sat bolt upright as Mac broke the news.

"Steve you okay, Steve talk to me mate." Asked a concerned Mac.

"Sorry Mac it's hard, really damn hard, I'm sorry thanks for coming to tell me in person, I appreciate it," said Steve quietly tears starting to roll down his face.

Andy returned from the kitchen juggling three hot mugs of tea.

"Come on mate have a brew, she'll be okay, she's going to get the help she needs now," consoled Andy.

Steve was devastated.

"I really don't know what I expected, I've been so confused it hurts. I don't want to loose my Anna."

Mac and Andy looked on slightly unsure what to make of Steve's emotions. Both of them had over the last seven months tried to put themselves in Steve's shoes and work out how they'd feel. Thoughts had ranged from wanting to inflict physical violence on the evil bitch to whisking her away to a far away land where extradition was impossible and seeking help from there. They felt deeply sorry for Steve and there was very little they could say to console him.

"Steve, Steve think about it," asserted Andy grabbing back Steve's attention. "A hospital order. They will help Anna and they can get her back on track I'm sure. Remember we've been there before at court although the restriction means the really dangerous mad ones can be kept inside forever, it also means as long as she is deemed to be cured she could be released one day."

Andy was right of course under the hospital order regime release was dependent upon the responsible authority being satisfied that the defendant no longer presents any danger arising from their medical condition. Steve knew from his experience about this type of sentencing. If Anna's mental health improved dramatically she could apply to a Mental Health Review Tribunal and could be released.

It was unusual for three experienced murder detectives to be discussing positively the aspects of a hospital order that allowed the potentially untimely release of a defendant they'd normally rather see banged up for the rest of their natural life.

"Thank you Mac, Andy," said Steve regaining his composure. "But Anna must face justice for the sake of the victim's families. A lot of years must pass before she's ever released. I really do appreciate your kind comments but she must be punished. You're being very kind given the circumstances."

"You chose the right place to escape from the world here Steve," commented Mac changing the subject. "How do you feel now Steve?"

"I really don't know Mac, I know one day I'm going to have to face the world again. I'll need to find a new job sooner or later."

"They might let you come back to work yet Steve." Said Andy optimistically.

"Nice thought Andy but now Anna's pleaded guilty the job will be looking to sack me before long."

"Don't say that Steve," Interrupted Mac. "I've squared most of it away. They're going nowhere with taking the police vehicle up to Norfolk and the neglect of duty when you went AWOL is a load of old bollocks. The best they'll get is you forgetting you'd taken your C/S spray home, that's it and I reckon if you take a written warning for that they'll have no choice but to find you a little office job in some corner of the yard."

"Thanks Mac but I don't think I will ever return to London even, let alone the yard. I've decided I'll offer them my resignation, bank the pension, sell up the Hertfordshire house and stay down here. My mum and dad have been great I can live here for as long as I need. Maybe I'll get a job as a postman in the villages round here or something like that; I'm getting used to my own company these days."

"You'll be alright though Steve won't you?" Asked a concerned Andy.

"I'll never be alright Andy, but life goes on and my folks need me, they're knocking on these days. This business has aged them considerably. Maybe I'll get a little dog or something, I don't know."

The three chatted away for a while as Steve began to relax slightly. The truth was Mac and Andy were the only visitors Steve had had since he left his parents to escape to the cottage.

"Shit are you guys driving back to London tonight?" Asked Steve realising darkness was closing in.

"I think we were going to do an overnight maybe in Barnstaple or somewhere nearby weren't we Mac?"

"Stay over here, I've got the spare room and the sofa, come on have a drink with me. There's some beers in the fridge and a couple of bottles of red in the rack. If you're really lucky I'll throw a couple of frozen pizzas in the oven as well."

It was a relief to see Steve lighten up a little. Whilst both men were dubious about the prospect of mixing alcohol with grief, maybe this was the tonic Steve needed to kickstart a touch of normality into his life. The three men enjoyed a sociable evening experiencing the full range of emotions as the alcohol flowed. Ranging from shared laughter to the occasional tears as Steve intermittently returned to reflect on the events of the previous spring. Overall Mac and Andy had made the right decision to spend the night at Steve's cottage knowing if they were honest that this would be the last time they ever saw him. Steve was serious about living in solitude it was the only way he would cope without his Anna.

Chapter 7

The Psychologist

"Anna you told the staff you're ready to talk?" Stated Vanessa from across the bleak and sparsely furnished side room. Anna just stared in silence looking through the grilled windows out onto the sun soaked grounds of Bramford Special Hospital. "Or have I wasted my afternoon coming here to see you again?" Asked the young phycologist.

Vanessa was a sharp young academic. When Anna had pleaded guilty to her crimes at court Vanessa had only just graduated at University. She had been practising now for nearly 13 months and in her eyes was privileged to have secured a placement at this notorious facility. From the outside it looked like a prison, physical security designed to keep some of the country's most dangerous mentally disordered offenders from posing a threat to the general public. Inside the walls the various efforts that had been made to modernise the old Victorian asylum had failed to lift its oppressive atmosphere. Anna had been a controlled but totally withdrawn patient. Unable to diagnose her true personality beyond the court reports Vanessa had vowed to get through to Anna one day and was not prepared to give up on her.

Anna liked to see Vanessa even if their conversations had been very one sided. Anna smiled and seemed happy in her company but said very little. In her mind, and unbeknown to Vanessa, Anna daydreamed that Vanessa was her long lost daughter who'd come to visit her socially, much like she visited her own sick mother in the Norfolk care home all those years ago. Of course Anna knew the real reason Vanessa sat opposite her and one day she had already decided she would open up to her. She quite often told the staff she was ready to talk to Vanessa then just clammed up the minute they were alone.

Anna turned and smiled pleasantly at Vanessa. "Thank you for coming my dear. It's been lovely to see you again. You better get going and enjoy that sunshine, you're looking a little pale, the fresh air will do you good."

This was an unusually long speech for Anna compared to previous sessions and although Vanessa knew that was it for today she knew she was getting closer.

"Thank you Anna it's been lovely to see you too, I'm coming back to see you again on Monday remember, we'll talk more then".

"Okay, take care dear, see you next week." Answered Anna pleasantly not wishing to upset her only visitor.

As promised Vanessa did return the following Monday morning.

"Hi Anna it's pouring down out there, why does it always rain on a Monday eh?" Greeted a slightly damp Vanessa.

"It was always raining on dad's farm, especially in the summer holidays."

"Oh yeah I remember my summer holidays, 7 weeks and no school, I loved them." Led Vanessa.

"I didn't."

"Oh Anna why not?" Asked Vanessa encouraged by this sudden willingness to talk.

"That's when it started, my horrible dad I mean, horrible nasty man, I hate him."

"What happened Anna?"

"He was a sick pervert. When he first started he used to say things like 'He loved my little boobies' and 'What a cute little bum I had' — sick bastard, I was only 12, I thought it was a funny joke. I hate him dirty, dirty horrible man. I just don't know how he made me think it was okay for him to do what he did?"

"What happened to you Anna?" Asked Vanessa risking a direct question.

"During those holidays he used to let me go and play in the hay barn, climb on the bales and jump off into piles of loose straw. It was fun, even if I was alone. When he'd finished work he'd turn up on his tractor and let me sit in his lap and drive around the field. The dirty bastard would get aroused, his hands everywhere pretending to stop me falling off as he hit bumps. I didn't even realise at the time, horrible fucking pervert. He just went on and on with things like that whenever he had chance."

"So when did it all stop Anna?"

Anna fell quiet, her gaze drifting back to the window.

"The rain's stopped Vanessa, what a beautiful rainbow look."

Vanessa had lost Anna again, it was pointless going on.

"Can I visit you again tomorrow Anna?"

"Yes please." She replied enthusiastically. Vanessa hoped this was Anna's way of indicating she would try and tell her more the next time they met.

Vanessa managed to reschedule some other patients and get back the following afternoon. "Raining again Anna, have you been out for some fresh air today?"

"No, I don't really like the rain. It started to rain on the day it happened you know."

"Okay Anna, tell me all about that day," asked a surprised Vanessa pleased to see a receptiveness in Anna that she hadn't seen before. Anna clearly wanted to pick up where she left off the day before and wasted no time getting back on track.

"I was 13 by then, a whole year had passed. I still looked forward to the long summer holidays despite having to keep that horrible man happy. He came to the barn one day and took me on a particularly long tractor ride doing all the normal sick things he did. I was glad when the heavens opened, he had to let me off then, it was only a small tractor no cab or anything like that. He just drove us straight into that hay barn and threw me in the big pile of loose hay playfully. The thing is there was nothing playful about his real intentions the dirty sick bastard couldn't stop himself."

Anna went quiet, was this going to be the end of today's very short session?

"He fucking raped me, I was just 13 and he raped me." Screamed Anna bursting into tears.

"Let me get you some water Anna," offered Vanessa.

"It's okay I need to carry on. It was ten weeks later on my 14th birthday that I nearly died because of that sick fucker."

"Why did you nearly die?"

Anna repeated what she had only ever revealed to two people face to face before. She had been suffering with sickness and tummy aches, her mother had put it down to her unstable menstrual cycle. Anna explained how she perked up on the day of her birthday party having managed to persuade her mum to let her have the small number of friends she did have around for a sleepover at the farm. Her mum was reluctant to have her friends sleeping over for some reason but finally agreed. After all the pizza, popcorn and copious amounts or home made soda-stream pop Anna got ill, very ill.

"Mum thought I had a ruptured appendix or something like that. I was bad, she even called an ambulance. I had a ruptured ectopic pregnancy, a baby was growing in my bloody fallopian tube. I had serious internal bleeding Vanessa. That bastard had got me pregnant. I had to have emergency surgery to save my life. The damage was so severe I had a full hysterectomy at the age of just 14, on my birthday for God's sake."

"What did your mum think had happened?"

"I don't know, I wouldn't tell her who got me pregnant when I was well enough to be grilled by her, I couldn't he'd already put a stop to that."

"What do you mean?"

"That evil man visited my bedside late one night in hospital, not long after the operation. I had drips, a stomach drain, I was a mess dosed up on heavy pain killers and everything. That bastard came to me, he just wanted to protect himself from the justice he should have faced there and then. He fucking threatened to kill me Vanessa if I said a word, kill me! I was petrified of him, he broke me." Cried Anna.

"Do you want to stop Anna?" Asked Vanessa realising how hard it was getting for Anna to re-live this nightmare.

"No, no Vanessa you need to understand why I killed him, you need to know everything."

Anna explained how it took months and months to recover from her surgery. She missed over six months of school and really got behind. When she did return she found out she had been labelled a 'slag' by all her old schoolmates.

"I was bullied, it was horrible, slag, tart, whore, horrible, horrible names they called me. I couldn't tell them I was raped, I just had to try and take it. I bunked off most days for the next two years and totally flunked all of my 'O' level exams. He ruined my life. The only good thing that happened was he stopped touching me, in fact he wouldn't come anywhere near me, that was a great relief. I wanted to kill him for so many years, I just didn't have the strength to. I worried about what might happen to me and mum if he wasn't there to keep the farm going. We didn't have a lot of money you know."

"So why kill him when you did?"

"Patricia… Patricia was a pen friend from when I was little. We kept in touch for years. I'd moved to Westhampton and seldom visited my poor mother and that bastard back in Norfolk. Of course when I moved I knew I'd be round the corner from Chisham where Patricia still lived. Chisham is in Westhamptonshire."

Vanessa knew Chisham was in Westhamptonshire, of course she did, she had the case papers detailing Joseph Fraser's murder, but she was prepared to wait until Anna was ready to go there.

"So tell me about your friend Patricia then?" Asked Vanessa.

"She was great I met her when me and mum visited my great aunt in Chisham when I was little. Patricia and I became friends, we used to write to each other about all sorts when we were growing up, but I never told her about my dad until that day. Pat and I had met up for coffee a few times after I moved to Westhampton, but that day she really needed someone and I was there for her."

"What happened?"

"She found out she was infertile. She had tests when things weren't going well with her husband; they were trying to start a family. She was distraught. There had been an almighty argument between her and her mum, she wanted to kill her dad as it was all that bastard's fault she couldn't conceive. All those years we shared a similar secret and we never knew. I never liked him he was creepy and far too keen to have her invite other kids round for parties at the pub."

"I don't understand why was it her fathers fault, what happened?"

"He fucking raped her just like my own evil father did me. When she was a young teenager as well. For years we'd kept these secrets and she had it out with her mum when the doctors gave her the devastating news."

"Okay, but why did that make her infertile?" Vanessa asked.

"Clamidia, that sick arsehole raped her several times and gave it to her. It was years later before she actually realised she had the disease. She found out when she thought she was pregnant. Patricia and her husband had been trying to have a baby for a long time."

"So what went wrong?"

"She wasn't pregnant the pains and discharge were in fact P-I-D."

"P-I-D?"

"Pelvic Inflammatory Disease, the undiagnosed Clamidia caused it. The fact that it wasn't diagnosed straight away resulted in damage being done to her womb and fallopian tubes, irreversible damage. Her mum didn't believe her, she went mad and threw her out of the pub when she went round. Poor Patricia couldn't bring herself to even tell her husband, he was working away for the week, so she called me in a terrible state. She came to my flat and told me everything, I broke down, I was useless. I told her everything, we were a mess."

"How did you cope Anna? That's terrible," empathised Vanessa as she watched Anna begin to quietly cry. "What happened next Anna?"

"Patricia stayed with me for a few days and I made her promise she wouldn't do anything to her dad, I'd have hated to see her get in trouble for that bastard. She wasn't going to mend things with her mum in a hurry but I wrongly thought her husband would stand by her. I encouraged her to tell him everything and maybe they could adopt or foster children if he really wanted a family. I only ever saw Pat again once after that day." Explained Anna with great sadness in her voice.

"Joseph Fraser not only ruined Patricia's life, it was also his fault that I lost the only friend I had to Australia, the other side of the world!"

"What made her decide to go to Australia?"

"He left her. Patricia's bloody husband just walked out the coward. He couldn't deal with it, none of it. She was devastated, her mum wouldn't speak to her any more, she hated her father and could now show it and her marriage had been destroyed. She visited just once before she left, when she had sorted out all of the formalities. Then not even a letter she might as well have disappeared off the face of the earth. In hindsight I think she needed to sever all links with her past, even the good ones, but I was devastated. I was lonely and so angry, the whole episode dragged up everything. I just went into a rage, got into my car and drove to Norfolk. I had to face that sick father of mine, tell him what he'd done to me and get my mother as far away from him as I could."

"What happened Anna?"

"She wasn't there, she was in hospital, taken in after a bad angina attack and that arsehole hadn't even bothered to tell me. I was mad I told him I was going to tell mum everything, the touching, the rape, the pregnancy and his evil threats at my bedside. I didn't care if he killed me he didn't deserve her anymore. He went mad, said she'd never believe me. We fought physically, he grabbed my neck and tried to strangle me. I kicked him hard in the groin and managed to escape. I just ran and ran, eventually I hid in that old hay barn I told you about. I think I knew he'd find me there. I climbed to the top of the bales and just cried; cried until I couldn't cry any more. Then I heard it the sound of that old tractor approaching. I looked around in a panic and thats when I saw that old rope. He shouted in his old croaky voice, "Anna, Anna where are you?" He knew I would be up on the bales. I quickly strung the rope around the roof beam and tied a sturdy slip knot on the end. I could hear the old man panting away as he struggled to climb up to me. I waited until his head popped up over the edge of the plateau of bales. Without even hesitating I dropped the loop over his head, pulled it tight and kicked the edge of the bales away. The entire leading edge collapsed and I grabbed my fathers body as we dropped to break my fall. He choked out his final breath. I let go and fell to the ground. I ran into the fields and back to the farmhouse panicking. I'd just killed my father. Something clicked in my head, I used my father's old typewriter in his office to type a very simple suicide note, mainly for the sake of my mother."

"What did you write?" Enquired Vanessa.

"I can't remember exactly but it was something like, 'I am sorry for what I've done I can't live with my sins anymore, good bye my darling.'

Of course I was safely back in Westhampton by the time one of the farm workers found the old nonse, still dangling from that roof. My mum was still in hospital when she was told, in fact she never got out of hospital. Two weeks later she had a stroke. Thankfully it was my Steven who was on duty when they needed a local police officer to break the news to me. Did you know that is how I met him?"

"No, I didn't Anna, when did you get together then?"

"Not for a long time, in fact it was just after the inquest. Steven always felt it was inappropriate to have a relationship with someone who he still had an official duty towards. Even when things concluded he was still nervous about the concept of dating someone he'd met through his job. He eventually plucked up the courage to ask me out for a drink. It was wonderful and despite everything that had happened I was so happy. I just couldn't quite get the sadness of Patricia's situation out of my head despite the positive turn of events. Joseph Fraser had to pay for what he'd done."

Anna paused, withdrawing into herself again.

"I'm tired, really tired sorry Vanessa can we finish please," she asked.

"Of course Anna, it has been a long session, you've done well. We do need to carry on sometime though, you know that?"

"Yes Vanessa I will I promise, can we do it next week though?"

"Yes, can I come back Monday I have all morning free?"

Anna agreed. Vanessa thanked her again and left satisfied thinking the hardest thing Anna had to talk about had now been covered but maybe she was wrong.

Vanessa had been distracted from her other clients for the rest of the week. Her weekend had been spent typing up her notes about Anna, going over and over the catalogue of events that signified the birth of a serial killer. Anna had a terrible time in her childhood loneliness, sexual abuse, life threatening injury, bullying and academic failure. Vanessa was beginning to really understand Anna and just hoped she could pick up where they left off and the six day break wouldn't effect the momentum.

"How was your weekend Anna, it was nice and sunny wasn't it?" Asked Vanessa as they settled down for an extended Monday morning session.

"Oh yes," she replied, "they let me go out and tend to the old flower beds. They said I can do more in the gardens now the summer is here as long as they have a spare staff member to go out with me."

"That's good Anna, I thought some of the outside areas looked a bit brighter."

"I know, I really miss my garden in Letchworth, I was just starting to get it looking nice when I had to leave."

Grabbing the chance to lead on from Anna's comment Vanessa asked, "Why did you have to leave?"

"Steven, I saw it in his face on TV before he ran out of that live press appeal, he was coming for me, I just couldn't face him. I'd hurt him so badly, I am an evil woman."

"Anna!"

"No, I should never have done that to him, if only I hadn't have felt so satisfied killing that old bastard Fraser I would have never gone on, I'm sure I wouldn't, but Joseph Fraser had to be punished. Somebody had to hurt him for what he did to Patricia."

"Are you ready to tell me about what you did to him Anna?"

"Yes," she answered taking a long sip of water and composing herself ready to begin. "I knew that old pub well. When I visited Chisham with mum she'd let me go off and play. It was only just round the corner and that's how I met Patricia and some of her friends at the time. I got to play in the pub and the accommodation as well. The layout hadn't changed when I went back for a drink one Sunday afternoon. Steve never knew I'd even been to Chisham before. He was in uniform back then and worked all sorts of shifts so it was easy to get away. He'd been posted to the rural sector after he'd finished his probation but I hadn't even realised he covered Chisham, I didn't plan for Steve to be the first officer to find that sick old man.

I'd finished my college course studying counselling and I think it was during that course that I realised I needed closure so far as Patricia went. I don't know why but at the time hurting Fraser seemed an acceptable option to me. I know now it was wrong but back then it didn't even cross my mind. I wanted to see him and I wanted to work out how I could hurt him so I went there two weeks before I started my new job with victim support. He was a frail old man and of course he didn't recognise me nor did Patricia's mum. I chatted to her, made small talk at the bar, she seemed very depressed. She didn't mention Patricia but did say she was going away for a few weeks to stay with her sister in Kent. She was older than her sister who was not very well at the time. That was it as far as my warped mind thought, my perfect opportunity.

I was away the week before I went back to the Wheatsheaf. On my induction course for the new job. Steve was working the following weekend so I stopped off overnight at the old caravan in Norfolk and went to have a long visit with my mum. You know when I visited her that Saturday all I could think of is the pain both my own sick pervert of a father and Patricia's horrible dad had caused these two women. Their lives were drawing to an end with nothing but sorrow and guilt to take to their graves. My mind was made up, I spent Sunday up in Norfolk and prepared myself heading down to Chisham that evening.

You know I was only going to crack his skull and brake his hands leaving him gagged and handcuffed or something until someone eventually found him. I wasn't going to kill him. I'd started to think about how I could do this and not ever get arrested. Steve had just got some new work boots that were quite expensive, money was tight back then you know. He told me how one of his colleagues had been lucky enough to have the job pay for their new boots when they over-stepped a suspects footmarks at a crime scene. Steve said that there were always police boot prints left at crime scenes. I was interested in that sort of thing anyway so I asked him about it. That's how I got the idea to take Steve's old boots and make sure any marks I did leave would be oversized and hopefully dismissed as made by police officers. I used my journey up to my course to divert to a couple of random towns and different shops. I got two sets of cheap handcuffs from some sleazy sex shop, a lightweight disposable set of coveralls from a DIY store and the set of Marigolds from the local supermarket near the caravan site. The weapon was easy, I found a heavy old rusty wrench bar. I think it was something to do with adjusting the legs on the static caravan but it made a great club. I dressed like a rambler, Steve's boots old jeans, a three quarter length padded Parker that concealed the bar just right. I wore a pair of my mums old glasses as a sort of disguise. I tucked my blonde hair away under an oversized woolly hat that was in fact a full face balaclava when rolled down. All I needed to do was casually walk through the busy Sunday night clientele, most of whom would be pissed and just think I was cheekily popping in to use the loos. No one would notice that I didn't leave, the only risk being that Fraser might have some kind of lock in and I'd be found out. Fortunately for me on that night he didn't.

I heard him lock the doors and begin to walk around the bar coughing and grumbling about the mess. I quietly hung the coat on the toilet door, slipped into my overalls, pulled on the gloves and covered my face with the balaclava, listening and waiting for my chance to surprise him as he took the next set of glasses behind the bar to the sink area. Of course I looked like some horrible armed robber he would have never thought a woman was inside that dominant attire. He was a frail old man and begged me not to hurt him as he turned around. I just lashed out with the wrench battering and battering the perv as he ran for the safety of the kitchen. As I went through the swing door after him I cracked him on the back of the head and he fell to the floor unconscious. I took a set of handcuffs from my pocket and clamped them to one wrist but he started to come round so I stepped back. He was dazed and began pulling himself up on the kitchen side. I cracked him across the back and grabbed his left hand clamping it into that griddle thing that was set to standby mode. As I locked it down it gradually heated up and Fraser began to groan. I locked the other set of handcuffs around his other wrist as his moans turned to screams. I just wanted to cuff him up to something and then leave him in pain to suffer but not die. Fraser pulled his melted hand free of the metal plates and lunged at me. I hit him around the head again and he staggered backwards incapacitated and punch drunk. That's when I saw the hanging pan rack and seized the opportunity to cuff him up to it spread eagled against the central steel table. He was in a right state by that point, pleading for me not to kill him. I don't know what came over me, I should have just left him, but there was no way I was going to be able to answer his plea. Its true what they say about when the red mist comes down.

I didn't care anymore, in fact I wanted him to know I was a woman and a friend of Patricia. I spoke for the first time. I told him he was a 'sick nonse' and he 'had to die for what he did to Patricia and the rest of her friends.' He just swore in defiance and said something like "Fuck off you little whore, you stupid girls asked for it."

That was it. I stripped a magnetic rack of knives and laid them out in front of him. He was still defiant and spat a mouthful of blood and teeth across the table at me. I used every single knife on him. From making the little slices and digs into his guts to slashing at his upper thighs. I knew for sure I'd nicked at last one of his femoral arteries. He was going to die that night, he had to, but slowly and in great pain.

It was when I set about his stab wounds with a meat hammer that his body dropped and the cuffs snapped open in quick succession unable to hold the body weight his legs no longer supported.

I just stood and watched him Vanessa, I don't know why but I let him drag himself through the back door of the inn backing away from me dragging himself towards that crumby old Wendy house. I picked my metal bar back up and stood over him on purpose until he'd backed all the way into the little house. He was done, exhausted his breathing laboured. I stood there and watched him die. It seemed like poetic justice that he died in the very location he'd previously touched up so many young victims. I kicked his floppy legs in and shut the door, not caring that his mutilated hand was still half out of one of the windows.

I wish it hadn't been Steve who found him, but it was useful when he got seconded to the murder enquiry. I was able to find out that no one suspected why Fraser had really been killed. I knew Patricia would never come under suspicion she was in Australia.

I washed up quickly back in the ladies loos but knocked the blood stained marigolds into the toilet by accident. Instinctively I just flushed it several times, stupid but they went down, even if it did flood the place. I wrapped the wrench in the overalls along with the balaclava. That lot went in Petesford reservoir after I left Chisham.

You know I felt so good that night back at the caravan showering the smell of Fraser's blood off of my skin. I had killed the two sick fucking bastards that had destroyed the childhood of me and my best friend and I was going to get away with it. I thought it would be easy to just get on with my life after that."

"Why couldn't you Anna?" Asked a now quite stunned Vanessa.

"I did, sort of. Once I found out the investigation was not going anywhere near Fraser's sex offending let alone me, I did get on with my life. I was very happy. Steve and I began to enjoy the romance in our life and I was able lock my childhood nightmares away in the back of my mind. Even visiting mum back in Norfolk wasn't so painful. When Steve and I drove past the old farmland once I could actually reminisce about the fun times I had there rather than the darker moments I'd endured. Killing my father and Fraser was the best therapy I could have hoped for. I know that no one will ever understand. They can't they didn't go through the nightmare I went through."

"Are you okay Anna," asked Vanessa noting Anna had gone quiet again after such a detailed outpouring of facts.

"Yes, I'm fine. I feel better, I need to tell you everything Vanessa, you need to understand why I went on, but I'm done for today, can we carry on later in the week please, I promise I'll tell you everything."

"I'll come back on Friday if that's okay and we'll see what we can get through."

"Please," replied Anna relieved she had someone she trusted to talk to. Vanessa seemed to understand why she did what she did.

Vanessa had succeeded professionally and given Anna the impression she was someone she could open up to. However once back in her car Vanessa just sat immersed in a mixture of conflicting emotions. If she was honest with herself she didn't want to have to hear such horrors from Anna ever again. It was challenging to deal with mentally ill offenders at the best of the times, but most of them generally only had one crime to admit to and face up to, not five!

Vanessa went back to her old University professor the following day and sought his reassurance that she was doing the right thing not challenging Anna's lack of remorse or recognition of wrong-doing. He confirmed Vanessa was following the right path and encouraged her to go back and finish the job as she was making real progress. Anna would be detained for many more years yet and the full and frank admission of all of her crimes was the most important foundation they could hope for. Everything else could be built on from there onwards in slower time.

Friday morning came and Anna was as pleased as ever to see Vanessa.

"I've been feeling so much better this week, I really am starting to feel in control again. I am so grateful for the time you take to listen to me Vanessa." Thanked Anna.

"I'm glad, you know we will have a lot more talking to do in the future don't you?"

"Yes, I know this is going to be a long road, it's just been so important for me to actually have someone to tell the truth to. I've never really explained what I did to anyone before, not even the court psychologist people. They just wanted to confirm I wasn't of sound mind, suffering from 'diminished responsibilities' and not a murderer. I think all that talk just made me worse you know."

"Okay good well shall we carry on and pick up maybe as to why once you had killed Joseph Fraser and your life started to move on you went back to killing again?"

"Victim support."

"How do you mean?"

"The job I took with victim support, I loved it. I was passionate about helping people deal with the effects of crime. You know I really don't think people realise how much some youth stealing a purse from an old lady's house can destroy a life. I spent an awful lot of time just trying to rebuild the confidence of a lot of the people I supported. It seemed like if it wasn't for a charity like victim support, no one else would care. As I got more experienced I helped out on some of the more serious cases, including sex offences; not as the primary support worker but as the assistant at first. We often worked in pairs when we had young victims or difficult families. The trouble is it was a double edged sword for me. I got great satisfaction from helping people, especially some of the young teenage victims, but I also realised justice was a rare commodity and this really began to frustrate me."

"But what got to you so bad you wanted to kill again Anna?" Asked Vanessa.

"Justice fails the vulnerable."

"How do you mean?"

"Well, all children are vulnerable in the family environment, it's where most paedophiles prey on their victims, some sick bastards even look for relationships with single mothers with ready made families just to get at the child. I know that from some of the harrowing stories I've come across through the NSPCC. It's only a mother who can protect their child in those situations, but outside of the home every child should be safe, especially in school. Richard Wilson destroyed that for two young girls and was going to carry on, he couldn't help it. He was the worse kind of paedophile I thought, one who wouldn't admit it. One who probably worked hard to qualify as a teacher just to get access to his target group, this man got a job at an all girls school for fucks sake, on his very first placement. Don't try and tell me he wasn't looking for someone to groom from day one. This man was intelligent but excused his activities as loving and affectionate relationships. He knew what he was doing was wrong. Now I only found out about that lot when he changed tack. You see Wilson had been caught in Nottingham and just walked away Scott free. He even kept his teaching career in tact. All this was in the victim support briefing pack for poor Brittany Doulton. I got to read it, so I know the Westhampton Child Protection Team and CPS knew all this as well. You see I met Brittany with a colleague Sheila Parks when she asked me to go along for support to Brittany's lively home. This was after the police had to tell her the CPS wouldn't support any further action against Wilson. I just watched her and took in the environment she was being dragged up in. It was obvious why Wilson had targeted her, of course she'd make a terrible witness. No jury would ever warm to her or believe her allegation against the word of a teacher even if the CPS had supported a prosecution. The thing is I believed her and I could see behind the hot air and rough exterior, Brittany had been damaged by Wilson's actions beyond repair. The state schools were full of Brittany's and Wilson was still in a position to exploit that.

All he had to do was accept his affliction and get help. Stay away from teaching or at least only work in all boy schools until he'd learned to control himself. But no, Wilson couldn't help himself, the two encounters he'd had with the law didn't deter him, they just made him stronger; he'd convinced himself he was doing nothing wrong? It was time for Richard Wilson to do the honourable thing, admit he was a paedophile and take his own life. I decided it was down to me to help him do that."

"So what did you do Anna?"

"Well, I thought back to Joseph Fraser. He was an old frail man but still put up a fight. I knew Richard Wilson was a younger fitter guy and I could never take him on in a fight. I also found out a week after seeing Brittany that his car had been vandalised so his details were routinely passed to victim support. That's how I knew where he lived and if I turned up on his doorstep as a victim support volunteer I knew he'd invite me in. I just needed a way to take control of him once I was inside. That was when it came back to me. Dad had a gun, a shotgun, I'd seen him use it when I was a kid. He even taught me how to fire it once, only so he could put his grubby hands all over me mind you. It hadn't been at the farmhouse when I cleared it out and Norfolk Police never seemed to ask about it so I guessed it wasn't something he had registered legally. I went on to realise I hadn't seen any of his tools when we cleared out the sheds at the back of the farmhouse. It was then that I recalled him talking about his workshop to my mum. I'd never been there but

I knew it must be tucked away on the land somewhere. The land was of course all sold off by then, bought out by the big industrial arable farm next to ours. They didn't seem to need the buildings just the fields. In fact they renovated and rented out the old farmhouse as a holiday let. So I went up to Norfolk on one of my routine visits to mum. Whilst up there I went wandering and that's how I found it. The old railway hut in the edge of the copse. It was padlocked up but I used a rock to smash that off. It was an old derelict shed, not exactly a workshop, even had a leaky roof, but it was obviously my fathers den, somewhere he worked and stored some not so legal things. Of course his old shotgun was there and a small quantity of shells. His tool box and lots of different old pesticides and potions were all stacked up. I found the Ketamine there, he must have got it from a vet because the instructions mentioned something about dosages for horses. I'd heard of Ketamine being used illegally as a party drug and in date rapes through my work so I took it to use on Wilson. I did a load of research in medical journals at Norwich Library and my plan for Wilson hatched out from there. I took a large hacksaw to the shotgun and sawed off the barrels. That was hard work and the end result was a bit ragged but it looked scary enough. It wasn't even loaded you now when I pulled it out from under my coat at Wilson's house. Don't get me wrong I did consider just shooting the bastard but it would have been far too noisy where he lived. I'd have never been able to slip away into the darkness after that."

"So tell me about the night you killed Richard Wilson Anna."

"Steven was on nights so I could go out anytime. I knew Wilson lived on his patch but my plan was always that he wouldn't be missed until he failed to turn up at school on the Monday at the earliest. I never wanted Steve to have to be the one that found him, it just shouldn't have happened like that."

"Does that bother you Anna?" Asked Vanessa sensing she was becoming a little troubled again.

"Yes, it does," cried Anna. "I know it doesn't make sense to anyone but I never wanted to hurt Steven in any of the shit I did. I miss him so much, I really miss him. Sorry Vanessa can we just take a break for a minute?"

Vanessa suggested she get some coffees and left Anna. She was grateful to be left alone for a moment to recompose herself.

When Vanessa returned Anna was calm, warmed and energised by the coffee and biscuits Vanessa had collected. They continued…

"So tell me about the night you killed Richard Wilson."

"Well, I knew I was going to do it that Saturday evening as soon as Steve left for work about 8. I had the shotgun and syringe full of ketamine all ready. I'd selected some old but tidy clothes that I could easily throw away later. I'd cleaned Steve's old work boots and put them in the back of the spare cupboard after Fraser so I dug them out again. I doubled up on latex gloves and made sure my hair was tied well back. I'd even been to the model shop and got a couple of cheap craft knives to fit in with the sort of school related bits and pieces you'd expect to find in a teachers pad. I drove to a separate part of the estate connected by a series of alleyways to Wilson's street. It was dark and fairly cold so I didn't look out of place with my old nylon parka on, the pocket lining slit inside to accommodate the sawn off. I didn't worry about Wilson seeing my face, he was going to die anyway, but I was able to conceal my face and features on route by keeping the parka hood up until I got to the front door.

It was about 8:30 p.m. when I got there. I simply knocked the door and waited for him to answer.

"Richard Wilson?" I asked. He confirmed. I introduced myself as Anna Lawson from Victim Support, crazy I don't know why I used my real name. I apologised for the late hour and checked it was convenient and if he was alone. Obviously I said it was about his car and rather reluctantly he let me in when I asked. He quickly went ahead of me towards the lounge. I thought maybe he'd picked up on something about me, maybe the shotgun shape, either way I instinctively acted and drew the weapon behind him following him close behind. The dirty pervert had suddenly realised a slide show of sick images were flashing through his computer monitor on the lounge table. I shouted "get away from that computer you sick fuck." That got his attention as he turned around with a start. He just pleaded with me, "please, please, take my money, my computer, have my car, please don't hurt me." He disgusted me, he was a feeble excuse for a man, no wonder he was too inept to forge a relationship with an adult female. If I wasn't determined to kill him when I went to the house I was after I saw the computer on the table surrounded by school exercise books he must have been marking whilst looking at that filth. Wilson cowered on the floor, it was pathetic. I grabbed a black marker pen from the pencil case on the table and threw it at him. 'Write your confession Richard it's time to die, write!' I insisted jabbing him several times in the back with the rough edge of the sawn off barrels."

"What did you make him write Anna?"

"Something like, 'I'm a dirty paedophile and I apologise for my sick fantasies. I have used my job as a teacher to get access to children and I have avoided detection and prosecution because the authorities are weak and don't protect children from evil monsters like me. Let God be my judge.' It took him ages, blubbering away. I took the opportunity to slip the cover off of the syringe and jab him hard in the upper arm with it just as he finished. He was in a real state then, panicked and pacing up and down the lounge insisting I tell him what I'd injected him with. Obviously I told him to 'stand fucking still,' but the ketamine kicked in really quick and he was soon staggering everywhere knocking things over. It was easy from there on, I didn't need the gun anymore, I just wrapped his arm over my shoulder and walked the intoxicated man up to his room. I had the choice of his bedroom or the bathroom, figuring most suicides that Steve had told me about took place in one or the other. By the time I got him up the stairs he was barely conscious so the best I could do was flop him down on his bed. You know that ketamine is powerful stuff, I think that might have killed him alone without all the messiness that followed. I'd remembered a girl I used to bunk off with at school sometimes when I was planning this. She used to self-harm making fairly superficial cuts horizontally across her wrists. On one occasion I was the one who took her to the medical bay at school. We had a particularly harsh school nurse back then. She was quite horrible even for those days, but I remember her saying my friend was just attention seeking, if she really wanted to kill herself she'd make proper cuts downwards not across. She was right of course and it's always stuck in my mind. It works as well; within minutes it seemed Richard Wilson had bled out peacefully in his drug induced stupor. That to me was more like euthanasia not murder. I placed the knife in his hand collecting the empty syringe and my gun from the lounge. I slipped out the back door. I even left it open like a considerate suicide victim might I thought. Hooded up I was able to slip into a back alley and escape unseen. I set off for Norfolk making good use of my new found bolt hole in the middle of the night and the half collapsed open fireplace it had to burn my soiled clothes. I was home, showered and back in bed smelling of fresh perfume before Steve was even thinking about finishing his nightshift."

"So how did you feel after killing Richard Wilson?"

"Brilliant at first. I know that sounds a little sick, but I'd been humane, I only helped him do what he would have done himself had he accepted his incurable affliction. Trouble is I didn't give his family a second thought when I killed him, if only Steve hadn't been given that family liaison job. He told me everything over time. It really upset him sharing their grief. He could only show it when he came home to me. All of the time I was providing an understanding ear all I could do is think that it was all my doing. I dealt with it, especially when Steve told me they were going to conclude the investigation was a suicide and the family knew the truth about their loved one. To me that was okay, I just needed to stop and learn to deal with things better. I couldn't risk dragging Steven into such an upsetting situation again. Especially when he went on to qualify as a full time FLO on murder enquiries."

"Tell me about London Anna."

"It was great, exciting, a new start. I'd been through quite a dark time when mum died. She'd done so well eventually recovering to a good standard from her stroke, then one winter she was struck down with pneumonia and that was that. Really quick; I suppose she was quite old and had done well to come out on the other side of a stroke. I had some nice visits with her before she went, it was just the sudden closing of that chapter of my life that knocked me off line for a short time. Steve was very supportive of course and eventually immersed me in flat hunting when we decided to move.

We had a really trendy place in E1 you know, right on the edge of the city near the top end of the famous Brick Lane, great restaurants and a lively night time scene."

"So London was good for you then Anna?"

"Oh yes and Steven of course. He was doing his dream job on the murder teams on a full time basis. I soon found the job with the NSPCC which was great. I was passionate about it, I loved it, they really make a difference you know. Did you know child victims are ten times more likely to report offences against them to the NSPCC than directly to the police. Of course we passed the referrals to the child protection teams and worked with them to try and bring offenders to justice. I was soon reminded though that the police and CPS had a high threshold for charging offenders, too high. So there I was all over again, looking for an alternative way to get those poor kids some justice."

"What do you mean alternative?"

"What I did to Costas Salvador was supposed to be alternative justice, but it was just a fucking mess in the end. It still destroys me thinking about it now. I should have killed that evil bastard Ahmed Akbar, it's so sad what I did, but Costas' blood is on Ahmed's hands not mine. Ahmed has to live with the fact he got Costas killed because he is an evil child abuser and that's that."

"So I know it's a little harder Anna but it would be really good to talk about how you ended up killing Costas, putting aside that he was in fact the wrong person in the end." Asked Vanessa sensing that Anna really didn't want to talk about this one due to the obvious regret she had.

"Okay, well I loved my job at the NSPCC and I was coping. Helping young victims in any way I could then moving on. It was when I shadowed a more experienced colleague dealing with poor little Ali that it just got to me again. That boy was in pieces, absolutely distraught. Even weeks down the line the best we could do was stop him running and hiding every time a male colleague appeared. His anguish of course was compounded greatly by the fact that the real offender was seen as a trusted adult and still had ready access to him until he was eventually found out. Of course we didn't know that at the time and just saw a boy whose trauma might never heal.

I was livid when my colleague told me about the police and CPS decision not to proceed. I knew Ali wouldn't speak to them at all about what had happened but I felt the physical evidence and statement from the home tutor was surely enough. Justice had to prevail so I planned my next move.

Steven had just started a three week course at Hendon so I needed to get this done while he was there and not likely to get involved in the murder enquiry. It took longer than I thought to get ready, I needed to meet Costas and see the layout of that workshop.

I knew Costas was a builder and the name of his firm was in our file. A quick internet search found his details listed under builders in East London specialising in home improvements. The idea of this man going into anyone's home made me mad, I had to stop him from taking advantage of anyone else's children.

I picked a Wednesday evening two weeks before the murder to do the reconnaissance. I just wanted to see if I could pull it off at that time and day. Before I knew it I was poking my head around that workshop door and looking at Costas Salvador working away at his workbench. I made some story up about having had a personal recommendation from a friend on the estate and was just dropping in on the off chance he could give me an idea how much fitting a new kitchen would cost. He insisted on taking some details on a pad he had in the office area. I quickly made up a false name using a combination of Eastenders character names, 'Dorothy Butcher' I think I used. I even used Turpin Road and the postcode E20 from the programme. I used to love

Eastenders back then. I had to use the phone number I had to hand that was for a charity shop in Bow when Costas asked for my number. We used to get decent toys from there for the NSPCC family centre. I knew he probably wouldn't get round to ringing me before I'd returned and killed him. It was useful going to the workshop for a number of reasons, not least to confirm the landline number for Costas' business did go to his workshop via an overhead line that fed into the building at the bottom of the wall near the outside tap. I couldn't risk going in there with that live so I knew I'd need to take a small pair of wire cutters to snip that when I returned.

So at an opportune moment over the next two weeks I grabbed my trusty old Magnums that Steve had still kept just in case he ever went back into uniform. I bought a new set of blue overalls from the local DIY superstore. I took a day off sick during the week and slipped back to Norfolk to get the gun. I was going to shoot Costas for sure but I still wanted him to suffer. That afternoon in Norfolk I practised using that shotgun at close range firing into tree stumps in the copse behind the old hut. Before I knew it I only had two cartridges left so I loaded them up and headed back to London.

The rest of the planning was fairly straightforward. I texted Steve on the Wednesday of the murder and told him I'd forgotten about a works drink that night so I'd be out before he got home at 7. He was going out with his course the next night so he didn't complain. It was kind off weird getting made up and putting on a nice outfit under my coveralls to go out and commit a murder. I knew I'd return to find Steven home so I even put a pair of heels and a bottle of Smirnoff ice in the boot of my car for when I returned. We had a basement parking area in the flats we were living in. So the car boot was an ideal location to store items for a quick change. Off I went wearing boots, coveralls and a long and bulky old hooded coat to hide the gun and help conceal my identity from the sea of CCTV cameras I'd noted on the estate.

I had worked out that I could walk through back streets and alleys to get to the estate that backed onto the railway arches and totally avoid public transport. Hood up I shuffled through the darkness until I stood opposite that workshop. Costas' van was outside and the lights were on. I moved closer, I could see his silhouette through the window in the workshop door. I quickly and quietly cut the phone line before taking out my shotgun and waiting for the next passing train. Then smash I kicked at those old wooden doors and bang, bang, he was down. It felt good and the noise was drowned out completely by the train overhead.

The poor man crawled away around the side of the central work bench and I just casually walked in and closed the doors behind me. I was like a woman possessed. I grabbed a large crowbar thing from the tool racks and just started smashing away at the back of him. He seemed determined to try and get up and face me. His strength and determination was unbelievable. He crawled behind the rear of the work bench and his left hand appeared on the wooden table top. I saw the nail gun, grabbed it and just nailed his hand to the table top. He screamed out in pain but still pulled his shattered body up. I think I said something to him about him never touching any little boys ever again and took his other hand symbolically flicking on the circular saw thing and slicing his fingers clean off. He cried out ripping his left hand free of the nails. I panicked at this point. I'd shot both his knees out, caused him some serious head injuries and blood was pouring out of his hand, but he just wouldn't lay down and die. I couldn't let him get to the door so I grabbed that left hand and secured it to the nearest object, the old vice. I clamped him in there to the tune of more screams. They were easily drowned out by the high arch of the ceiling and regular overhead trains. That's when I mucked up."

"What do you mean?"

"That's when I left my DNA at the crime scene. As you know that was the beginning of the end for me, I just didn't realise it. I saw an open tool box, I needed a sharp blade, so I shoved my gloved hand into it to grab a Stanley knife. I nicked my finger on the blade. I didn't realise at first, I just carried on tightening the vice and slicing Costas' wrist so he started to bleed out. Then I saw it, blood oozing from a small ripped section in the glove on my finger. I was horrified. I looked around and found a bucket and an old rag. I had to venture outside briefly to fill the bucket with some water. Costas was still stuck in the vice, the last of his blood rapidly draining from him. I could see the pulsating flow weakening as he started to die.

When I came back into the workshop I was shocked to see he had moved again. I quickly looked around and saw him virtually dead slumped in his office. In his dying moments he must have ripped his crushed hand free from the vice and made a final effort to get to his phone. Probably where he was trying to get to all along. Anyway I quickly washed down the surfaces that I thought I had touched including the Stanley knife that I totally submerged. I threw the water out and shoved the bucket back under the side. Obviously I now know that I left my blood stained print on the rim; stupid woman. I was in a bit of a fluster by now and I don't know why but felt like I needed to get out of the area fast. I grabbed Costas' keys and left in his van. I just hit the A12 and kept driving. I ended up north of Romford and drove around a large council estate until I chanced upon a massive derelict hospital site. I could see old CCTV cameras, but I concluded there would be no way they were still in use. I wanted to burn the van out there and then but couldn't find any flammable liquid in the back. I thought about a local garage but had to kick myself at the foolishness of the idea. Not only might I put myself on CCTV but I'd stink of smoke and petrol, not the kind of odours you pick up on a night out. So I just left it locked and tucked in an old yard area right in the middle of the complex. I took an old tool bag from the back and stowed my gun and blood stained coveralls away in it. I added a load of heavy tools and packs of nails to weigh it all down really well.

Heading into Romford I found a canal or drainage channel type of thing to dump the heavy tool bag into. I'd walked a couple of miles from the hospital so there was no way the police would routinely search this bit of dirty water. I noticed blood on my boots still but I couldn't just get rid of them. I had to rinse them on my feet beneath a drainage pipe feeding the channel. It was about 10 p.m. on a Wednesday night. It was easy to buy a ticket with cash and anonymously head back to Liverpool Street from Romford. I walked home from there and did the planned quick change at the boot of my car, opening the Smirnoff and deliberating spilling half of the bottle down my front for effect. Steve had gone to bed early, obviously tired from his course. It was a good job really because even in the half light of the bedroom he said I looked a mess, then joked that it must have been a good night. "It was," I said thinking I had just rid the world of one of the most evil paedophiles I'd ever come across. I was so sad when I found out the truth a week or so later."

"So when did you go back to the van?" Asked Vanessa recalling somewhere she'd read about it being burnt out.

"The next night, it was simple really. Steve was out drinking as planned, I stopped off at a different DIY store in Leyton and picked up a two litre tub of white spirit. I figured that was less conspicuous that buying a container of petrol at a garage. I drove my own car but parked just short of the hospital in a quiet residential street. It was easy to slip through the alleyways from there into the old hospital estate. All I needed was my carrier bag with the white spirit and some matches. I ripped the plates off of the van to make it hard to initially ID before dousing the cab well with white spirit and torching it. I was little 'Miss Innocent' walking through the adjoining estate back to my car, well before the smoke from the flaming van was even visible. I was home, showered and watching Eastenders on Sky plus before I knew it and long before Steve rolled in drunk."

"So how did you feel when Steven got involved in the investigation into Costas Salvador's murder?"

"I was devastated; that wasn't supposed to happen. I even complained at the time when he took that call. I obviously didn't reveal why I was annoyed, but Steve shouldn't have had to deal with that. As the first few days went on I did feel a bit better. Steve was really enjoying his exhibits work and it was strangely satisfying knowing that I had created such an interesting crime scene for him. That didn't last long though, not when I found out they'd found my blood and a partial print. I felt sick with worry, I ended up taking time off of work. For some stupid reason I thought they were closing in on me. I tried to carry on as normal but it was hard and I did make myself ill. Steve did his normal thing worrying about me not being well.

It just went from bad to worse when he told me about the father actually being Ali's abuser and not Costas Salvador. I changed my thoughts to secretly hoping they'd find me, lock me up and throw away the key. I thought I deserved it. After a while though I moved away from those thoughts. I rationalised things and shifted the blame in my head to Ali's sick father. As time went on I managed to put the whole thing behind me and made a promise with myself that that was it. No more killing. I even moved offices to the central London team where I had a managers job supervising the call centre operators for Child Line and didn't have direct contact with victims any more. It was less front line really and better for me. Steven's career took off and we enjoyed some wonderful times together. We even moved out to our first house from that London flat. I had my garden and had escaped from the hustle and bustle of London that I'd grown tired of as I got older. Of course when Steve went back onto the murder squad in the middle of 2012 It wasn't so bad because he was one of the bosses by then. He didn't seem to spend quite so many hours at work as he did when he was a DC.

I think I'd have been fine if it wasn't for that corrupt bastard MP. I read the story when it broke and also saw the obviously false retraction a week later. It made me mad, really mad, but it didn't tip me over the edge at all. I was able to control it, put it out of my mind and move on."

"So why did you kill Bernard Lyle then Anna?" Asked a confused Vanessa.

"Shona, she was one of my members of staff. Shona came to me distraught one afternoon. She'd taken a series of calls from a young girl named Rosie who was in absolute pieces. Shona had worked out that this girl must have been the same girl whose mother had featured in the tabloids about a month before back in December 2012. Rosie had been calling everyday after school so I hung around the next day and listened in when Rosie rung again. This poor girl had lost her innocence to that fat old bastard, he'd destroyed her life. To make matters worse the one supporting adult in her life, her mother, had chosen to make money from the tabloids rather than support her daughter and make a proper allegation to the police. The media circus had destroyed any chances of a successful prosecution and the poor young girl was alone, she'd even lost all of her friends being dragged up north by her mum. I couldn't bare the thought that so much damage had been done by a man who stood a chance of being a key member of the next government if the opposition won the 2015 general election. He had to be exposed at the very least. I didn't plan to kill him you know; that came later.

I'd learnt a lot over the years just chatting to Steve and following crimes reported in the news. I'd seen documentaries where technology had been a criminal's downfall, but I needed technology to get at Lyle.

Rosie had been groomed by Lyle through the children's charity he was the patron of. They organised outward bound activities and Rosie had loved all that when she gave it a try. Lyle then took her out hill walking and things like that, but not with the charity just with him alone mostly. Rosie had trusted Lyle like the father she never knew. In between trips he'd chat with her online via a schools dating site she'd suggested they used. Rosie had mentioned in her calls about Lyle setting up a strange user name, something like 'sugar daddy.'

That's how I knew, I just needed to find him online and take it from there. I figured that as the internet side of his grooming hadn't come out in the press reports he might still be using it to find new victims. I just needed to get him on the end of a computer and pose as a naive young teenager agreeing to meet him face to face. If I achieved that I could properly expose him and get him to confess his sins to the world.

I got hold of a second hand Samsung Note smartphone from one of those cash exchange shops in E1, didn't need any ID to buy it. I bought a 3G SIM from a Whitechapel market stall and did all my top-ups at this shitty little newsagent I knew off Brick Lane where there would be little chance of anyone remembering me or capturing me on CCTV if the police ever checked.

I spent several weeks logging onto the teen dating site as 'Sassygirl13' fending off what were obviously young boy's advances before one day a 'sugardaddy317' logged in. That sick arsehole didn't even hide the fact he was a man rather than a boy. He went on about being a child at heart and enjoying socialising with younger people rather than those his own age. He talked about his love for some of the more fun London shows like Lion King, Billy Elliott and Wicked. He talked about how he just fancied a night out but had no one to go with. He suggested Nandos, shopping and a show; his treat. He really knew how to temp a young vulnerable and deprived youngster like Rosie was. Someone whose parents didn't have any money or just didn't spend it on their children, a kid who just wanted someone to take an interest in them and care about them a bit. I played along, it was easy, I let that sick pervert groom me for a few weeks keeping him well away from real young victims. I couldn't just keep his interest for ever if I didn't meet him. My plan to expose him online was not working out. He'd just deny being 'sugardaddy317.' He wouldn't use a webcam or any type of face time type of app showing his face. It was at this point that I changed tack. I needed to stop this horrible paedophile, I wanted to hurt him as well now and I knew what that would mean."

"You would end up killing him?"

"Yes, I think I knew that would be the end result, I just didn't admit it to myself at the time. I needed to cover my tracks, I'd be in central London, it was awash with modern digital CCTV systems. I'd read a few stories about criminals using and exploiting female Muslim attire to move around fully covered. I actually felt a little guilty about this, I'd lived and worked in East London for years mixed in with its vibrant Islamic community and didn't want to create more unnecessary racial tension. I rationalised it according to their faith in the end concluding I would have Allah's full support removing the evil that hid behind the wealth of this man. It was easy to buy a niqab by going back to where I used to live. I chose an Arabic Abaya as the most authentic robe to buy. I could pose as an Arabic tourist in central London. I took a risk buying it but there were so many market stalls to choose from I thought surely they wouldn't remember me. I even covered my head with a standard head scarf and put on an Albanian accent to convince the stall holders I was an Eastern European Muslim woman looking for a more traditional form of dress in preparation for a pilgrimage. With this disguise purchased I could walk away from the scene and take the nearest underground system away from the area and head east without drawing any attention to myself whatsoever.

Fortunately I'd encouraged Steve to keep his old boots for the garden when we cleared out the flat and moved to Letchworth. 'The size nines had served me well.' I thought, so they were due one last outing. The trouble was I'd dumped the gun, when I'd used up all the shells previously, and although Lyle was a fat arsehole he'd still be able to put up a fight. I was sure of that from past experience. That's when I remembered how Steven had brought a bag home with his stab vest, handcuffs, baton and gas in. I remembered because he said not to say anything about it as he shouldn't really bring his C/S home but it was only for a few days before he moved to his new office at Hendon. Of course he forgot to take it into work and I forgot to remind him. It was a risk but I decided to take it. Anyway I needed to do this when Steve was away from home with work staying overnight in London or somewhere else. He did this occasionally now we lived out in the counties.

I was going to get Lyle to confess over the internet via the smartphone. I would then hang him to death. So it was back to the DIY shops for a good strong length of rope, some plastic ties, a heavy duty face mask to minimise the effects of C/S on me and more latex gloves. It was easy to get Lyle to meet in London. I told him I lived out in Essex and asked if he could book me a room to stay in overnight. I acted all innocent and asked him to book tickets to Grease 'my favourite musical' I said. I suggested a date when Steve was away at some national conference or something. I knew Lyle would book something swanky and made excuses about needing to drop my overnight case there before we went out. I could picture the horrible bastard virtually drooling at the mouth just thinking about the opportunities the innocent 'sassygirl13' had offered up. He fell right into my trap gave me the apartment address he had pre booked. He said he'd meet me there at 7:30 p.m. ready to go straight out. This was a couple of days before the murder and it was easy to slip out of work at lunchtime to go and take a look at my options. I needed a discreet route back to Westminster underground station where I could catch the district line from. This fitted with my plan to escape via East London in disguise. That's when I found the fire door out of the rear of the complex and decided I could use to leave the building.

On the day I committed the murder I drove from home right round to the end of the district line at Upminster. I made sure I was slightly later than requested just to make sure Lyle would be inside the apartment and waiting when I arrived.

I filled a large handbag with the coiled rope, C/S spray and police baton. I'd worked out how I would video Lyle's confession and email it straight into Sky News, an outlet that I trusted to report the truth. I had the Abaya and Niqab ready to put on and easily found an empty carriage to do so before we reached the next station.

So there I was at around 8 p.m. that night still fully robed for effect, spray in one hand baton extended in the other tapping gently on that sick man's apartment door. Of course he opened it, enthusiastically without even asking who was there. I'd looked at the website photos of the rooms, I knew about the original features and old metal roof beams all painted up to look trendy. My plan worked perfectly. First a face full of C/S gas, followed by a couple of hard and effective baton strikes forcing him back towards the bedroom. I dropped the prepared loop around his neck and threw the loose end of rope over the bar pulling hard on the end until Lyle was on tiptoes half choking to death. I was in control. I kicked the dressing table stool over to where he stood and shouted at him to stand on it pulling the rope tightly as he did so. He was a heavy man and it was a little harder to haul him up than I'd anticipated. I now know of course I must have shredded part of my glove at some point. I tied the rope off to a sturdy old Victorian style radiator. He was still choking gripping the rope at the neck trying to plead for his life but not doing too well still coughing and spluttering from the gas. I whacked him a couple more times and secured his hands with the plastic ties. I then slackened the rope just a touch. I needed this man to be able to talk. His first clear words were "please don't kill me, I'll do anything you want. I have plenty of money, how much do you want?" I'd written out a script for him based on the original newspaper article I'd still managed to find online. I told him to read it, that's what I wanted. He said, "he couldn't," so I told him "he'd have to die then," and tightened the rope again. He could barely splutter "ok,ok." I loosened it again holding the script and phone's camera up to his face.

Just hearing those words from that snivelling idiot as I recorded his confession made me really want to hurt him. As soon as he'd finished I went straight back to the rope pulling it hard and making sure it was really secure. I smashed his knee until it shattered and watched him struggle to keep up on one leg before the stool eventually gave way. Lyle twitched and jerked dying quite quickly really soon after that. I deliberately uploaded the video using the flat's wifi, I needed him to be found, just not too quickly.

My plan worked like clockwork, I was out of the fire escape and back on the district line before I knew it. I got off the train as planned looking like any other woman at Upminster, everything tucked away in my bag. The rest was simple, round the M25, up the M11, then heading cross country via a secluded old lake I'd found just outside Baldock. I ditched the smart phone and burnt my disguise away.

I thought I'd got away with it, I was just disappointed Lyle's confession never got aired.

It was hard when I realised I was going to be found out. I was terrified when I saw Steven on the TV that day leaving the press conference. I knew he was coming for me, that's why I ran."

Anna paused as a member of staff came to the door.

"Sorry Vanessa, sorry to disturb you," she said.

"That's alright Helen I think we've reached a good point to wrap it up for the day, what do you think Anna?"

"Yes, can we talk again soon please Vanessa?"

"Of course you've not got rid of me yet," she smiled.

"You've got a visitor Anna," announced Helen.

"A visitor?" Responded a surprised Anna.

Anna followed Helen into the day room and stood stunned, riveted to the spot like a statue, just staring at her beloved Steve. The gap between them like a no mans land she just could not cross.

"Anna," was all he could say.

She stood in silence tears beginning to roll down her cheeks not knowing what to do.

Steve slowly walked across the room and wrapped his arms tightly around her.

"I can never forgive you Anna, you know that; but I can't just stop loving you."

She melted into his arms and knew she would always regret the hurt she had caused this wonderful man. The only man she would ever trust…

THE END

Out Now..

If you enjoyed 'Man Slaughter - A Detective's Story,' why not try my second book 'Gap Year - A Detective's Story,' already out...

When newly retired Detective Superintendent Andy Porter discovers his friend's daughter Helena has gone missing on her gap year travels he heads off to the East African coast to try and find her. No longer surrounded by a team of New Scotland Yard detectives Andy struggles to solve the mystery of Helena's disappearance.

When he subsequently finds out it may be linked to other missing youngsters he decides to enlist the help of an old friend...

Copyright

Disclaimer

Printed in Great Britain
by Amazon

78854395R00231